MVFOL

The Burke Series Book 1

Lyle T. Burchette

D0942946

WINEPRESS WP PUBLISHING

ISBN 1-57921-304-9
Library of Congress Catalog Card Number: 00-102724

To Phyllis Kay Burchette, my loving wife and partner, whose love, encouragement and help made it possible for me to finish this book . . . a life-long dream fulfilled . . . I Love You!

AND

To the late Oliver Thomas Burchette, my father. Many of the teachings and concepts written in these chapters were taught to me by him as we talked and walked over the same hills in Louisa, KY that you will read about in the following pages.

Acknowledgments

It is difficult to thank everyone who has influenced and encouraged me in the endeavor of bringing about this first story of the Burke family in Lawrence County, KY. However, I must pause to mention a few.

First of all—to God be the glory for inspiring me and giving me the talent. I would also like to thank the College of the Ozarks, Point Lookout, MO for the use of their excellent library and museum; Rev. and Mrs. Martin Jones, Pastors of the New Life Church, Arkedelphia, AR; Mr. Bill Hartman of Green Lantern Antiques, Hollister, MO; Tony and Carolyn Scott, Branson, MO; Sue Houser, Ozark, MO; Michelle Crawford (my sweet grand-daughter), Hollister, MO; Louise Devers, (Pastor Martin Jones' mother) who lives in Indiana; the wardrobe department of Silver Dollar City for the use of Civil War clothing; and Josiah Williams who created the front cover art for this book.

Last but not least, thanks to my mother, Violet Damron Burchette, my sister Mrs. Paul Prince (Frances), and my wife and partner Phyllis Kay for all the special encouragement and assistance along the way.

Contents

Service and Sacrifice

"OH, GOD—HELP—ME—I'VE BEEN HIT," SCREAMED A TORTURED VOICE. John Burke was lying on his back in a ditch, hugging his Sharps rifle when he heard the desperate cry for help. Bullets from Rebel rifle fire were whizzing overhead like hundreds of hornets, but he knew he had to get to that wounded soldier. The ditch was filled with a mixture of cold January mud and ice. He quickly rolled over, trying to keep his rifle breech dry as he peered out through the dreary noon haze. He breathed a sigh of relief as he looked around and no one else seemed near.

"Where are you?" he called, endeavoring to locate the voice.

"Down the hill from you—I think," the voice called back, noticeably weaker than before. "I think I'm dying." The voice trailed off into the noise of battle. Canister shells from twelve-pound cannon fire were exploding to the right and left of John and his company, which was spread out all across the steep hillside. "Oh, God," John prayed out loud, "help me get through this terrible rain of bullets to my wounded comrade." Even though he prayed in a strong voice, the noise of battle diminished his words to the sound of a whisper.

"Hold on, friend—don't give up, I'm coming," he called as loudly as he could. Perhaps his comrade really was dying. *Maybe he's already dead*, John thought, yet he knew he had to make the effort to render aid.

John rolled over rocks and wet rugged terrain down the hill until he figured he was about level with the sound of the man's voice. He began squirming on his belly, using his elbows and knees to propel him through the winter slush. More than once his mouth filled with cold, wet earth, and a whimsical thought crossed his mind. *I know what a gopher must feel like.* In spite of the dampness all around, his mouth was dry and there was a metallic taste on his tongue and the roof of his mouth. He recognized the taste all too well. He had experienced it once before when he came face to face with a huge black bear in the Virginia wilderness. It was unadulterated fear, plain and simple! *With all my faith in God, I didn't think this would ever happen*, he reflected. With bullets flying, cannon shells bursting and men dying or shot all around him, there it was again—terror. He knew that if he were standing, his knees would be knocking.

"I'm close by—where are you?" he called out. Nothing but the constant, unrelenting noise of battle answered him.

"What's your name? What company are you with?" He strained to listen through the din, but a scattering of Confederate mini balls made it impossible to hear a thing.

Dear God, I wish I had my horse. His company commander, Captain Drury Birchet, from his own hometown of Louisa, Kentucky, had ordered that the mounts be tethered at the foot of the hill across Middle Creek. "The terrain is not given to horse battle," he'd said. "They'll be raining hell out of a cannon barrel down on us."

Well, Drew was right. But, I still wish my horse was here. I'd mount and get out of here. The minute the thought passed through his mind, John knew it was a lie from the devil. As scared as he was, he would not quit; he would fight to the end if that's what it took to get the job done. He was a rugged man who thought he was afraid of nothing. Evidently he was wrong.

"Sowers," the moaning voice filtered through the din. "Tha's my name—I'm from B Company." Again the weak voice trailed off. John took heart and suddenly the fear left him. He began to maneuver himself toward the young man with renewed vigor. *What a soldier I am! All this and I haven't even got off a round by rifle or pistol.* Moving his hand to his side, he took comfort as he touched the Colt just as he squirmed point-blank into a body. It was still warm, and as he felt for a heartbeat, he whispered, "Thanks be to God." Sowers was still breathing.

He propped the wounded man against a fence post then carefully ripped open his jacket to examine the wound. John's heart sank when he saw a gaping hole in the stomach, still flowing with blood and other matter that made John sick at his own stomach. He turned away as he retched, but nothing came up. He knew the young man was dying and there was nothing he could do. John wanted to weep when he recognized Private Sowers as one of the recruits from Louisa, but he fought his tears. He took the dying man's hand and spoke to him softly.

"I'm right by your side, soldier; I won't leave you. We—we'll see this thing through together; you and me," he comforted as he looked into the youthful face.

Private Sowers looked up into John's eyes with difficulty, struggling to speak, "I—I have—I—," he started. John could see his eyes, crusted with frozen earth. He blinked as John helped clear them off; then they focused on his face. Private Sowers moaned, and his eyelids closed. They opened again and he clutched at John's jacket. He sputtered and a bloody froth spewed out on his lips. He writhed in pain, trying to speak again. "I've bit the bullet—isn't thet right, Burke?" he asked, recognizing John.

John bit his lower lip, fighting back his emotions. He lowered his eyes, not wanting to face the hazel ones of his friend, but forced himself to reply.

"I—I believe you have, Brett," he said, using the soldier's given name. "I'll stay right here with you until it's all over if you want me to." John spoke softly, still holding Sowers' hand.

"Would—you s-ay someth-ing k-ind ab-out me to my—my folks—and—and wo-uld you say the L-ord's Pr-ayer with me ri-ght now?" Brett asked, coughing and gasping between words as tears formed small streams through the grime of battle on his face.

Choked up as John was, no words came at first. He held himself in check and nodded as he began. "God's provision, Brett, is heaven when we die—you follow with me. 'Our Father which art in heaven . . .'" Brett's weaker voice joined following John's. "Our, Fa—ther wh—ich art in hea—ven . . ." It seemed to grow stronger as they both took faith from the prayer that was God's Word.

Unusual strength came into Brett's hand until it seemed to cut off the blood flow in John's hand. As both men concluded the prayer and uttered "Amen" in unison, Brett Sowers breathed his last breath. He had a smile fixed on his face as John closed the glazed eyes. At this point John lost himself and fell across the boy's body, beginning to sob. The tears flowed while his body shook involuntarily. It was a cleansing type of weeping mixed with joy and sorrow, for he knew Brett was out of pain and with the Father. He wept for the loss of a friend and also for Heaven's gain, for that is surely where Brett Sowers had taken up new residence. John was acquainted well enough with the young man to know of his faith in God through Jesus Christ His Son.

When John regained his composure, he laid his slain friend next to the split-rail fence, crossing the boy's hands after he straightened out his jacket to hide the wound. He took Brett's rifle and stuck it into the hillside, bayonet down, to mark his resting place. He lifted himself slightly to look around when he realized there was a lull in the Confederate firing, and noticed other Union soldiers, some sitting up, some on their knees, and others beginning to stand. It seemed all were looking toward the crest of the hill where menacing barrels of cannon could be seen. At last he could see the enemy to shoot back. For the first time since the battle had started in this sector he could see several Rebel soldiers—perhaps two to three hundred yards away. This was the enemy front that had been sending a murderous assault of gunfire down on them. *They must have ceased firing to survey the damage they've done,* John thought. This was his opportunity and he grabbed it, taking careful aim at a Rebel soldier outlined on the horizon.

"Let's get 'em, men. Now's our chance to take the hill," he shouted. His voice echoed just as he squeezed off a round and he watched the silhouette disappear suddenly.

The battle cry had sounded! John took the initiative and the men in his sector followed. A blitz of Union gunfire began to play havoc on the Confederate front line.

"Advance, men—advance!" shouted Captain Birchet. The men recognized his voice and began climbing the hillside, halting only to fire and then moving ahead. Several accurate volleys rang forth before the enemy collected themselves and began to fire back. At first it was just the rifle fire, followed by the ferocious cannons, some filled with grape, some with canisters, and some with exploding shells.

John paired up with young Aaron Short from Company G. They crawled, they ran and they jumped, sometimes just a few feet at a time. Then they would hunch down before the next advance. Each time they came up to their knees they would squeeze off a round, then load and repeat.

"I got me a Reb that time, John. I saw him fall," Aaron whispered hoarsely.

"Good going, Shorty. Keep up the good work," John answered.

John had indeed noticed several men fall due to his deadly accuracy, but he said nothing about it. He wasn't exactly sure how he felt about shooting—and killing—his fellow man. He knew these Rebel men believed in the cause they were fighting for just like he believed in his cause. Also, he knew that many served and worshiped the same God that he claimed.

"Brett Sowers was killed jus' awhile back," John reluctantly informed Aaron. Both young men were about the same age and knew each other. He hated to give the news to Aaron, but felt he should.

"Oh, oh no!" he cried out, openly devastated. He collapsed into a sitting position. "Are—are you sure about that, John?" he inquired, his mind whirling with shock.

"Yep, I'm sure, son," John said, using the kinship term to convey affection and consolation. John was about ten years older than twenty-year-old Short.

The Rebel firing was growing worse again. Cannon shells exploded everywhere. John, Aaron, and others spent their time floundering in the cold, muddy terrain. John's beard was matted with mud and ice driblets. He was hungry and aware of an advancing fever. In spite of the cold, he was burning up; perspiration beads stood out on his forehead and his uniform was soaked from the inside. A few times he felt dizzy, but didn't have time to think much about it. He checked his pocket watch. Two o'clock. Suddenly his mind cleared and he remembered it was the 10th of January 1862. They had moved from the outskirts of Paintsville early that morning and met the enemy on a ridge south of Middle Creek at nine o'clock. John, in his fevered condition, could not understand the clarity of his mind as he recalled the events of the day. Led by General James Abram Garfield, they were ordered to "take that ridge held by the enemy."

Fighting had started at ten o'clock. By noon the Union forces were all pinned down, and an exploding shell mortally wounded Private Brett Sowers.

"What am I to do now?" John shouted feverishly as he stood up without regard to his safety.

"What'd ya say, Burke?" he heard Aaron shout back, almost off in the distance. "Get down, Burke," came a shout. Then there was a huge explosion and John felt something burst in his head—like spirals of fire—then excruciating pain—then complete blackness!

Floating. There was a sensation of floating in a pillow of whiteness. Blessing! There was no pain, but John felt so light! Suddenly his eyes began to focus and he was high, very high, looking down on hilly terrain. There was smoke filtering up. He could smell the powder and sulfur mixture as his eyes focused on the scene below. *Hey,* John thought, *I know where that is—it's Middle Creek; over there lies the Creek—winding, winding, ever winding.* He spotted movement as two men far below looked for something. *What are they looking for? If I could only get closer.* And suddenly he was closer.

"This man is dead," he heard one of the men say. Then he knew—these men were looking for bodies. *Who have they found dead?* he wondered as his vision telescoped onto the man lying on his stomach. He saw the shattered clothing; his eyes focused on the torn left leg caked with dried blood and mud. *The man surely is dead!*

"I'll turn him over," the other man said.

John watched as he rolled the man over face up. *My dear God—That's me! I'm dead! Is this heaven? Where am I?*

"Wait a minute," the first soldier shouted excitedly. "I detect a heart beat—this man is still breathing!"

"It must be a miracle! I'll go get a medic and stretcher for him," the second man said. "Who is it?" he called over his shoulder as he took off running for help. "Why it's John Burke, a trooper from K Company," answered the soldier who had turned over the body.

If I am still living, what am I doing up here watching this? John wondered. As he centered on that thought, John felt a pulling toward the body. At first it was like light gravity. Then it grew stronger until finally he was back in the body. Suddenly he was aware that pain had returned as his eyelids fluttered. His head felt like it was going to split; his left leg throbbed violently, and he heard voices as someone lifted his head.

"It's all right, soldier. You're lucky to be here. You're alive—and with God's help, you'll stay alive. We are with you and . . ." the voice faded as John drifted again into unconsciousness.

The smallpox fever that had started on the hillside developed in John as he lay in the Union medical tent outside of Paintsville. In the next week he faded in and out of blackness, with a mixture of dreams and thoughts of home. He would feel himself floating again only to be sent hurtling to the ground like a star falling from the sky. He felt hands bathing him in cool water and then he felt as though he were burning, as the fever climbed high in his body. He felt people working on his leg and he heard voices.

"The wound seems clean now, but if gangrene sets in . . ." The voice faded.

"Amputate—must be amputated!" the man's voice declared. John shook like he was having convulsions and he heard his own voice scream out, "No! Don't touch my leg—God help you if you cut my leg!" And again he heard the voice in the background speak of amputation.

"I don't see how we can guarantee total healing unless we take the leg off!" He heard his own voice ring out again in defiance, "Leave it alone. It's my leg—don't you dare cut it off!"

At these times John knew he was in turmoil. He felt his leg quiver as if trying to get out of bed. Then suddenly a peace came over him. He heard the same voices in the background speaking in lower more hushed tones, "Well, Doctor, maybe we could hold off one more day—it will be touch and go, but if we can save this man's leg, let's try."

"Yes, one day—and we'll see," said the other doctor. The two men left the room and John was finally able to rest, exhausted from the ordeal.

Once, before becoming coherent, John dreamed of his family—though it seemed more like a vision. Elizabeth, his wife, and Sue Ellen, their eldest child, dressed in pretty spring dresses, were walking through a grassy field. They were so cheerful and almost buoyant as they walked, turning back and waving as they went. Across the grassy slope a stream separated his son, Ollie, from his mother and sister. He was frantically waving both arms at them. Elizabeth and Sue Ellen seemed carefree as they walked toward a bright light, too bright to look at with his naked eye. When he awakened, a cheerful matronly looking lady was sitting beside his cot bathing his face with cool water.

"My goodness, Private," she remarked with a pleasant smile, "it sure is good to have you back with us. You've really had a rough time of it—but the fever has broken and I think you threw off that old smallpox germ."

"I—I guess I was dreamin'," John said. "Where am I?"

"Well, you're in Paintsville in a Union medical tent. I'm Nellie Clavin, your nurse, and you sure were dreaming, young man! Is Sue Ellen your wife?"

"No, ma'am, Sue Ellen's my daughter. My wife is Elizabeth," he answered with a weak smile.

"Well—you called her name out too—also someone called Ollie."

John tried to sit up, but got up to one elbow and his head fell back on the flat pillow.

"Now listen here, soldier, you are far too weak to try that stunt again. You have been here fighting infection and fever without so much as a bite of food for a week. I've just been able to get a little broth and some water down you since they brung y'all in," she gently scolded.

"Ollie—that's my son, the other one I spoke of. I'm sorry to cause you such a frightful problem," John apologized. "My leg? What about my leg?" He suddenly remembered his fear from the half-heard conversations.

"You've still got it, son," she said. "You sure did give that sawbones 'what for' when he tried to take it from you. Mind you—there's still a hunk of metal in there that we couldn't get out. You'll have lots of pain and a frightful limp, I'm aguessin'—but you still got your leg!"

After Mrs. Clavin left his bedside John thought more of the vivid dream and it left him a little perplexed.

The winter of 1862 was a difficult and life-changing season for both Union and Confederate troops and many Lawrence County citizens. The Battle of Middle Creek, as it came to be called, was a decisive victory for General James Garfield and the Union forces.

John had ridden with Company K mounted troopers and close to 1,700 Union soldiers from Louisa to meet the Confederate forces of General Humphrey Marshall, who was advancing towards their town. They met south of the Peach Orchard area of Lawrence County, not too far north of Prestonburg, Kentucky.

While John was recuperating, he learned that the victory had earned Garfield a promotion to brigadier general. He soon found out the Confederate troops had backed off—but they also claimed the Battle of Middle Creek as a victory.

John Burke had been struck in his left leg by a piece of shrapnel from cannon fire as he and his company advanced under orders to take and occupy a strategic hill. Private Sowers and others—on both sides—went to meet their Maker on that hill. John realized that he had come within a breath of that himself. While fighting infection from his wound, he came down with a case of smallpox and hovered between life and death. John's memory went back to the day he was wounded and he remembered the burning fever and all the perspiring he had done just before he was hit. He found out that an epidemic of smallpox had swept through Union Troops and many soldiers were buried there without ever having fired a shot. He was one of the few stricken men that had lived through it.

"Hello there, soldier!" A friendly voice called out to John as he sat propped up on his cot. A Union captain approached from the opening in the tent. He pulled over an empty powder keg and seated himself next to John.

"Hello yourself, sir," John responded weakly. "I'm Private John Burke, 14th Regiment Company K. Sorry I can't get up for you." John extended his right hand. The captain took it and gave him a warm handshake.

"I'm not the chaplain, but I am here in his place," said the officer. "By the way, I do know you, Private Burke. At least—I know who you are and I came here from the garrison at Louisa. My name is Samuel Lyons and I thought it was time you had a visitor from home," he chuckled.

"Well, I'm sure proud to see you, Captain. I've been kinda hankerin' for some news from home."

"Well, John, I can't give you actual news about your family, but I can tell you that General Marshall is retreating south and for the time being our hometown of Louisa is safe."

"That sure is good news jus' by itself, Captain—everything else OK?" he asked.

"Not everything, John. Louisa has been hit by that terrible disease that gave you such a hard time. Lots of families have felt the loss of loved ones and it has been a hard winter so far." Captain Lyons hesitated. "Private, the real reason I'm here is for you. Are you feeling whole and complete—not only in your body—but also in your—your mind?" he asked.

John laughed with some effort for he was still extremely sore. What the good captain asked had struck him funny.

"Do you mean—have I took leave of my senses? Leastways that's what I think you're askin', Captain." John caught his breath then continued, "I think I'm gettin' stronger each day, sir. My leg hurts mighty like sin, in spells—but that's to be expected with the extra metal I'm carryin' around. My bout with the fever left me weaker 'n a newborn kitten. But—my mind? That's somethin' else agin," he laughed. "Some folks would allow thet I never had one anyways," he concluded with a wide grin.

Captain Lyons turned slightly red at John's inference concerning his mind, but truthfully that is what he was concerned about. John was definitely shell-shocked by that tremendous blast from the cannon and the doctor and nurse had relayed concerns to the command post.

"Well, John—I wasn't exactly asking if you were crazy. I just wanted to find out if you have had some unusual thoughts," he inquired more softly.

"Oh, I don't mind you askin' that question, Captain." John smiled. "As a matter of fact I did have a couple of things happen that was purely different. Leastways it seemed that way to me when it happened." John leaned more toward the officer and asked, "Captain, are you a religious man?"

It was apparent that Captain Lyons was caught off guard with this question, but he could see it was an important question to his wounded subordinate.

"I guess you could say I'm not extremely religious—although I do believe in a God, and I do go to services on occasion," he ventured cautiously. "Why do you ask?" He cocked his head to one side with a puzzled look on his face.

"Well, sir, I'm what you would call a Bible-believer. I try to serve the Lord and teach my family to do the same. The reason I asked is simply to decide if I should tell you about two experiences I had that might be hard to understand. "Even if you are a Bible-believer, like me, Captain, you may have a hard time understanding what I'd tell you—I still don't understand!"

Captain Lyons knew John's background and had read his Army personnel file, which wasn't very complete. He was aware that this man was a trapper, a hunter, and a woodsman who knew more about this Tri-State area of Kentucky, Ohio and western Virginia than any man currently living here. What he was finding out in this interview was that John Burke is not just a country yokel!

"John, I'll be honest with you—I don't know whether I can understand what you experienced or not, but I do know this—you can trust me to be discreet. And I will do my best to understand—if you want to tell me."

Warmth came through John's blue eyes as he began to relate what happened after being wounded and how he seemed to float above the hillside at Middle Creek as if he was transferred out of his body and was seeing the battlefield from the air. He kept his attention on Captain Lyons' facial expressions the whole time.

He explained that it seemed like he had been lifted above the feeling of pain and suffering. Then, as he looked down, he saw himself being looked upon and handled as if he were not the person who was lying there, cold and still. And when he looked closer he saw his own face and the expression of death. But then he sensed the pain and suffering come back as his spiritual body felt the pull of his physical body. When he re-entered his own body, the pain was tormenting and real. As he recounted the pull of his body—to attract what seemed to be his spirit—and then the return of pain and feeling, he could see moisture form in the captain's eyes. He paused, took a deep breath, then began speaking again.

"Captain, before you comment on what I just told you, I'll tell you of another experience that took place after I was brought to this medical tent. This one happened just before I became aware that I had been battling a high fever. It may have been due to the fever—I don't know." John still held Captain Lyons' interest as he told of the dream he had about Elizabeth, Sue Ellen, and Ollie. "It may have been a dream or a trance—I'm not sure. Anyway, these two things are all I know to tell you that was new to my mind.

"Oh, yes, there was one other thing! Fear ran through me like I have never had before—except one other time. I've always considered myself to be fearless—pretty much, until now. But I know that's no longer true. I did overcome it—and I don't know if it will ever return. I sure pray to God it doesn't!" he concluded.

Captain Lyons spoke slowly and carefully. He did not want to upset this man who had been through such a terrifying ordeal and was obviously very sensitive.

"About your fear, Private Burke. I know something of war—and battle fear. We sometimes tritely ask the question, 'Have you seen the Elephant?' This deals with that question. What we mean is: 'Has one seen the battle up front and felt the fear?' We all have—those who experience the edge of battle. The difference between a coward and a hero is—one runs away; the other stays and fights! Both have the same fear; both desire to run away—one doesn't and the other does." He paused, studied John's face, and felt satisfied that he had offered some consolation.

"Yes, sir," John said with a wry grin. "I've heard that expression before—now I sure know how to answer it!" He relaxed back on his pillow as the captain continued.

"About your—your personal dream, John! I don't know how to comment. We all have them at one time or another. This one was evidently more real to you than other dreams you have had in the past. Your guess on its meaning, if there is one, is as good—no—better than mine. In times of war we are all preoccupied with thoughts of family and home.

"The other experience seems to me a real and personal 'out of body experience.' I heard of something like this one other time. I don't doubt for a minute that it happened just as you said. I would say that you were very near death—or—or maybe you died. I happen to know that what you saw was not a dream. It actually happened! I have met those two men and the scene you described happened—just as you saw it. All I can say is—God was not ready for you to leave this world—not at this time. I can only surmise that you left your body for a short time and then returned." It was very quiet as both men pondered the officer's words. John felt that the captain had more insight than a lot of men who claimed to be religious.

"John, what you told me will go no further than right here. I would not share those experiences with just anyone! I will tell you that the Army is going to give you an honorable discharge for medical reasons due to the condition of your leg." He stood and saluted John as he said good-bye.

"When you get back to Louisa please look me up, John. You still have a future with the Union Army—if you want one. The Army is not finished with you yet. But that will be up to you." John smiled at him weakly and Captain Lyons was gone.

When John was well enough to travel he was given honorable discharge papers and allowed to go home to Louisa. He took gifts for Sue Ellen and Ollie. It was with an anxious and happy heart that this wounded soldier rode home with visions of greeting his loving family. He could still picture Sue Ellen by the fireplace as she prayed that sweet prayer just before he left. *My dear God—how grateful I am to be alive*, he thought as he rode along, realizing that if that shrapnel had hit him in his back or spine instead of the leg, he would be dead.

Every step of the horse brought him closer to home, but each step also brought him excruciating pain from the metal cutting like a knife inside his leg. He stopped by the garrison to turn in his military-issue horse. One of the guards was assigned to take him the rest of the way by buckboard. John was grateful for that kindness for it would save him time. Soon he would be in the sweet, tender arms of his beloved Elizabeth and greeted by his loving children. As they neared the small cabin, John thought he would just slip in on everyone. He called to the driver. "Jim, jus' let me off here. I'll go in on foot to surprise everyone."

"Whoa," Jim reined in on the team. "Don't blame you a bit, John, they'll all git a kick outa yer surprise."

John thanked him as he took his gear from the wagon and walked the last one hundred yards. Jim gave him a knowing smile and waved as he rode off toward town. There had been no mail delivery to or from home since he left, so this would be a real surprise for everyone.

"Elizabeth," he shouted. "Sue Ellen, Ollie." No one answered his call. When he put away his gear, he looked around and noticed that no one had been in the cabin recently. An eerie feeling started in the pit of his stomach; one that he could not explain. *Something isn't right*, he thought. Naturally, he went to the home of his nearest and closest friends in Louisa, Armsted and Rebecca Birchet. It was an agonizing two-mile trip on foot and John was sorry he let the Union driver return so quickly. His mind was fixed on his family and the nagging uneasy feeling that he could not shake. He finally made it, limping all the way. After catching his breath, he stepped up on the front porch.

Rebecca Birchet heard his steps and came out the front door, running to greet him. She hugged him and as she stepped back, John read the sadness in her face.

"Rebecca, what is it? What's wrong?"

"You haven't heard from anyone have you, John?" she asked, her eyes filling with tears. John sensed disaster. He swallowed hard, but the lump that had risen in his throat would not leave.

"Becky, what are you tryin' to tell me?" He tried to make himself rigid enough to receive her answer. Tears were running down Rebecca's cheeks and she brushed a strand of hair from her face.

"John—Elizabeth—" She choked and hid her face. She tossed her head back, but was not able to hide her pain. "Elizabeth and Sue Ellen are—Oh, my dear God," she gasped. "John—they are—they are with the Lord!" John suddenly became as limp as a rag and fell into her arms, grabbing her to keep from falling. His body convulsed, wracked with pain as he sobbed uncontrollably. Rebecca found herself supporting a grieving husband and father, using the porch post for support. Suddenly the front door flew open and a dark-haired lad in buckskins rushed to his side and grabbed him around the waist.

"Daddy, you're home. Daddy, you're home—Oh Daddy, Mother and Sue Ellen have left us. Daddy—Oh Daddy." John bent down to Ollie, taking him in his arms. They wept together as Rebecca tried to give comfort. She had several daughters at home and they all gathered around, weeping together.

Finally John lifted his tear-stained face and asked what happened. Rebecca pulled over a hickory chair on the cold front porch and explained that Elizabeth and Sue Ellen, along with a number of other town folks, had succumbed to the smallpox epidemic. They had died within hours of one another just ten days before, and were buried by caring friends. Ollie was grief stricken. He had been staying with Rebecca Birchet and her family since the tragedy.

John buried his haggard face in his hands and began to moan unabashedly as he staggered into the house. The tears flowed through his fingers and fell in great drops to the floor as he sank into the nearest chair in a pitiful heap. Ollie was right beside him with both his arms wrapped around John's shoulders. Silently he too let the tears flow, consoling his dad the best he knew how.

The Burkes had known tragedy before, but not this close to home and not so much at the same time. John visited the graves of his wife and thirteen-year-old daughter in the town cemetery. Ollie never left his side, giving him support as he limped up the hill. They stood together over the graves, grieving in silence, each trying to cope with the heaviness in his heart. Finally, John spoke.

"Let's do it together, Ollie," he said, choking back more tears. Ollie joined in and together they quoted the 23rd Psalm.

The Lord is my Shepherd; I shall not want.
    He maketh me to lie down in green pastures:
He leadeth me beside the still waters.
    He restoreth my soul:
He leadeth me in the paths of righteousness
    for His name's sake.
Yea though I walk
    through the valley of the shadow of death,
I will fear no evil:
    for thou art with me;
thy rod and thy staff
    they comfort me.
Thou preparest a table before me
    in the presence of my enemies:
thou anointest my head with oil;
    my cup runneth over.
Surely goodness and mercy shall follow me
    all the days of my life: and I will
dwell in the house of the Lord
    forever.

John and Ollie Burke looked at one another and in unison said, "Amen!"

It was a long, silent, tortured walk back to the empty log cabin. Just a few hours before John had rushed home with eager anticipation. Now he was trudging homeward—empty and forlorn. Dark clouds threatened overhead and it was bitter cold, with a hint of snow in the air. He had been grieving just long enough to believe Elizabeth and Sue Ellen were really gone. In the process, without realizing it, he had shut young Ollie out, which was not normal for the big woodsman who dearly loved this young man. And that is exactly what he was: a young, stalwart, ten-year old—going on twenty-one.

Before John came home, Ollie had been through this death and burial alone not knowing where his dad was or when he would return—or even if he would return. The Birchets had told him about John's wound and illness, but didn't have any idea just how badly his father was hurt until John walked through the door. He stood by his dad through the hours of his grief and was a comforting friend, allowing him to mourn in silence. And now he was marching along in stillness trying to keep up with his six-foot frame. He sensed the reason for John's silence, but he was aching and confused inside too.

For the first time John thought about the dream he had when his fever broke. He now had insight to what God was trying to tell him—that He was trying to prepare him for this loss. *I'll tell Ollie about this some day, but not just yet,* John thought. They were almost to the cabin when he broke the silence.

"The rain falls on the just and the unjust," John quoted from the Bible. "Oliver," John said, rarely calling Ollie by his birth name.

"Yes, sir," Ollie answered, looking up at his dad, startled by the way he had spoken.

"You are one to ride the river with, son!" He looked the youth in the face and went on, "What I mean to say is, it takes a lot of gumption to go through what you have gone through in the last month and not fall apart at the seams. I don't know where we will go from here, son, but one thing is for sure, I will be proud to have you as my partner and to be right here beside me.

"I remember the last night we were together as a whole family." John gave a deep sigh as he caught his breath and blew into the cold air that formed a cloud in front of his face. His voice quivered as he continued.

"Th—That sweet prayer that little missy prayed. Do you remember?"

"Ye-es, sir," Ollie said, choking back his quivering voice. He knew his dad was holding back his grief and more tears, and so was he. "Some-thin' about all that—that—we had to be thankful about, wasn't it?"

"You got a—a—pretty good memory, son. She thanked the Lord, as I recall, for the gift of life and somethin' about that if this was all we had in life we would still be blessed—remember that?"

"Yes, sir, I—I remember, now that you mention it, and you said some-thin' about we may never be this way again! It was like as if you knew all along—Did you, Dad? Did you?"

"No, Ollie—not really. I guess I just had what some folks call a warning. I was really thinking more about myself—and the coming battle. It never entered my mind that tragedy would come from the direction of home. That was a complete surprise to me."

Ollie bowed his head as they came down the path toward home. Mournfully he asked, "What do we do now, sir—I mean with Mom and Sis gone 'n all?"

"We'll have to think on that, son. I jus' don't rightly know. I do know this, God will provide for us, he always does." *Oh, God— what ARE we going to do?* John thought. "Better bring in some wood, Ollie, lots of wood! It looks mighty like snow t'night."

T W O

 # Before the Battle

W AYNE COUNTY, VIRGINIA, WAS THE "STOMPING GROUND" FOR JOHN
Burke, a mountaineer and woodsman. Mill Creek and
Twelve Pole Creek area in the lower Appalachians seemed like his
back yard, where he spent his days tramping through the woods. He
fished, hunted, trapped, and lived off the land just as free as the air
he breathed. This love for the woods came from his father, Thomas
Christopher Burke, known as "T.C.," who was a roving mountain
man. His woodsman heritage also came from his grandfather Damron
on his mother's side of the family, who was of the same nature.

John's rugged good looks followed his father's likeness—a
strong, six-foot frame and raven-black, naturally curly hair flowing down his face into a matching full beard. He had an angular
face with a well-formed forehead. Thick dark eyebrows gave way
to full cheekbones with dimples on either side, though hidden by
his beard. Thin small lips, which looked larger because of his raven
mustache, seemed recessed from an average-size nose. He was lean

through the waist, but his loose buckskins could not hide his strong chest and muscular arms. His outdoor lifestyle suited him and it was evident that he was happiest in the woods.

John taught his two youngsters well. From the time Ollie was four years old, John took his young son into the lower Appalachians of Virginia, teaching him the ways of the woods and, more than that, how to survive by living off of the land. Ollie was a willing student and with his strong ancestry of mountain folk, it came natural to him and he loved it. The animals, shrubs, trees, and flowers, as well as the beautiful birds, were all part of his wilderness education.

This, of course, was not all that Ollie and Sue Ellen were taught! The Burkes were hill folks who believed in book learning; especially the Book of Books, the Bible. Many hours were spent by the fireside or lamplight with their mother Elizabeth, as well as John, learning letters, memorizing verses in the Bible, and telling the familiar Bible stories. The teachings of Jesus were also taught faithfully.

Then came the big war. Some called it the War Between the States; others called it the Civil War. One day John invited a couple of friends from across the river to go fishing with him and Ollie near Doan, to relax and discuss the volatile situation.

"I don't see anything civil about it—families fighting families— all about someone owning another human jus' because he's a different color," remarked John to his close friends.

Armsted "Smitty" Birchet baited his hook and dropped it into Twelve Pole Creek. "I know jus' what ya mean, John. I get more upset about it all the time. We're going to have a come-uppance about this hyar war pretty soon." John was admiring his string of fish when Drury, Smitty's cousin, put in his opinion.

"Boys, I'll tell you what, we better enjoy today—it may be the last time we get together to fish for some time. John, when you going to move 'cross the river? If th' war comes, Louisa will be a prime target for the Rebs, and we need all the good men we can get over there with us." Drury deliberately put him on the spot because John had mentioned doing just that several times. Ollie moved up beside his dad to see if he had caught more fish than John had. He also was curious about his dad's answer to Drury.

"Soon, very soon," John replied. "I have a meeting with Lafe Hewlett next week to look at a place. It's a nice piece of property with a late garden that'll need harvested before first frost," he concluded with a smile. That night these men and their families all joined at Smitty's for a fish fry.

Consequently, in the fall of 1861, John traded for five acres with a log cabin across the Big Sandy River near the small town of Louisa, Kentucky. The cabin was near Two-Mile, boasting a native stone chimney and a well-built lean-to shed for livestock. There was also a good fresh-water well near the side door. John was pleased to move his family into their new surroundings.

The rumblings of war, along with the military step-up in the county and surrounding area, made John want to do something to get involved. General James A. Garfield had been sent in to occupy the town and area with a frightful number of Union troops. Southern sympathizers were spread throughout the whole area of eastern Kentucky and the western Virginia Appalachian hills. Most of the Louisa town folks were holding to the North, especially many strong friends of the Burkes: the Birchets, the Carters, the Boggs, as well as the Taylors and Shorts. Smitty Birchet was at the point of joining a regiment under General Garfield's command as they were garrisoned at the location, which was to become a fort. There was strong talk of an expected raid from Confederate troops and everyone was on edge.

A small group of Smitty Birchet's friends had gathered around the forge fire in the blacksmith shop on this cold December day as Smitty poured his heart out to them. He was a well-respected man in his mid-forties, with a grown son as well as a wife and smaller children at home. Smitty had called this meeting himself and it was plain to those friends present that Smitty Birchet was visibly concerned.

"I tell you, boys, we got to do something—an' I mean quick—like right now!" There were beads of sweat on his brow—not from the anvil or the fire—and his browned face showed real signs of concern. His strong right arm clutched a mighty hammer and he hit the anvil to emphasize his point.

"I was over to the Union camp jus' t'day and I saw the general prancing around on his stallion rustling up his men to get ready for battle. I tell you he is one to tie to."

"I have a question for you, Smitty," cousin Drury commented. "I have heard that General Garfield hasn't had a lick of military experience. He was just a senator or some sort of political man from over Ohio way. Is that true?"

"Partly true," Smitty replied. "But that don't mean the man don't know how to wage warfare. I have no military background, nor do the likes of all of you, but I'll bet yer a dollar you'll all fight for yer homes and yer town!" There came a round of assenting grunts and nods of approval. John backed Smitty whole-heartedly.

"Men, you all know me! I'm a hunter and a woodsman and would rather be out treein' an ol' coon than bein' with a whole wagonload of folks. Jus' th' same, I moved over here for two reasons. First, I wanted a safe home closer in for my family and second, 'cause I see the need to join together so we can fight th' enemy if they try to take over. So—I'll say what I have to say loud enough for you all to hear me—I'm with you, Smitty," he said as he raised his musket in agreement. "When do we go?"

John, a Bible-believing man, found himself agreeing with Smitty's convincing argument. After all, the Burkes didn't hold to slavery. Nor, for that matter, did most of the folks in these hills, even though Kentucky was considered partly a southern state. All of Lawrence

County had fewer than one hundred slaves in total—and most of those who owned slaves did not really hold to the slave market. John also believed that his home was about to be raided by men carrying guns, and he had his wife and children to think of, as well as his friends. That was his thought as he voiced his commitment to his friend, who he believed was a man of integrity.

Smitty smiled warmly at all the faces as they nodded approval at John's last remark. It was plain that these men were with him. Sturdy pioneer family men, all with wives and children except for Aaron Short, a young man of twenty. With Smitty, John Burke and Drury Birchet was John Boggs, Samuel Thompson (a man of education like Drury), William "Bill" Taylor, Levi Sparks and, last but not least, John W. Prince from the Webbville area.

Aaron Short was very fond of the Burke family and had been at the new homestead to help when the family moved from the Cassville area on Mill Creek across the Big Sandy River.

"I know if it comes to war, I'd rather be with men like John and Smitty. Also, Brett Sowers couldn't be here tonight, but he'll be with us fer sure," Aaron offered.

With one accord these men agreed that they would follow Smitty and join the 14th Regiment under General James Abram Garfield, a man with no proven military record. He was a thirty-year old Senator from Ohio who had been an educator before that. All responded in unison that commanding General Buell, who sent Garfield here, must have known what he was doing.

And so it was the next morning that John Burke and Armsted "Smitty" Birchet, along with the company of friends who had been at the blacksmith shop, went to the garrison of Union soldiers and enlisted in the Army. General Garfield himself gave them the oath of allegiance to the Union as they affirmed commitment to the northern cause and against slavery. Although a rather small man in size, a little wide in girth, General James Abram Garfield was an impressive figure of a man. He carried himself with dignity and had an eloquent style all his own. A full, handsome face with a Roman nose and a well-trimmed mustache and beard set off his finely fit uniform. He spoke with perfect diction and a style that was both proud and oratorical.

Everyone tried to stand in perfect attention as the general dismounted and passed through the ranks looking each man up and down. He stopped in front of Brett and Aaron and looked them over with a smile.

"You two young men are about the same height. Where are you from?" he asked.

"We're both from right here, sir," Brett answered with a faltering voice. "Lawrence County," he added.

"Very good, soldier. I am sure you will both do well. God bless you!" Then the general shook hands with each man. John, standing near Aaron, smiled from ear to ear. He was pleased that the general took a special interest in his two younger friends.

All the men were impressed as they vowed allegiance to the Union Army and were placed into the 14th Regiment by request. No particular reason—just that many of the Lawrence County friends and acquaintances were in that particular regiment. Their families were allowed to look on as they were sworn in. Young Ollie Burke was struck with awe at the dramatic event, one he would never forget.

Training started immediately and continued non-stop for the next two weeks until Christmas Eve. They were equipped with uniforms, boots and weapons, depending on supplies on hand, and were also allowed to bring their own firearms. They learned military command procedures, some close-order drill and how to follow orders. Southern forces were advancing somewhere to the south of Prestonburg, Kentucky, headed this way and they all knew they didn't have much time to prepare; but they all had a willing spirit and there was a sense of readiness about them.

Almost immediately the Birchets' background and training, mostly that of Drury, brought them to the front. He was promoted to captain and Smitty advanced to sergeant, serving under Drury in K Company. John Burke was put with the Birchets in K Company and the others were put in different companies as they were needed. Samuel Thompson was made first lieutenant and Bill Taylor was given the rank of corporal in Company D. The rest were privates and glad to serve wherever needed. All these men were excellent marksmen and both Drury and Smitty were exceptional horsemen. Drury kept his own horse, Beauty, a beautiful bay with a glistening black mane. Ollie loved to see that horse prance and watch Drury as he sat in the saddle like he was part of the horse. What a grand sight it was! John Burke was an excellent horseman as well and Ollie felt grateful that his dad had taught him the art of riding and caring for horses. Although Ollie was not envious, he looked forward to the day that he could have a horse of his own and ride like Captain Drury Birchet.

It was a cold Christmas Eve in 1861 when John Burke placed his six-foot-plus frame into a hand-made hickory rocking chair close to the crackling fire in the Burke's one room log cabin. The smell of oak and hickory wood filled the cabin with a sort of rough fragrance mixed with the aroma of fresh pine. A floor-to-loft Christmas tree with homemade decorations of strung popcorn, mistletoe and holly berries gave a cheerful reflection as the dancing chimney fire and the half-burned candle in the window played ghostly shadows on the rough cabin interior. It was a peaceful scene and John's family hovered close about him in a semi-circle around the fireplace.

"Ollie, you be careful with that hot wax," his mother warned.

"Yes'm," he respectfully answered.

Elizabeth Cooper Burke's busy hands were nimbly placing scraps of colored cotton cloth together in a pretty arrangement as she worked on a quilt for Ollie's bed.

Sue Ellen was threading a needle through popcorn to finish off the tree decorations and ten-year old Ollie was dipping candles as layer after layer of wax coated the wick. There were already eight finished candles hanging between two stakes with a stout cord tied from top point to top point.

"Sue Ellen, don't you think you have about enough popcorn strings for that tree?" Elizabeth asked.

"Almost, Ma'am, I'll just finish up this last one."

John reached over to a small stand behind his chair and picked up a well-worn family Bible. He flipped through the pages quickly with the assurance of one who knew where he was going and had been there many times before. His blue-gray eyes glanced from family member to family member and each knew exactly what that look meant.

"Everyone gather around. Stop whatever you're doing—it's time for God's Word!" John ordered softly.

Elizabeth's hands immediately folded on her quilt work and pushed back a strand of black hair seasoned slightly with streaks of gray. Ollie leaned against the bricks to the right of the fireplace and Sue Ellen leaned back against her mother's legs. All eyes came to rest on John as his deep voice filled the room with the words from Saint Luke, chapter two:

> And it came to pass in those days, that there went out a decree from Caesar Augustus, that all the world should be taxed. (And this taxing was first made when Cyrenius was governor of Syria.) And all went to be taxed, everyone to his own city. And Joseph also went up from Galilee, out of the city of Nazareth into Judea,

unto the city of David, which is called Bethlehem; (because he was of the house and lineage of David:) To be taxed with Mary his espoused wife, being great with child. And so it was, that, while they were there, the days were accomplished that she should be delivered. And she brought forth her firstborn son, and wrapped him in swaddling clothes, and laid him in a manger; because there was no room for them in the inn. And there were in the same country shepherds abiding in the field, keeping watch over their flock by night. And, lo, the angel of the Lord came upon them, and the glory of the Lord shone round about them: and they were sore afraid. And the angel said unto them, Fear not: for, behold, I bring you good tidings of great joy, which shall be to all people. For unto you is born this day in the city of David a Savior, which is Christ the Lord. And this shall be a sign unto you; you shall find the babe wrapped in swaddling clothes, lying in a manger. And suddenly there was with the angel a multitude of the heavenly host praising God, and saying, Glory to God in the highest, and on earth peace, good will toward men.

John reverently came to a halt, with moist eyes, and called his family closer to him as he joined hands with Elizabeth on his right, Ollie on his left; Sue Ellen, between her mother and Ollie, completed the circle.

"Sue Ellen," John began, looking her in the eyes, "on this night we celebrate the birth of our Lord. I know each one of us has something to be thankful for, and something to ask the Lord for, so let us begin in prayer with you. OK, darlin'?"

"All right, Daddy," Sue Ellen said and she began, "Dear Lord, we love you so very much and we are thankful to be together here at our home as a family. We thank you for the many blessings you have given us and even if everything was to end in this life right now, we have been most blessed. I thank you for my brother. I thank you for my sweet Mother and her gift of life to me and Ollie.

I thank you for my Daddy and I pray you will be with him as he goes off with the soldiers to fight for our land and our rights. Please protect him, O Lord, 'cause we will miss him so much. And, and . . ." Her eyes began to fill with tears and she could say no more.

After a long silence, John finally spoke softly, saying, "I think the little missy has prayed a prayer for all of us tonight, for we'll probably never be just like this ever again—not that I wish it, but I sort of feel it."

With this heavy statement, John turned to Ollie and said, "Son, I need to have a man-to-man talk with you."

"Yes, sir," Ollie replied, straightening up at the seriousness in his dad's face and tone.

"Ollie," he said as he placed a large brown hand on the youngster's shoulder. "You're the man of the house now. You know how to hunt and bring in meat; you know how to cut wood and stoke the fire; you also know how to keep lots of water brought in and supplied for your mother. I want you to do exactly what she tells you and make me proud of you. You're too young to go into this strife they call a war, and so it is only fittin' that you take care of the women folks and keep the cabin up for all of us. Do you understand what this means, son?"

Ollie looked down at his feet with a gnawing feeling inside. He struggled not to let it show and after a few seconds of hesitation looked his dad full in the face.

"I won't let you down, sir. I'll do my dead-level best to take care of all you put me in charge of."

A warm smile broke out on John's ruggedly handsome face as he shook his son's hand acknowledging this man-like statement.

"I know you will do just that, son—and God be with you!"

At that moment John's mind flashed back to August of 1852, when his own father was at the point of death. T.C. Burke loved his family, but was never close to them until just before he went to meet the Lord. He and John's mother, Amanda, had found the Lord some time before, but T.C. never learned how to communicate with John and Marcy, his sister. Ollie and Sue Ellen never really knew their grandparents, so this tender time together made John extremely thankful that he had always held his family dear and shared with them. His father had taught him a lesson—of what *not* to do—which he never forgot.

Just after Christmas, on the 26th of December, General Garfield mustered his troops and, after many tearful good-byes, set out on a slow march leading them up the Livisa Fork of the Big Sandy River. After a few days they cut across in line toward Prestonburg, Kentucky, with plans to camp in the Richardson area.

New weapons had replaced many of the smoothbore muskets the hill folks had used for years. The .58 caliber Springfield rifle-musket was by far the most plentiful. It was made over from the US Rifle Model 1841 and boasted a forty-inch bright steel barrel. It weighed nine pounds and used a paper-wrapped mini-bullet charged with sixty grains of black powder. This weapon combined the percussion system with the musket in rifled barrels, which was much more accurate for a longer distance. A trained soldier could load and fire one of these popular weapons up to six times per minute.

A limited number of Sharps rifles were also issued and were valued by those men lucky enough to receive one. This weapon was a breech-loaded rifle, which used a linen-wrapped bullet. The trigger guard served as a lever which, when pulled down, lowered a block and revealed the breech. The cartridge was inserted and the act of placing the lever back clipped off the back of the linen exposing the powder. The percussion cap was used to ignite the powder. This weapon was much in demand, but there were not enough of them to supply all the troops.

A good number of men were issued the Army Colt handgun, a single-action revolver developed in the 1840s. It was an accurate percussion revolver with smooth hardwood handles, and each man who received one felt honored. Drury and Smitty both were in that lucky bunch, and John boasted a new single-shot Sharps rifle for his scabbard.

John Burke and many of these down-to-earth hill folks marched off toward an enemy they had never faced. Most, including General Garfield, had never fired a firearm at another human being. They had never experienced the fear and emotion of an all-out battle with hundreds of men engaged in mortal combat trying to annihilate one another. If they had been asked before the battle, most would have said they were not afraid. But all would soon discover that war was so drastically different than anything any one of them had ever experienced.

THREE

He Restoreth My Soul

B Y THE TIME OLLIE HAD BROUGHT IN FOUR BIG ARMLOADS OF WOOD, John had a roaring fire going and it was dark outside. The wind had picked up, whipping around the cabin from the southwest and whistling through the split rail fence that made up the walls of the shed.

"You know, Ollie, God really does restore and provide for our souls. Even after all this loss I feel Him working on my soul, my body, and my mind right now," John said as he lowered himself into his chair. He noticed that his words seemed to have a calming effect on Ollie.

"Yes, sir. Me too, sir—and you do too, Dad. You being here sure means a lot to me! I was really up and down—mostly down until you got home."

John took a great deal of encouragement in the words of his son—the only family he had left.

The log cabin was snug, with a lean-to shed and two stalls on the south side. It was a simple structure used mainly to shelter

41

domestic animals, which at present included one Jersey cow that afforded the family milk and butter. It was Ollie's chore to care for her.

"I reckon I ought to feed and milk Daisy," Ollie sighed. "She was missed getting milked a couple o' times while I was bunkin' over at th' Birchets', 'n she don't take kindly to that for sure."

"Keep warm, son. This leg of mine ain't too good yet and it didn't like all the walkin' I did today. Anyway, go ahead and I'll jus' sit here by the fire to warm it up a spell."

Ollie went to the barn with the wind blowing straight through his trouser legs. It made his spine chill and he shivered involuntarily. He lifted the leather loop on the pole gate that swiveled on two leather hinge-straps, carefully raised and moved the gate enough to edge around it to the back part of the shed. Daisy heard him coming, mooed softly, and tossed her head as if to say, "It's about time!"

"I know, I know, Daisy," Ollie said. "I'm gettin' there and I'll give you an extra helpin' t'night for being so patient with me. 'Sides, it's goin' to be plenty cold."

Ollie forked a healthy helping of fodder with lots of corn nubbins to make Daisy happy enough to moo her thanks. He got the galvanized pail and milking stool from wooden pegs on the wall and in a short time returned to the cabin with a ten-quart bucket three quarters full of warm milk loaded with butterfat. John turned from staring into the coals in the fireplace to watch Ollie set the bucket of milk down and pull off his heavy coat.

"Brr-rr, it's really getting colder out there. Already some flakes of snow, jus' like you said. That fire sure does feel good," Ollie said, his teeth chattering as he moved close to the fire holding out two red hands to get warm.

"Not too close," John remarked. "If you get hot too fast, your hands will start burnin'."

An hour later father and son had eaten a meal of broiled rabbit, heated canned beans, and cold biscuits warmed over the fire. This was topped off with two healthy glasses of fresh warm milk straight from a grateful Daisy who felt relief after the milking process. Ollie had put the rest of the milk into a crock, covered it with cheese-cloth, and set it into the cold section of the cabin away from the fire. He looked at two other crocks with soured milk and thick cream on the top.

"Guess we'll hafta churn tomorrow, Dad, or we'll end up just throwing this clabbered milk to the hogs 'n chickens."

John had two fattening hogs not too far off from killing time and about a dozen chickens that roosted in the rafters of the shed. That was all the livestock the Burkes kept. Being a woodsman and a good hunter, John kept fresh meat on the table from the forest, streams, and fields. They all had worked a small garden, raising a few vegetables; John and Ollie had done the preparing of the soil and planting, and Elizabeth and Sue Ellen had done the rest, including the canning and preparing of jams and jellies. Mason glass jars had become common just a couple of years before and Elizabeth took advantage of the canning process like a lot of other hill folks. Their pantry was well stocked with the canning that the women did from the two gardens, one on Mill Creek in Virginia, and the one they inherited when they purchased this five-acre parcel.

Sitting back in his chair, warm by the fire and full from supper, John realized just how much he was fighting off the loneliness from the absence of his women folk. He knew he must go on with life for the sake of a young boy who relied on him, but he also knew it would be very difficult.

"Ollie, go over to the coat rack and bring me my saddlebag. Watch out now, mind you—it's a trifle heavy."

The coat-rack was just a few steps away so Ollie reached up to the well-worn saddlebag. Something struck him funny and he mused to himself, *Hmm, a saddlebag with no saddle, nor nary a horse?* It was heavy, but he carried it to his dad.

"Stay handy, Ollie," John said as the lad was turning away, then quickly turned back. "We have been so carried away with the loss of your mother and sister that I nearly forgot jus' how important you are to me."

A bit embarrassed, Ollie looked down and twitched a little nervously. "T'was nothin," he said.

"Yes, it was somethin' and I'll be the first to admit it! You're not only my son, you're a good son, and you have been a stand-up son to the women folks and to me. I'm proud of you and I jus' want to show you that I am."

He worked with the cold leather a minute, then opened a bulging compartment and pulled out a plain leather belt with an army holster and a Confederate buckle inscribed "C.S.A.". Very carefully he took the revolver out of the holster, released the revolving cartridge cylinder, and removed the live, paper-wrapped bullets one at a time until he held six in his hand. Ollie's eyes were full of expression and his mouth formed a big "O," which he did not utter. John watched the expression on the youngster's face as he worked with the cylinder.

He left the percussion caps in place, and put the cylinder back to normal position. He then handed the weapon to Ollie handle first, and said, "Ollie, this is my present to you just as soon as you learn how to use it, respect it, and treat it like what it is—a killing machine."

At first Ollie was speechless! His eyes got so large that John thought he was going to lose them.

"Me, Dad? It's for me? I—I can't believe it—wow, I do believe it. You brought this home for me?" he repeated. "Oh, Dad! It is beautiful. It is—is it real? It's not a toy is it, Dad? I mean those are real bullets aren't they?" he asked breathlessly as he turned it over and over, looking at its shiny barrel, the beautiful wood handle, the cylinder, and the movement of the hammer as he cocked and released it without allowing it to hit the striking nipple. John could see he was overwhelmed with gratitude. Suddenly Ollie let loose, unable to contain his excitement any longer. He jumped up shouting, "YIPPEE, I mean WOW," and went running around the cabin pointing the pistol at the hewn log walls repeating "Bang—Bang—Bang." Then abruptly he stopped and looked at his dad, somewhat embarrassed.

"I'm sorry, Dad! It—it just got the best of me. This is about the best gift a person could ever get, and—I guess I got excited." John could not control himself at this impulsive outburst. He laughed as he reached out and caught the lad, pulling him close and hugging him tightly to his chest. He was thinking of what a prize this boy was to him. He had never seen him get so excited before and he was genuinely pleased that Ollie liked the gift so much that he put on such a demonstration. As John loosened his grip, Ollie backed off, still enthralled with the Colt.

"It's heavy, Dad! Real heavy," he finally managed to say.

John took the weapon and slipped it back into the holster.

"Yes, son, it's heavy. But more than that—it's dangerous! You are worthy of it, but you need to be taught how to use it proper and it will get lighter as time goes by. You have learned how to shoot a shotgun and musket and soon you'll have a rifle of your own. You're a dead shot and know how to hunt and fish, but learning to use a handgun? Well, that takes a different kind of thinking! It's not used for hunting food so much as for protection, law-enforcement, and survival in these times.

"This weapon is a Colt Army .44 caliber and it's used by both Confederate and Union troops when they can get 'em. You have to pull th' hammer back each time you shoot and it takes a percussion cap like this one on the cylinder and a cartridge. They're called bullets. These are paper-wrapped, but they have linen ones for th' rifles. That's a type of cloth. I'll show you one another time."

Ollie raised his head with a quizzical look on his face, looked down, then back up at his father.

"Dad, you said I'd have a rifle. Don't I already have one?"

John chuckled. "Son, if you mean that musket that you hunt with—no, that ain't no rifle! That's a good shootin' ol' long gun, that's for sure, but the hand-gun revolver I jus' gave you is closer to a rifle than that ol' musket."

He could see the clouds of confusion come over Ollie's face and he knew he had created more questions.

"Let me give you a lesson about small arms that may help you, Ollie. Now, go get me a musket ball."

Ollie obediently went over to a nail beside the cabin door and brought back a leather pouch. He sat down near his dad and reached into the bag for a smooth round musket ball. John, in the meanwhile, took a bullet from the belt of the Colt and handed it to Ollie. "Look at the difference between the two." He paused, giving his son the chance to look it over. "Tell me about the difference, Ollie."

"Well," began the youngster, "one's smooth and round; the other is sorta pointed." He glanced up at his dad.

"This is true, son, but they both do the same job. Now, there's also another difference. Can you tell what it is?"

"One has a covering and a small holder with it?" he queried.

"Yep! Now why do you suppose they both don't look alike?" John asked.

"I don't rightly know," Ollie said with a shrug, looking to his father to fill in the gaps.

"OK, now comes the lesson." Taking the two missiles from Ollie, John began to explain, holding up the ball first.

"You see, son, this is round and smooth 'cause it fits into—and is fired through—a smooth-bore barrel shoulder gun. You know what I mean. When you clean your musket and look down the barrel after she's nice and clean you see smoothness and light—like looking through a tunnel, isn't that right?"

"Yes, sir, I remember that."

"Now, in order to force this ball out that barrel you need powder, wadding, and a primer cap, don't you?" Again the boy nodded his understanding. John took the six-gun from the holster, held the unloaded pistol toward his eye and sighted down it, looking toward the firelight. He handed the weapon to Ollie indicating for him to do the same thing.

"What do you see there, boy? Look close now! Tell me what you see."

Ollie eyed the cylindrical hollow barrel carefully and said, "Well, sir, I see a sorta smoothness. It's clean an' all, but—it's grooved inside—at least that's what it looks like?" He looked up at his dad and John smiled his approval.

"You got it, son! Them grooves is what makes it a rifle, 'cause that's what they call 'rifling.' Now, they don't call that revolver a rifle because of it's size—but sure 'nough that's what it is. You see, a rifle is not necessarily what a gun is—it's the way it's made. Now listen to me, son. This bullet I'm holding here in my hand is the primer, the powder, 'n the wadding all in one piece. 'Sides that; the lead ball is in the end—only it's shaped with a point. When everything in the casing is set off by th' percussion cap, a powerful explosion takes place inside this paper case 'n it burns up th' paper and forces the lead missile, called a bullet, down the barrel of the rifle in a fierce speed. The grooves cause the bullet to spin, and the spinning keeps the bullet going straight to hit the target you aimed it at! Now if you fired this bullet out of your smooth bore musket—that is if you could—it would tumble through the air and not hit a dad gum thing."

Picking up on the lesson quickly, Ollie added, "An' that's why the other one is round, so's it won't tumble." The light had come on in this young but alert mind.

"That's exactly right, son! And that's why a rifle is more accurate, shoots farther, and is a lot handier than the musket. An' that's what I'm goin' to git you soon as I can afford one."

Leaning back in his chair, John pulled out his pipe, filled it with tobacco, and lit up a smoke, something he didn't do often. He was well satisfied with his lesson and, most of all, with his student. He was a simple woodsman, educated better than most, and had few vices, but once in a great while he enjoyed a pipe and was known to occasionally take a sip of corn liquor, especially if he didn't have to pay for it! He gritted his teeth on the pipe stem for his leg was throbbing, though for a while he had forgotten it.

"Ollie, I don't know when I have ever felt so plumb tired out. Almost like I been following a stubborn mule and an ol' plow all day."

"I'm frazzled too, Dad—and even though it's been partly sad, for me it's been a good day too."

Ollie banked the fire then pulled his birch bunk over close to the hot chimney stones. John was already set for the night in his chair, where he slept on occasion. Ollie picked up the quilt his mother had just finished putting together before she died and wrapped it around his dad, who had already kicked off his well-worn boots. Before long Ollie was sound asleep after he had said his nightly prayers thanking the Lord for taking care of their needs and for receiving his mother and sister into His arms.

It was a blue-cold morning when they awoke. Ollie was chilled to the bone as he rolled out of his bunk and was grateful for the heat from the fire John had already stoked up. He quickly put on an outer coat and stomped his cold feet as he warmed his hands at the edge of the chimney. John was busy fixing something to eat while Ollie peered out their one window, seeing nothing but white. He pulled the door open and sure enough, there were acres and acres of fresh snow.

"It appears to be about eight to ten inches, Dad," Ollie guessed.

"Don't surprise me none," John said, glancing at the open door. "Close 'er up, Ollie, or you'll let out all the heat." Ollie shuddered involuntarily as he willingly complied.

After a good breakfast of biscuits cooked in an iron skillet, bacon and scrambled eggs, Ollie washed it all down with ice cold milk while his dad sipped steaming coffee, cradling it to keep his hands warm with the heat of the cup. Ollie set out to clear a path to the shed, where an anxious Daisy mooed a welcome. He fed her, milked her, and fed the hungry chickens as they clucked their pleasure at the shelled field corn that was much better than trying to scratch out breakfast in the snow.

John Burke was in a reflective mood about his family and things of the past. He had lost track of his sister, Marcy Frances, just before he married Elizabeth. Marcy was a well developed young woman by the time she was fourteen and was wooed by a local young man who talked her into running away with him. Before T.C. and Amanda knew what was happening, Marcy was gone, leaving in the middle of the night. This tore John's heart out when he heard about it, for he had been very close to his tall beautiful sister.

He had become a bare-knuckle fighting champion and was away at a fight in Logan, Virginia, when she left. John always blamed himself for not being at home, for he felt Marcy would have come to talk to him if he had been there. After John found the Lord, he began to pray for her and Ira Blankenship, her young man. It was rumored that they went west, but they had not heard from her again.

He lost his father and mother not too long after Marcy's leaving, so it closed a whole chapter of Burkes in John's mind. Even though he had relations on his mother's side, he still felt alone. John married Elizabeth a few years later and when Sue Ellen was born, he felt that a new generation of Burkes was well on the way. Ollie enlarged the family and John thought they would have one more child. Now, that was all gone, and it was just him and Ollie—all alone! As he thought on the family history he walked over to the window, looking out on the snow, and called out to the Lord.

"Oh, God! I am not ungrateful—I love you with all my heart and I know that Dad, Mama, Elizabeth, and Sue Ellen are with you. But what do you have for Ollie and me, Lord? It is so lonely here without my Elizabeth and Sue Ellen. We miss them so much. I know, Lord, that you are our provider so I trust that you have it all under control. I also know that you will never leave us or forsake us. That is your promise. So, I will be expecting your answer—In your time, Father. Amen."

We Will Serve the Lord

THE BURKES HAD NEVER BEEN FARMERS ALTHOUGH THEY DID SOME gardening and canning, raised a few pigs and farm animals for their own needs, and sometimes a little trading. What they excelled in was hunting, fishing, and some trapping of fur-bearing animals for clothing or trading the furs. They never trapped just for the furs alone since John believed that every animal he killed was meat for the table, either his own or someone else's. Therefore, he always had something to trade, barter, or even sell to get the necessities for his family. One day, not long after his return, John was deep in thought concerning Ollie's ability to hunt. When the youngster entered the cabin, it prompted a question from John.

"Ollie, have you been keepin' up with huntin' while I was away?"

"Yes, sir, been huntin' mostly for squirrel and rabbit 'bout once or twice a week," Ollie replied.

"That's good, son. You're not wasting th' meat now are you?"

"Oh, no siree, I got customers in town for the meat—dressed and such!"

John smiled to himself and just shook his head. *Customers! What an imagination.* He limped off without asking for an explanation.

Ollie was already on his way to being just like his father. He had been able to handle the musket his dad had marked as his since he was old enough to load, cock, and shoot it, and had become an expert shot, hunting rabbit and squirrel almost daily. John hadn't found out yet, but young Ollie had been hunting for money from the time John marched off with the Union Army. His "customers" were the Smith family, the Wheelers, as well as two other couples from town who paid him weekly to supply them with wild game. Two dressed rabbits or squirrels a week had earned one dollar each in silver coins from four families.

While John was still mending he walked each day, trying to get his leg stronger. For the most part he stayed around the cabin. He knew he was preoccupied and did not spend enough time with his son, but Ollie seemed to cope very well. He would disappear from time to time, but John was never concerned because the lad was very responsible. John actually appreciated the time alone with his thoughts. He spent a lot of time in prayer and in thought about the spell of terrible fear he had experienced on the battlefield. One afternoon when Ollie returned from one of his outings, John asked him about his schooling. He had not touched on Ollie's education in some time, which made him realize how much he had depended on his wife to follow up with the children.

"Ollie, how have you been doing with your studies? I mean readin' and arithmetic 'n all?"

"Doin' fine, sir. I keep up with school in town 'n attend whenever Mr. Truestone calls class. He is absent some though. Them's th' days I hunt." Then Ollie added a comment that sent John into fits of laughter.

"Master Truestone keeps himself warm these winter months with somethin' from a fruit jar. He tells us students it's medicine, but to me—well, it sure does smell almighty like one hundred percent corn liquor!"

John was satisfied Ollie was doing fine in his schooling so turned his thoughts to something else that had been on his mind—the Union Army. He had been thinking a lot about the challenge Captain Lyons left him with at Paintsville.

The final winter months and the spring of 1862 were busy for both John and Ollie. Ollie was kept busy in the midst of two more sizable snows with his hunting business, practice with his new handgun under his dad's supervision, his chores, and some school. His eleventh birthday, on March 25th, was uneventful. It came and went and not much was said about it.

John received his medical/honorable discharge from the 14th Regiment Kentucky Volunteers, but still was in and out of military headquarters a good deal. He did not tell his son, but he was working for Captain Lyons and the Union Army. His frequent visits to the Army base seemed odd to Ollie. And then there were those frequent mysterious trips to Cherokee, Sandy Hook and over to Carter County. John would be gone sometimes for several days at a time, come back tired, and would seem to be deep in thought. At least, Ollie noticed, his limping seemed to improve and John didn't complain as much as before, but Ollie still had a lot of unanswered questions.

On one of these trips he was gone for nearly three weeks, leaving Ollie in town with Rebecca and her children. The Birchets also had questions about John's absences. Ollie could not answer them, and John never offered any explanation. He left on April 5th and did not return until the 20th. Ollie was very concerned. When John did come home, and without any explanation, he grabbed Ollie and held him up giving him a loving hug.

"Where have you been, Dad? I've been powerful worried 'bout you. So has Becky and the girls." John just acted as if he didn't hear the question. Instead, he produced a beautiful Sharps breech-loading rifle with several boxes of shells. The bullets were enclosed in linen casings instead of paper.

"This is for you, Ollie. It may be late, but happy birthday, son! I know you think I forgot, but I didn't—not really."

Ollie took the beautiful, long rifle and, remembering how he had acted when his dad gave him the revolver, held back his emotion. After all he was in the presence of Rebecca and the girls and he didn't want to act like a kid. John had something for everyone, including Rebecca, but his chief interest was in Ollie's reaction, and he noticed how Ollie was holding himself in check.

"What do you think of her, son. Isn't she a beauty?"

"Oh, Dad, it isn't like any ol' long gun I've ever seen! I can't wait to try her out." Again his eyes showed his excitement as he fondled the nine-pound rifle.

"Pretty soon, son, pretty soon. I'll have to show you some things about that gun that are a lot different than thet ol' musket of yours. You'll pick it up fast though. You've a natural knack with firearms."

"By the way, son, I don't want you to use it for hunting yet. Just git familiar with it and keep it good 'n clean," he said with a glow on his face as he watched Ollie's eyes. They told the whole story of how pleased the lad was.

John wore his regular clothes on these trips to military head-quarters, his deer skin outer garments and coonskin cap. He almost always wore moccasins and rarely boots anymore. One day after his long absence in April, he rode in on a pretty sorrel mare with the Union cavalry brand. When Ollie asked about it, John's reply was curt and defensive.

"Sometimes I take the loan of a horse from the fort. After all, son—I *was* in the Army, you know!"

Ollie decided to mind his own business and leave his dad alone. *Probably he's still hurting from Mom's death. Maybe his leg's bothering him more than he lets on.* Anyway, with all the time Ollie was spending alone, he was learning to do quite well. He was large for his age and seemed to be older to most people. He was seldom around other children so he acted very mature for his age. He thought of himself as an adult more than a child, and was not known to buddy up to anyone in particular, even on the days he was in school. When the children would gather and play "Andy Over" and other such games at the schoolhouse once in awhile he would join in, but most of the time he would just watch.

There were special times toward spring when he and John would do things together, like going to Blaine Creek to fish. Ollie had learned to make a hickory spear Indian fashion, wade into the water, wait, and spear fish in the small streams so abundant in Lawrence County. It was also nice to just sit on the bank with his dad, holding a pole cut from a sapling with store-bought hooks and homemade sinkers made out of lead. They would dig earthworms, which to him were just plain "fishworms," then go fishing for the day. They would boil some eggs, take a piece of salt pork, some cornbread, a jug of buttermilk and it would be a picnic. It was one of these times together late in April when John finally confided in his young son.

"Ollie, I need to apologize to you for bein' so private this past winter. You have taken to it real well, but I jus' need to explain to you." John hesitated as if fumbling for words. "You see, son, I'm still not supposed to tell you—but most don't realize what a distinct young man you are; you're more like a man than a boy, and that's the way I always treat you. What I'm goin' to tell you is not to be told to anyone else, and I am tellin' you 'cause you're my closest friend as well as my son. You understand, don't you?" Ollie nodded and knew this was very serious business.

"Ollie, you see, I'm not out of the army at all!" He waited to let that take effect, watching Ollie's expression before going ahead.

"What do you mean, Dad? Didn't they give you a discharge 'n all?" his eyes widened as he waited for an answer.

"Well, it's kinda hard to understand. I do have a discharge, but the army came to me and asked me to work for 'em. So, even though I'm free to go and do my druthers, I am a hired man to the Union Army. The truth is I have been working as—well, sort of a spy for the government."

"A spy? Really, Dad? Really?"

John smiled at the boy's excitement.

"Yes, Ollie, really. They picked me because of my knowing the wilderness 'n all. I know this area very well and make my way in the woods better 'n most; so I was a natural to be able to move around in these hills to check on Confederate troop movements and also enemy undercover activities against our side. In other words, I am still almost the same as in th' Army, jus' not so much as anyone else knows, do you understand?" Ollie was filled with wonder, and a feeling of pride for his dad was building up inside.

"I *knew* somethin' was goin' on!" Ollie exclaimed, kicking the dirt with his foot. "Now it all makes good sense to me. Sure, Dad—your secret is safe with me and I won't mention it to no one."

Ollie was pleased to be taken into his dad's confidence, and John was relieved that his young son would understand his absences, in case—God forbid—some misfortune would befall him and he would not return from one of these trips. On the long trip in April he had a very close call that almost took his life, so he felt he should give his loyal young son some information. John knew that the army had a larger plan in mind, which might necessitate Ollie's involvement. This is why he felt it important to prepare the lad with some knowledge of his military activities.

"By the way," John remarked, "didn't we come out here to do some fishin'? Betcha I catch th' biggest one—I betcha!" The race was on.

It was a good day for fishing. John caught two large bass and Ollie caught a catfish that was larger than John's bass, so he was the winner!

It didn't take long to start a fire after gathering some dry branches and bark off a nearby birch. When it decreased to a slow burn, John buried two large potatoes in the glowing coals then helped Ollie practice handling the six-shooter. He was becoming very comfortable working with the weapon, though he had not fired it much yet. John felt there was time for that. They went from working with the Army Colt to sharing some memories and good times about Elizabeth and Sue Ellen.

"Do you remember that time we came here with your mother and Sue Ellen?"

"Yes, sir—I sure do." Ollie giggled then added, "You got mad at Sue Ellen 'cause she started making noise and throwin' sticks in the creek. She was scarin' all the fish away."

"Yep! She loved to go fishin'—but hated to fish." John laughed. "She sure was good at cleanin' and fryin' 'em though."

"Yeah, I'll always remember her," Ollie said. John noticed that the remark was cheerful. It wasn't sad at all. *This is good*, he thought.

When the potatoes were nearly finished they roasted the cleaned fish over the fire with a sharp hickory stick and the feast was on. They ate the eggs, fish, baked potatoes seasoned with salt and pepper John had remembered to roll up in some paper before they left. They added buttered cornbread and washed it all down with grateful swallows of buttermilk. John figured that with such a feast he would save the salt pork for another day.

Ollie spent the next few days firing his Sharps rifle, improving with every shot. He was impressed with the accuracy of the weapon and, although he had to steady the gun to take aim, because of its weight and his size, he could hit anything he aimed at 150 yards away and even further.

He loved the ease of just placing a cartridge in the breech. He raised the lever that prepared the linen-wrapped bullet for firing. He then pulled back the hammer to half-cocked position, placing a cap on the nipple and, bringing the hammer to full cock, he squeezed the trigger. The cartridge eliminated all the work of using powder, wadding, and setting a primer cap in separate functions. It increased his shooting ability by several times for rapid fire and accuracy. John watched him and shook his head in awe at the ability this eleven-year-old had with a firearm. He decided it was time to break him in on the Colt as well. The belt and holster did not fit Ollie, so John buckled it on himself and handed the glistening .44 caliber six-shooter to the boy, who had already learned the procedure for slipping the percussion caps and bullets in the cylinder.

"Hold it straight out, Ollie, just as if it was your finger and you was pointing it at something. That's right! Use both hands, sight right down the middle of the barrel, hold your breath, and squeeze the trigger. Don't jerk it."

Ollie did just as he was told and a fearsome bang sounded as the six-shooter flew up when it recoiled. He had aimed at the fork of a low branch in an oak tree and couldn't see where the bullet hit. John saw it well, looking over Ollie's five-foot-two-inch height.

"It was a might low and to the left, son, but if it had been a man, he'd a been hurtin' for sure. You pulled down or jerked a little just as you fired the gun. The weight it takes for your finger to pull that trigger is still a little heavy for you. You'll just have to practice 'till you can shoot without thinking about it."

Ollie continued to practice by carefully cocking the pistol, taking aim and shooting at objects at a distance of about twenty five yards. He did get better and finally was hitting his mark, or within inches of it, every time.

My dear God, John thought in a private prayer, *what would have happened to Ollie if I had fallen and not returned from the battle, or from the recent missions I have been sent on. What is Ollie going to do, God, without a mother, without a sister and a family— other than myself?*

John was standing by a weeping willow tree as he prayed silently in his spirit, which he did often when he walked in the woods and frequently had a strong sense of God's presence. Many a time he had knelt beside a rock or a tree and prayed out loud or sometimes would pray silently and God would speak to him in his spirit. It was not as if John would hear an audible voice, but at times he would hear sentence communication deep within and knew that God had answered. At other times he knew he had to wait and would indeed know the answer—in God's time. John always practiced patience with God and loved these great communion times alone with his Maker, knowing that God was watching over the both of them. He sensed that God wanted to speak to him—here and now! He prayed silently again. *Yes, Lord, I am here. Just like Samuel—Here am I, Lord, your servant—John Burke! Speak to me, Lord. I am listening. Amen!* And John remembered his earlier prayer as he said amen.

John watched and listened and, on the breath of God, the answer came—within his spirit.

I am your family, John Burke. You are my servant and Ollie is my servant. You are my sons, as Joshua was my son; you and Ollie are my sons as Joshua declared, "*and if it seem evil unto you to serve the Lord, choose this day whom you will serve; whether the gods which your father served that were on the other side of the flood, or the gods of the Amorites, in whose land you dwell: **but as for me and my house, we will serve the Lord.**" You have also chosen my house and as I protected and fought for Joshua—so will I fight for you. I will restore unto thee, John Burke. I will restore unto Ollie. He will have sisters and family—he will have a mother. I will perform my word, John Burke.*

John thrilled at God's word. He knew within himself that God's word to him was true. Just as true as the written word out of God's book, this word he heard was God talking to him. He remembered one of his favorite stories from Genesis 22. God had sent Abraham to slay Isaac, his only son from Sarah, his wife. He remembered how God withheld his hand as he started to strike his son dead. He remembered how God provided a ram caught in the thicket to offer up a sacrifice after Isaac was spared. He also remembered how Abraham called that place on Mount Moriah Jehovah-jireh which meant "God will provide." And He did. God always provided and for this reason John knew that the word he heard in his innermost being was true. God never lies!

FIVE

A Wise Son
Heareth His Father

THE HILLS WERE ALIVE WITH SPRINGTIME IN LAWRENCE COUNTY. LEAVES were bursting forth, flowers swayed in the breeze, and here, where western Virginia meets eastern Kentucky at the waters of the Big Sandy River, it was hard to believe there was a war going on nearby—but it was. The river was busy with push boats bringing war supplies and cargos to Louisa and on up the river to the area where battles were being fought closer to Prestonburg. The steamer *Sandy Valley* and other steamboats were loaded with barrels of flour and pork earmarked for the Fighting 14th Kentucky Volunteers.

Small pockets of Rebel soldiers were scattered here and there throughout the county especially to the west and south. This prompted a secret meeting between John Burke and Captain Samuel P. Lyons, who was responsible for military intelligence directly under the commanding officer. General Garfield was no longer with this Louisa Garrison, having been sent toward Tennessee just after the Middle Creek battle. Two o'clock in the afternoon found them huddled over a map of eastern Kentucky, including Lawrence County, talking in low voices.

"Burke, we have reason to believe that a company of Rebs is bivouacked in the Sandy Hook area over towards Morgan County. Our sources believe that those troops are an advance party of a much larger force that may be heading this way to occupy our garrison at Louisa."

"It may be so, sir. I have some Damron cousins from the Twelve Pole Creek area of Wayne County that are part of the Rebel forces. Family gossip is that at least one of them is somewhere over west or south of Louisa territory. I don't know much about where, but—well—you know how family rumors are. I guess it leaked out to me 'cause they all think I'm no longer attached to the Army."

"That's good, Burke, I mean the part about them thinking you're out of the Army now. That's why you're so important to us and why we count on your loyalty," Captain Lyons volunteered thoughtfully.

"By the way, were you aware that two Damron boys have joined our forces from over Wayne County way?" Captain Lyons added.

"Well, I'll be dang busted," John called out, which was just about as close as he ever came to swearing. "I didn't have any idea. They must be Spurlock Damron's sons, Lewis and John, his older brother."

"I wouldn't know about that part, Burke, but I do know the younger one is a sergeant and they're with the 39th Mounted Infantry in K Company. I doubt that you'll have time to look 'em up now though, which brings me to the reason I sent for you. I want you to reconnoiter the western area and on into Morgan County, winding north and coming back through Carter County. Can you do this and be back in a month?"

"Well, sir—that's a tall order! I do know all that country pretty well, but that's pretty wild terrain and, well—on foot 'n all."

"Take a mount and pack animal if you need, Burke. We simply have to acquire this information. It may make a big difference in our defense here in Louisa."

"Well, sir, a mount and pack animal would help, but I have another consideration—an eleven-year-old boy. He is pretty able for a youngster his age, but a month is a long time to let him shift for himself." Captain Lyons seemed to have all the answers.

"Take him with you, John. After all, you're a civilian out hunting and trapping; he'll just add to your cover and may be suitable company for you. Why—we may even work out putting him on the payroll," he said with a twinkle in his eye. With that Captain Lyons stood, which told John that the meeting was over and he was dismissed. He also knew the captain considered the job done.

Captain Sam Lyons was a stocky man, muscular and just under six feet in height. His brown hair was receding at the forehead, much to his dismay. He kept his dark mustache neatly trimmed. Sharp gray eyes, a warm easy smile with a decisive manner and a strong handshake caused most men to notice him, if they got that close. John had become very fond of this officer and had a growing respect for him.

John accompanied Captain Lyons to the administration building, where he filled out the necessary request forms for the armory and stables. He proceeded to pick up a Sharps rifle and adequate ammunition for the Sharps as well as his Colt. Then he went to the stables for mounts, saddles and other necessary equipment.

"Howdy, Glen," John greeted. "I need your help again to select a couple of good riding mounts with all the trimmin's. Goin' to be gone awhile. And, Glen, they need to be civilian animals," he said with a twinkle in his eyes.

"Glad to help you. You're one of my good customers. At least you know how to take care of th' animals, not like some o' these ornery knot-heads thet don't know which end o' th' horse to git on," Glen called back.

Glen Adkins was a burly, bearded man with a winsome smile, who knew that John meant mounts and saddle equipment without military marks if possible. The army kept a few horses and mules as well as western style saddles just for the purpose of scouting and civilian use. It didn't matter as much with the weapons, for both Confederate and Union forces had enough of their equipment circulating in non-military use to avert any suspicion. In just a short time he had selected two good horses for himself and Ollie, a mule for pack, saddles, blankets, and pack bags for the mule—all standard issue that could have been purchased anywhere. He had bills of sale with non-military insignias or markings for everything as well as a ten-day supply of feed and fifty dollars in cash to purchase anything additional he might need.

John had mixed emotions when he took these field assignments, for there was always the chance of meeting up with some of the Damron family members who were Confederates. They were cousins on his mother's side of the family that he knew and loved. None were slave owners, just men who lived in the South and enlisted in the Southern cause because they felt it was the thing to do. Each of these men in the border states, as they joined and picked sides, faced the same decisions: knowing that at some time they may have artillery or guns facing each other with the possibility of killing some family member. Still a man must do the job he hired on to do, and sometimes the thing he must do was not a pleasant task.

As he rounded the bend to Two Mile, the area where the small cabin was located, John turned his thoughts to Ollie and the task he would have to get ready. John was riding the black gelding leading a beautiful bay and the mule. *Ollie will be excited about going on this trip and he will sure be a comfort and help to me with this bad leg of mine. I'm glad the captain was so agreeable about Ollie coming along.* As John approached the cabin, Ollie turned the corner of the shed and started running toward him, shouting excitedly.

"What did you do, Dad, trade for 'em? Did you buy 'em, Dad, did you?"

"Hold your horses, son, jus' hold your horses!" John grinned as he tied the animals then took Ollie by the shoulder and led him into the cabin. Settling into his chair to rest his leg, he explained their mission. Ollie felt very important and sort of awed at the aspect of traveling with his dad and being an aid to the military effort.

"Ollie, Rebecca and her kids are our closest friends and they live only a couple of miles away. I need you to ride the bay over there and ask them to take care of the place for us. They can have all the eggs and milk, but Daisy needs cared for and food put out occasionally for the chickens. Also, get word to your customers that you'll be away on a hunting trip with your dad. If anyone asks about the bay—by the way, her name is Ginger—jus' tell 'em she's borrowed, which is the truth, Ollie, and don't say anything else about where we are goin'. You understand, son?"

"Yes, sir." Ollie climbed on the mount using a piece of rock to gain access to the stirrup. Off he went at a trot toward Louisa, with his mind full of excitement.

John began to busy himself packing the mule with dried meat and nut meats from last fall's collection of hickory and black walnuts. He fondly remembered Ollie and Sue Ellen dutifully cracking all those nuts without a thought to what the future, so near, would hold for the Burke family. Now those nuts will be used as staples for a trip on the fringes of war and he thought of that saying he thought was from the Bible: "Only God knows the future." He included a slab of bacon, two of the molds of butter that Ollie had so religiously prepared from the churn with clabbered milk, plenty of salt and some pepper.

John knew the life of a woodsman so he prepared what they would need to keep them well off the beaten track. Shooting game would be restricted because they were in a war zone. That thought caused John to pack a musket with ample ammunition for hunting purposes. If an opportunity for hunting presented itself the popping sound of a musket would attract less attention than a .52 caliber Sharps. The roads to all the areas they would be reconnoitering were primitive, but he felt that he could find out more by being out of sight as much as possible. John included a packet with emergency bandages and some small tools in case of injury. *Just in case,* he thought. Finally he packed the bedding, although not much was needed since summer was coming on and the weather was quite warm already. A couple of Macintosh rain slickers topped off the mule's gear and he was done.

In spite of the throbbing pain in his leg, he endured the effort of packing the mule better than he thought he would. His leg felt at times as though someone was chopping on it from the inside. He had learned to bear the pain and figured he was going to face it for the rest of his life.

Ollie came galloping back on Ginger just as the sun started setting. He quickly dismounted and filled his dad in on what he had accomplished.

"Becky said they'd be glad to help out, Dad. She didn't even ask 'bout th' horse and—what's next? What do you want me to do?" he asked all out of breath. John could see his excitement and the flush on his face. It warmed him to see the youngster's anticipation.

"Take care of Daisy 'n the chickens, Ollie. Jus' figure on doin' your chores and if anythin' else is needed, I'll let you know," he said with a smile.

Ollie enthusiastically took care of the assigned chores, caring for Daisy and putting out some feed for the chickens.

John's plan was to get started early in the morning since he had already decided to go north part way using the woods then take a heading toward the mouth of Deephole Branch. There he would cut across John Birchet's farm and head west toward Cherokee, either by way of Twin Branch or toward Pleasant Ridge. He was acquainted with all the farmers in that direction and knew he could count on them not to ask about what he was doing.

After a good supper they both drifted off to a sound sleep. The emotion of the day and their excitement did not prevent them from a deep slumber.

Before daylight the two travelers were rolling up their bedding and preparing for departure.

"Ollie, go into the tack room and get a small supply of kerosene. We want to take our lanterns 'n I almost forgot it. Not too much now, we can pick up more along the way if we need it," John called out.

Soon the horses were brought out saddled and the rifles were placed in their scabbards. John buckled his Colt around his waist and told Ollie to put his in his saddlebag.

"I don't know how much silver you have, son, but if you don't have it put away safe, now's the time to do it."

"I got it in a can in the corner of the cabin, Dad. It's under those two loose boards, kinda buried. Is that all right?"

"That sounds safe enough, son. The cabin should be fine while we're gone with Becky and th' girls lookin' in 'n all."

The black gelding snorted out a warning and the mule pranced nervously, signaling that someone was coming. Silhouetted in the early dawn a horse and rider were approaching the cabin front.

"Hello the cabin—is that you, John Burke?"

John immediately recognized the voice. "It shore is me, Johnny Allison, what 'n the world are you doin' out here this early?"

John Allison, sheriff of Lawrence County, reined in and dismounted. "Wal, I heerd you 'n the boy was takin' off on a huntin' trip or somethin' and jus' thought I'd catch you before you left," he said, shifting his cud of tobacco. He turned and spat before continuing. "Two men roughed up some folks over on the Point and took their belongings—what little they had—'n was headed toward Blaine. Since I didn't know which way y'all wuz headin, thought I might warn you."

"I appreciate the tellin', Johnny, I'll keep my eyes peeled and watch out for them fellers. Sorry I can't ask you for a bit of breakfast, Sheriff, but we ain't eatin' yet. Sorta planned on fixin' somethin' on the move down the road apiece. You're mighty welcome to travel with us a spell, if you have a mind to."

After the sheriff found they were going toward the mouth of Deephole, he declined. He thought he'd head across the hill toward Smoky Valley to see if he could cut the thief's trail. John Allison was a determined man and the two ruffians, whoever they were, had him to reckon with unless they had fled his county.

"Why didn't Sheriff Allison bring a posse with him to catch them two fellers, Dad?" Ollie asked with a curious look.

"Son, John Allison is a posse all by himself. He is an apt man for the job of sheriff 'n if he runs into them two he's after, they better jus' give up peaceably 'cause they won't have a chance," John answered with a grin.

So it was, on the fifth day of May 1862, that John and his son headed north with the sun coming up over the Big Sandy and the taller Virginia hills in the background. John led the horses single file, staying on the well-traveled trail heading into bottomland country. The hills on either side were covered with large oak trees. Occasionally a poplar peeked out among the new oak leaves and several large sycamore trees stood tall reaching skyward.

Daisies and morning glory flowers abounded over the rich bottomland, already high with rye grass. The air was fresh with the smell of early summer, and it was a good morning to be out enjoying nature and God's creation. The animals led off in a quick step as the terrain began to change and John had to pick a winding path as a steep grade increased in front of them. After what seemed to be a long hard climb between sassafras shrubs and sumac bushes, plus several encounters with blackberry vines, Ollie found himself alongside his dad. He noticed the look on his face as John enjoyed the scenery below. As far as the eye could see to the north and to the west was valley after rolling valley cradled by an endless chain of hilltops covered with huge oaks and dotted with occasional giant pine trees. Looking back toward Louisa, there was a blue haze filtering the morning sun, as it appeared to be about ten o'clock in the morning. Ollie was deep in thought thinking it was hard to believe how late it was and how much he had enjoyed the ride when John's words interrupted.

"Well, son, we'll stop here to eat a bite 'n let the horses rest a spell." John slowly dismounted to the right instead of the customary left, favoring his left leg, which obviously was giving him some major discomfort. Ollie saw him wince as he involuntarily let out a moan between his tightened lips.

"It'll take some gittin' use to—this horse ridin' for me, son, 'specially with this sore leg o' mine."

Ollie simply answered, "Yes, sir!" He wanted to reach out to his dad, but simply did not know what to say. He dismounted, dropping the bridle reins for Ginger to graze, then immediately began to pick up dried branches and twigs for starting a fire for he knew his dad would want coffee. Ollie found a nice clearing, pushed back the high grass, and gathered some rocks to form a fire circle. Before long John had the fire going and two thick slices of bacon starting to smell mighty good. Water in a pot was just ready to boil so he put some coffee into a piece of cheesecloth, waited for the water to boil, then dropped it into the water. Soon the aroma of coffee mixed with the smell of bacon filled the air. Ollie took two cups of flour, some butter, a pinch of salt, added a little water, and shortly had a batter ready to drop into the pan when the bacon was done. It wasn't long before the travelers enjoyed biscuits with rich butter and preserves along with a hunk of bacon from the hog they had butchered in February. They had salted down one hog away for their own use and traded the other for fodder and shucked corn for Daisy and the chickens.

John pulled out his pipe and packed it, took a light from the dying embers of the campfire, and sat back against a big oak.

"The animals will do to feed on that sweet grass a little, Ollie, 'n I want to take some time to talk to you about the business we're doing for the Army. We may not have time to talk later on, and I jus' want to make sure you understand what we're about."

Ollie scooted up close and nodded his head.

"You see, Ollie, it will seem to you at times that we are jus' visitin' folks, when all the while we are working. Spy work is kinda like doin' a lot of listenin' and not much talkin'. Some times I will jus' ask innocent family-type, friendly questions and hear all that is said. I might say no more than, 'Wal, I'll be' or somethin' like that, but pick up a lot of stuff to remember. It'll be after we git alone, jus' you 'n me, that we will write down what was said that's important. That's where you'll come in handier than a coonhound on a trail. I'm goin' to use you to do my writin' and map makin'. You see, part of what we're to do is make maps. Do you have any questions, son?"

At first Ollie shook his head, then changed his mind, blurting out, "What do you want me to say or do, Dad?"

"Ollie, don't say much at all unless I ask you to or you're takin' the lead from me. In other words, jus' mostly listen and sometimes it's OK to ask a question. Jus' don't give your opinion, even if you have one."

Ollie understood and was satisfied with his role, although he thought it probably was not an important one. After all, he was just delighted to be here with his dad, riding out into country he hadn't been in before. Ollie was a good woodsman for his age and had never been lost in all his hunting trips, even over unfamiliar land. His natural ability caused him to take notice of things in the woods—and also in the heavens.

It was time to get on the road again, so Ollie caught Ginger and Silky and rubbed them down a little before putting the blankets and saddles back on. They had rested about an hour and a half and he figured it was probably close to noon although he did not have a watch. His dad had a pocket watch, but he could pretty well tell what time it was by the sun. They mounted and rode off in a northerly direction around a ridge where the terrain leveled off as they reached the top of the hill. The land was clear as they looked off to the left into the valley below where grazing cattle dotted the land. Thirty minutes or so later Ollie noticed a family plot with some rock and slab markers. Seeing his interest, John filled him in on the location.

"This is the Carter family graveyard, son." Ollie glanced at the markers, but John noticed how quickly he changed his interest. "Who's all them cows belong to, Dad?" he asked looking south to the hillside dotted with cattle.

"They all belong to your Uncle John Birchet, Ollie. Matter of fact we're on his land now and jus' about all the land you see in any direction belongs to him."

"My goodness, he must be a wealthy man, Dad," expressed Ollie. "How much land does he own?"

"I don't rightly know, son, but it must be over a thousan' acres. As far as bein' wealthy, I suppose you could say so in land, but he's a sight more wealthy than that in jus' bein' a good man and followin' the Good Book 'n the Golden Rule, about doin' for others. By the way, son, he's not really your uncle, but you can call him that in due respect. We are close to the Birchet family and we may be relatives somewhere back. Seems so at times."

Another thirty minutes of riding found John and Ollie descending rather sharply as they came off the crest of the hill and Ollie had to lean back in the saddle to put a strain on Ginger's reins. John had shortened the stirrups for his height, but it was still a long reach. Finally they began to level off a little as they came up on a small clearing off to the right and Ollie noticed they were following the trail beside a bubbling branch of water making its way over the large rocks.

The well-worn wagon road was very rocky. On the left was a small hill with lots of brush, briars, and small saplings. The path continued to descend to a nice clearing and the trail crossed another stream of water flowing from the spring rains. John reined up as he let the animals drop their noses in the cool water to drink their fill. Another few minutes of riding found them at the point where the branch of water they had been following emptied into the larger creek.

"This is Deephole Branch," John said, turning to his son. "It's where this area gets its name."

"Why do they call it that, Dad?" asked his inquisitive son.

"Well, I guess I knew that one was coming, Ollie," John said with a big smile. His teeth glistened through his black beard.

"You see where that hill comes down sharp and the creek bed seems to turn agin' that hill?" he said pointing off to the right across a section of cleared bottomland. Ollie nodded.

"As I understand it, there is a deep hole of water there underneath that big cliff-like rock stickin' out. They say you can't find the bottom in that water hole. It's dangerous! They sometimes call it a 'suck-rock', 'cause the current will suck a man in and he'd drown."

Ollie seemed impressed by his dad's story, but his mind turned elsewhere.

"How about the fishin', Dad? Is it any good?"

"Actually, son, about a half mile further down Deephole Branch, you'll find better fishing where it dumps into Blaine Creek right at a bend in the larger body of water. Mind you, it's pretty good in Deephole, but where it ends into Blaine is much better. Maybe we'll get to try it sometime." With that remark John turned his horse and headed up the trail in a curved pattern toward the crest of the next hill with Ollie right behind him.

A House Divided?

A<small>T THE TOP OF THE HILL</small> O<small>LLIE NOTICED ANOTHER FAMILY CEMETERY IN</small> a clearing off to the right, and just down the hill he spotted a big white two-story home with barns and out buildings.

"That's Uncle John's place," explained his dad. "Let's go down and pay 'em a visit." As they headed down the hill toward the Birchet farm, a young lady came out on the porch, drying her hands on the apron she wore over a print dress with a full skirt. Ollie noticed two things about her. First, she was very pretty and second, she wasn't any larger than he was, even though she looked older. Her hair, braided and crossed up over her head, was almost black, with chestnut highlights that looked smooth as silk in the sun. She flashed a big smile across her face as she looked at Ollie.

"Get down for a spell 'n come on in, John Burke," she said. "That must be your young'un, Ollie."

Ollie was surprised she knew who he was. He could not recollect ever seeing her.

"Well, 'pon my soul, if it isn't Eliza!" his dad answered. "My great day you have grown to a fine lady since I last saw you. Where is Rhoda? Is she as lady-like as you?"

"Oh, she's down at the barn gatherin' some eggs," Eliza said. "Pa and Ma will sure be glad to see y'all. Like I said, get off and come on up on the porch; I'll have Wiley see to the horses."

A tall Negro man came around the corner of the house, acknowledging John with a big smile and nod.

"Aftanoon Mista Burke. Been a month o' Sundays since I done seen you," the old gentleman said, walking toward John and Ollie, who had just dismounted. John dropped his reins and walked over to the man, extending his hand.

"Well, Jim, it sure is good to see you. You're lookin' fit as a fiddle. How's your wife doin'?" As he shook his hand vigorously, John continued without waiting for an answer. "Meet my boy, Ollie, Jim. I don't think you've ever seen him." Ollie took the man's hand and the black man almost shook his arm off, pumping it up and down like a water pump.

"I do declah, Mista Ollie, you sho look like your paw. You's a fine lookin' boy." Ollie noticed the hardness of Jim's calloused hand. Jim turned to Eliza. "Don' you go t' botherin' Mista Wiley, little missy, I'll take care o' Mista Burke's horses 'n sech." Before they knew it, he had taken the reins from Ollie and was leading the animals down the hill toward the barn yelling back over his shoulder, "I'll tend to feedin' and rubbin' 'em down while I's at it, so don' you no nevah mind now!"

Ollie and John stepped up on the porch to join Eliza, who had placed two chairs for them. Eager to show some hospitality, she offered them hot sassafras tea.

"I'd be down right pleased to have a cup, Eliza. How about you, Ollie?" John said without hesitation.

"I think I'd rather have a cup of nice cool water, if you'd point me toward the well."

Eliza took Ollie by the hand, led him to the corner of the porch, and showed him the well, which was out a ways from the side of the house, then turned to go inside for John's tea.

At the well, Ollie dropped the long chain through a squeaky pulley until he heard the bucket hit water. After a few seconds he felt the tug on the chain as the bucket filled, then he quickly pulled it up hand over hand until the leaky bucket was sitting on the edge of the well box. A long handled dipper hung from a nail on the well box; Ollie availed himself of it, taking a long, deep drink of the cool, almost icy water.

While Ollie was filling up on cold water, a handsome young lad with curly dark brown hair came from the back of the house toward the well. He was disheveled and dirty from working in the field, and streaks of perspiration made muddy trails down his cheeks. He carried a porcelain basin in his hand and spoke to Ollie as he advanced, "Howdy, my name is Wiley Birchet. What's your name?"

"Ollie Thomas Burke."

"You kin to John Burke over Louisa way?"

"One 'n the same. My dad's John and he's up there on the front porch right now."

Wiley poured the water left in the bucket into the basin, saving enough for a good long drink. The two boys walked over to some large chiseled stones at the rear of the big house. A wooden washstand showed signs of much use. Wiley set down his water basin, picked up a brick of lye soap, and began to wash himself almost to the point of bathing. He sputtered and soaped, and washed from his kinky hair to the back of his neck and ears, over his face until water ran down the front of his shirt that was partly unbuttoned. He grabbed a family towel hanging to the right of the stand and dried vigorously.

The final touch was when he picked up a comb with a few teeth missing, obviously part of the wash stand equipment, and ran it through his curly locks until some semblance of order was on his crown. Also part of the equipment was an old mirror that you could almost see yourself in—if you looked real close. When Wiley finished, his handsome young face was clean and he had a big smile that made Ollie think of Eliza's smile when they arrived.

"Jus' came from the corn field over toward Blaine where Pa was plowin' an' me 'n Susan was a thinin' and hoein'. Terrible dirty work 'n I don't mind to tell ya' I don't like it nary a bit."

"I guess Susan is your sister and your pa is Uncle John?" Ollie asked.

"Yep, there's a whole mess of us Birchets countin' uncles, aunts 'n cousins, not to mention brothers and sisters. Here at home there's me—I'm ten—and Susan she's next and twelve. Rhoda is sixteen; Eliza is seventeen. The rest don't live here, but I got seven more brothers startin' with Robert." Wiley stopped, almost winded at this family chronology sketch. Ollie blurted out, "'Pon my honor, Wiley, that's a big family." Too late he realized that might not sound so good, so he quickly apologized. "I really didn't mean that the wrong way, Wiley, I jus' guess I was surprised 'n all. There was jus' me 'n Sue Ellen and—and—she's gone." He looked toward his feet and Wiley quickly jumped into the conversation.

"Oh, that's all right, Ollie. We all know it's a big family, but us Birchets are known for big families. I also heard about your ma 'n sister. We're all sorry about that. Happened last winter, didn't it?"

"Yes, they both went the same day 'n dad was off fightin' in the war. I was home with the women folk and it seemed like there was nothin' I could do but watch it happen. I did pray some, though, but I don't know wuther it helped none."

"Oh, it did, Ollie, it really did. Pa says it always helps to pray; though sometimes ya' can't see what it's doin'. It probably eased the sufferin', or helped your pa come home sooner. Thet's it, Ollie—look, your dad did come home from the fightin', didn't he?"

"Yeah, Wiley, he sure did. Even though he was wounded 'n all—he did come home."

"Ya' see, Ollie, he may not have come home at all if ya' hadn't o' prayed."

Ollie took some comfort at those words. Both boys were the same age, but Ollie was not around other children much except at school and he was mostly a loner because of his very serious nature. Wiley seemed to be of a kindred spirit, for he was a loner as well where boys were concerned! All his brothers were considerably older, so he was closer to his sisters; mainly Eliza more than the others simply because she loved to be with Wiley and was not bothered by their age difference. He was the last child of John and Mildred Birchet, who were old enough to be his grandparents. John was fifty-eight and Milly, or Milla, as she was sometimes called, fifty-five.

The sun was beginning to set and the shadows were getting long as the boys climbed the steps to the big porch in front of the two-story house. John was still visiting with Eliza, and Rhoda and Aunt Milly had joined the circle.

"C'mere, Ollie," his dad called out. "I want ya' to meet your Aunt Milly and Rhoda. I see you 'n Wiley have already met."

"Howdy, Ollie," said Aunt Milly. Rhoda smiled and nodded at him.

Aunt Milly was a pleasant woman to look at, though her years as a frontier farmer's wife left signs of a hard life. Her excess weight seemed to suit her and she was still a very attractive, motherly woman. Even though her hands were rough from hard work, she had a pretty round face with a chin that disappeared with her tapered neck. She had beautiful hazel eyes, alert and full of expression. Her almost-black hair displayed streaks of gray threaded through it and she wore it piled on top of her head.

Rhoda was less outgoing and expressive than Eliza with complexion lighter than Eliza's. She seemed to be quite a thoughtful, beautiful young lady who was also very tiny. Perhaps a little taller than her sister, her hair was more blond than brown, which made a nice frame for her tiny turned up nose, pale cheeks, and light blue eyes.

Ollie was taking all this in, listening to the remarks about himself. The comment that 'he took more after his father' and other light chatter was interrupted by a jingling harness. Through the failing light they could see Uncle John and Susan at the barn giving instructions to Jim, who nodded his understanding then led the horse away. They walked toward the porch, their gait displaying their tiredness. Uncle John was carrying a large-brimmed straw hat. In spite of their weariness, they both broke out with big smiles when they saw Ollie and John on the porch.

John Birchet was a fine looking man for his size, which was around two hundred and fifty pounds. He did not have a large stomach, but for all of his six feet he was solid and strong, crowned with pure white hair that lifted and waved in the soft evening breeze. He was a proud man, rich with a heritage of family that spoke of character and a strong belief in God.

He was the grandson of Burwell Birchet, who fought under the command of General George Washington at Valley Forge and died of wounds received in action at the end of the Revolutionary War, still serving under General Washington in New Jersey. Burwell left a widow and four small children on a farm he owned at Walker's Creek, Virginia. Benjamin Birchet, his eldest son, was John Birchet's father and, although John was born at Walker's Creek, as an infant traveled with his father through the Cumberland Gap into Virginia and settled in Kentucky.

John had been back to the old home place once, when his maternal grandfather Herron died. Ben and Susannah Herron had sent him with official power of attorney to settle the Herron estate. Uncle John was also related to Drury and Armsted Birchet in Louisa through his father's brother, Uncle Burwell, Jr. John Burke thought of all this family history that he was privileged to know about this man he both loved and respected. *I must tell Ollie about this some-time soon. He will respect this family even more,* John thought.

"Well sir, John boy, it's about time you come by and paid us a visit. You had us real concerned about you 'n th' boy here. My, he is a fine lookin' one! Stand up, son, let me look ya' over."

Ollie dutifully obeyed. "How are you, Uncle John?"

"Well, I'll be. Why I'm jus' fine, boy, jus' tired. But that's normal for me this time o' th' day. I'll be fit as a fiddle soon's I git some o' this dirt offen me." With that Uncle John shook hands with Ollie and John, taking hold of the man's shoulder with a genuine show of affection.

Susan, tanned from a lot of sun and with radiant brown hair, was all smiles. Although there was plenty of dirt on her, she was pretty as a girl could be. She shook hands with Ollie, boy-like, and he felt the strength of her long fingers as she greeted him warmly. Her remark was like her father's, "I need to git some of Blaine Creek's dirt offen me too."

Being dressed in a pair of boy's overalls and high clodhopper shoes did not hide her girlish comeliness. She was tired and dirty, but still radiant with a smile that lit up her whole face. Her naturally curly hair was close-cropped and hung loose about her face.

Ollie quickly headed toward the well and called back over his shoulder, "I'll fetch y'all some water for washin'."

"Fine," Aunt Milly said. "Jus' bring it to the back door of th' kitchen, Ollie. I've got some hot water simmerin' on the stove and they both like ta use hot water for washin' up."

He went to the rear of the house and picked up two pails to bring in the water. Before long he had filled the big wood and coal stove's tank full of water and left two full buckets standing in the kitchen.

"Ain't a lazy bone in that boy's body," he heard Uncle John remark. This made Ollie feel sort of warm inside, although he didn't let anyone know.

Both Susan and Uncle John looked clean as could be as they all sat down at the long kitchen table, hand-made of seasoned oak. The woven chairs of hickory wood were also homemade. The aroma of fried chicken filled the room turning thoughts and appetites toward the bountiful food prepared by Milly and a black lady named Martha, Jim's wife. John and Ollie had just been introduced to her and she, like her husband, seemed to know John.

Uncle John took the head of the table and asked his guest to sit at the other end, with Ollie sitting between Susan and Wiley. Martha was kept busy bringing in water, pitchers full of buttermilk and sweet milk, as well as biscuits and hot cornbread. Uncle John had planted his garden early, so there was already fresh new leaf lettuce that had been garnished with hot vinegar and bacon grease. They also enjoyed green onions, radishes, green beans canned from last year's garden, mashed potatoes with thick chicken gravy, as well as a platter of fried eggs.

After Uncle John asked God's blessing on his guests, his household, and the table before them, everyone was busy eating almost at once.

"Pass th' taters please," Ollie asked of Wiley.

"Shore, Ollie, ya want some gravy to go on top?"

"I'd sure love to have some. I don't think I like anythin' better 'n mashed 'taters 'n gravy."

"Now come on, son," Uncle John remarked. "Ya mean ta tell me you like 'taters better 'n fried chicken?" he teased, laughing as he spoke.

"No, sir, I got to admit—I can't say 'taters are better!" Ollie smiled back shyly, "but 'taters sure do make fried chicken taste better." Everyone thought that was a good comeback and joined him in laughter. Uncle John looked at Ollie's dad and just shook his head with a big grin.

"I believe ya done raised yerself a bantam rooster, John Burke. Thet boy's got vinegar fer sure." Working on the farm does a lot for making healthy appetites and after all the preliminary discourse, everyone settled down to the business of eating.

During the meal, Ollie found himself looking across the table, studying Eliza's beautiful features. She had long black hair, a creamy complexion, and blue-green eyes that flashed with long eyelashes. She was about the same height as Ollie, which was five-foot-two, but very tiny and feminine. Ollie noticed earlier that she had the smallest waist he believed he had ever seen on a young lady. Most ladies in Ollie's circle of friends did not wear form-fitting dresses, but this one that Eliza was wearing sure complimented her figure. She seemed to have a pleasing personality as near as Ollie could see, but he had just met her this afternoon. His thoughts embarrassed him and he quickly looked around to see if anyone could see what he was thinking. She looked his way several times and each time gave him a beautiful smile. *I sure wish I were older*, he thought. This wish made him blush, and he hoped no one was looking at him. He quickly turned his mind to his meal, trying to avoid eye contact from across the table.

Dessert was stacked pies, which was a first for Ollie; he'd never seen them fixed this way before. Several apple pies with thin crusts were baked then stacked like a layer cake. You simply cut through all of them and each person got a very big slice of pie. Ollie really liked this way of cooking pies.

"John Burke, come join me in the parlor fer some visitin' and a smoke," Uncle John invited as he pushed his chair away from the table.

"Don't mind if a do, Uncle John, I need to let thet meal shake down some."

Ollie and Wiley were also finished eating so they pulled their chairs up close as John and Uncle John settled down with their pipes to visit in the big front room. You could look out the window onto the front porch and see the rocker and porch chairs as well as the big hay barn beyond. Uncle John had lit a big lamp with a tall smoky chimney and set it on the mantle above the fireplace. The ladies were busy cleaning up after the meal, and Wiley had talked Susan into doing his late chores of feeding the animals, milking the cows and locking up the brooder house. Rhoda had offered to help her.

"John, tell me about th' war 'n bring me up to date on you'uns," Uncle John invited as he settled into his chair. "I ain't heerd no outside news fer a spell, and haven't been in ta town in a coon's age."

"To start with, Sheriff Johnny Allison came by real early this mornin' and told us about a couple of fellers thet beat up on some folks over on the Point. I guess purt-near killed 'em and robbed 'em. He thought they headed this way—or maybe over to Smokey Valley," John related.

"I'll be dad-gummed," Uncle John commented. "Gettin' to where folks can't keep what they work fer and raise! Did anybody know them fellers?"

"Don't think so. Might be Army deserters, I'm thinkin'," John suggested.

"Wal, we'll keep a shotgun with us in the field and keep our eyes peeled. It's a dad-blamed shame thet folks like them are to be watched—all the time! We outa take 'em out and shoot 'em," Uncle John added.

"Well, to be truthful, I think thet's jus' what Johnny Allison's got in mind," John said with a chuckle.

"John, I'd like to hear about this battle you went on. Could ya share a little about it—I mean if'n you don't mind?" Uncle John requested.

"Before I start talkin' on the war, Uncle John, I need to ask where your sympathies are—to th' North or th' South? I sure wouldn't want to offend you—I love you all too much," John asked with a hint of concern on his face.

John Birchet leaned his six-foot frame back in the chair; his white hair outlined in the lamplight. He worked hard all day. Even with his weight, and at fifty-eight years of age he could work younger men to a frazzle. No one in his family could keep up with him. His blue eyes narrowed softly and he ran his fingers through his white beard as he considered John's question.

"Son, that is a fair question and it deserves an honest answer. As you know, I have two negroes here—Jim and Martha! I had others and let 'em all go some time back, giving them their freedom. Jim and Martha stayed with me 'cause this is their home and they even call themselves by my name—Birchet."

Uncle John paused a minute, emptied his pipe into the fireplace, then continued. "I don't hold to slavery and I never will, but I somehow feel this here war is about more than the freedom of the black man. Anyhow, I don't hold to war. I've had both Rebs and Yankees here as guests and think a lot of 'em all. As far as I'm concerned, they're all welcome. I treat them the same. I've listened ta both sides, and they both think they're right. I try to live by the Bible and take care of my family—'n that is the most I think I've ever said on the subject." He began to laugh amiably as he ended his speech. Ollie and Wiley, as well as John, joined in with him. In fact, they laughed so much that Aunt Milly came in to see what was going on.

It was now John Burke's turn to answer, so after the laughter subsided he got very serious and took his turn at speech making.

"When I enlisted in the 14th regiment," he began, "I was skeptical, if not cynical, about this war. I was sort of encouraged to join with Drury and Armsted Birchet—your relatives—along with several others. My justification at th' time was to protect Louisa and my family 'cause the Confederates were advancing toward town by way of the river. I s'pose I hadn't thought too much on the subject 'til then.

"After bein' in for the short time I was, I got a different view on the subject, mostly by hearin' others discussin' th' war. I came to believe in the northern side more than before, Uncle John!" The younger man looked his friend full in the face and continued.

"I'm not sayin' that them other fellers don't have a good cause. Many of them feel like they're fightin' for their homes and the way they have lived fer years, but I have come to believe that the Union cause is a better one. It wants to hold our country together instead o' makin' two countries out of it. I'm bound to stand with President Lincoln in that matter. Even though my stay with the Army is over, because of gettin' hurt 'n all, my belief has become stronger in th' Union cause.

"Now, about war 'n killin'—there ain't nothin' I like about it. I am a man that fears God 'n believes in His word—and always have. You know that Uncle John! The problem is, I know thet the men I was havin' to shoot at prayed too, 'n believed in that same God, and most o' them felt God was on their side jus' like we did. I had to do some serious reckoning on this subject before I went into battle; tho' I kept it mostly to myself. My final thinkin' on it was a part I remembered in th' Bible in Jesus' words. Do ya remember, Uncle John, where He said, *'a house divided agin' itself shall not stand'*—or somethin' like that?"

"Yes, sir, I remember that in th' Bible."

"Well, that was my justification to help me aim down my rifle barrel and pull a trigger—to fire on another man. I had three thoughts in my mind. First, I knew he was pointing his rifle at me and would take my life if he could. Next, I had a family and friends at home that he was comin' agin', and finally, I knew that he was a part of those that divided our house so it wouldn't be able to stand, 'n I was fightin' with Mr. Lincoln to put it back together. That's the way I come to think, Uncle John, so I loaded and fired, and I loaded and fired, and I know I took more than one or two Reb's life with that rifle, 'cause I don't miss what I'm shootin' at very much." John had everyone's attention as he continued.

"The way I got this here piece of metal in my leg happened this-a-way. A troop of our men was climbin' up a rocky bluff th' north side of Middle Creek hill and we was bein' blasted by Reb artillery really somethin' fierce. Captain Drury had ordered us to take the top o' that hill, where the shootin' was comin' from. I picked off two or three of th' enemy as I was climbing—mostly on my belly. Now we were a troop of mounted Infantry, but th' hill was too rocky for our mounts. All of a sudden there was an explosion over my head and the next thing I knew, I was in a medical tent where a doctor was considering takin' off my leg. I saved him that decision 'n told him, 'Leave it on, Doc—I'd rather limp through life on my own leg, even if it hurts, than have one of those wooden legs.' So I still got some metal in back of my knee thet he couldn't git out. Sometimes it hurts like blazes, but I thank God I still got both legs."

"Amen," said Uncle John. "Ya know, John, I appreciate you tellin' me about that experience, 'n specially givin' me an idea about your thinkin' on th' North. I'm goin' ta put some real hard thinkin' on that myself. I never did have it put ta me thet way before."

John had deliberately omitted the part about his experience with fear and also about the death of the Sowers boy. He didn't want to call attention to himself.

After a brief pause, Uncle John made a request.

"Read me some in the Good Book, Boy. I always did like to hear your readin'."

John Burke reached over and picked up the family Bible on a table by his chair, and proceeded to read the third chapter in St.

John. By the time he had read through the whole chapter, the senior John's eyes had become heavy and he was feeling the wearing of the day. They ended the evening with a family altar and prayer.

"Boys, we better git to bed. A farmer's life starts early and, after we help with the chores tomorrow, we'd best be on our way, Ollie," John suggested. The Burkes stood up in unison and Aunt Milly came in with a lamp. Uncle John said good night as Aunt Milly led John and Ollie up the steep stairs to a musty smelling room with a big bed in it.

"You boys can sleep here and I'm sorry fer the musty smell; it's been some time since I opened up and aired it out."

"It's fine, jus' fine," John assured her. As soon as father and son got into bed and pulled up the covers, they were fast asleep.

Before daylight, the smell of biscuits, bacon, and breakfast fixings were sending an aroma up to the room where John and Ollie slept. *What a delightful way to wake up,* thought John as they pulled on their pants and shoes. They rushed into the cool pre-dawn morning to the washstand, where they doused their faces in cold water from the well and rinsed out their mouths with baking soda water. Ollie rubbed his teeth and gums with a clean forefinger and ran a comb through his black curly hair.

"Come 'n git it," was Eliza's call, and the Burkes came in to find Uncle John and the others just finishing their breakfast.

"Sit down, boys, 'n git some good food before you're off again. Where you all headed, John?" asked Uncle John as they pulled up to the table and began to eat a good country breakfast.

"Well, I think we'll go over toward Pleasant Valley and the old Babbitt farm 'n then take a bearin' towards Blaine country," John answered. "I jus' want to spend some time with my young'un here and teach him about campin', do some huntin', and try to stay away from the war." Uncle John nodded his affirmation.

"Well, it suits you and Ollie. It's your way of life, John, and a man can do no better than follow the Good Book, n' teach his craft ta his sons. Now you don't pay any mind ta the chores here, jus' git out there 'n git on your way. Wiley 'n Jim will tend ta things here, and I'll take Susan 'n git back ta that cornfield. Don't you worry any about them deserter fellows. I'll take my musket and Susan can bring th' shotgun along, but I allow we won't need 'em, 'cause I ain't cut any sign here of any strangers cuttin' through."

Seeing the closeness of the Birchet family put John's mind into a reflective mood. As he ate quietly, his mind drifted back to the experience he had when he and Ollie were spending some time together. The fact that God spoke to him was an exciting thing. The experience left John trembling and wet with perspiration. God's voice had sounded so loud, so definite. He looked up the quotation God had given him in Joshua, the twenty-fourth chapter and verse fifteen. He never had shared this with Ollie, but it occupied his mind much since it happened. *What about the family God promised?* he wondered. *Isn't this quite a bit for God's provision? Who— and where will Ollie get a sister? More importantly, where will he get a Mother? Wouldn't that mean God is going to give me another wife? When will this happen? Elizabeth has not been gone six months yet.* Sometimes he wondered if he just imagined it all. But then he would remember that Scripture. It wasn't even in his mind before then. It all happened right after he prayed, asking God questions—so it had to be real. He decided it was best to just turn things over to God and let Him do it in His time.

John and Ollie finished their meal and were soon on their way, saying good-bye to this loving family and good friends.

SEVEN

Did You Ask for a Family?

J OHN AND OLLIE BACKTRACKED FROM THE BIRCHET'S FARM TO THE DEEPHOLE Branch, crossing at the foot of the hill. There they reigned Ginger and Silky up stream, staying close to the north side of the hill. The trees were thick, hiding them from view of the bottomland. Although the terrain was rocky and much more difficult, it was more to John's preference because he did not want any more meetings with friend or foe. He chose the path across the Babbitt farm because the old home place had been deserted for some time. He hoped to cut across Pleasant Ridge, staying to the trees and away from the hill tops, at least until they reached the outskirts of Blainetown about mid-afternoon. They would have covered some twenty miles from the Birchet farm, traveling by way of the woods.

"Hold up, Ollie," John whispered. Ollie stopped Ginger in her tracks.

At the ridge gap, on the low spot across the Babbitt farm, John reined up and quickly dismounted, motioning for Ollie to do the same. Quietly they led their animals through the gap. John pointed out the old farmhouse off to the left. Slowly they came around the west side of the farmhouse through what had been an apple orchard, but was now overgrown with weeds, thorns, and thistles. Suddenly John stopped and knelt as Ollie watched him, wondering why he just seemed to be looking at the grass and weeds.

"Look here, son, notice how the tall grass is bent. Which way would you say this horse is going?" he asked, again in a whisper.

"Looks like toward the east," Ollie said, pointing.

John looked up at Ollie and pointed to the thick rye grass, where Ollie could see faint impressions leading off toward the farmhouse.

"What else did you notice, Ollie?" he asked, making a teaching lesson out of the circumstances.

"Th' horse isn't wearin' shoes," Ollie said quickly. "He's goin' barefoot," he added with a grin. John patted his son on the back and noted the joke with a nod.

"You're exactly right, son, I'm proud of you."

The grass was not dug up or damaged or even cut, such as a shod horse would do; nevertheless the tracks were there and, as Ollie looked over his shoulder, he could see that the horse had come out of the woods to the north along the crest.

"Stay right here, son. I'll check things out and come right back."

The Sharps rifle slid easily out of the scabbard and with sign language John told Ollie to keep very quiet. Ollie watched his dad slip off silently through the underbrush toward the house as he followed the trail left by someone's animal not too long before.

It seemed forever before any sign of life was forthcoming from the direction of the old house. Just as Ollie was beginning to feel anxious in the pit of his stomach, that familiar face appeared and motioned for him to come.

Ollie gathered the reins of the horses and pack mule from where they had been enjoying the tall grass, and approached the house.

His dad led him around to the rear door, which was no longer a door, but just an opening where the door had once been. When Ollie dropped the reins of the animals for them to continue grazing, he noticed that the grass and weeds had been mowed pretty thin by other horses; some shod and some not. Fresh horse droppings indicated that several animals had been tethered there recently.

As he stepped through the door into shaded light, his dad spoke to him.

"Well, Ollie, you can see—not just one unshod pony has been here, but several shod animals as well. Look over here." John pointed to the old stone fireplace.

There were signs of a recent fire and a stack of cans and jars, evidence of camping. The garbage and fetid odor had attracted a host of flies, making the room far from pleasant. Covering their noses and mouths with bandannas, John and Ollie gladly stepped outdoors.

"Son, this is what we're about. It looks to me like this is a camp for two or three Johnny Rebs—or we've stumbled onto the hide-out o' those thieves 'n roughnecks. Either way, it's our job to check it out. They'll be back 'cause there are two bedrolls in the other room. I don't know th' story o' that unshod pony we followed in, but looks like to me it met up with two others 'n headed off toward Blainetown or cut back toward Louisa. I followed their trail a ways out on foot. That's what took me so long. From the amount of checkin' I was able t' do, I can't rightly decide if the one thet come in was with 'em before or not; I jus' know he's with 'em now, and for sure they'll be back—prob'ly by night fall. We need to find a place we can watch for 'em without being seen. There ain't nothin' we can do until we find out who they are."

John led the way along the trail of the unknown threesome about a hundred yards or so then stopped and headed off to the east, up a hill through some huge oak trees. The dense oak branches

91

and leaves obscured the sun from view. Climbing up the rocky landscape through the trees brought them to an overhanging cliff.

"This is the spot, Ollie! We'll camp here and wait. There's good shelter, it's well hidden from the cabin, and we can keep watch of the trail."

The huge rock formation was made to order for John's purpose, but he acted like he had been there before. He directed Ollie to take the animals over to a cleft in the bluff that disappeared under an overhang and gave good shelter. Ollie started taking off the animals' saddles, but they were a little heavy for him so John helped. Once the animals were tied, John gave Ollie some instructions. They were both to check out the different ways in and out of the farmhouse and trail locations, good vantage places to watch and not be seen, and also to find at least one or more ways to exit without being seen from the downhill direction. John explained to Ollie that their function was not one of confrontation, but observation.

"If'n we can move in here 'n not cut any notice to the campin' party, see who and what they're up to, report on their activities to whoever needs to know, and be out o' here without them ever knowin' about us—we've done a good job."

Ollie was alert and nodded his understanding. He knew he was to leave the terrain exactly as he had found it, without any sign of his presence. Having been taught the ways of the woods while hunting for deer and other game, he knew just what his dad had ordered.

It was high noon before the two woodsmen met again and debriefed one another on their findings. John was pleased with his young son for locating an exit through the cleft in the rock that led out to a small ravine and down the other side about a hundred and fifty feet behind where the horses were staked. John didn't indicate that he already knew of that exit. He had found another one on the down side of the cliff, up the hill over pretty steep soil, but a good way to exit. John had also found several good places to observe quietly without being seen. One path led within two hundred feet of the east side of the farmhouse.

"Ollie, it's time for a bite to eat," John said. "We'll have to have a cold camp, mind you; can't risk any smoke bein' seen or smelled."

So it was a lunch of some cold cornbread from Aunt Milly, boiled eggs she had packed for them, topped off with a handful of hickory nuts.

"OK, son, in my saddlebag on the left side you'll find a long narrow leather case. Bring it to me, please."

Ollie dutifully brought the case to his dad, who opened the flap and pulled out a slender telescope. He held the small end to his eye and turned the other end while Ollie watched him.

"You've never used one of these, boy, but I want you to get used to it now." He handed the device to Ollie, who put it to his eye and jerked it back quickly with his eye watering.

"Try it again, son. It makes things seem to be real close to you. See that blue bird out there sitting on the oak limb? Point it that way and look at the bird through the glass."

Ollie did so and at first it was a blur, then he began turning the end and the bird came into focus. It seemed so large and close that Ollie unconsciously reached out to touch it.

"Now, son, you have the first watch. Take that glass 'n go to the lookout spot I showed you down by th' house and listen as well as watch. Use the glass in watchin' and if ya see anything of our travelers, slip back up here 'n let me know."

After Ollie left, John went to the mule pack and brought out a rolled up piece of cowhide with a belt and holster in it. It was a surprise present he was making so the boy could wear his Colt around his waist. John began to sew painstakingly around the edge of the four-and-a-half inch brown cowhide belt that was soft and pliable because he had worked lanolin into the hide. The thin strip of rawhide he was sewing into the border of the belt was more to decorate than for any practical purpose. The belt was made to fit Ollie's slender waist, with a large section to lap under on the buckle side to give room for expansion as he grew. John had purchased a silver buckle and belt loop in Louisa, but had not gotten to the place of putting it on as yet. The holster leather was carefully cut out to fit the colt, and also sewn together with the red rawhide. This was his first endeavor at such an undertaking, but so far it was looking good. As John stitched, the already dim light had become very faint, making the close work difficult. He glanced up through the giant trees to notice that the sun had disappeared.

John pulled out his silver Waltham watch and noticed it was close to three thirty. He methodically wound the watch with the small key in the case then dropped it back into his watch pocket by the end of the silver chain fastened to his vest. He thought about his young partner, put the holster-belt away and swiftly went down the hill slipping from tree to tree until he located Ollie. It had become increasingly darker and John heard the first rumbling of thunder not too far off. The storm seemed to be coming from the northwest. This was typical of the season in eastern Kentucky, and this looked like it was going to be a regular gully washer.

"Ollie, let me spell you, son. I should have thought ahead, but didn't. Go back to th' pack and bring me my slicker and you better put yours on too. We're 'bout to have a cloud-burst I'm a thinkin'."

Ollie gave his dad the telescope and wasted no time getting back to the camp, where he dug out the two Macintosh rain slickers. Having donned his, he hurried back to his dad just before the rain started. As John slipped into the raincoat he gave off an involuntary shiver, just as large raindrops began to fall.

"That rain shore does have the edge of winter still in it; it's down right cold. Son, I'll stick it out here for a while. You go back and see to the horses—make sure everythin' is in the dry. Check th' pack 'n all, 'n I'll keep as dry as I can here, but I got to keep a watch fer them fellers. It may be fer nothin', but seein' that's our job, I'll do my best."

Ollie made it back again to the rock overhang and moved the horses a little deeper into the crevice, giving them a portion of mixed corn and oats. He was moving the pack to higher ground just as a bright flash of light split the sky, accented with a clap of thunder a few minutes later. Ollie flinched but was not frightened; he was always a little awestruck with the effects of nature in a thunderstorm. He had a deep respect for it, but at the same time enjoyed seeing it happen. It appeared that all heaven opened up, with the thunder bellowing out a response to the brilliant flashes of light, and poured barrels of water out on the Kentucky hills. Drops of water became trickles, trickles became streams, and streams became rivulets cascading down the hill over rocks and around trees until the culmination gave off a rushing roar.

It was as dark as night and only the occasional flashes of lightning gave illumination. He found himself counting between the flash of lightning and the clap of thunder: one—two—three—four—five— crash! "Only five miles away where it struck," Ollie said out loud. One time it was even closer. Silky strained at his halter. He stomped, let out a snort and neighed showing dislike for nature's attack on his surroundings. Ollie restrained him talking in soothing comforting tones, but he was still wide-eyed and nervous.

"Whoa there, boy. Easy, big fellow," Ollie comforted, rubbing his nose then stroking his mane and shoulders. Finally the beautiful animal began to settle down. Ginger seemed less nervous and the mule apparently couldn't have cared less. After awhile flashes became more distant and the rumbles more faint, but the steady rain continued.

It was after five-thirty when, through the dim light, Ollie spied his dad coming under the overhang into the dry. He took his slicker off and Ollie took it from him, draping it over a protruding ledge to drip dry. All in all John was not that wet; the slicker did its job well, but the curls on the ends of his raven black hair were turned up from dampness around the edge of his coon-skin cap.

"Great day, I'd shore like a cup of hot coffee right now," he said. "Jus' can't take the risk tho'. They're back, son."

Ollie pricked up his ears as his dad explained that three men had returned, although he couldn't make out much about their clothing or conversation due to the dim light and bad storm.

"Looks like they had a bundle of somethin," John said. "Couldn't tell much 'bout what it was, though."

He had waited until he saw signs of a fire in the house, then he returned to their camp knowing the men were in for the night because of the weather.

"This is a good time for our supper, too," John allowed.

Ollie immediately began to fix something for them. They had water from a canteen to drink and felt much better after eating.

The rain had subsided and the clouds had cleared until a moon could be seen peeping through the oak leaves. The branches in the large oaks were bending and swaying as the wind picked up and whistled through the trees.

"Ollie, I'm goin' to sneak down to the other side of the cabin and see if I can get close enough to listen," John said. He shifted his weight to his right leg, wincing at the pain in his game leg. "I know they been up to no-good; I'd just like to find out what," he concluded.

The old farmhouse was basically a large one-room cabin that had been added onto at either end. There was one fireplace in the original part that served as a kitchen, living, and dining arrangement. The additions had been intended for sleeping rooms, but the present inhabitants had thrown their bedrolls on the floor in front of the fireplace. There was a door frame with the door missing in the rear and another door on the opposite side of the room.

One wall had two window openings, just holes without glass or curtains. A table and some chairs stood in disarray in the center of the room.

John felt his best chance to hear anything was from the open window on the north side, so he carefully descended to the east side of the house and crept silently to the far corner, directly under the window, within hearing range of any conversation inside.

After Ollie got the two bedrolls fixed, he watered the animals from the water dammed up in the hillside runoff and rubbed down the horses and the mule. This adventure was new to him and even though he had perfect confidence in his dad, and was obedient to a fault, he could not help but be a little apprehensive about him going off to the house alone. Without the luxury of a lantern or campfire to see or read by, there was nothing to do but wait. So he washed up in some rainwater, rinsed out his mouth and rubbed his gums with a forefinger. He curled up in his blanket with ten thousand thoughts. Soon he drifted off to sleep.

He was awakened suddenly by a cold, wet hand over his mouth. He shook inside with fear until he recognized the huddled form over him.

"Shh," John said softly. The lad came straight up in the bedroll immediately alert and very relieved.

"Well, son, we have a serious situation on our hands! These men are Army deserters and the ones Johnny Allison warned us about. They've been campin' here since th' mischief on the Point. But that's not all. It gets worse. It seems they have murder to add to their stealing 'n sech. They've jus' come back from over Busseyville way where they killed a man and woman and took their young'un."

"What!" Ollie exclaimed. "They—they took a baby?" Ollie's expressive eyes grew wide at the thought of someone hurting an innocent child. He had a sensitive nature, always caring about smaller children, although still a child himself.

"Well, purty close," John replied. "Remember that bundle I told you about earlier? I believe that was the child, a little girl, I think! Anyway, it seems as if they was stealin' in a house and was found out so they killed the folks that lived there, not knowin' the young'un was around. I think she was asleep in another part of the house 'n got woke up by the racket. One o' the men wants to kill her even now 'n the other two are holdin' out. The little one's life is in danger. There's no tellin' when they'll give into the mean one. Th' point is—we got to do somethin' first."

Ollie spoke up with a suggestion. "What if I saddled up Ginger 'n go back to the Birchet's farm and git Uncle John and Jim?"

"Good thought, son! That was my thought too, at first. But I couldn't forgive myself if'n they hurt that little one while we was waitin'. I think we got to do somethin' more drastic—and that means th' two of us. I heard a sayin' once that stuck to me. Divide 'n conquer! That's what we've got to do."

Patiently, John laid out a plan with his eleven-year-old son, in whom he had the utmost confidence. He cautioned him about the violence of these men, and that they would not hesitate to kill; they had done so already and had nothing to forfeit. John carefully pulled out Ollie's Colt, loaded it, and cautioned him not to use it unless he had to. But if he did—then point it intending to do damage, not just to wound.

"Fire it like you were firing at a wild animal," John instructed. "Remember, son, we're here to save that little girl! She's tied up over in the right-hand corner of the room away from the kitchen door. If you have the opportunity to get her out, don't wait for me to tell you—jus' do it!"

Ollie had a lump in his throat, but it was subdued by the excitement of the moment. John asked, "Do you have the plan straight?" Without hesitation Ollie said, "Yes, Dad, I do!" John knew he would rather have this young son of his aiding him than lots of grown men he knew.

"Let's go do it, partner!" John gave Ollie a pat on the shoulder.

Ollie circled around to the eastbound trail the men rode in on and John went in the opposite direction. Ollie crossed the trail and was thankful for the moonlight that helped him see as he crept silently toward the rear of the house where the horses were tied. As he approached the house, he could see light from the lantern through the open door threshold that illuminated the area around it. He slipped over the hill into some wet shrubs that had him soaked in short order. He knew his dad was correct when he told Ollie not to wear the light-colored slicker. Ollie felt the six-shooter in his belt and patted it, as if taking comfort in its presence. As he became parallel to where the horses were, he edged his way up the hill toward them and a large sorrel snorted as he drew closer. He stopped and froze in his tracks when he heard a coarse voice speak from inside.

"Sam, what is wrong with those horses?" A large bearded man appeared in the lantern-lit doorway and glanced outside.

"Aw, it's alright," he said. "Prob'ly jus' a varmint spooked Ol' Charley. He's kinda skittish anyway."

Ollie waited a good five minutes without moving a muscle, carefully controlling his breathing. Then he quietly slipped up on the left side of Charley and loosened his reins. Charley readily followed the lad as he led him off down the hill, circling around toward the old apple orchard where he and his dad had ridden in. He knew that the advantage of surprise was with them as he led the animal further away from the farmhouse. So far as he and his dad knew these men did not have the slightest idea they were being spied on or that there was anyone within several miles of them. The old Bernard Babbitt farm had been vacant for some time and hardly anyone came through this way, so the men felt quite safe.

Ollie took the horse several hundred yards from the men into the thick undergrowth. The ground was soaked enough so there was no noise. All he had to be careful of was the horse's hoof striking a rock.

Satisfied with his location, he slipped the bit out of the horse's mouth, hobbled his front legs, and let him graze. He cautiously made his way back, repeated the performance with the second horse, and silently prayed that his luck would hold out until all three animals had been led away from the men. Ollie knew luck had nothing to do with it. He knew God was all for them saving this little girl from the wicked men that had killed her parents.

Meanwhile, John was busy with his thoughts and concerns for his son. He had given him a man-sized task and although he knew Ollie was up to it, he was still just a boy! John had the advantage of knowing where Ollie was for he was able to see his movements from time to time. Ollie was doing great, so John's thoughts fell to the little girl who must be frightened out of her wits although he still had not heard any crying. *Perhaps she's sleeping*, John thought.

It took about an hour to move the horses in various spots away from each other. Ollie had made sure to take each one in a different direction away from the farmhouse, but they all ended up in the general vicinity of one another. His dad would take over when the men came out to search for the mounts. He had the satisfaction of knowing that his dad was waiting patiently from the other side of the farmhouse for him to do his part and get back into place by the back door.

Ollie eased back to the east side of the farmhouse and went to a medium-size sycamore tree. He climbed up into the wet branches, where he had a commanding view of the back door and the place where the horses had been tied. Now, all he had to do was wait.

Ten minutes went by and he heard one of the men say something about turning in. The man they called Sam said, "Are ya gonna feed that young'un?"

"Naw, let her starve," another voice said. With that a stream of profanity came from one, then it was quiet again—except, off to the left and over the hill came the mournful, blood-curdling squeal of a panther. Its howl sounded almost human. As a matter of fact, Ollie knew it was human and he smiled to himself. Sam came running through the door blurting, "What in God's name was that?"

"Nothin' but an ol' painter, Sam." But, by now, Sam had seen that the horses were missing.

"Thunderation," he snarled. "The horses has done been spooked off!" Sam stepped outside, looked to the right and left, then advanced toward the tree where Ollie was hidden. He stood directly under the tree, looked to the front of the house, then turned, and retraced his footsteps to the door. By this time another, smaller, figure had joined him in the lamplight. As he spoke to Sam, Ollie recognized the voice as the one who had wanted to let the little girl starve.

"Did ya see anything, Sam?"

"Nary a blasted thing! Looks like I'm goin' to hafta round 'em up. In this light it'll be hard, but we ain't got any choice in th' matter. Listen up. Greg, you'n Wayne stay here with the girl 'n I'll see if I can rustle 'em up," Sam ordered, obviously annoyed with the situation.

Sam stepped back into the house, mumbling something about getting a light. He returned in a few minutes with his hat on and a rough leather jacket. He carried a lantern in his hand and Greg walked a few steps with him, both looking at the ground to see if they could spot any signs of where the horses could have gone. In less than five minutes Greg gave up and went back into the farmhouse flipping the lit butt of a cigarette into the night. The sparks flew in an arc as the butt came to rest and Greg disappeared indoors.

Sam finally discovered a print in the wet grass and started over the hill in the underbrush, thrashing and cursing under his breath. Occasionally he would whistle and call out for the horse.

"Here, Charley, come on boy." He made a clicking sound with his mouth, whistled again, and called out, "Charley, here boy. Come on boy—Charley."

Ollie shifted his position, knowing he had to play the waiting game and just be patient. The sounds of Sam had died away as he went further from the house and finally he heard nothing at all. A good fifteen minutes went by before that awful, mournful panther howl was heard again.

Greg appeared in the door, visibly scared. It was discernible in his voice as he shouted, "Hey Sam—Sam! Where are ya Sam?" There was no answer. Just silence except for a few tree frogs chirping away in the night. He turned and spoke to the other man in the house. "Damn it, Wayne, somethin's goin' on out there! Sam don't answer a'tall. I don't like this one bit." He disappeared back into the farmhouse.

Wayne said something that Ollie could not distinguish. He finally appeared in the doorway then stepped outside with Greg right behind him. They both scanned the area, allowing their eyes to adjust to the darkness, cocking their heads to listen. Then suddenly, there it was. The panther call came again—almost like a child crying this time. Wayne looked at Greg and it was obvious he was petrified.

"Puts a shiver right down yer spine, don't it?"

"Yeah," Greg said, shaking his shoulders. "Look, thet kid ain't goin' nowhere the way we got her tied 'n all. We're goin' ta hafta find Sam 'n th' horses, ain't we?" he continued.

"Wal, we ain't got but one other lantern so we can't split up ta look. I allow all that's wrong is Sam can't find the horses 'cause they's been run off by that painter," Wayne reasoned. "You take th' lantern after I light a candle or two 'n I'll wait here fer a spell, and if ya can't find nothin', come on back n' git me," he continued.

"Dunno why it's got ta be me ta go," mumbled Greg as he went inside. Shortly he came out dressed for the wet brush and carrying the remaining lantern. A faint glow and flickering came through the doorway, indicating that candles had been lit indoors.

Greg crashed through the underbrush and wet limbs like a clumsy ox, showing his displeasure that he was the one that had to go look for Sam. He took a straight westerly course that was more level and easier walking. Every once in awhile he called out for Sam and the horses.

The plan was going just as predicted, although John had thought they would both venture out on this last go around with the panther.

After another ten minutes or so of silence from Greg, Wayne came to the door. He listened and looked as he smoked. It seemed to Ollie that he was very nervous. He went back inside, soon appeared in the doorway again, and tossed the butt to the ground. He placed his hands on his hips causing Ollie to notice a six-shooter on his left hip with the butt end facing out. He was tapping his boot on the floor now, showing his anxiety. Ollie could tell he was dressed, in part, with confederate infantry clothing. He went back inside and Ollie prepared to make his move.

Ollie slid down the tree very quietly and hid himself at the corner of the farmhouse closest to the tree as he and his dad had planned. He cautiously peered around to see the exit where the light was flickering from the candles. He heard movement in the house, but Wayne did not appear. He remembered that his sole job was to get the little girl and move her quickly into hiding. He was holding his breath when suddenly he felt a hand on his shoulder. At that point, under the tension of the moment and all his blood pulsating with excitement, Ollie thought he was going to die of fright. He pulled and cocked his Colt and turned abruptly into a big man's chest. It was John Allison! The sheriff quickly slid his hand over the hammer and put his finger to his lips saying,

"Shh, I'm yore friend, son. Shh."

Ollie's blood began to flow again and he felt tingly all over, letting his breath out slowly.

"Great day, Mr. Allison, you done went and scared the life right outa me," Ollie whispered softly as he buried his head into the sheriff's arms. Sheriff Johnny was patting him to calm him.

"I know, son, I know—but I was surprised ta see ya here, too! I follied these men from Busseyville where they did in some good folks, 'n I didn't know I was goin' ta have help." He hunkered down and Ollie followed suit when they both heard a noise inside. It was Wayne cursing and kicking something around. Ollie thought he heard the little girl whimper.

"Tell me th' plan, Ollie! Where's yore dad?" inquired the sheriff.

Ollie quickly told what he had done, what had happened, and what his role was.

"Dad has been makin' sounds of an ol' panther and he plumb has those men scared silly. Th' plan was to draw them out one at a time—'n it's worked! I jus' don't know where Dad is right now," Ollie said.

"Sounds good, son. I'll jus' folly this last man and see if'n I can give your pa a hand."

The sheriff nodded, indicating for Ollie to go ahead as he had planned and he would lend some assistance. Just as this suggestion was made, the panther let out another mournful howl. It sounded like it was very close, just over the hill.

Wayne came running to the door with his revolver in his right hand. He had pulled on his Johnny Reb cap and had a candle in his left hand. He was cursing and obviously bothered as he flew out the door, almost extinguishing his candle. He stopped, looked both ways, and ran straight ahead over the hill through the wet brush.

Ollie heard the sheriff say quietly, "Wayne Ballard!" Then he slipped over the hill to the east of Wayne and Ollie could see him no more. This was Ollie's cue and he sprang into action, moving along in the shadows of the house, headed toward the door. He entered without hesitation, stopped for a few seconds to get his bearings, and then advanced toward the bundle in the corner. He spotted the little girl as she saw him approaching. She was frightened and turned her pale face away as if she were about to be struck. Ollie reached over and patted her on the head as he spoke to her.

"Don't be scared little one, OK? I'm here to help you, not to hurt you. I've got to get you away from these bad men—do you understand?" The child looked up into his face with big brown eyes and reluctantly nodded.

"Let me see your hands," Ollie said.

She held out her little hands, which were tied together so tightly that the blood had stopped flowing. Ollie pulled out his hunting knife and carefully cut the ropes.

"When th' blood starts to flow you will feel like your hands are on fire. Jus' rub 'em together like this," Ollie said softly as he showed her how to rub her hands together. She did so very awkwardly while Ollie pulled back the wrap and saw her tiny bare feet in the same condition as her hands. He also cut those bonds.

"Honey, you're jus' goin' to have to trust me," he said to the little girl. "You won't be able to walk on your feet for a while so I'm goin' to carry you. I've got to get you away from here quick before one of those men come back, OK?" She nodded her head but still did not say a word.

Ollie quickly bundled her up and made it out of the room, leaving the remaining candle as it was. He ran out the east end of the farmhouse and began to climb the hill through the trees toward their hideout in the rocks. As he hurried, he silently prayed, asking the Lord to be with him and protect this little child, as well as his dad and the sheriff. The boy took some comfort in knowing that Johnny Allison was there with his dad. Out of breath, Ollie rested against a tree and felt the warmth of the package he carried. He felt good about what he had done and knew that she was safe now—he just knew it!

Silky and Ginger greeted him, snorting and prancing as he entered the cover of the big cliff. He went to the back wall, where his own bedroll was laid, and carefully placed the small girl on it. He could barely see in the dim light, but already his eyes were adjusting slowly to the dark. He took both the child's hands in his and began to rub them tenderly, blowing on them so his warm breath might help restore the feeling and circulation. He then repeated this remedy to her cold feet. Afterward, he took his coat and wrapped her in it until nothing was showing except her head.

"Do you feel better now, honey?" Ollie asked softly not even aware of the term of endearment he was using. It just seemed to be the thing to say and wasn't even thinking about it.

The child seemed more relaxed as she spoke for the first time. "What's your name?" she asked in a small sweet voice.

Ollie smiled all over to hear the girl talk to him.

"Why, my name is Ollie Thomas Burke. What's your name?"

"My name is Cindy Lou Smith, and I'm six y'ars old—and I'm thirsty," she added.

Ollie quickly got the canteen and offered it to Cindy Lou. On second thought, he jerked it away surprising her. He left for a second and returned with a tin cup.

"Since you're a lady I figured I better give you a cup." He smiled and poured a cupful of canteen water for her. She drank it down without it leaving her lips, and Ollie could make out a faint smile in the dim light.

"Now you stay right there to rest a spell and warm yourself up, Cindy. I'm goin' to get somethin' for you to eat." He found some cold cornbread left from Aunt Milly's, then opened up some butter and a jar of honey. He prepared it for her painstakingly and returned to the bedroll. As she ate, he realized how hungry she must have been. She ate the small meal quickly, took another cup of water, and spoke again.

"Thank you, Mr. Ollie. You are very good to me, and I like you."

"I like you too, Cindy. Come on now let's me 'n you get some rest until Dad comes back," Ollie said, feeling a glow inside.

After bundling Cindy up Ollie put the food and utensils away before returning to her. He then sat down with his back against the cliff beside the bedroll and scooped up Cindy Lou, cuddled her against his shoulder and just held her tight. She put her curly, disheveled locks on his chest and soon was fast asleep. Ollie felt good, as if all the ugliness for this little girl was behind her. Certainly she had had enough for one lifetime at the ripe old age of six. Ollie wondered if she knew her parents were dead and this thought led him to think of the sheriff and his dad. Somehow he knew all was well—it just felt that way. He cuddled Cindy in his arms, wrapping the blanket around them both, and soon he drifted into a nervous sleep.

Both Ollie and Cindy were still sleeping when John and Sheriff Allison came up the hill to the cliff hideout. They had four horses including Sheriff Allison's mount. The sheriff led the other three, which were saddled with full gear and had three disgruntled, sore, murdering thieves handcuffed on them.

Ollie was awakened by their arrival and carefully put the little one down, leaving her still asleep. He greeted them both and turned to his dad. "Is everything OK, Dad? Did you get them fellers? Boy-ee I was really sleepin'!" he said, stretching as he yawned.

"It's all OK, son. Sheriff Allison was right in time, but—so was you!"

"By th' way, what time is it, Dad?"

John pulled out his pocket watch and leaned over to the lantern Sheriff Johnny was carrying.

"Looks like 1:30 in th' mornin', Ollie. By th' way, son, you did a good job with th' little missy and she sure seemed to take right to you."

"She seems to trust me all right, Dad, and she is sweet as can be. She didn't say anythin' about her folks 'n I didn't mention them either. I wonder if she even knows about 'em?"

"I don't rightly know, Ollie. Thet'll have to come later. We caught these bad ones, and Sheriff John is goin' to take 'em to town to th' jail. We're goin' to have to back-track a piece and leave the girl at Uncle John's for th' time bein'." John turned to the sheriff, reached out and shook his hand, expressing his appreciation for coming along at the right time. The sheriff shifted his cud of tobacco and looked directly at John.

"Wal, John Burke—'n you too, Ollie—I should be thankin' you fer doin' my job so well for me. If'n I ever need a deputy I'll sure by dang know where ta git 'em," he said with a broad grin.

"I hope ya don't mind, John, I'm goin' ta move on even though it's still nighttime. I'd like ta have these fellers in the jail by mornin'. Soon's I can I'll take care of the funeral for the girl's folks and find out somethin' about her kin if I can. From what I know right now, she ain't got any a'tall. Anyways, I'll git any belongings she might have and git 'em over to John 'n Milly. I'll leave word for you there, since yore goin' ta keep on travelin' with th' boy."

Once the sheriff had gone Ollie wanted to know what had happened.

"Ollie, I'm plumb tuckered. If'n you don't mind, we'll catch up on th' questions 'n answers at daylight," John pleaded. "I feel like catchin' forty winks or so and then we'll talk."

"That's OK with me, Dad. I know you must be plenty tired. How's your leg doin'?"

"It'll be all right once I get off of it a while; I sorta forgot about it in all th' excitement. Thanks for askin', son."

They both turned in, Ollie lying down quietly beside his newfound friend. Ollie was asleep again very soon. John could not get to sleep right away. He turned over and looked down at the little girl.

"God, here she is, a little sleeping beauty, it looks like—without anyone in the world," he prayed aloud. "What shall I do with her, Lord? I need guidance from you, oh Holy Spirit!" In his spirit, almost immediately, God's Word came:

"The Lord is not slack concerning His promise, as some men count slackness; but is longsuffering to usward, not willing that any should perish, but that all should come to repentance." This child now needs family, John—did you ask for a family?

John bowed his head and began to weep. He knew the word that came to him was a Scripture in II Peter 3:9. It had not entered his mind before now. He knew God was answering prayer.

109

Of Such Is the Kingdom of Heaven

I T WAS JUST AFTER DAWN AND THE SUN WAS PEEPING THROUGH THE FOLI- age when the aroma of coffee and bacon reached John Burke's nose, hunger stirring him in his bedroll. He sat up, yawned and stretched, and was surprised to see Ollie busy fixing breakfast. *He sure knows how to wake a man painlessly* John smiled to himself. When he moved, he winced. The pain in his leg was bad.

"Good morning, Dad. Thought you'd like a good hot breakfast since we had a cold camp all day yesterday. Cindy is helpin' me."

"Well, sir, you sure do know how to get to my good side," John smiled. "So Cindy is this pretty miss's name, huh? Found myself wonderin' about that." Cindy was sitting at Ollie's feet watching every move. John caught her glance momentarily as she flashed him a big smile.

Well, God—if you mean for her to be my child, and a sister for Ollie, you sure can pick well. A sobering thought hit John in the face. *Dear Lord, I didn't want this young'un at the expense of her parents. You know my heart, God.* As he reasoned with himself, back and forth, his thoughts continued. *The death of this child's parents was set in motion by circumstances surrounding those men, her parents, and only God knows what else long before I lost my family. It is sufficient to say that only God knows the future. We must live with what comes to us and accept it, giving thanks to God for it.* As John pondered these things, he accepted just what he saw, as it appeared to him.

John made himself move around on the stiff leg until the blood started circulating. He noticed the horses eating some grain and saw evidence that they had been watered and walked. *Some kind of a young'un I have; there just can't be another to match him.* Gratitude almost overcame him as he moved to the breakfast fire just as Ollie was ready for them to eat.

There was fresh biscuits, butter, honey, thick strips of crisp fried bacon, and gravy, all topped off with hot coffee.

"You'd make someone a good wife, Ollie," John joked.

"Awe, Dad, quit your teasin'." Cindy Lou giggled as she finished off a biscuit soaked with hot gravy.

After breakfast the little campsite was busy with cleanup, saddling up the mounts and putting the pack on the mule. They were ready to go except for the morning talk that John had promised.

Another thing on John's mind was to have time for devotions with his young audience. He had some decisions to make concerning his new passenger who had so easily attached herself to his son. He felt God had spoken to him, but he must not take things for granted. John found a comfortable spot to recline against a giant oak and called the children over to him.

"Well, Cindy, you're goin' to have your first meetin' with the Burke family, and you're our most honored guest," John began.

Ollie and Cindy sat listening to John tell how he maneuvered around and caught the bandits off guard and apprehended them.

"First off, all credit belongs to the Lord for the victory for He was with me all the way. Ollie couldn't see me nor th' front side of th' house from his position, but I could see him take the gang's horses away one at a time. You did as good a job as me, or anyone else could do, son." John told his story dramatically with gestures. He even gave his imitation panther howl.

"Then Sheriff Johnny filled me in on the encounter with you, Ollie, and how he scared the daylights outa you. We placed the saddles and gear on the horses and the sheriff handcuffed the men, who had started coming around by this time. We were both happy that not one shot was fired and, with exception of some severe headaches, even the deserters came out OK." Ollie and Cindy were sitting very still listening, so John continued.

"The two men, Sam Densmore and Wayne Ballard, were deserters from some Confederate outfit in the south, and that Greg was a younger brother of Wayne. He came in from Olive Hill way to join them here. Another deserter who left the ranks with them had got the message to Greg to meet them here."

"How did they know about the Babbitt farm, Dad?" Ollie inquired.

"Can't say as I can answer that, son, but I'm sure they knew about it afore they robbed th' folks on the Point though."

"What's goin' to happen to 'em, Dad?"

"Well, son, thet'll be up to th' law in Lawrence County to decide. What they did was real bad, but I'd rather talk about that later"

"Sure, Dad," Ollie said "I was jus' wonderin'."

John turned his eyes on the new member of their party and flashed a big smile at her.

"And how is Cindy gittin' along right now?"

"I guess I'm OK," she answered. "If you mean, how do I feel 'n all? Oh, I was just thinkin'—I'll never see my Mama and Daddy agin, will I?" Her large brown eyes fastened on John as she waited for an answer.

John looked at her a full thirty seconds before he ventured any kind of answer, not knowing exactly how to deal with this subject. Silently he was praying and asking for God's guidance in how to approach this tragic situation. He knew he had not one, but two sets of young ears waiting for some explanation. John drew his face down close to the child and touched her cheeks.

"Cindy, if your own dad was sitting right here and you asked him thet same question about your Mama, supposin' she was th' only one thet was gone, what do you think he'd say?" John added while Cindy was hesitating, "Jus' use your own words, honey. Try to think out what he'd say to his little girl."

"He would prob'ly say Mama has gone home to heaven. That Jesus came and took her home, and I would get to see her when I got up to heaven—I think!"

Cindy's answer gave John just what he needed to continue his counsel. It showed him that the child had a Christian upbringing and that no doubt her mother and father were folks who believed in God's Son, Jesus the Christ. John thought to himself, *thank God for answered prayer and for the wisdom He gave.*

"Cindy, that's a lot like the answer I'm going to give you about your Mama and Daddy, only I want to explain it by tellin' you a Bible story. Do you like Bible stories?" She nodded and so did Ollie, even though he wasn't asked.

"Do you remember who Adam and Eve are in the Bible, Cindy?"

"Yes," she said. "God made Adam and then made Eve for a wife for Adam, and they got kicked out of th' Garden of Eden."

"That's right," John nodded. "And after they got kicked out of the garden they had some children. The first two children they had were boys called Cain and Abel. Now these boys were farmers like prob'ly your dad was, and one raised grain and stuff out of th'

114

garden, 'n th' other had livestock like farm animals. Now Abel was th' one who had animals, and he brought a sacrifice to God to worship Him. Cain brought some of his stuff to worship God with, too. Now men and women, boys and girls like all of us, can only see things on the outside, but God—because He is God—can see on the inside—like our heart and our attitude. Well, God saw both Cain's and Abel's hearts and was pleased with Abel's heart, but wasn't happy with Cain's. Cain got mad, 'cause he was jealous, and he turned and killed his brother, which was a bad thing to do—just like those men who killed your folks. Now, Cindy, I'm goin' to ask you another question. Do you think God told Cain to kill his brother, or do you think Cain jus' did it on his own?"

"That's easy, Mr. John. God wouldn't tell Cain to do that, he did it by himself."

"Child, thet is exactly right. But do you think Abel is in heaven?" John again directed the question to Cindy.

"Yes, he's in heaven, 'cause he was good and God took his sacrifice."

"Right now, honey, you have helped answer your own question. You see, the Bible tells us that th' rain falls on th' good and th' bad. This means that bad things happen to the good folks as well as the bad folks. God didn't plan to take your mama 'n daddy away from you, and he didn't tell those men to hurt your folks either. Like Cain, they were just mean 'n did it. It was at that time, once they were killed, that God stepped in and took them home to be with Him and to also wait there fer you. I hope you can understand what I said, honey. God didn't kill your mama 'n daddy, but He has had them in His care ever since those men took their lives. And those men will have to pay fer what they did—maybe with their own lives."

Cindy was thoughtful and then rolled her big eyes, now wet with tears, up at John and then over to Ollie. "If Ollie and you, Mr. John, hadn't come along I would prob'ly be in heaven too, with

Mama and Daddy." Before she finished, her little shoulders began to heave with uncontrollable emotion that had not, as yet, been expressed. "What—what—am—I—going to do? What's—going to happen to me?" The tears were flowing and she was sobbing as if her heart was broken—and, indeed it was.

John picked her up in his strong arms and held her close, patting her and kissing her cheeks as he consoled her; understanding exactly what she was going through, as did Ollie who was standing close by with tears running down his face unashamedly. John Burke had always taught him that a man who could not—or would not—cry, was a man who would have a difficult time giving sympathy to others.

"The Burke men are not ashamed to shed tears, even as Jesus shed tears for us," John had stated more than once.

After the tears subsided and John was sitting against the big oak again, he put Cindy on his lap. Ollie sat by his side holding Cindy's hand.

"Now, little darlin', about your questions." John smiled tenderly. "You're goin' to be a part of our family until some of your own kin show up. If they don't show up, you're goin' to be my little girl and Ollie's goin' to be your own big brother." Cindy's big eyes got even wider as she smiled through the few tears that were still coming.

"Really, I mean really, Mr. John?"

"I mean really—and let's stop this Mr. John business. From now on it's Daddy John, thet is if'n you want to call me that. I'll never be able to take th' place of your real daddy, but since he's gone, I don't think he'd mind if you wanted to call me Daddy John."

Cindy put her arms around John's neck and kissed him. "Yes, Daddy John. I love you, Daddy John." John put her down and she ran to Ollie, her new brother, and kissed him, saying, "I love you too, Ollie." Ollie blushed crimson and mumbled, "I love you too, Cindy Lou."

After this much needed relief, John and Ollie decided it was time they made their way to Uncle John and Aunt Milly's. Ollie pulled the horses around and put Cindy on the horse in front of him in his full-size man's saddle. Ollie only weighed about one hundred and ten pounds and Cindy was not much more than half that, so they both filled the saddle very comfortably, and Cindy loved the comfort of Ollie's arms about her. Ollie didn't mind it much either. On the journey back, following the winding trail to Deephole Branch, John told Cindy about Uncle John and Aunt Milly and their children, and how they were like family. He clarified that in families, sometimes men had to take business trips and that was what he and Ollie were doing when they discovered where the gang of outlaws was hiding. He went on to explain that she would be alone with the Birchets for a while until he and Ollie returned for her. He assured her it would not be for long and he promised they would return for her. He also explained that the sheriff would probably be out to see her and bring any of her things that were left at her home place. John told her the sheriff might also have to ask her questions about the things that happened in her home when the men came and hurt her parents and carried her off.

Cindy seemed perfectly content and was enjoying the ride as they came up the hill that overlooked the Birchet home. Since John and Ollie had left the Birchet's, just twenty-four hours before, a lot had taken place. In Ollie's mind it seemed like such a long time, but really was just a short while since they left.

John was surprised at first to see Uncle John and the whole family at home on a workday until he remembered the big rain last evening. Of course they wouldn't be in the cornfield because of the wet ground. Uncle John and Wiley were mending fences at the side of the barn and the ladies were all in the house.

Cindy Lou Smith was introduced to everyone and made a big impression on the Birchet family. The clothes she was wearing when she was abducted were tattered and the simple homespun dress was worn out. Her feet were bare. Eliza noticed the child was dirty and was suddenly embarrassed for her appearance. She decided to remedy the situation.

"Well," she said, "we ladies have to take care of some very lady-like business, so if you will excuse us . . ." With that she scooped up Cindy and went off into the house.

"She is something special, Uncle John," John Burke commented.

"Yes, she certainly is a purty little girl," replied Uncle John.

"Yes, she is, but I was talking about Eliza—seein' th' need of the young'un and takin' it on herself to tend to her."

"Oh, I see what ya mean. By the way, fill us in on all the happenin's in this recent adventure."

John began with the time they left the farm yesterday morning and led right up to the capture of the gang and Ollie's part in the rescue of the child. He went on to say that Sheriff John Allison would be getting in touch with them in a matter of days, if not hours, to let them know about any of Cindy Lou's family. As far as they knew, the family of three had no relatives in these parts; they had moved here in an old farm wagon with very few belongings. They were probably God-fearing folks on the move from Virginia and came across the Cumberland Gap. The farm, according to the sheriff, was just a few acres that Clyde Spellman had let them live on for just a share of the stuff they would grow on it. He was glad to have someone living on the old place just to take care of it.

Ollie interjected a thought about the Burke family keeping the little girl if it turned out she didn't have any relatives to claim her. John confirmed this and added that she would sort of help fill the void in their lives left by the passing of Elizabeth and Sue Ellen. He omitted the experience he had with God, his prayers for himself and his son, as well as the answers. He felt God would prove Himself in this matter all by Himself.

John Birchet was a family man and appreciated the idea of Cindy coming to stay with these two worthy friends, who were much like his own family. He said as much to the two of them.

"Well, they'll probably hang those fellers that killed the youngster's folks," speculated Uncle John.

"No doubt about it," added John. "They'll prob'ly have them hung before Ollie and me git back. I told Johnny to keep the little girl out of th' fracas if'n he could, but she's prob'ly th' only eye witness. However, he's got my sworn statement thet I heard them talkin' of it while we were snoopin' on them up at the Babbitt farm, 'n them havin' th' young'un tied and threatenin' to kill her should be enough to hang 'em two times. Ollie 'n me both are privy to that talk."

"I don't hold ta killin," said Uncle John. "But I believe if men take another's life out of greed and deliberate-like, they ought ta die themselves. It don't bring back the ones they killed, but it keeps them from killin' any more which they are jus' as likely ta do as not."

"Amen," said John Burke, with Ollie and Wiley as his echo.

Shortly, Eliza came out with a brand new little lady. Cindy was scrubbed clean, her pretty light brown curls gleamed, and the new cotton dress she had on made her pretty as a picture. She had little button shoes on her feet and she simply shone. John assumed the dress was one that had belonged to one of the Birchet girls. Ollie was the first one to comment.

"Look at that—she's jus' beautiful, isn't she, Dad? John nodded his agreement as he took her in his arms for another hug.

Cindy was blushing very prettily with a smile on her face that made everyone sit up and take notice. John thanked Eliza again, knowing this little lady was in excellent hands.

NINE

In the Valley
of the Shadow . . .

BY EARLY AFTERNOON JOHN AND OLLIE WERE ON THEIR WAY AGAIN AFTER having dinner at Aunt Milly's insistence. They were quietly making their way over very familiar territory. As they passed the old house on the Babbitt farm, Ollie could not help but think of the drama that had played out here a few short hours ago, one he would never forget. Another hour or so found them on a crest that John called Pleasant Ridge. When they stopped for a stretch and to rest the horses, John handed Ollie a pencil with a tablet of paper.

"While it's fresh in your mind, Ollie, I want you to write down all th' things that happened in th' last few days. Use your own words, draw any maps you want to, but record th' date and times as well as what happened. This is a journal; some people call it a diary. We want this book to be our memory on this trip so keep it up to date on our little rest stops, like this 'n others. Everything you remember and put in it is important. Don't be afraid o' details. It may be very important to us some day—or someone else. Every once 'n awhile I'll tell you to write down somethin', jus' fer me. Remember this book is private, jus' fer me 'n you. No one else is to have it except us; it's our record of things on this trip. Keep it hid in a safe place 'n only tell me where it is."

Ollie took the tablet and pencil, said he understood and would do just as his dad said.

"Son, I didn't mention this in front of the Birchet family or Cindy, but I want you to know this 'n also record it in that book; not now, but when you have another break. I sent word back to Captain Lyons by the sheriff about this encounter we had and my thinkin' on the subject. The only thing I told Johnny was that Captain Lyons was a friend of mine at the Garrison and he might be able to put a trace out on th' little girl fer me. My main reason was to make the captain aware of where we were and what was goin' on without betrayin' our real mission to the sheriff. You should know this now, to put in th' book."

Ollie put the book and pencil away for he could see his dad was ready to hit the trail again.

As they rode through the underbrush and trees, they occasionally came to a split rail fence that John would carefully take down and then restore after they went through. When he wanted to communicate, he would talk in low tones or whisper to Ollie. They crossed several low valley areas and had to ford creeks that were swollen with the recent rain. They crossed one where the water was up to the horses' bellies.

"This is Greenbrier Creek," John said from the other side as he and Silky waited for Ollie to cross with the pack animal.

Ollie was amazed at all the places his dad had been, and how he remembered the names of small creeks and areas he had visited or hunted. Ollie had an inherent ability that showed those same woodsman qualities. He was proud of this instinct that evidently was a gift from God, as well as from his dad.

They moved into an area with large oak and elm trees interspersed with thick underbrush on the hillside as they gradually gained elevation. Ollie could see the crest and skyline that opened into a clearing. They were obviously on the west side as he could see the evening sun beginning to set through the heavy branches and leaves. John dismounted and motioned to Ollie to do likewise. As Ollie slid off Ginger he dropped her reins that anchored the trained horse. Fred, the mule, swished his tail at an aggravating fly and seemed glad for the rest. John sat on the damp ground with Ollie, and in low tones began to talk to his attentive son.

"Son, we are on a hillside that overlooks Blainetown if you could see past the trees. I mean it's still a pretty good walk downhill to town, but we are close. I am not expectin' any Rebs to be in this area, but you never can tell. We need to spend the next little time before dark settles in scouting the area on foot to see if we cut any sign. We could raise suspicion ourselves since we have been stayin' away from the regular traveled roads, 'n I don't want to do thet if I can help it. Now you head around to the north 'n I'll check th' south. I want to find a campsite where we can have a hot meal and visit a spell, but only after I'm sure we are in a good spot."

"I understand, Dad. I'll tie th' mounts over there at that tree in case somethin' spooks 'em."

Each went a different direction and it wasn't five minutes before Ollie found what they could use for a campsite, but he continued weaving up and down the hill until he was satisfied there wasn't any sign of other travelers. He had been gone about thirty minutes or so when he returned to find John already waiting at the horses.

"I found a spot and no sign of anyone around up and down th' hill, Dad," said the youngster.

"Good," John said. "I didn't come across any sign either, but I found a spring coming out of rocks where we can water th' animals 'n fill our canteens."

John took the animals to water after Ollie explained where the spot was for the campsite. He told Ollie to find some dry wood and start a small fire so they could rest and have supper. He was confident that the boy had found a suitable location as he walked off, smiling to himself.

It was another fifteen minutes before they rejoined and Ollie went to help his dad remove the saddles and unpack the mule. John went to the fire while Ollie attended to feeding the stock and rubbing them down with dry grass. John was pleased with the location; there was a natural windbreak of large rocks and a natural shelter to sit and lay out the bedrolls. Of course, it was under the giant oaks and the stars, but there did not seem to be any sign of rain on this warm spring night. Ollie had designated himself chief cook on this expedition, and John had no trouble at all accepting the lad in that role. He despised that part of camping himself, although he was very adept at it when he had to do the job.

As he fixed the meal and as they ate together, Ollie thought ahead to the "visit" part his dad mentioned earlier. He always learned from his dad on these occasions, and he had a question or two tucked away to ask in an appropriate moment.

They both ate well and Ollie wasted no time cleaning up. After getting rid of their waste, he washed the utensils in the spring then put them away. His dad had mentioned that they would ride into Blainetown in the morning and buy a "town breakfast." Ollie looked forward to that for he didn't get a town breakfast very often. John wanted to be friendly and listen to some town talk to see if anything particular was on the folks' minds concerning the war and its progress. Basically, all the small towns in these parts were pro Union, but there were a few folks around for whom secession was a popular option.

"Dad, I know I got to start bringin' that book up to date, but I just thought you might answer a question for me—about your job with the Army 'n all?"

John smiled at him. "Sure, Ollie, you certainly are a part of my work now and you deserve any answer I can rightly give you. What's the question?"

"Well, if you are in th' army—or not in th' army but work for th' army in this spy business—do you have a rank, like private or somethin'?"

"Good question, son. I'll try to answer this way. If the Confederacy caught me, there is nothing to show that I am in—or attached to—the Union forces. If I was found out, th' Yanks may not even admit thet I work for 'em to save my hide. This is for my own protection, 'cause if'n they found thet out, they would hang me right on th' spot. That is the punishment for bein' a spy. That is if they can prove it, or sometimes even if they think on it real hard! If, on the other hand, I was in a Union camp and given a uniform, say at the end of th' war, I would be in a captain's uniform. That's my civilian rank. But no one knows thet except Captain Lyons and his superiors in th' intelligence branch of our government. That's my civilian rank Course now you know it."

"Great day in the mornin', Dad, I sure am proud of you for that! Do you get captain's pay, too?"

John laughed and said, "I sure do, Ollie, if and when they ever decide to pay me. I've only been paid once since I started in this position. The pay in the army is slow in comin' sometimes, but you do git it eventually."

Ollie was now full of questions so he fired off another one.

"Well, Dad, when did this all take place? Can you tell me that?"

John thought a moment and looked deep into the fire's dying embers as if remembering something he didn't really want to remember. Then, looking at his inquisitive son, he thoughtfully answered.

"Ollie, I wasn't sure I'd tell you about this at your age, but all in all—I suppose you've got the right to know! I'm goin' to tell you a story about somethin' that happened jus' last month and it was why I was gone so long. Th' reason I held off tellin' you had to do with the fact that, for th' second time in this war, I almost lost my life. I suppose the reason I didn't—well—was the will of th' Lord. He surely had His mighty hand on me, or I wouldn't be here to tell th' story."

Ollie turned a little pale at the thought of losing his dad. He found himself pulling a little closer to John, anxious to hear this adventure his dad was about to relate.

"Dad, was that the time you brought me home the new rifle?"

"That's exactly right, son. I gave you your late birthday present when I returned."

John took a deep breath of fresh air, looked around, and patted Ollie on the shoulder. He moved his stiff leg to a more comfortable position, then started his story.

"It actually started on the fourth of April, when I went into the garrison to check in with Captain Lyons. There was a flurry of activity at the camp and a group of men were all standing around the administration area where the captain's office is, 'n I knew at once somethin' was in th' wind. I called out to th' captain 'n he answered fer me to come on in. I went in and several fellers I didn't know were standin' around. I knew one feller there, Bill Campbell, 'cause we'd talked about th' Lord a few times 'n we had hit it off purty well. I nodded at him, and Lyons told me to have a seat. I felt a little funny about thet 'cause there was only two fold up seats, 'n I felt kinda strange takin' one.

"Captain Lyons began by talkin' to me as if all th' others already knew about th' subject. He told me thet there was a difficulty with enemy supplies comin' into th' north to replenish th' Rebels, and th' source of those supplies had presented a big problem fer our side. An informed messenger from General Garfield, who was near Chattanooga, Tennessee, told us that a lot of th' problem was a Confederate railroad that comes out of Atlanta, Georgia up to Chattanooga. This was a big part of th' enemy supply line. A group of boys from Ohio, thet came over with th' general, had volunteered to dress like southerners 'n go down and try to do th' railroad in." John paused a moment and Ollie took the opening.

"Do you mean destroy th' train, Dad?"

"Well, th' thought was more to destroy th' tracks 'n bridges, I guess. Th' track was about one hundred miles long with trestles 'n bridges, and Confederate troops guarded it all th' way." John stood and stretched, changed his position, then continued.

"Well sir, fifteen men had volunteered to travel by horseback dressed as southern civilians and meet a gentleman in Marietta, Georgia, to try 'n carry out th' plan. This was where they needed me, if'n I'd volunteer to go with them. They needed someone that was familiar with th' ways of th' woods and knew how to live off th' land if needed. They knew I was familiar with the territory all th' way down through Tennessee, 'n none of those Ohio boys had ever been over th' ground. This would speed up th' mission considerable. Well, of course, I said yes and th' captain wanted us to leave as soon as we had drawn supplies and dressed in suitable clothes. My wilderness clothes were more practical, but didn't look much like a southern gentleman. I ended up packing some to change into when I got closer to Marietta." John caught a question in Ollie's eye and hesitated.

"Where did you get th' extra clothes?" he asked.

"Thet's easy, son. An Army headquarters set up th' size of Louisa is prepared fer all kinds of things. I picked them up there," he said with a smile.

"Well, th' captain said to treat our mounts 'n equipment as expendable if'n we couldn't sell 'em or anything. He also told us this was a dangerous mission and it may be a one-way trip in case anyone wanted to change his mind. Them boys were determined and willin' to die if needed. He asked if there were any questions, but the only question that was asked was, 'When do we leave?'

"Th' captain said thet would be up to Burke, he was th' captain on this trip, therefore, was in charge of all following arrangements and departure time. His orders were for every man to follow my orders until I had delivered them all safe into James J. Andrews' hands in Marietta. At that time Andrews would take command. I was a little surprised at this command business, but I could understand th' reason why." John moved to stretch his leg, wincing with pain, then continued.

"I took over and saw to it thet we all had good mounts, very little grub, and even light in weapons. I couldn't' see any reason to weight us down taking weapons thet we might have to leave to the enemy. I met with th' men jus' before dark and asked if they had anyone to say good-bye to. I had decided not to let you know about it, 'cause I didn't want you to worry about me. No one had any other business to tend to, so I told them to ride in twos wherever they could, and we would travel fast, staying away from main roads whenever possible. I told them to eat light, take small sips from their canteens, and avoid talkin' above a whisper."

Ollie interrupted again. "Jus' like us, huh, Dad?

John smiled. "Right, Ollie. Jus' like us."

"I followed th' Big Sandy as much as the terrain 'lowed me, and we arrived at the headwaters o' th' river after midnight. We camped there and slept a few hours, takin' turns at watches and was up jus' before dawn on our way to th' Cumberland Gap. All in all, it took five days to git to Marietta and we were tired and wet 'cause it rained off and on purt-near all the way. We were plumb wore out.

We only had one encounter and that was near Calhoun, Georgia a little town on the Railroad Line.

"We really needed a hot meal by this time, so we broke down and made fire, cooking up some beans and coffee. It was evening and a squad of Rebs seen our fire and came along. They kinda made us nervous 'cause they came pointin' their muskets. 'Howdy,' I said, in my best southern drawl—which I don't have to pretend too much. 'We're jus' havin' a bit o' beans and coffee, would y'all care to join us?' There were ten men in the patrol and th' leader was a corporal who spoke to me.

"'Where did you men come from?'

"'Down from Chattanooga way,' I said. Figuring what he'd ask next, I said, 'We're all neighbors headin' t'ward Atlanta to join up.'"

"Were you scared, Dad?" Ollie interrupted with wide eyes.

"Yep, son! You could say I was scared, but not nearly as scared as I was at the Middle Creek Battle. All I had to do was say one wrong thing and th' trip would have been over right there!" John answered.

"Well, goin' back to where I left off—with that last remark the Rebs relaxed a little and the corporal said, 'Well, have a good trip, boys. We're with th' First Georgia Confederate Volunteers and kinda watching this section of th' rails over closer to Calhoun. Thanks for th' invite for coffee 'n such, but we'll git back over toward town. We'll probably run into you sooner 'n ya think.' After that, we relaxed and even laughed and talked a little. It was the afternoon of the tenth that we arrived on th' outskirts of Marietta. We had been comin' downhill, so to speak, as we traveled into town from Big Shanty, a little railroad town at th' foot of a pretty good-sized mountain. We learned later this was a famous landmark of the area named Kennesaw Mountain. Marietta looked like a fairly nice-sized town so we traveled to the east a ways out of th' city limits. We picked a good spot to stop and we all changed and spruced up some.

"I called out Bill Campbell and sent John Scott from Ironton, Ohio, with him to see if there was a market for the horses to be sold. 'Not all at one place,' I cautioned, 'but see what the market in several places will bring and perhaps we could salvage some of the Union money out of the south.' I told th' boys I'd meet them back where we changed in two hours. Everyone else was to stay close by and not wander too far away until I located our contact.

"James J. Andrews was described to me as a man who looked like a southern plantation owner—with a vested suit, well-trimmed tapered dark beard and a clean upper lip. The password from me would be, 'I wonder what the weather is like up in Chattanooga?' Then he would identify himself. Andrews was a dealer in contraband and lived in the South, spying for th' North. It was his plan that we were workin' on." Ollie had another question, so John paused.

"What's contraband?"

"Another good question, son. Contraband is a term for trading merchandise thet's not legal—like guns, rifles, or bootleg liquor. This could all be contraband. In fact, dealin' with anythin' thet's not legal is usually considered contraband. In this case, Andrews was probably dealin' in stuff th' North could use against th' South, 'cause he was devoted to th' Union."

"Is he still dealin' in contraband, Dad?"

"No, son. Mr. Andrews is dead!" John said sadly.

"I don't want to get ahead o' my story, so let me go on." Ollie nodded, anxious for John to continue.

"I proceeded straight into town on foot and found my way to a nice tree-lined street called Whitlock that had several fine homes on it and even a big hotel called the Whitlock Hotel. The Marietta Railroad Station for th' Western & Atlantic Railroad turned out to be on th' corner of Whitlock Avenue and the railroad rails, with another red brick hotel next to the train depot. The depot was a bustling place with pretty southern ladies dressed in frills and bonnets and carrying fancy parasols, business people, farmers, and Confederate troops—both officers and enlisted men. You could get lost in watchin' people, but it wasn't long before I spied a likely candidate, who could be our contact. I did exactly as I was supposed to. I walked up to the gentleman, who had his back turned to me, and said, 'I wonder what the weather is like up in Chattanooga?' Th' man turned slowly and looked me over.

"'I quite imagine the weathah in Chattanooga is exactly as it is right heah, suh! By the way, mah name is James J. Andrews,' he said and extended his hand to me. I took it and shook his warm, firm hand, saying, 'My name is John Burke, sir. I'm mighty pleased to meet you!'" Ollie let out with a giggle as his dad mimicked Mr. Andrews' southern drawl.

"We sort of moseyed over to the big hotel across th' street and I told him in low tones that I had fifteen men plus myself to put at his disposal. He smiled at this, then I led him to our meeting place. As we walked he told me he had six other men in town who would join us and that they were stayin' at the Whitlock House. Back at our meeting place, I introduced Mr. Andrews as our leader to the men present and we waited for a bit until Bill and John made it back. They appeared before long with th' news that they had four different livery stables to sell the livestock 'n saddles to, and for good prices. I told Bill to take care of that the next day by selecting whoever he needed to help. We would use the same place to meet again at three in the afternoon. I then turned th' meetin' over to Mr. Andrews.

"'Ouah mission is simple,' he said, 'but dangerous, and we all may not make it through; it depends on the providence of the Lord.' Again, we were all given the opportunity to back out of th' operation, but th' men all stayed true and seemed to admire Mr. Andrews.

"He told us to 'pa'ah off in twos and just casually buy a ticket to Chattanooga on the train that leaves at dawn on the 12th, th' day aftah tomorrah. We will all be passengahs on the train called

The General. This is a 25-ton engine capable of speeds up to 60 miles per hoah.' We all looked at each other and I reckon some of th' men were like me—never been on a train before in our life. Two men were to help Mr. Andrews at the engine to run th' train. They were Wilson Brown and William Knight, both engineers."

Ollie again sounded off with giggles as John attempted to mimic Mr. Andrews.

"Th' plan was for us all to leave th' train at a whistle stop up the road a piece. The other six men would be positioned north of th' place a few hundred yards and would cut the telegraph lines then join the train after we pulled out. The place was called Big Shanty, 'n thet's where all train passengers were to have breakfast. At that point all us Union fellers was to unhook th' train from all the cars except three, take off up the track a ways, pick up th' other fellers, and proceed on, burning th' bridges and tearing up rails as we went. We were to destroy—or slow down—th' source of Confederate supplies comin' to th' Rebs from there. Tools would be on the train n' some o' th' men were trained how to take up rails.

"Well, Ollie, it sounded simple all right. It jus' depended on th' timing. It was later that I found out Mr. Andrews made a dreadful mistake. You see, we were supposed to leave on Friday, th' 11th, but our leader decided Saturday would be better. Thet decision probably cost him his life. If'n we had left on Friday, we wouldn't have met the oncoming trains thet cost us valuable time. Anyway, we all shook hands and left at different times for th' town. Bill and John Scott attended to th' livestock 'n we got rid of anythin' we didn't need to take."

Ollie was spellbound as his dad held his attention with this thrilling story out of real life that happened such a short while back.

"I stuck with our leader and we talked, and I'll be dad blasted if he didn't look th' part he was playin' so much—well, I had trouble believin' I was with a Yankee that was as loyal as he was. We ate at the fine elegant hotel where he was stayin', called the Kennesaw House, after th' mountain I mentioned earlier. To eat with linen on th' tables for a table cloth and napkins, and everyone there dressed prime—I don't mind tellin' you, I felt a little out of place. It was kinda like I was in a fancy New York or Paris place thet you read about 'n never see. Mr. Andrews told me not to feel thet way. He said southern gentry folks were just thet way. So I enjoyed th' meal and we both listened to th' war talk.

"It was all about the Confederate victory at Shiloh in Tennessee. This had happened just a day or so before, and it didn't make me feel too good, I tell you. I also learned thet General Garfield was there, at Shiloh, which surprised me. Of course, this total Confederate victory was not exactly true, but I didn't know the Union side of thet 'till I got back. Anyway, Mr. Andrews took me to the main desk of this hotel, where he had already been staying, and I rented a room there too. I never slept on a bed with coverings like those ever before. It was nice and I did sleep good—after I got used to my luxury."

"It's hard to believe people live like that, huh Dad?" Ollie asked.

"You sure got thet right, Ollie. Someday I'll take you to a fine place like thet!" he said, watching Ollie's eyes widen with anticipation.

"Well, anyway, next day we all got our tickets to Chattanooga, which cost us $3.60 one-way for first-class fare. We moseyed around town and could have enjoyed it if we weren't so wrapped up in our mission. We met at three in th' afternoon as planned, and everyone was ready with their tickets. John and Bill turned two thousand dollars over to me from th' sale of th' equipment. I gave about three hundred back to th' boys, replacing money outa their own spendin' for hotels, meals and tickets. They all said that I was to see it got back to th' garrison if'n they didn't make it.

"It's kinda funny, Ollie, with all th' danger I was in, I didn't ever consider not comin' back! I put fifty dollars in my pocket and was thankful th' boys had th' foresight to get gold coins instead of Confederate paper money thet I'd heard about. I took Bill with me and we strolled a couple of miles outa town on th' north side toward Kennesaw Mountain. I hid th' money in a leather pouch in a shallow hole under a flat pink granite rock, with Bill as my witness. It was very near a switch lever for a railroad siding. After we went back, we described where it was to two other o' th' boys, jus' in case somethin' happened to us.

"Bill had a room in th' same hotel as me, and we had a devotion and prayer together about th' raid next day, wishin' each other well as we departed for th' night.

"The General pulled in from Atlanta right on time at dawn th' next day. My, it was a pretty sight—all shiny and spewin' steam, a clankin' and hissin'. We all boarded and th' conductor, a big man all full of smiles and pats on th' back, picked up our tickets. His last name was Fuller and he was sure proud of thet big steam monster. Not thet I blame him; it was somethin' to behold. Mr. Andrews, all elegant in a new suit, was in th' same car with me 'n Bill, and several others from our mission. We were closer to th' engine and th' others were in th' next car back. It wasn't long until we were steamin' along, listenin' to th' noise of the train.

"It was a very short time before th' conductor came through callin' out, 'Big Shanty—Big Shanty—all off for breakfast!' Mr. Andrews caught my eye and nodded, did th' same to others, and we were committed."

When John had cupped his hands, saying, 'Big Shanty—Big Shanty,' Ollie could picture himself on the train, as if he was living it with his dad. He didn't say anything for he knew there was more of the story to come.

"We, th' Raiders from North, poked along 'til all th' regular passengers got off. As Bill and I got off, we rushed to th' front to check out th' rails. All was clear. Th' engineer had jumped off to get some food, so Mr. Andrews 'n two others took over th' engine.

We ran back to th' car they was uncoupling—'n th' job was done. So far, so good. I gave a signal to th' front o' th' train. Mr. Andrews saw me, 'n off we went. Bill 'n me jumped on th' end boxcar jus' as we saw Mr. Fuller come runnin' out o' th' station. He was wavin' his arms, shoutin', 'Come back heah with mah train!' Come to find out, he was a Confederate officer."

"Dad, I hate to bother you, but what's a 'conductor'—like Mr. Fuller?" Ollie asked.

"Son," John said, laughing a bit at the question, "I'm not sure thet I can tell you, exactly. Thet's what they called him. He was sorta in charge of th' train. Collectin' th' tickets, bein' nice to th' passengers, and pretty much givin' orders to everyone workin' on th' train. Thet's 'bout as near as I can come to an answer, OK?" Ollie nodded and John continued.

"Well, as I was sayin', some other folks followed Mr. Fuller, 'n then th' soldiers started shooting at us. Some of the bullets were hittin' close so we scooted down as th' train began to pick up speed and then we were outa sight. We all gave a cheer and waved our hands. But I knew it wasn't over.

"Our plan was to stop a few hundred yards north while we picked up Robert Buffum 'n James Wilson an' the other four who had cut th' telegraph lines, then we were off again. We traveled pretty fast, but Ollie, what we didn't know at that time was th' Rebs had got another engine and were in hot pursuit. What ruined it for us was that we met an oncoming southbound train and then another and that's where we lost time while they passed. You see, on Friday, we could have gone straight through, but on Saturday, we had to pull off on another track to the side and watch 'em go by.

"Well, son, we gave 'em a run for their money, but wasn't able to do any damage to th' line. We didn't have th' time and, after a run covering some eighty plus miles, mostly in a downpour of rain, they caught up with us before we crossed into Tennessee. We had run outa fuel and there was too many of them for us. We hit out for th' trees, but they were all around us and it was all over. All of us were caught."

Ollie was nervous with anticipation at this point. He knew his dad was here telling the story, so he was OK, but as John told the story Ollie relived it with him.

"We were all taken back to Atlanta, where things happened fast. After a quick trial, we were found guilty of spy work and sabotage. We all talked while we waited, knowing th' result would be death—a climb of thirteen steps up to a scaffold, a rope around our necks, a blindfold, a drop to th' end of th' rope—and—and—eternity. But, you know, son—in all this talkin' 'n thinkin', I had an inner peace. Bill 'n me both did, and some of th' others made peace with th' Lord, includin' Mr. Andrews.

"Well, I don't know how it happened, but they came into th' room where we were held, took Mr. Andrews and seven other men out, and led 'em to th' scaffold. We didn't know what was goin' on. Bill was one who was taken with Mr. Andrews; also John Scott 'n others. Shortly, they came and got th' rest of us 'n took us to see th' hangin'. We all had to stand there 'n watch our friends die at th' end o' thet rope. I cried as Mr. Andrews, Bill, and th' others stepped off to meet th' Lord—and not one of them made a sound.

"I know what you're thinkin', son! Me, too! Why did they hang only seven men? Why th' seven men that they picked? Why did th' rest of us git left to watch? We discussed thet too, asked ourselves a dozen or so times. Th' only thing thet we could figure out was—th' Lord. I remembered what Mr. Andrews said about the providence of the Lord. Their work here was over, 'n th' Lord had somethin' else fer us to do. At least thet's all I could come up with.

"Th' very next day, towards dusk, they were taking us to new quarters with two guards. They prob'ly felt we were downhearted, seein' our buddies executed 'n all, so they were very lax. I was in front of a single-file line with a guard in front, carryin' a musket. There was eight of us in line with a guard at th' other end, also with a weapon. We still had on our street clothes so I felt it was now or never if'n we were to break out. I looked around to th' raider back o' me and I winked. I pretended to stumble 'n bumped th' guard. He fell to th' ground 'n I knocked him out with my fist." Ollie was getting ready to interrupt, so John waited.

"How hard did you have to hit him?" The boy asked anxiously.

"Oh, about like this." He drew back a fist as if he were going to hit Ollie.

"Never mind, Dad—I get the point. Go on with th' story." After they both laughed a little, John continued.

"Well, by this time th' boys behind had caught th' signal and over-powered the second guard and we escaped. As we scrambled away, one of th' fellers shouted, 'Every man fer himself.' I heard th' rush of soldiers come by in pursuit, 'n I didn't run. I just made myself as small as I could and sat right down against th' building and acted like I was asleep or somethin' 'n they rushed right past me. After it quieted down and I could see nobody else comin', I just stood up and walked slow, kinda hummin' a tune, and no-body paid me any mind. A little later, at a hitch rail at th' north end o' town I sorta borrowed a 'southern horse,' who didn't' seem to mind th' borrowin', and walked him out of town headin' north along th' same railroad. After I was out of sight of the city lights, I climbed aboard and me 'n thet roan horse jus' headed north against th' rails."

Ollie noticed he had been sweating. His head was wet with perspiration as he had been so caught up with this close call his dad had had while he was out "hunting," without Ollie having any knowledge of all his dad was going through. "God was so good to bring you home, Dad, safe for me."

"Th' rest is pretty much scattered—at least, my knowledge is. I know James Wilson 'n some of th' others made good their escape, but some were caught and held. I made it back thet same night to north of Marietta, where I hid th' coins with Bill. They were still right where we hid them. Seventeen hundred dollars in twenty-dollar gold pieces in a leather pouch was pretty heavy—'n I think more money than I ever carried any distance. Thet's eighty-five gold pieces, Ollie, in case you ain't counted 'em up. I made it up to Kingston town, where I paid for a good horse, one thet wasn't borrowed. I also picked up this Colt to match yours and th' rifle I brought back to you.

"By th' 19th I was back in Louisa where I spent some time at th' Garrison givin' my report. They thought I was gone for good, so were pleased to see me, especially Captain Lyons. I turned in th' money thet was left and gave an accountin' for how it was used. I have been a captain since thet trip—at least an under-cover captain," John added to his spellbound son.

"Dad, that was th' most excitin' story that I ever heard."

"Yeah, Ollie, right now it seems jus' like a dream as I sit here 'n tell you about it." John added quickly, "But it wasn't a dream, son. Those men are with their Lord, and for some reason th' good Lord kept me here. The reason He kept me here may be you, son—it may be you!"

Both John and Ollie were silent for a time; Ollie's mind went back to Cindy while John was still reliving the Georgia adventure.

"Dad," Ollie said, "do you really think Cindy will become part of our family—like you said to her?" He bent over and wrapped his arms around his knees, waiting for his dad to answer.

"Yes, Ollie, I think so, though I don't know for sure. I have an inner peace about it," John answered. "You see, I asked God to give us a family—two times! Once when the big snow came last winter. Remember, right after I got home? The other time was when we went fishing and you were target shooting. I felt that God spoke to me and gave me a special word, straight from Him."

"What did he say, Dad?" John smiled. He was expecting that question.

"Well, He gave me a Scripture word about Joshua when he said, 'As for me and my house we'll serve the Lord.' And He said He is our family—that you are His son as well as I am His son. He also said He would restore sisters, mother, and family."

"More than one sister, Dad?" He asked his eyes bright.

"That's the way I heard it, Ollie." John answered honestly.

"And—and a mother, too?" he asked.

"Yes, and I wondered about that, too! But that's what He said, as I understood it."

"Dad, that would mean you'll be getting married again, wouldn't it?" Ollie asked with a grin.

"I guess it would, Ollie—unless the Lord plans on replacing me too!" he said, laughing as he said it.

"Aw, Dad—don't be silly, God was talking to you!" Ollie leaned back and started humming a tune, thinking over the recent answers. He was glad about Cindy already.

After the long story, John Burke decided to turn in. Ollie asked if it would be all right if he used the lantern to do some journal work and make his first entries. He just cautioned his young son to keep his eyes open and his ears sensitive to the sounds.

Ollie worked late, making his first entry on May 5, 1862. He tried to be complete and exact to detail, without overdoing the wordiness. He was a good young scribe who was well read for his age. This had helped him in learning to spell and was also a big help in correct grammar. Ollie knew that some words he and his dad used were just the way people in these hills talked. They followed the path of least resistance. His mother used to caution him about that path, but never said anything to his dad. Ollie could discern the sound of a squirrel running and jumping, and climbing a tree. He was familiar with the clumsy jaunts of a skunk, possum and many other small animals.

Ollie's thoughts drifted back to his dad as he made another entry in this diary of the Burke men. He found himself wondering if his dad would ever seek another woman in his life. If he was to have another mother, it seemed to Ollie that his dad would have to marry again. Ollie knew he could deal with that. If it happened he knew it would be God's plan. Ollie closed the journal, as he was becoming drowsy, and his last thought before turning into his bedroll was, *Time will tell.*

TEN

Strength and Honor
Are Her Clothing

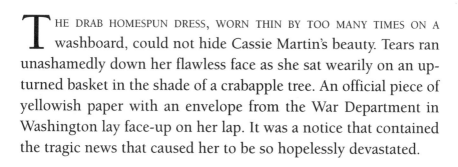

THE DRAB HOMESPUN DRESS, WORN THIN BY TOO MANY TIMES ON A washboard, could not hide Cassie Martin's beauty. Tears ran unashamedly down her flawless face as she sat wearily on an upturned basket in the shade of a crabapple tree. An official piece of yellowish paper with an envelope from the War Department in Washington lay face-up on her lap. It was a notice that contained the tragic news that caused her to be so hopelessly devastated.

Dear Miss Martin:

This is to notify you that on the 6th day of April 1862, your father, Captain Jacob Martin, was killed in action at the Battle Of Shiloh. Your father was heroically leading his men in a Cavalry charge at the time of his death and has been interred in the National Cemetery at Pittsburg Landing, Tennessee.

> Regretfully,
> Simon Cameron
> Secretary of War

A postman from Blainetown, more than five miles from the little Caines Creek farmhouse, had delivered the news to Cassie this beautiful spring day in April. Cassie was alone! There was no one to share the news with. No sister or brother—and her mother had been dead for many years. Of course, that was the story of Cassie's life, one filled with a series of tragedies. As a young girl, before nine years of age, she had wished many times that she had never been born.

A traveling preacher had come through Caines creek and held a revival at the one-room schoolhouse where Cassie now taught school from time to time. He was an old-time United Baptist "Hellfire and Brimstone" preacher who could preach you into hell, and let you smell the smoke. One good thing about old Brother Williams—he also had the love of God for the sinner man and woman. Although he preached a strong message about hell, he wrapped it in the love of God, and he cried honest tears when he asked the man, woman, boy or girl to walk that long path down to the bench, which was turned around to make an alter.

Cassie remembered that cold winter as if it were yesterday! Matilda, her mother, had talked Jacob into attending the revival with her, and of course Cassie was happy to go. That night so long ago, she, her mother and father Jacob felt the call of God on their lives and as a family trod that old trail so many sinners trod. They knelt side by side and gave their hearts to the Lord. Their tear stains were left on the alter bench that night as they repented and asked Jesus into their hearts. And one thing she knew right now—her dad was with her mother in heaven.

Jacob was a good man, fair as a businessman and good to his neighbor when called upon. But, he became almost a recluse, a bitter man. His one obsession was to have a male child. Cassie was his firstborn, and Matilda lost her health and then her life trying to bear a son for Jacob Martin. She went through six miscarriages, the last one being a stillbirth of a male child, and she died giving birth to that child. Each pregnancy was a tragedy for Matilda Johnson Martin. Because of an infirmity she was not able to bear children. Even Cassie's birth was a miracle and almost cost her mother's life. The local doctor advised her not to attempt to have any more children and, except for her husband, she would have stopped trying. But she sat condemning herself, and instead of standing up for Cassie to be a little girl child, she allowed Jacob to have his way in treating the child like a boy.

Jacob was a man gifted with musket and rifle, and was the best man with a six-gun in the countryside for miles about. He could throw a knife and light a match with it and split a straw with a hand axe. Consequently, he wanted his boy to be able to master the same weapons. So Jacob, in his blind ambition to have a boy, made a boy out of Cassie, his daughter. He taught her to ride, to shoot and to throw a knife and a hand-axe, or hatchet, like a man. She had a sharp eye and a willingness to learn, so she became better than most men at an early age. Jacob kept her hair short, dressed her in boy's clothes, and took her everywhere with him. At this early age, Cassie did not know any different, and she enjoyed being with her dad. To Jacob, she was Cass. He never treated her, referred to her, or regarded her as a girl until after she was nine years old. With the childhood loss of her mother, and a father that denied her own sex, Cassie went from being called tomboy to being shunned by the girls at school, which caused her to be withdrawn. Though she was a faithful student, by the time she was nine she was an unhappy, melancholy child, particularly when with other children.

In late winter 1851, after Cassie had turned nine, her mother gave birth to a stillborn little brother and died in childbirth. This deep tragedy shook Jacob Martin more than any other. He closed Cass out, as well as the whole world, becoming hermit-like in existence.

Matilda had corresponded with a close friend in Boston: Prudence Ison Milsap, who had married into a wealthy family. Joab Milsap, visiting the eastern Kentucky hills, had married Prudence and moved her out of abject poverty into a wealthy Bostonian environment, but she never forgot her school chum of years before. When she heard of Matilda's death, she made a trip all the way back to Caines Creek to talk to Jacob. Jacob was at a loss to talk to anyone, make any decisions, or even to be sociable. However, he consented in writing to turn custody of Cassandra over to Prudence so she could take her back to live with her in Boston.

The elegant but sickly lady took Cassie with her. They traveled by buggy to Blainetown and on to Louisa, Lawrence County's county seat. Blainetown was the largest community Cassie had ever seen and Louisa seemed like a big city in comparison. She then traveled by steamboat with "Aunt Prudence" all the way to Pittsburgh, Pennsylvania. Prudence purchased some girl's dresses for travel. The disheveled nine-year-old, when cleaned up, turned out to be a beautiful young girl, but she didn't seem to be aware of it. The trip however, was exciting for Cassie—first by the steamer *Tom Hackney* to Pennsylvania, then by rail to Boston. Prudence took the pretty youngster aside and instructed her.

"Cassie, please feel free to call me Aunt Prudence. I may not be your real aunt, but since your dear mother (God rest her soul), had no living kin, please consider me your aunt."

Aunt Prudence was good for Cassie! She was not a well woman and she was very strict, but she brought Cassie into the world of women, which she had never even visited before. She attended proper schools for girls, always dressed in the finest, and she was allowed to read anything in the library. She was obviously intelligent and by the time she was sixteen, she was easily one of the most beautiful young women in Boston.

Cassie spent long hours in the library, reading literature and novels. She was fascinated by the world of make believe and used to spend time dreaming of a prince who would come and carry her away into a world of romance and love. She was sheltered much by Aunt Prudence and never saw much of boys—or even much of the Milsap family—except for servants. They all resented Prudence bringing this "country trash" to Boston. Meanwhile Prudence was fast losing her health to constant bouts with ague. A deep, hacking cough racked her through and through, and never seemed to leave.

As strict as Aunt Prudence was, she was lenient with Cassie concerning the time she worked in the church. Aunt Prudence was deeply religious and Cassie attended regularly at Boston's famous Trinity Episcopal Church.

Here Cassie developed spiritually into a young woman who was healthy in her experience with the Lord. It was the ministry staff of the famous church that helped chase a way the gloomy disposition of her childhood and the influence of her mother. She became personal and victorious in her experience with the Lord, overcoming the nightmares of her past tragedies, learning how to deal with them. She only regretted that her mother didn't have the inner peace before she died that she now came to have on this earth. She realized that her mother was with the Lord and happy now, but her life on earth could have been much easier if she had spent more time in God's Word, understanding Him!

Her love for Aunt Prudence grew and she found herself transformed by the bedside care she was able to give her adopted aunt during the last year of her life. She went occasionally to the theater, and twice to a circus. She attended several presentations by the symphony orchestra and all the while she became a faithful student and a regular to teach God's Word and academics at Trinity Church. Aunt

Prudence died just after Cassie turned sixteen. Another tragedy. This time Cassie was mature enough to handle it and realized that this dear woman had lived her last years just to help develop her best friend's child. She had personal knowledge of what the Lord meant, when He said in John 15:13:

> Greater love hath no man than this, that a man lay down his life for his friends.

Almost immediately the Milsap family forced Cassie to return to Caines Creek. In no uncertain terms they made her realize that she was not needed, and had been tolerated only because of Prudence. Cassie was a new person now and it did not even make her angry. She was happy within herself, and happy to be with herself. She enjoyed her own company and felt a whole person because of the relationship she had with God. It hurt not to be wanted, but Cassie found herself thinking, *It's their loss more than my loss. I am a good person and they are losing out by not getting to know me.* When she had this thought, she was embarrassed for having thought it, but God swept her inner person clean of this thought, allowing her to feel it was not a vain thought. It was an honest thought, although she had a loss too! She didn't have a chance to know them or help them.

Little did Cassie know that she was developing a Bible-based philosophy that would not allow her to feel sorry for herself: Laugh with those who laugh, mourn with those who mourn. But like Paul, the greatest teacher in the New Testament,

> *"Brethren, I count not myself to have apprehended; but this one thing I do, forgetting those things which are behind, and reaching forth to those things which are before, I press toward the mark for the prize of the high calling in God in Christ Jesus."* Philippians 3:13 & 14.

Actually, Cassie was ready to return, she had no ties to Boston except for Aunt Prudence, and she was no longer there. Cassie longed for her father, even though he had never written. She held no grudge toward him for the difficult childhood he had forced upon her. She didn't regret the things she had learned about weapons. Somehow, she looked upon her experience as a circumstance that God had His hand on and someday she would find it useful.

As Cassie steamed down the Ohio River on the *Tom Spurlock*, she realized she was a much different person than the frightened little girl, who thought she was a boy, some seven years before. She was allowed to keep just a couple of the dresses afforded her by her benefactor, and she didn't know what she was coming home to. She had very little cash, and she knew she would need that to buy some clothes more suitable for Caines Creek and the hills of Lawrence County.

Jacob did not know she was coming home, and she didn't know how she would be received. After purchasing some overalls and other clothing in Louisa, she barely had enough money to hire a buggy ride to Blainetown. From there she walked the five and a half miles to Caines Creek, once she found out that her father still lived at the same rented farmhouse. When Jacob saw Cassie coming he just waited. He did not know this beautiful young woman coming up the dusty trail. She was five feet, five inches tall and had beautiful auburn hair, naturally curly and falling around her shoulders. She had eyes as blue as the sky and a creamy white, flawless complexion. There was something about her that he knew, but he couldn't put his finger on the "something."

"Daddy," she said as she walked up to the fence, within twenty-five feet of him.

"Cass? Is that you? My dear God—I—I—don't believe it." He started toward her and as she met him they embraced. He drew back with tear-stained cheeks. "Honey—you're the most beautiful creature I ever laid eyes on. I mean it." He hugged her again picking her up and squeezing her. She had forgotten just how much she loved him, and was very pleased that she was welcomed home as she was.

Before long Jacob dropped back into his old ways. She was never Cassie, always Cass. He spent time helping her brush up on her skills, which she did readily. When she was eighteen, he purchased her a beautiful horse and a shepherd puppy. The three of them, Cassie, Shep, and Spot, a spirited gelding of black and white coloring, spent lots of time together. At the circus in Boston Cassie had watched a pretty young showgirl do trick riding. She made up her mind that if she ever had a horse of her own she would learn those tricks. She spent hours learning and developing her skills with Spot. The animal was patient and seemed to enjoy his young master. They learned together.

She spent time also with Shep. He became her protector, and could attack upon command. She taught him communication by hand signals, and he had a nose for tracking like a bloodhound. These three were inseparable, and Jacob let them be. He was content just to watch them with amusement. He made barely enough money to keep them in food, and Cassie raised a garden, canned and cooked, taking care of her father. She became tanned and physically fit, able to run through the woods for hours, as well as keep up with the household activities for herself and Jacob.

Cassie had suitors, young men of her community and nearby Blainetown. The outside rumblings of war, which seemed to have nothing to do with them, began to pull these young men into the core of it. The suitors narrowed down and no one seemed to be that one she held high in her dreams.

She felt God was saying no to those who came calling with marriage on their mind. He seemed to be saying to her, *You would know him when you see him.* She kept her dreams about her proverbial knight in shining armor. She knew this was a fantasy world, but she also believed God would give her the desire of her heart. She held on to that.

Soon Jacob was caught up in the romance of the war. One day he disappeared for two days and when next Cassie saw him he was in Union uniform. He had enlisted in Catlettsburg, Kentucky as a first lieutenant. Her father was all smiles, and all Cassie could do was kiss him good-bye. It never even occurred to him that he was leaving her alone and without money. He left her a small amount, but a precious little. It was probably all he had.

Now Cassie picked up the telegram from the war department, went through the house and saw nothing there that she wanted to keep. She had a few weeks' worth of food left, a couple of changes of clothes, rickety furniture that would be suitable for firewood, and a rented farmhouse with a few outbuildings that had nothing for her to hold on to. Shep was by her side when she knelt by her bed with the telegram, her worn Bible and her memories. She picked up her Bible and read the fourteenth chapter of St. John's Gospel, and concluded with the 91st Psalm, and than she prayed.

"God, my Father—here I am again. This is your handmaid, Cassie! My father now rests with my mother in your presence, and I am alone except for the animal companions I have. My good dog Shep, my faithful horse Spot, and me. I have the most important thing, right here in me. That is your Holy Spirit, your presence and therefore, I am not alone. I put my complete trust in you! It seems I must turn a page in my life. I will do this knowing you are holding my future. I have prayed many times Lord—you know me well—for a—a—prince. A knight—a man for my life who I can serve and who will love me. You can send him along just anytime Lord. I'm ready! If this sounds like a foolish prayer, forgive me. I love you, Lord, and I want what you have for me. I know you will give me the desire of my heart. The reason I know this is because your Word says it. It says if I delight myself in You, that You will give me the desire of my heart. It's your promise, Lord—Psalm 37:4. I have delighted in you, my Lord, now I ask for you to fulfill your promise. I thank you Lord. Amen."

ELEVEN

Blessed Are They That Mourn

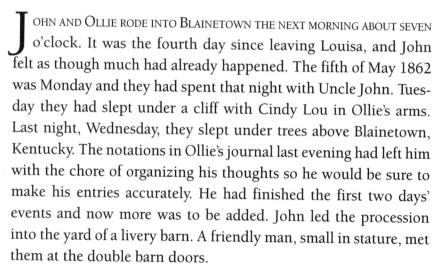

J OHN AND OLLIE RODE INTO BLAINETOWN THE NEXT MORNING ABOUT SEVEN o'clock. It was the fourth day since leaving Louisa, and John felt as though much had already happened. The fifth of May 1862 was Monday and they had spent that night with Uncle John. Tuesday they had slept under a cliff with Cindy Lou in Ollie's arms. Last night, Wednesday, they slept under trees above Blainetown, Kentucky. The notations in Ollie's journal last evening had left him with the chore of organizing his thoughts so he would be sure to make his entries accurately. He had finished the first two days' events and now more was to be added. John led the procession into the yard of a livery barn. A friendly man, small in stature, met them at the double barn doors.

"Howdy there. Mah name is George Johnson 'n I run this barn. How can I hep ya?"

"Howdy back to you, George. I'm John Burke from over in Louisa 'n this is my boy, Ollie. What's yer rate fer feedin' 'n such?"

"Good rates. Real good rates." George followed up. "Be a dollar a day a piece fer th' mounts, which includes feed 'n grain, take off th' riggin', curry 'em down and walk 'em, plenty of water and I'll throw in doin' th' mule fer free. Weekly rate is less of course."

"Sounds fair enough, George," John said as he dismounted. Ollie took his lead from his dad.

"Actually th' nightly rate will do us this time, but I'll throw in another half-a-dollar for an extra measure of feed fer the animals; we'll prob'ly be here all day at least."

"Consider it done, Mr. Burke. By th' way, Shirley Bradley serves up a good breakfas' down th' other end o' th' street. Good as any place around these parts."

John smiled. "You read my mind that time, George. Is Shirley still at th' same place as last year?"

"Same as th' last five years near as I can recall," George answered.

After turning the reins over to George, John reached into a leather pouch that he carried on his belt and pulled out three silver dollars. He handed them to the livery man saying, "The extra fifty cents is a tip for doin' a good job, which I know you will do." George gave him a big smile, showing a mouth half-full of empty spaces where teeth used to be.

"Thanks a bunch, Mr. Burke, 'n by th' way, since I'm th' only one tendin' th' barn, if y'all come back when I'm gittin' some grub or somethin' jus' go ahead 'n hep yourself to yer animals. I'm not usually gone too long," George explained as he began to unsaddle Silky.

John and Ollie strolled down the middle of the main street toward the place George had directed them for breakfast. John had already told Ollie about the mouth-watering steak and eggs, with home fried potatoes, country gravy and biscuits that Shirley was famous for. As they enjoyed the walk, they passed a general store that also served as a post office. Several people were out on the street, a couple mounted on horses, other town folks just getting up to a new day. Three or four children were playing chase around a board crosswalk, and they stopped to stare a bit at Ollie.

Blainetown wasn't large, so it wasn't long before they stood in front of an older house with a front porch where several folks were enjoying the morning. They were seated in rocking chairs, straight-back hickory chairs, a glider, and a swing. John and Ollie climbed the steps and John nodded respectfully to the folks on the porch as they cast curious eyes on the two strangers.

"Sure is a fine mornin'," John cordially said to a couple who were local farmers, judging from their appearance.

"Yes, sir, it sure is just thet," one acknowledged, and added, "We left y'all some breakfast in there, but we was sure tempted ta eat it all." He chuckled at his own jest. John and Ollie good-naturedly joined the laugh as they stepped through the door into the parlor that had been turned into a nice dining area. John and Ollie were not prepared for what happened next.

A beautiful young lady greeted them, stopping John dead in his tracks. She spoke ever so sweetly with a little curtsy. John was staring into the bluest of blue eyes adorned by long, dark, curly lashes and framed by perfectly shaped brows. She was a sight to behold, with glorious soft auburn hair in curls, natural rosy cheeks on a bed of flawless milk-white skin. She stood about five feet five inches in height and her simple print dress, which had been washed many times, clung to her every curve. She was beautiful and radiant.

John was speechless and frozen in time—as was the lady. They both seemed paralyzed. Ollie could see the mutual attraction and was glancing first to the lady then back to his dad, back and forth. Neither was speaking and Ollie was beginning to feel embarrassed. He felt he needed to break the silence.

"There's a nice table over there, Dad." Ollie gestured toward a window table.

John returned to himself, shaking his head. He endorsed Ollie's choice by heading toward the window; he turned toward the lady who was following them and asked, "Is this table all right, ma'am?"

"Yes, sir, it will be fine. You gentlemen be seated and I'll bring out some good hot coffee."

As she disappeared into the kitchen, John got his bearings and realized there were several tables in the room with people eating breakfast. He paused to reflect on what had happened. It was as if he and all surroundings were at a standstill while he gazed into the eyes of a young woman he had never seen before and was so smitten by her beauty that he could not speak. The perplexity of this situation was that such a thing had never happened to him before, even in his courtship of Elizabeth. This bothered him and made him feel guilty. This incident had happened in front of God and everybody else, including his son. John collected himself just as the young lady returned with two mugs and a pot of hot coffee. She placed the cups in front of John, then Ollie, and began to pour for John.

"How about you young man, do you drink coffee, or would you like something else?"

Ollie nodded. "Coffee will be fine, ma'am. By the way, my name is Ollie Burke and this is my dad, John. We live over at Louisa."

Back came the radiant smile and another curtsy as she acknowledged first Ollie with an outstretched hand, and then John.

"I'm glad to meet you, Ollie," she said politely, "and you too, John Burke," as she warmly shook his hand. "My name is Cassandra Martin, but everyone calls me Cassie. Now, what can I help you gentlemen with in the way of a good meal?"

Having collected his thoughts and his behavior, John answered Cassie with a smile.

"Cassie, give us two orders of steak and eggs with all th' trimmings. Make the eggs over easy on both of the orders and fry the steaks medium." John glanced at Ollie. "Anythin' else, son?"

"Only a glass of milk, please."

"I'll get this order on the way right now. I can tell I have two hungry men to feed," said Cassie as she headed back to the kitchen.

For John the dining room was back to normal, although he could not testify to what had happened earlier. He didn't know what the folks all thought of his entrance. Being himself once again, he began to notice his surroundings. At one table were four men who showed evidence of recently being military. The uniforms they wore, in part, were from the North. Their talk seemed to be engrossed in war developments, and John noticed that one man kept looking toward him. The man looked familiar, but John could not place him.

At a table over to their right two rude young fellows kept giggling and making gestures as they watched Cassie moving around the room pouring coffee, serving breakfast, and attending to her customers' needs. She was plainly annoyed by these two rowdy men, but nevertheless tried to ignore them. They had untied her apron more than once and one even tried tripping her by sticking out his boot. Ollie was totally disgusted with these two bad examples of mankind and wished he could do something about it. Four men sat at another table just sipping their coffee and discussing spring crops. They were farmers, no doubt, John figured.

Cassie brought their platters of breakfast, and what a feast to behold! The Burkes didn't have beef very often. Sometimes they had venison, which both dearly loved, but most of the time it was wild game, chicken or pork. This steak was made to tickle the palate, and indeed it did. It was topped off with fried apples and a cool glass of milk.

Then, suddenly, an incident happened to mar the ending of their breakfast. It occurred so quickly that Ollie would later have trouble recounting exactly in what order things happened. Cassie passed by the two obnoxious men and one pinched her backside.

She let loose with her left arm and swung an open hand at the one who offended her. He ducked and her hand kept coming, hitting John in the side of the head. John's head hit his plate on the table and he was dazed. By this time the eyes of the whole room were watching, sort of holding their breath. The two rowdies were the only ones laughing. Cassie was crying, knowing she had hit the wrong party. John stood, picked up his napkin, and was wiping his face and beard when the man who caused the problem shouted, laughing at John, "Thet'll teach ye—pinchin' th' little gurl thet way." He laughed again.

The last laugh was caught in mid-course when a brutal blow jarred the ruffian senseless and dropped him to the floor, clearing the table as he went. John's left hook put him to sleep quickly. The other roughneck was not idle. He pulled a knife, advancing toward John, waving the knife wildly, when suddenly he stopped and looked down at the handle of a shining Colt, with the barrel buried in his stomach. He noticed in a glance the cocked position as his ears heard the sound of blue coolness speaking to him.

"Now, Mister—you can put your knife away and say I'm sorry to th' lady. Pick up your sleeping friend, and mosey out of here. If you do that very quickly, you can avoid me havin' to pay for a cheap funeral—which would purely ruin me 'n Ollie's breakfast!"

The man knew John was dead serious even though he spoke with a touch of humor. He put away his knife and muttered an apology to Cassie who was still weeping. John patted her and gave her a quick hug, saying, "It's all right, Cassie. They'll not be back and I know you didn't mean to hit me. Everything is OK."

The roughneck dragged his groggy friend to the door, making a hasty exit. John and Ollie sat down and sort of cleaned up the mess on the table where a coffee cup had been knocked over and John's plate had overturned. Cassie disappeared into the kitchen still sobbing and Shirley herself made an appearance with a damp towel to help with the table.

"I'm sorry about those two. They're nothing but trouble wherever they go," Shirley said as she cleaned up the mess. "I'll tend to Cassie later," she added with firmness in her voice.

"Don't blame her, Mrs. Bradley," John quickly defended, "She had no intention to hit me at all. The other man ducked and she jus' lost her balance. Why, she's a fine waitress," John added.

Mrs. Bradley's lips were firm and just nodded at John's attempt to defend Cassie. John reached for his pouch and pulled out two silver dollars. He knew the meal was .75 cents each and, as he handed it to Shirley, he said, "Th' rest is a tip for Cassie, and it was sure a fine meal, as always."

Shirley tried to refuse the money but John insisted, as he picked up his cap from the rack and started toward the door. It was then he noticed the room had cleared except for the two of them. The excitement must have been too much for everyone. Ollie looked around for Cassie but didn't see her, so he followed his dad into the street.

John's thoughts were all of Cassie. Not so much the stimulation of the last few minutes, but rather of their initial meeting. He had mixed feelings about the guilt he felt in being caught off guard and exposing his bare inner emotions in front of his young son, in front of Cassie, a perfect stranger, and everyone in the restaurant. He could not imagine what had possessed him to behave that way. The knowledge that this had never happened with his wife of almost fourteen years troubled his mind even more. He and Elizabeth had married young and never were in any doubt of his love for her. He had never looked at another woman. *She has not been gone six whole months yet, and I haven't been thinking of anyone else. My Dear God,* he thought, *what must Ollie be thinking?* But worse than that for John was that he did not even know how to approach the subject with his son. He was reminded of the prayer he had prayed and the answer he received.

As they walked up the street without a word John spied a shoemaker through a glass window, hammering on a shoe heel, and it brought him back to the present. He stopped dead in his tracks and turned to Ollie.

"Son, I want you to do a little spying on your own for me— backtrack to th' place where we ate and see if you can git a reckonin' on those two men and where they went. Just mosey around and see if you spot 'em. Don't do anythin', just kind o' keep your eye on 'em. I don't think they're the type thet will follow up on thet fracas, but jus' in case, it's better to make sure, OK, son?"

"Sure, Dad, I'll check 'em out and trace you down. Don't you worry none, I'll be jus' fine," answered Ollie, always feeling very important when his dad gave him an assignment.

John waited, watching the youngster walk off down the street. He quickly headed to the livery stable where they left the horses. George was not visible, so John discovered where the saddles were placed along with the pack. In a short time he found the holster and belt, and located the silver buckle with matching rivets and snaps. Gathering them all up, he walked back to the cobbler's shop. The pleasant-faced man with a closely trimmed white beard and a shiny pate where hair used to be flashed a big smile at John.

"Howdy friend, how can I help you?" The businessman said.

John reached out his right hand and they shook hands introducing themselves. The cobbler's name was Donald Osborn.

"I've been makin' a holster and gun-belt for my son, and I need to get the buckle and fixin's put on to finish it up," John said, holding out the colorful new leather belt.

Donald took the belt, unrolled it full length and glanced back at John, giving him a full smile.

"I can see you have done a fine job, Mr. Burke—even allowed room for future growth. He must be a fine young man to deserve such a gift as this. Do ya have th' gun to go with it?"

"Yes, sir," John said, as he pulled out his own revolver.

"It's th' match for this Colt here, Donald, 'n by th' way—jus' call me John."

"Well, let me have the buckle and we'll see what we can do. If you want you can mosey around town and come back in awhile and I'll have her all fixed up for you," he said, turning to finish up the shoe he was working on.

John thanked the man and went out to the boardwalk, looking up and down the main street. He crossed to the general store and post office, where a group of men were gathered around a huge pot-bellied stove, although the stove was not fired up at this time of year. This was the town meeting place. As he moseyed in he saw two of the four men from the breakfast parlor there. They nodded at him with a smile of recognition. The only problem for John was—what were they remembering—his meeting with Cassie at the door or the fracas at the table? He didn't have long to wonder.

"How sore is th' side of yore haid?" sheepishly asked the one who had kept looking at John earlier from across the dining room.

John shook his head, unconsciously feeling the spot where Cassie thumped him, as he laughed good-naturedly.

"I'll tell you what, boys, if thet blow would have landed where it was aimed at, I wouldn't have had to hit him at all. Thet little lady would have laid him out for sure!"

This broke the ice and they all began laughing. It was plain that they had been discussing this when John entered. After all, that was a lot of excitement in this little town. John introduced himself to the two men from the restaurant, Wilbur Van Horn and Gene Yates. Gene was the one who kept looking toward John and, as it turned out, they did know each other casually from the garrison in Louisa.

Both were wounded at Middle Creek and Gene still had severe complications from a stomach wound. Wilbur was exempted from the military because he was operating a farm deemed too important to the war effort to be shut down. There were two other middle-aged farmers who had been on the porch when John and Ollie came in for breakfast. Gene asked about Ollie, and John told him that he had sent him to trace down the two rowdies.

"My reason was really double-sided," John said. "I'm gettin' a belt and holster I made for Ollie finished up over at th' cobblers shop 'n I wanted it to be a surprise. Th' other side is, I really thought it wouldn't hurt to know about those two. I'd hate to be blind-sided by 'em."

Gene nodded. "Not a bad idea, John, but you really had them two figured right. They're dodgers of the army on both sides and don't have much nerve when it comes right down to it. They prob'ly hit th' road lickity split as soon as they came outa Shirley's place."

Just as Gene finished his remark Ollie entered the store, nodded to the men and came up to his dad. John put an arm around his son, introduced him to the group, then mentioned the mission he had sent him on. Ollie confirmed what Gene had said.

"Well, Dad, the two men are long gone and are not likely to come across the person of John Burke again—not deliberately anyway."

John chuckled, patting him on the shoulder. "Good job, son. Why don't you look around to see if we need anything in the way of supplies." Ollie seemed to think their supplies were OK but he would look around anyway. He ended up getting a two-pound sack of sugar.

While Ollie was shopping, John's thoughts again drifted to Cassie. He was so taken with her. He didn't know how he was going to see her again, but he sure wanted to.

John had mentioned he'd like to get a haircut and have his beard trimmed while in town. Gene offered to show him to the barber, which presented him with the opportunity to be alone with John. He had something important to tell him. John, on the other hand, knew a barber was good for information if he was willing to talk; at least, that was his justification for the haircut and trim.

An hour later, after John's haircut, Gene and Ollie seated themselves with John in front of the barbershop. Gene looked at John slyly and said,

"Thet pretty waitress, Cassie, sure took a tumble for you, John. Did you notice thet?"

John could not help blushing as he quickly came back with, "Aw, you're surely kidding, Gene. Why she's jus' a youngster compared to me."

Ollie had pricked up his ears and was watching the two men with interest. Gene nodded his head with a smile. "Don't you go kiddin' yerself, John Burke. She is a woman full grown and th' purtiest I've ever seen. I have been around these parts fer some time and I never seen her look at anyone th' way she looked at you. You mark my word. I ain't kiddin' a bit!"

Gene went on to say that he had been at the garrison infirmary in Louisa, where he had seen John going in and out of the administration area and surmised John was still active in some way with the Union Army.

"Anyway thet's what I wanted ta mention ta you," Gene said.

John was relieved for the change of direction in the conversation; he was becoming mighty uncomfortable talking about Cassie in front of Ollie.

"I am not asking you to admit or deny it," Gene went on. "Jus' take this information and use it, or pass it on ta someone who can use it."

John nodded and invited Gene to continue. He told John and Ollie about a group of Rebs that had been operating in the Blaine area, as far over as Caines Creek and as far south as Cordell.

"What do you mean by 'operating'?" asked John.

"Wal, as near as I can tell, they's about a dozen of 'em, and they're stealin' food and animals from th' local farmers in this area. What I think is—they're either stashin' it or carrying it to a larger Reb group somewhere to feed their troops. Ya see, it's a well-known fact thet this geographical area is mostly all pro-Union in feelin's. Them thet are Confederate sympathizers keep it to themselves. I know this—them thet live here is pretty upset about the siti'ation and don't know whether to take it to the sheriff over in Louisa (since he's th' law in Lawrence County) or to th' military." Gene paused. "I don't know even if I'm right in tellin' ya about this—and if'n I'm not, jus' tell me and I'll be outa yer hair."

"Let me ask you this, Gene, before I answer thet question— how do you know for sure it's Rebs doin' th' stealin'?"

"Oh they ain't no doubt about thet—at least in th' mind of the locals. Chet Rice, one o' th' farmers in th' store this mornin', saw them running away after raiding his chicken house. They was three of 'em, all with full Johnny Reb uniforms. There was Confederate markin's on the horses. He saw 'em plain." Gene further explained how he had seen them himself in Wilbur's molasses cane field just after Wilbur turned up with two steers missing. Gene had taken a shot at them before they headed their horses into the timber.

"Well, I'll tell you this, Gene—you got th' information into someone's hands that will see thet somethin' is done about it. Don't you fellers git riled up enough to take matters into your own hands jus' yet. Give me two or three days to get some help. Mind you, I'm not admittin' to anythin' except thet I'll see thet you get help. Thet's my promise, and I'll leave it up to you to get word to th' other fellers. Now, one more question! If 'n a feller was to try and spy out th' land to watch these raiders, which way would he head out to be th' most likely to succeed?" John asked.

"I'm not dead sure, but my best guess would be over towards Cordell. I was headed up Brushy Creek a week ago and I saw a horse crossing thet had a lot of use. I saw lots of prints of shod pony's and plenty o' droppin's where they been waterin' 'em. They's nobody over in thet country what lives there, thet's got all thet many horses. Now if'n you head back toward Louisa on th' main road, jus' go till ya come ta Brushy Creek and head up th' creek towards Cordell. You'll spot th' place, plain as day," Gene elaborated, adding the bonus of partial directions.

At one point John interrupted Gene and sent Ollie to the livery stable to get his journal. When he returned John told him to take notes on all that had happened today, especially the information Gene had given them, including the directions. John and Ollie shook hands with Gene and thanked him for the information. They had started down the street when suddenly John remembered the holster. He smiled to himself and headed toward the cobbler shop, with Ollie quick on his heels. Ollie was used to following his dad without question, so he was right behind him when he climbed the wooden sidewalk up to the cobbler shop and went in.

"Well, sir," the cobbler said as he advanced toward the Burkes, "is this the young man this present is for?"

"Yes, indeed. Donald, this is Ollie. Ollie meet Mr. Donald Osborn. He has something for you to put on."

Ollie waited while the cobbler brought over a beautiful new belt and holster. "Try this on for size, Mr. Ollie," he said, holding out the pretty prize.

"For me?" Ollie shouted. His eyes widened with delight as he fumbled with the buckle and strapped on the new present. He placed it high on his right hip and slightly forward for an easy reach and a quick draw.

"Dad, you are the best dad in the whole world to buy me a holster all of my own." He wasn't too proud to hug his dad. And hug him he did, with Donald Osborn, smiling widely, looking on.

"First off, Mr. Ollie, your dad made that holster for you. He didn't buy it from me; I just put the buckle on. Secondly, I don't think I ever met a young man your age that was ever given such a nice gift. This means that you must be a particular boy to be honored with such a great gift."

John paid the cobbler and, thanking him for finishing so fast, he and Ollie went on their way. John had placed his weapon in the holster, allowing Ollie to get the feel of the weight of a gun. Ollie kept pulling it out and placing it back as he practiced on the way to the stable. It was now close to one o'clock. John put his hand on the youngster's shoulder. "How are you doin' for stomach timber, boy? Do you feel up to eatin' dinner?"

"Naw, Dad, I had all I could do to eat most o' that steak this mornin' and I am still workin' on that meal," Ollie replied as he placed the Colt in the holster for about the twentieth time.

"That was my feelin' too but I was jus' checkin'. It might be your last chance to get a town meal in awhile," John said, although his thoughts were of Cassie as they approached the big double barn doors at the livery stable.

"George—oh, George," John called out, but no answer was forthcoming. They went into the dimly lit barn to the stalls where their animals were placed side by side. Ginger snorted a greeting and Ollie allowed her to nuzzle him while he stroked her forehead. They slipped on the bridles and brought the horses out of their stalls to put on the saddles and saddlebags. Together they put the pack on Fred, and Ollie slipped the journal back into its place. The rifles stood in the corner by the double doors and Ollie went over to get them while John tightened the girth on Silky. As Ollie was on the way back with the rifles they both heard a noise. It sounded like—sniffling?

John motioned to Ollie and he froze in his tracks. Another sniffling sound came from the rear of the barn. John couldn't figure it out. Was it an animal or could it be a human? Then it seemed to stop. John indicated to Ollie to advance and he did so, moving quietly. He handed the Colt to his dad, handle first and John handed the animals' reins to him while he lifted the Colt in the air barrel first and softly and slowly moved toward the direction where he had heard the noise. Again, they heard what sounded like a sniffle, as if someone were crying. John lowered the weapon and came to the last stall, where a spotted gelding pawed the straw. John was not at all prepared for what he saw. There, huddled in the corner, was Cassie Martin, sobbing as if her heart would break.

"There, there girl," John said. "Nothing is as bad as all thet." He waved his arm to Ollie to come toward them. Ollie tied up the animals and came to his dad. John had thought a lot about this young woman today, but certainly did not expect to find her here, not like this.

John hunkered down beside her and was stroking her hair, trying to make her respond to soft talk. That's when he heard a throaty, threatening growl and noticed a large shepherd dog by her side. Cassie put her hand on the animal and said, "It's OK, Shep. It's OK." The animal laid his head in her lap and was quiet.

"Miss Cassie, we mean you no harm. We're your friends—you can trust us. So just tell my dad what the trouble is. I am sure we can help!" offered Ollie, as he scooted up to the pretty lady.

Cassandra Martin responded to these kind words and looked at Ollie with her beautiful blue eyes, now moist and rimmed with red.

"Oh, thank you, Ollie. Thank you also, Mr. Burke. I know you mean well and I know your intentions are to help, but—but I don't know how anyone can help in my situation."

John sat himself down on the opposite side of the stall, made his stiff leg comfortable, and spoke to Cassie.

"Well, little lady, we are not in such an all-fired rush that we can't sit down and at least listen to your problem. After all—anyone who packs a wallop like you do deserves my attention!" The smile on John's face indicated good humor. Cassie broke out in laughter and her face turned red.

"I guess," she said, after controlling herself midst tears and laughter, "that if anyone deserves an explanation, it's you two—John and Ollie Burke."

John's invitation was sincere, so Cassie told her story. Shirley Bradley had called her in after the fracas of the morning was over and gently but firmly fired Cassie from her job of about two weeks. The reason—"flat out" as Shirley put it—was that Cassie was "too pretty to work for her." Shirley liked her, and Cassie was a good waitress, but she was attracting the wrong kind of customers, and Shirley could tolerate it no more. She absolutely knew that Cassie had good morals, but those men who created the upset in the restaurant were not the first. It had happened three times in two weeks with these silly flirtations. She also knew this was not Cassie's fault. Cassie was just "too uncommonly pretty" for such work, not being married and all. At least this was Shirley Bradley's opinion on the subject and she was the boss. And so Cassie was let go, but this in itself was not the dilemma.

Just three weeks before, Cassie had been notified that her father, her only living relative, had been killed in the battle at Shiloh. Jacob was a federal officer under General William Nelson. She had been alone in a small farmhouse on Caines Creek since her dad left late last year, and she had no livelihood. She had started toward Louisa on this horse, which was hers, and Shirley Bradley had intervened and talked her into staying in Blainetown to work for her. She offered her room and meals as payment for waiting tables, and she could keep her tips for wages. At this point Cassie paused and thanked John for his generous tip this morning. After John waved it off, she continued her story.

"That's why I don't know which way to go or what to do."

"Cassie, is anything keeping you in Blainetown, now that your dad is gone?"

"No, Mr. Burke, the farm we stayed on was rented and I can't even afford the rent there, which was cheap enough."

"Do you have any belongings at all?"

"I have this loyal dog, Shep, my beautiful horse, Spot, with a saddle and bridle. I have this comfortable bedroll, some cold biscuits and $5.50 in hard-earned money and—most important—I have the Lord," she added.

John stood up, turned to Ollie. "Saddle her horse, son." Then he turned to speak to Cassie.

"You're rich young lady! You just don't know how rich you are yet. You also have two new friends and you're coming with them for the time bein'. And besides thet, God has your life under control. I just want you to know—you can trust us. As a matter of fact, you're th' second lady in distress we have had the privilege of rescuing this week. This must be God's plan and right now we're leavin' this place—and you're comin' with us.

Cassie Martin picked herself up, brushed off her dress, followed Ollie, and John out the big double doors, and said only one thing.

"Thank you, John Burke. And I also thank you, God!"

TWELVE

Behold Thou Art Fair

O LLIE WAS BUSY THINKING AS THEIR CARAVAN TROTTED OUT OF Blainetown single file. Shep was out in front, sniffing and running from horse to horse; then back out front waiting. Next came John, followed closely by Cassie, riding astride her horse like a man. She had a good, well-worn western style saddle and had tucked her dress carefully for maximum decency. Ollie brought up the rear of the small procession, leading the mule and thinking back over the last seven hours as they headed toward Blaine Creek.

Shirley spotted them and waved when they passed the diner, as did the cobbler and others who were strangers to John and Ollie. Ollie rode on ahead for a minute or two, stopping at the store to pick up the sugar he had left inside. He ran out, put it in the pack, and was ready to go again.

As they rode along, Ollie was reliving the episode in the dining parlor where Cassie and his dad had met and locked eyes. It was like a spell was cast over the two of them and, although he looked back and forth at them, they were oblivious to him being there. His dad had been smitten by this beautiful woman—totally off guard and unprepared for the shock of it. He could see the others in the room and knew it was time for an emergency procedure. That is when he suggested the table and returned them both to reality. Yes, both of them. Cassie was caught in the intricacy of the moment as well as John.

His father was a handsome man—over six feet in height, with wavy black hair, blue-gray eyes, and a handsome face with a full black beard that he kept well-trimmed. Ollie smiled at the recent haircut and trim. He was grinning to himself as he thought about his dad this way; John would be embarrassed if he knew the thoughts of his young son. His dad had not mentioned the occurrence of this morning all day long, but Ollie knew he was thinking about it—and Cassie. He knew his dad just didn't know how to approach the subject with his son. As Ollie looked Cassie over again, he decided that she was the most beautiful lady he had ever seen, even more so than Eliza Birchet. Up until now Eliza had been at the top of the "Ollie beauty scale."

Cassie Martin was also involved with her thoughts of this strange entourage. *A chance meeting in a restaurant this morning and here I am following a handsome stranger with a son who is about ten to twelve years of age but acts like and has the manners of an eighteen-year-old. Only God knows where this will lead.* However, she felt a deep peace inside her bosom that said, "all is well." She had just had her twentieth birthday on January 26, and already folks were looking at her as an "old maid." She had slim pickings indeed around Blainetown these days with all the young men in the service. This had started two years ago and had increased, until none were left except draft dodgers and misfits to her way of thinking.

The eyes and looks of this man, who could even have a wife at home, had electrified Cassie. Somehow, she knew that this was not so. The morning's encounter suggested to her that he was alone except for his son. She knew one thing for sure—this was the man she was waiting for. This was the man she had prayed for. She always felt she would know him when she saw him, and this was the one she was waiting for. There was not one doubt in her mind that the morning's experience was love at first sight. God had answered her prayer and, whether John Burke knew it or not, he was her man!

Somehow she felt he did not know it yet, but she sensed that Ollie did and would be the one to help his dad understand. That is why Cassie felt a peace on the inside and was now delighted that she had been fired this morning. It was as if Shirley Bradley was in on a giant conspiracy with her and Ollie and God. The only thing left to do was help John Burke discover it. *I am your destiny, John Burke, and I will make you forget your loneliness that I can see, and the tragedy that I can sense has been in your life, so help me God!* This was the promise she made to herself as she followed this dear man God sent her.

John led his party north toward Blaine Creek, not far out of town. Because of the addition of another passenger he had not discussed with Ollie the plan forming in his mind. He did not want the small number of folks who saw them leave to have any notion of his real direction of travel either. Cassie's joining his group was his idea, and he was excited about her being with them. He no longer felt the guilt he was feeling before, because he knew that this young lady was put in his path intentionally by God. Just as surely as Cindy Lou was put in Ollie's and his life, so was Cassie Martin. He would deal with the "why" as time went on, but right now he was content to accept the inevitable: Cassie belonged! Perhaps she was the lady God was going to answer his prayer with, perhaps she wasn't. God would let him know in due time.

John turned back east when he reached Blaine Creek and followed the rushing water of the shoals into the quietness of deep water as he made a path where there was no trail. They proceeded slowly along the bank, up the hill, over the draw, back to the creek, and continued this course for about five miles. John often wondered why Blaine Creek was called a creek. He had seen other bodies of water that seemed to him to be smaller than Blaine, but were called rivers. As John led his caravan into a little clearing, which was blessed with shelter as well as good visibility, he pulled on his reins and spoke.

"This is the place, Ollie. Let's make camp here. Picket the horses and relieve them of their gear."

Cassie made herself useful picking up dry wood for a fire, and spotted an ideal place to build one. As John took the pack off Fred he smiled to see Cassie pitch right in and make herself at home. He knew the next order of his business would be a private family meeting and a time of getting acquainted with this new addition to their family.

In a short while a nice campfire was burning and a pot of water was on to boil as Ollie showed Cassie where things were kept in the pack. Ollie said he had a taste for fish, being so close to Blaine. John and Cassie agreed, so he took hooks and line and some pork rind for bait and headed down the creek to find a good spot. Before long, John and Cassie were relaxing and enjoying a cup of black coffee.

Cassie was first to break the silence.

"John, do you remember earlier—you said something about me being the second lady you rescued this week? Who else did you rescue?"

John laughed and hesitated a moment then began the story about Cindy Lou and the tragic loss of her family. He went into detail about the rescue, especially Ollie's part, and the trip back to Uncle John's, where Cindy Lou was left in the capable hands of Eliza and the Birchets. He also told her about his and Ollie's part in agreeing to give her a home. At this point Cassie asked, "Do you mean that you are taking Cindy to be your own daughter and Ollie's sister?"

"Well, that depends on whether Sheriff John Allison can trace her relatives or not. I also have a friend in the Union Army looking through his sources. In the meanwhile, I told little Cindy thet if we didn't find any kinfolks, thet she could call me 'Daddy John' and we would be her family."

Cassie's face brightened. "Why, John, that is admirable of you and Ollie, and this little Cindy must be adorable as well as a very fortunate little girl."

"Well, we are blessed, too! You see, Cassie, while I was away in the Army fightin' last winter, in January to be exact—I lost my wife and thirteen-year-old daughter to smallpox. I came home with a wound I got in the Battle of Middle Creek and found only Ollie left."

Cassie thought, *This is confirmation of the loneliness and tragedy I saw in John's eyes.* John continued the story of the loss of his dear ones, Elizabeth and Sue Ellen, and about that lonely cold day he and Ollie climbed the hill in Louisa to visit the recent graves. He felt that in Cindy, and now perhaps even Cassie, God was replacing what had been taken away by tragedy.

"I do hope you won't think me presumptuous," John ventured, "but that is what I meant when I told you that you're comin' with us."

"Not at all, John. I feel I belong here and I also believe God has a hand in all this." She said with a tear trickling down her cheek. Cassie did not want to assume too much or say too much. She decided just to take her lead from John's leadership and his guidance.

"At first it was very difficult for me, even knowin' thet, as th' Bible says, 'th' rain falls on th' just and the unjust,' I had a hard time acceptin' my loss. I sorta hung on thet Scripture, but Ollie has really been my mainstay. Also, I continued to work for th' Army in a civilian capacity, which made the lonely times seem more tolerable. You must know this in jus' losin' yer pa—as time passes, it gets easier. So it has been with Ollie an' me; we have actually come to be closer now."

"Yes, John, I do understand and realize that your loss must have been much more difficult than even my own. My dad and I were close, but I remember more my loss at nine, when my mother passed away. It probably was easier because dad was away when this happened in the war. I had been here on the farm alone all those months since he enlisted. I suppose what you mean about Cindy and myself filling those empty spots is somehow replacing Elizabeth and Sue Ellen?"

John answered Cassie's question. "Cassie, you're a well-read young lady and it's plain you have some formal education as well as havin' a Bible background," John commented. After a pause he continued. "I know you must remember the Bible story of Job—how he lost all he had, even his family. You will also remember how God restored everything Job had until, at the end, he had more than in th' beginnin'. I sorta feel God is in th' restoring process with me and Ollie right now, and I am willin' to let Him do whatever He sees fit with me. Do you understand, Cassie, what I'm tryin' to say?" John was perspiring and a little uncomfortable. He was willing to let God do what He wanted to do; he just felt uncomfortable in taking a hand in it himself.

Cassie did not answer immediately. She knew what he said as well as what he meant, but Cassie wanted to see John Burke come to the place of acknowledging that he loved and was attracted to her on his own. She could see that right now John Burke was placing the responsibility for her and even little Cindy coming into his and Ollie's life onto God. He could accept this easier than the knowledge that he had anything to do with it. It was easing his conscience because he was still mourning his loved ones and he was still, in a way, married to them.

In John Burke's mind, Cassie thought, *he can more readily accept God's role in our fateful meeting and coming together than he can his own realization that he has fallen in love. The fact that he was physically smitten by his meeting with me, as I was with him, has escaped him because of probably several reasons. He has to deal with my being much younger than him. He has to deal with the fact that social attitudes dictate that he has not mourned long enough. He probably even has to deal with his own morals as to the man-like feelings that he must have for me—thinking they are wrong because of all of these other thoughts. It is much easier putting all the responsibility on God.*

True, she did see God in what had taken place; He did have His hand in answering her prayer. But she also knew John fell in love with her just as she had fallen for him. Right now she saw John as looking for an easy way out by saying it was all God's doing. She was not going to let him get off that easy. John must come to terms with his own feelings and be honest in expressing them. Cassie began an evasive action.

"John, you're right. I do have a formal education. My mother had a close friend back in Boston who took it upon herself to pay my way back east after Mother died when I was nine years old and Daddy allowed me to have an extended stay with Aunt Prudence. I came home to Kentucky after she herself passed away when I was sixteen. I also had formal Bible school in Boston and finally taught Bible lessons to younger students while I was there. I do remember the story of Job. One of my favorite quotations from Job is found in the first chapter, verse 21; I believe it says, 'Naked came

I out of my mother's womb, and naked shall I return thither: The Lord gave, and the Lord hath taken away; blessed be the name of the Lord.'

"I—I think—I know what you are speaking of, John. You're comparing yourself to Job. I said before I feel like I belong here and I feel like God has a hand in me being here, I just must find my role."

As Cassie finished her explanation she became quiet and looked toward Blaine Creek. Her inner impulse was embarrassing even to Cassie. She would like to walk over to this beloved, generous man and take his bearded face in her two hands. She wanted to look into his eyes and say, "Wake up, John Burke. I love you—I love you. I want you to take me into your arms and tell me that you love me, too; that you want to love me, caress me—and never let me go. I want to kiss away your tragedy and bring new life and happiness into your home until death do us part! I want to help you with Ollie and fill empty spots in his life, I want to help you raise Cindy, if that is your lot, and be a mother to her. I want to bear you other children, John Burke. I don't want to take the place of Elizabeth. I want to have my own place. And, so help me God— I will have that place!"

John Burke was shaken by this woman. There was no doubt about it. He had seen her outward beauty and was taken by surprise and bewildered by the occurrence that he had no control over. Now he found that she is not only the loveliest creature he had ever laid eyes on, but she is also exasperatingly intelligent. John was in a dilemma for a comeback to this last bit of conversation that had been hurled at him, but he was saved from having to do so when Ollie came strolling on the scene with a string of nice fish. It was dusk, so he lit two lanterns and hung them to add to the light of the campfire.

Ollie cleaned the fish while Cassie put some potatoes into the glowing coals to bake. She also mixed some flour and meal, salt and pepper together and put a big iron skillet on the fire to heat up with some butter. The timing was perfect. Just as the butter was bubbling she had the fish coated with the flour mixture and put them on to fry. Before long a delightful aroma filled the air and John was enjoying the work of the lovely lady and his son fixing a meal together. They teased and laughed and mixed cornbread dough as if they had been doing it for years.

It was dark now and the pleasant glow of the campfire and the lanterns cast a nice light around John, Ollie and Cassie, as well as Shep, as they enjoyed a plentiful, delicious supper. John topped off his meal with a spoonful of molasses and butter melted over hot crisp cornbread. *My dear God, she can cook too,* he reflected while Cassie and Ollie were engrossed in "get acquainted" chatter.

Shep stirred and his ears stood straight up. The hair on his back bristled and deep in his throat was a rumbling growl as he looked toward something in the forest, unseen but heard by his sensitive ears. There was the sound of a tree branch snapping, and John became alert as he stood. Neither Cassie nor Ollie saw it happen, but his revolver was already in his right hand, his left hushing them to silence.

"Hello th' camp," came a voice. "I's a friend, not a enemy. Can I approach yo' camp?"

"Come on in with your hands high and empty. We're glad to have you—come on in," John answered.

A black man wearing a Confederate uniform walked in slowly with his arms straight out and nothing in them. He was turning them slowly as he came in so John could see in front and back. He was a man of medium stature, about five feet ten inches in height. He had a very deep shade of dark skin, a ruggedly handsome face with a square-set jaw, and was clean-shaven except for a couple of days' worth of stubble. He carried no visible weapons, only a shoulder strap holding a small leather pouch about the size of a single saddlebag. He had a half-smile on his face and spoke to John as he advanced.

"Mah name is Zeb Peters and I wuz a plantation slave in Alabama. I wuz 'n inside house slave and they made me jine up in the Rebel Army and put me in dis unifom. I don' know if'n you all is Yankees or Rebs, but I is hopin' you is Yankee. I been runnin' no'th fer three, maybe fo' days, 'n terrible hongry. The smell o' that fish cookin' just plumb got to me; I had to come 'n ask fer a bit to feed mahse'f with."

John put away his weapon and spoke to the man.

"Zeb, jus' put yourself down here and we'll fix you something to fill thet empty spot. We got plenty left and you're welcome to it."

Even as John spoke Cassie had moved into action and fixed Zeb a plate with two whole bass fish, baked potato and cornbread with butter and molasses. Ollie poured him a cup of coffee and they all sat back as he ate. With all of his hunger, he ate politely and gratefully. John visited with him as he ate.

"We didn't answer your question, Zeb, but I will now. We're civilians from over in Louisa. I'm John Burke, and we're family. This is my son Ollie and close friend Cassie Martin. We only raised a gun at you because, in these times, as you know, a man can't be too careful. Your uniform is not too welcome in these parts, 'cause a group of Rebs has been raidin' the local farms here abouts and they are on the lookout. We just had heard about thet today so we're a little nervous."

"Hey, Mr. John, yah don' hafta 'splain ta me. I wuz takin' an all-fired chance in comin' in heah like this. I been watchin' ya fer mos' an' hour and finally decided you all didn't look or act much like th' Rebs I has been with. Havin' a hansum boy and purty

twelve: behold thou art fair

missus kinda tole me y'all was genteel fo'ks. I jus wuz too hongry to fight it anymo'."

"Is that enough food, Zeb?" John asked, as he saw the plate just about empty." We ain't got anymore fixed, but if you're still hungry we'll find somethin' else."

"No suh, that's plenty an' y'all are mos' kind. Thet'll hold me fine," Zeb answered.

John asked the man his plan and basically he had none to speak of. He was just trying to find his way to the Union Army and was going to ask for sanctuary and even offer to fight for the North if they would have him. John found out that Zeb knew where the Rebel camp was in the Brushy Creek area that Gene Yates spoke of. John decided he could use this man if he was willing to stay with him.

"Zeb, I'm formin' a plan that has to do with th' work me and Ollie are doin'. If'n you was to stay with me, I'll see thet you get to meet those Union Army fellers you are lookin' for. I could find you right handy to me if you have a mind to stay around."

John was pleased with Zeb's reply.

"Mr. John, I's at yo' service. Jus' tell me what to do and I'll do mah best."

John turned to Cassie and Ollie. "This plan is going to take th' two of you to play out your parts jus' as I ask and put your trust in me. Cassie, this especially means you, for you are new in the Burke family 'n our way of doin' things." John turned directly to her.

"Cassie, I'm sending you to Louisa tomorrow with Ollie. He'll take you to Rebecca Birchet, the wife of a close friend of mine who is a sergeant in the Union Army stationed out of Louisa. He'll then take you to our cabin outside of Louisa and I'm going to ask you to stay there until we return from this business trip thet we're on. What I mean by stay there is—th' place is yours. It's a small log cabin and there is a cow named Daisy to milk and chickens to tend to. Th' Birchets have been tendin' to th' place and will turn thet over to you. There is a stall for your horse and plenty of feed. There is food in th' pantry as well as in th' smoke house. With th' chickens, eggs, milk 'n butter, there is enough to live on. We have a good well close to th' door. Mind you th' cabin will be dusty and such; we've been livin' alone since th' ladies have been gone, but th' place is comfortable 'n I can picture you in it. Th' Birchets are jus' a short piece down th' road so you can get help or visit. They'll jus' love you to death if'n you let 'em."

Cassie looked John straight in the eyes. "John Burke, it will be my pleasure to attend to your house and I will do you proud. When you and Ollie finish your business, I'll be there to welcome you home."

John turned to Ollie and told him to take Cassie home by way of the Birchets and then take a letter, which he would compose later, to Captain Lyons. This letter would tell about Zeb Peters, express his need for the captain to send him a small troop of horse soldiers, which Ollie could lead back, and meet his dad at the forks of Brushy Creek and Blaine two nights from now at eight o'clock.

John told Ollie he would show him the exact place where to meet tomorrow. He explained to Ollie his dependence upon him to protect Cassie and to help her discover their little place, showing her around before he returned with the soldiers. John took Ollie and Cassie over to the picketed horses and asked them a question.

"Could the two of you ride double back to Louisa on Spot and let me hold Ginger here for Zeb? He can be a big help to me. I'll keep your rifle in the scabbard and let you wear your Colt, Ollie, in your new holster. We may have need of th' rifle; I doubt if Zeb has ever fired a revolver at all."

Cassie and Ollie looked at each other and Cassie said, "That's fine with me. How about you, Ollie?"

"Aw, you know it's all right, Dad, I'd do anything it took to help you. Me 'n Cassie will be fine."

"Good, son. I knew I could depend on you. You bring back another horse from th' Army for Zeb, an' also a change of clothes out o' that Reb uniform. Right now I want you to take your rifle and break Zeb in on it—loadin' 'n such. He prob'ly jus' knows about muskets. Jus' don't fire it." Ollie removed the rifle from the scabbard and walked back to the campfire.

The night was not well lit with a moon, but there was enough light that John could see Cassie and make out her soft features. He reached out and took her by the hand and led her within a few feet of Blaine Creek. The water's movement made a rippling sound, merging with the melodious night noises of crickets, frogs, and night birds. John was full of things to say to this lovely woman that were motivated by their pending circumstance, as well as inner feelings that he did not understand or know how to express. A word in the Bible, the Song of Solomon came to him, "Behold, thou art fair, my love." He felt the strong impulsive desire to hold her close to him, to stroke her soft hair and touch her lips and cheeks. John also felt his heart pounding in his chest and knew she must be able to hear it. With all this collage of feelings running rampant, John nevertheless controlled himself in the presence of this woman whom he just met this morning. He nervously reached out his right hand and touched Cassie on the cheek ever so gently.

"Cassie, I am a little mixed up right now with all I have to do in th' way of responsibility to Ollie and to my job, 'n now to you. I am also mixed up about sendin' you away from me so soon and a part o' me wants to keep you here, when I know th' right thing to do is jus' what I'm doin'. Honey—if I can call you thet—jus' be patient with me and believe I am tryin' to do what is right for us all." With this John stopped, almost feeling he had said too much. Cassie reached her hand up to the hand on her cheek and pulled it down to her lips and sweetly kissed it. She looked into his eyes, which she could see even in the darkness.

"John, I understand more than you think. I feel more about the words unexpressed than you think. I have utmost confidence in you doing the right thing and I have patience to wait for you until the time is right." With this she took his hand, placed it under her neck, and hugged it to her as she squeezed the nervous fingers, then kissed his hand again.

"Cassie, I will have Ollie show you where all of Sue Ellen and Elizabeth's clothes are kept. I hadn't the heart to get rid of them before and now I know why. You may have to take a tuck here 'n there, but please make use of them. I know you don't have too much now and these will get you by until we can get you some new ones. I hope this don't offend you—them bein' gone 'n all?"

"Not at all, John Burke, not at all. If you and Ollie don't mind, I'm not a proud lady in the sense of wearing someone else's clothing and God knows I need to have something to change into besides this dress, which is almost worn out. I am grateful to you—and Ollie." She gave him a big hug.

Cassie and John strolled back to the campfire, linked arm in arm, and found Zeb excelling in loading and unloading the Sharps. Cassie excused herself after getting a lantern, a bar of soap, and a towel from John, and headed toward Blaine Creek to "freshen up" as she politely put it.

"Ollie," John said to his son, "would you have any objection to giving your mother's and sister's clothes to Cassie, seein' she only has about what she is wearin'?"

"Not at all, Dad. It seems to me a terrible waste not to let somebody wear 'em. It's for sure you 'n me will never use 'em," he said, grinning.

"Good boy, son, I knew you wouldn't mind, but I still had to ask. When you get Cassie home, show her where they are and you might mention it to Rebecca in private so we don't have any embarrassin' moments for either one of them." John turned to Zeb to explain.

"My wife and daughter passed away in the smallpox epidemic last winter, Zeb, and thet's why we're helpin' out the little lady."

Zeb laughed and slapped his knee saying, "Mr. John, ya sure don hafta 'splain ta me. Appears ta me she is fambly anyway. Thet's what y'all said when I jined up wit th' fambly!" John laughed also and remarked to Zeb that he was absolutely right.

John told Ollie to see to the horses for water and the nightly rub down while he composed the letter to Captain Lyons. Zeb offered to help and they took the horses downstream apiece so there would be no chance of interrupting Cassie. Cassie came back while John was writing, and cleaned up the supper utensils, putting them all away. John noticed her as she worked around the fire, and admired her slender looks and beauty. The fire dancing in the night made the edges of her hair come alive as if she were rimmed with a fiery halo, accenting the red in her hair. He could hardly help but notice the silhouette of her shapely legs as she worked on this side of the campfire and the lanterns. Her soft print dress of multitudes of washings was very thin and allowed the light to come through freely. A Scripture passed through John's mind in the Song of Solomon: "Behold thou art fair my love." *I'm glad no one knows how embarrassed I am,* John thought.

He was wrong of course. Cassandra Martin knew. She was using the thin dress, which was no deliberate doing of her own, mind you, and the campfire light to the best advantage her innocent modesty would allow her. She knew exactly what she was doing and also knew who it was for and why. She wanted her man to have a lot of thoughts about who was waiting for him in Louisa at journey's end. She thought it also all right to hurry up patience just a tiny bit. After all, she had waited a long time. As she finished around the campfire, she moved over next to John and smiled radiantly. "John, can I please sit here next to you while you write? Will I disturb you?"

"Why, of course, Cassie, that kind o' disturbance is always welcome," John said with a mischievous grin on his face.

Cassie blinked her long lashes, flashing John a radiant smile as she sat down. She used his left shoulder as a backrest, allowing her auburn curls to fall over his chest. Enfolding her arms around her knees, she braced herself with bare feet, so she seemed perfectly relaxed as she leaned against John and allowed him to write—and to notice her, of course.

The sound of horses and voices announced the arrival of Ollie and Zeb, who both noticed the satisfied scene and smiled as they finished their task. Ollie got out the journal without a word and began to update it by lantern light. Zeb apologized for being so tired and explained he had not had a peaceful night's sleep for some time, so he retired. John, after finishing his composition, picked up his blanket and returned to his former position, allowing Cassie to nestle against his shoulder while he placed his arm around her. They were shielded from the damp night air and coolness from Blaine Creek by the blanket, and very soon Cassie was asleep. She had two adoring eyes watching her sleep for a long time before John also drifted into dreamland. Neither the pretty lady nor the handsome father was aware that two young eyes had watched the both of them as they were innocently enjoying their closeness.

Ollie was pleased with what he saw and found himself approving. He knew Cassie was unique! She had manners, and extreme love for his dad that showed all over. That is what his dad needed and, he deserved the best. In the providence of God and in the absence of his mother from this earth, Ollie felt like God had given John the best—Cassandra Martin.

THIRTEEN

The Lord Will Provide

T HE UNUSUAL BURKE ENTOURAGE WAS UP BEFORE DAYLIGHT, FIXING breakfast, saddling horses and breaking camp. Ollie and Cassie were on the breakfast detail while Zeb and John took care of the horses, saddles, and pack for Fred.

"Make sure we do a good job of destroying evidence of our camp as much as possible," cautioned John, knowing it would be done without his warning. By first sun the group was heading toward the mouth of Brushy Creek, which meant backtracking a ways. Again Shep was out in front, running back and forth, sniffing bushes and running back wagging his tail as if to say, "Hurry up, slow pokes."

John led the group, followed by Ollie and Cassie both riding Spot, with Zeb bringing up the rear, leading the pack mule. He was riding Ginger and she had trouble getting used to the new man and heavier weight. She was not too excited about it at first, but finally settled into Zeb's gentleness. Before they knew it, they had arrived at the place where they would go their separate ways. John called Ollie and Cassie over to him for instructions.

"This is the place, Ollie. Remember I'll meet you here tomorrow night, which is Saturday. Allow Captain Lyons to decide how many men to send, but I don't feel it calls for many. Are you all settled as to what you should do?"

"Yes, sir, I have the letter right here and it will all be fine."

"Do you remember what to do with Cassie and what to say to Rebecca?"

"Yes, sir." Ollie grinned. "I'll see that Cassie gets taken care of and everythin' will be fine, Dad. Now stop worryin'."

"OK, Ollie." John smiled. "I see you got it all under control. Keep to the main road; should anyone git nosy, you're brother and sister on th' way home to Louisa. The two of you should not give rise to any suspicion so all will prob'ly go well and you should be home way before dark. Good bye, son, and God bless you." John extended his hand to his son and received a tight handshake.

He then turned his attention to Cassie and as he extended his hand to her, their eyes met. She eagerly took his hand and clutched it momentarily squeezing tightly with both hands.

"God go with you, John Burke. I—I'll miss you," she said, breaking up a bit with moist eyes. She turned quickly and looked at Zeb, blinking to try to hide her tears, and said, "God go with you, too, Zeb."

Cassie turned her horse up Brushy Creek, heading toward the main road to Louisa. She and Ollie both looked back and waved, then were out of sight.

Zeb smiled at John, shaking his head as he spoke, "Mr. John, that is a hansum lady. I say, she's done got th' mos' beautiful eyes I has evah seen."

"That she does, Zeb. I feel th' same way and I am sure goin' to miss her, and Ollie, although we'll be seein' Ollie tomorrow night. Now, tell me what you know about these raiders, Zeb!"

"I done cut their trail a couple days ago, Mr. John! I fust was scared they wuz on mah track, but aftah watchin' 'em real careful like, I done foun' out they had sum othah mischief in mind."

"How'd you know about their stealin', Zeb?" John inquired.

"I hid and sorta followed 'em. I saw 'em take five steers that I knew nevah belonged ta them. It wuz outten a big bunch of cows." he answered.

Zeb explained to John that he had watched these men drive the cattle toward their hideout which was an old cabin in the woods. They had constructed a makeshift corral out of hickory saplings and it was nearly full of livestock; mostly cattle. As near as he could count, there was probably ten to twelve men, and they would have to be doing something about the cattle soon for they had a good many of them when he was there.

"When did you see them last, Zeb?"

"It wuz yestiday, Mr. John. I had come from that place to where you was campin', but 'member, I wuz walkin' and cuttin through th' heavy trees so's not to leave any track and so's nobody cud see me."

"Well, you lead up Brushy and I'll follow with Fred. When we cross the main road I'd jus' try to go back th' same way you came to us, and we'll be extra quiet jus' in case we run into someone. You jus' keep your ears open good."

Zeb led off, following John's instructions. John couldn't help but notice the fresh tracks at the Blaine road where Ollie and Cassie had turned off. His chest felt as if it was still warm from where her head had been as she slept last night. He shook his head to shake off the "Cassie spell." He needed to be alert at this point and keep his mind on the job. He was glad God favored him with Zeb; he knew this man would be valuable to him.

In about an hour they came to the crossing on Brushy Creek that Gene Yates had referred to when he gave John directions. Zeb dismounted with John right behind him. Zeb began to move quietly across the creek to the west, leading Ginger. He was listening and slowly working his way up an incline thick with brush more than just large trees. As they neared the crest of the hill timber was thick again and Zeb zigzagged down a gradual slope and around to the south. He seemed to know exactly where he was headed. He soon came to a cliff that sheltered a cave large enough to ride a mounted horse into. John knew this area abounded in caves, but had never discovered this one. Zeb dropped Ginger's reins, which stopped her cold in her tracks.

He came over and whispered to John that this was the place he stayed in while keeping an eye on the Reb raiders. What he really had wanted was food and had hoped to steal it, but the leader of this group was clever and the cabin was never without someone inside.

John and Zeb left the animals and went down the slope to see the cabin. It was a good-size cabin and seemed in good state of repair. The corral had been emptied and had only a couple of horses, the cattle having all been moved elsewhere. John found a good location to observe the surrounding area without being seen and removed his telescope from his inside vest pocket. Slowly and methodically he scanned the area to see if there was any activity from Confederate soldiers, but the cabin seemed all but deserted. One soldier was outside cutting wood, and he thought he caught a glimpse of movement through the open cabin doorway. He told Zeb to return to the horses and wait for him in the cave. He was going to try and get a closer look or substantiate the number of Rebs here and elsewhere. Zeb gladly complied and returned to attend to the horses and find a comfortable place to relax.

Ollie and Cassie soon made their way to the road that went to Louisa.

"Ollie, I would feel more comfortable if you rode in front of me. After all, you know the trail better than me. Is that OK?" Cassie asked.

"I don't mind if I do, Cassie. It makes sense to me." Ollie slid off and climbed in front with the aid of his new friend.

Cassie gave him the reins as she put both arms around his slender waist and held him close to her. This was very comforting to Ollie as he felt the warmth of her arms about him. Spot was sure-footed and seemed to not be bothered with Shep darting in and out, sometimes coming right under his feet. It was obvious the two animals were friends and accustomed to each other. They rode for perhaps an hour in silence. Ollie was buried in his own thoughts, and Cassie was lost in her dreams. They both had much to think about. Ollie broke the silence first, mentioning the saddle in which they were so comfortably seated.

"This sure is a soft saddle, Cassie. It seems almost like a big ol' cushion."

"Yes, Ollie, I think so too. That is actually the reason my dad got the saddle for me. He wanted me to be happy and noticed the extra padding that had been added. He offered to get me a side-saddle, which I also know how to use, but I preferred a gentleman's saddle. So he just smiled at me and got this one." She laughed, remembering her father's reaction.

"Well, I have seen the ladies around these parts ride on those contraptions and I don't understand for anything how they stay on a horse at a gallop," Ollie commented.

"You're right, Ollie. It's not easy and you sure have to get used to it. I know some of the 'proper' lady folks in our area turned up their noses at me for riding a horse like a man. I just ignored them. I felt my comfort and enjoyment were more important than their prudish noses."

This time Ollie laughed and shook his head. "You're something else, Cassie—one of a kind."

Not being able to see him full in the face from where she was riding, Cassie just squeezed him a little as she threw a question to him.

"Why, what ever do you mean, Ollie Burke?" she asked impishly.

"Well," said Ollie thoughtfully, "you are a straightforward sort of a lady and you don't try to hide behind words you don't mean. What you say is up front and you speak it out it seems to me. That's not like most grown-up lady folks I've met. Just like this saddle for instance. You could have done the proper thing so most folks would look at you well, but you didn't want to, so you didn't. That may not set well, but you jus' don't pay any attention to what other folks think. You did what you wanted. I guess that's what I mean, and—I like it!

"I guess that's one reason why I like you. Like when you aimed at that roughneck yesterday at Shirley's. It landed in the wrong place and it cost you your job, but you felt like giving that poor-excuse-for-a-man a wallop and so—you tried to do it. Oh, how I wish it had landed where it was aimed." Ollie began laughing again, as he remembered the bewildered look on John's face when the blow landed on his dad.

Ollie could not see the humiliated look on Cassie's face. "I wanted to run to John and clean the food off his beard and—and hold him—and tell him I was sorry."

"You like my dad, don't you, Cassie?" Ollie surprised her with this straightforward question.

"Well—well, why of course, Ollie, I do like your dad—and I like you, too," she stammered, trying to regain her thoughts and composure. Ollie's question had taken her off guard.

"Aw, Cassie, you know what I mean. Of course you like me, but now you're answering me like one of those other ladies—not like th' Cassie I was talkin' about before. You are talkin' to me like

I was a ten-year-old kid that don't know too much, or see too much, but I figure you know me better than that by now."

Cassie Martin sighed very deeply and spoke straight to Ollie after this impudent, but true, comeback.

"How foolish of me, Ollie! Of course I know better and you are anything but a normal eleven-year-old boy. I think that at times you are older and wiser than John and myself. I had noticed this before, but your question caught me by surprise and I was evasive. I apologize to you and will give you a straight answer.

"Yes, I do like your dad. I more than like him, Ollie. I have fallen deeply in love with him and want to be his wife and share a home with him as well as you and Cindy Lou. There, I've said it just like the Cassie you said you liked. Now you answer me back the same way. What do you think of that answer?"

Ollie reined up Spot and turned sideways in the saddle so he could see the face of this openhearted woman he had put on the spot.

"Cassie," Ollie offered, looking into her eyes, "I already knew your answer and I have done some considerable thinkin' on it before you spoke. I feel you will be good for my dad and me too. I think you are God's pick for John Burke, and I think the only thing that he is dealin' with right now is how quick it happened after Mother's passin'. As you said, I caught you off guard. But you caught dad and his feelin's off guard! He loves you, Cassie. I can see it all over him. He still is holdin' off, partly because of me, but I'll help that out—when the time is right.

"Now, about your question—what do I think of that answer? I think I am very happy about it. You're a great lady and I know we'll be good friends and I know you will do my dad right and make his loneliness disappear—mine too. That will make me very happy."

Cassie was weeping by the time Ollie finished, and she hugged the young man, kissing him on the cheek as he finished his confession. They clung to each other a whole minute or longer, saying nothing, then Ollie turned and set Spot in motion again.

It was getting on to 3:30 when Ollie and Cassie reined up in front of the Birchets' home in Louisa. They had moved at a fast walk most of the way except for a couple of rest stops and a break or two to water the horse. They had passed cordial greetings to two sets of teamsters, one a merchant bound for Blaine with supplies for the general store. The driver of the team of horses knew Cassie and they passed the time of day visiting for ten minutes or so. The other was a farmer bound for Busseyville.

"Howdy, Becky," Ollie greeted, as he slid to the ground. He turned and offered Cassie a hand, which she took and slid off behind him. "This here is Cassie Martin, she's me 'n dad's friend and gonna be stayin' over at the cabin while we're out campin' 'n all. Becky, meet Cassie. And Cassie, this is Becky and her girls," Ollie introduced.

Rebecca was delighted to see Ollie. He brought Cassie up to the porch in his introductions. He explained that while they were gone she would be taking over the responsibilities at Two Mile, attending to the cow and chickens.

"Dad said he sure would appreciate you'uns lookin' after Cassie for him."

Rebecca was taller than Cassie, rotund and very jolly. She had a winsome smile and laughed a lot. She was in the process of fixing supper so she asked Cassie to join her in the kitchen. Cassie said she would help if Rebecca would just show her what to do.

"Rebecca," Ollie said. "I have an errand to run for my dad, if you and Cassie don't mind. I'll take Spot, Cassie, but you had better keep Shep here." Cassie went over to pet Shep and hold him before Ollie rode off.

"Now listen, son, you be back in time for supper about six or so. You and Cassie will eat here before you head off toward the cabin," Rebecca ordered good-naturedly.

"Sounds good to me, ma'am, we could do with a good home-cooked meal, huh, Cassie?" She smiled and nodded as Ollie rode off toward town.

Ollie was let in at the Garrison and asked directions to Captain Lyons. Shortly he rode up in front of the administration building, which had been recently constructed. Captain Lyons was bending over papers in his office when Ollie was led in.

"Captain, I'm Ollie Burke and I bring you greetings from my dad, as well as a message." Captain Lyons stood and beamed as he reached across his desk to shake hands with Ollie.

"So you're the youngster that rescues ladies in distress," said Lyons. "I mean, Cindy Lou Smith, of course."

Ollie blushed and was visibly embarrassed. "Yes, sir, at least I was able to help a little. Dad and Sheriff Allison did most of it. I was just lucky to be with them."

"Well, sit down, Ollie. Let me at least tell you this so you can fill your dad in when you get back to him. It looks like Cindy will be your sister, and John will be able to raise her, if you both desire that task. She doesn't seem to have any known relatives that we can find. I have worked with the sheriff these last few days and can come up with no leads at all. In the meanwhile, Sheriff John has taken clothes out to the Birchets, what few things he could find at the house.

"There wasn't much so the sheriff and I, as well as the Damron boys, threw in a few dollars and purchased some things for her. We really didn't have to do that, for Eliza Birchet has taken over the project and the little girl is living in tall cotton right now. She is a doll, I understand, and they all fight over who gets to make over her.

"Anyway, what do you have for me?"

Ollie reached into his pocket and produced the neatly folded letter his dad had written.

"This will explain, sir."

Captain Lyons read the letter quickly, and then read it again.

"OK, let me see, you need a complete outfitted horse with rifle, a uniform or clothing for a man. What size do you think, Ollie?"

Ollie looked the captain over. "About your size would do fine, sir. Zeb would fit your size just great, I believe."

"Great!" Then to someone beyond his door Lyons spoke loudly. "Private King—front and center."

A broad-shouldered private suddenly appeared in the doorway and saluted. "Yes, sir, Captain, you called?"

Captain Lyons introduced Ollie as one of the Garrison scouts, which made Ollie feel two times taller than he was. Lyons then began barking orders to Private King.

"I need these things right away, Private, in this order: First, find me Sergeant Lewis Damron and have him report here immediately; next, go to stores and get me a complete private's uniform, boots and pack. Get my size—I think that would be medium. Make the boots size ten, if we got 'em. Next, go to livery and bring me back a horse with saddle and complete riding gear, rifle boot, saddlebag, and so forth. Next, pick up a Sharps and ammunition at the armory. As you go by the mess tent, send someone back with a pitcher of milk or lemonade for our scout. You got all that down, King?"

"Yes, sir." King saluted, and was off.

While Ollie was waiting he filled the captain in on the incident that had happened at Shirley's diner, and about finding Cassie and bringing her back to care for the farm. Just as Ollie finished, the lemonade arrived with a platter of cookies, baked army style—sweet, crisp and hard as a rock. Nevertheless Ollie nibbled on a couple and enjoyed them.

"How old is this second lady you gentlemen rescued, Ollie?" The officer asked.

"Well, sir, I believe she said she was twenty,"

"Describe what she looks like, Ollie—just so I might recognize her, you know, should I meet her," the captain urged with a curious grin.

Ollie wasn't dumb; he knew what the captain was trying to find out. He gave a full description of Cassie. Ollie figured he might as well be completely open with the captain; you sure can't hide someone who looks like Cassie.

"I see," said the captain. "I think by that description that you would call her a pretty girl, wouldn't you, Ollie?"

"Captain Lyons, sir, if I have led you to believe Cassie is only pretty, I've not been fair to her. Mind you I'm only eleven, but I have never seen anyone that is as beautiful as Cassie—including my mother and sister."

"Well, Ollie, she will be around longer than just awhile, I'm willing to wager. John Burke is a distinct kind of man, Ollie. He's gone less than one week; he rescues two ladies, takes in a Confederate soldier defecting to Union ranks, locates a band of Rebel raiders and catches a band of murdering renegades. Of course, all this was with your expert help. I think in the process, he has found a daughter—and a wife." Captain Lyons laughed and Ollie joined him.

"You are probably right all the way around, sir, but my dad has inside help. He has the Lord with him, meeting his needs. Dad has always said, God will provide!" Ollie explained.

"I believe you are totally right, Ollie. Anyway, speaking for myself and the Union Army, I'm glad you're all on our side; to God be the glory!"

Just then a handsome sergeant appeared and saluted the captain. "You sent for me, suh! Sergeant Lewis Damron reporting, suh."

Captain Lyons saluted loosely and pointed to the other chair.

"Have a seat, Sergeant. I don't know if you have met your cousin here. Meet our youngest scout, Ollie Burke. I understood from his father, John, that you are related."

Lewis's young handsome face beamed through his hazel brown beard. He had eyes to match and they sparkled as he reached over and shook hands with Ollie.

"Pleased to meet you, Ollie. You sure look like your dad, as I remember him. I haven't seen John since a family reunion over in Wayne County along time ago. I believe you were at home with your mother at the time."

He turned to Captain Lyons and said, "Yes, suh, we are sort of shirt-tail relatives through my father and John's mother, whose maiden name was Damron. John's great-grandfather and my great-grandfather were brothers. We sort of lose track after that." He paused and laughed. "Ollie, you might like to know about your great-great-grandfather Lazarus, though. He was a scout in the Revolutionary War when he was not much older than you."

Before Ollie could comment on this news, the captain brought them back to the business at hand.

"Sergeant, I want you to hand pick six men—some of your best horsemen from the 39th—and prepare them to go with young Ollie here. John is doing some work for us and Ollie is prepared to lead you back to rendezvous with Burke by tomorrow night. The two of you can decide where you'll meet. Make sure the men are well armed and have provisions for five days. The rendezvous point is near Blainetown at eight o'clock tomorrow night.

"You will be in charge of your men and young Burke here will be in charge of getting you there. You will then work under John Burke's orders. By the way, John has a colored man there working with him who will join your command. After your mission is finished, whatever that will be, you will report back to me and bring the new man with you." Captain Lyons saluted Sergeant Damron and, by that salute, dismissed him. Lewis saluted, then spoke to Ollie on the way out.

"Ollie, see me before you leave the garrison. I'll watch for you."
Ollie nodded as the sergeant left.

"Good man, good man," the captain said. You may want him
to pick you up out at your cabin when you get ready to head out,
Ollie. By the way, how did you ride in. Are you leading the extra
horse back?"

"No, sir," Ollie replied, "Dad had me ride double with Cassie
on her mount. For now Zeb has my horse and rig, as well as my
rifle. I'll go back on the horse you have for Zeb and we'll exchange
when we—ah—ron day voo?"

Captain Lyons laughed, slapping his knee, until he noticed Ollie
looking a little sheepish.

"I'm sorry, son, I'm not laughing at you—I admire you. Not too
many would try to use a new word that quickly. You have guts,
son, I like that in a man. The word is R-E-N-D-E-Z-V-O-U-S, and
you didn't do too badly at pronouncing it. Just say it more quickly.
It's a French word that means 'a meeting place.' It could be used as
a place, or time. You won't forget either will you, son?"

"No, sir," Ollie said, blushing a bit, but I kinda liked the sound
of it and appreciate th' teachin' on it." The lesson was interrupted
by Private King, returning to tell the captain that the orders had
been carried out and Ollie's new mount was ready just outside.
Glen, the livery man said, please deliver his greetings to Mr. Burke.
Ollie smiled and stood up, sensing it must be time to get back; he
was feeling hunger pains tell him so. Captain Lyons said good-
bye, shaking his hand again, reminding him to "rendezvous" with
Sergeant Damron on the way out as well as tomorrow. This got a
chuckle out of Ollie, and the captain patted him on the shoulder
as he went out.

"Just call the horse Billy, Ollie. He'll answer to that," Private
King told him.

The mount was tethered at the hitching rail and the private gave him a hand in mounting. Ollie spotted Lewis and walked the horse over to him. Ollie said they should leave no later than two tomorrow afternoon. He told the sergeant how to find the cabin at Two Mile, and Lewis said he would be there with his men at one P.M. Sharp.

It was just past six o'clock, the designated suppertime, when Ollie dismounted and tied Spot up with Billy at the Birchets' place. He could smell the aroma coming from the house. It was mouth watering to one so hungry. After all, the cold meal he and Cassie had on the way from Blainetown seemed like a long time ago.

"I'm back," announced Ollie as he came up on the porch and entered the house. Rebecca and Cassie greeted him and he noticed the flush on Cassie's face from the heat of the kitchen. She hugged him. "We missed you, but you're just in time for a great hot meal. We've had fun, especially me, because they let me help."

Rebecca spoke up proudly, "What a help she was too. Let me tell you, young man, she is great in the kitchen. I believe this young woman can do anything to do with makin' food taste good."

"Doesn't surprise me none at all," said Ollie. "Let's eat, I'm as hungry as can be."

As they sat at the table, Ollie felt a little outnumbered by the ladies. With Armsted gone and twenty-year-old Danny also in the military, that left Rebecca, who was about fortyish, with six girls. Ollie was closest to Pamela, a tomboy who was his same age. Sarah was seventeen, followed by Rosette, who was fifteen. Isabella was thirteen; then there was little Rebecca and Laura at six and three. It was, therefore, no surprise to hear mother Rebecca say, "Ollie, since you are the man at this table, will you please offer thanksgiving?"

He gave thanks as they all joined hands then enjoyed hearty laughter and the blessings of a table full of good things to eat. It reminded Ollie of other times, although he did not say it out loud. He thought much of his dad and wished he could be here, too.

By eight o'clock Ollie and Cassie were at the cabin on Two-Mile Creek. Ollie lit the lamp and showed Cassie where to find other candles and lamps, then excused himself to tend the horses. After bedding them down in the shed, he patted Daisy, who recognized him and gave him a welcome "moo" and swished her tail. He fed the horses and gave them a good rub down, finishing with a little currying.

In the meanwhile Cassie delighted herself discovering her new home. It was cozy and, although bachelor-like as John had said, much to her liking. It seemed to be complete with things to satisfy her curiosity for some time to come. Shortly Ollie joined her and allowed her to continue her quest uninterrupted.

"Let me show you where Mom and Sue Ellen's things are, Cassie." Then he showed her his dad's double bed and told her she could make use of his bed. Cassie was a little embarrassed, but Ollie seemed not to notice and showed her a spread draped over twine for a partition. It could be pulled out for privacy whenever needed. Ollie excused himself, saying he was going to catch up on his journal entries. Cassie was so full of her own thoughts for John that she welcomed the chance to be left alone with her dreams.

It was Ollie who received a surprise early in the pre-dawn morning. He awakened to start his busy day, but found Cassie already out of bed and out of sight. Ollie pulled on his buckskins, which he felt appropriate wear for the day's activities, and searched for her. He found her milking Daisy in the shed. She had made herself right at home and had already fed the horses a measure of grain. Ollie was pleasantly surprised to find this beautiful lady who was so full of ambition, comfortable in her new surroundings. Ollie did not announce himself, he simply slipped out unnoticed and went back inside to start a breakfast fire in the fireplace. Ollie and John had talked about getting a new, store-bought stove like Aunt Milly's but they had just made do with the fireplace.

By the time Cassie came in with a pail full of milk, Ollie had breakfast well on the way. She pitched in, full of giggles and fun, and before long they had eaten a good hot breakfast of bacon and pancakes topped off with molasses and Daisy's butter.

"Ollie, we make a good team." Cassie laughed.

"We sure do, Cassie. I was real surprised to find you out milkin' already this mornin'! I think you'll find your way around without me showing you a thing. I will anyway though, 'cause Dad will ask me! I'm agoin' to saddle up Billy and run into town for a spell and when I come back, I'll show you whatever you haven't already found." Ollie chuckled, then went on. "I'm supposed to meet Sergeant Damron and his men and head back to our *rendezvous* place with Dad when he gits here."

Cassie pretended not to notice Ollie's use of the new word, but she did and turned away smiling. Ollie handled the word perfectly; it was only his little hesitation before and after that gave him away.

"Fine, Ollie, I know you have a lot to do, and I want to heat up some good hot water and have myself a luxurious bath. Then I'll try on some of those new clothes you and your dad have been so gracious to provide. Don't concern yourself with me. I'll be fine and dandy."

Ollie excused himself and went out to saddle Billy. He had put on his new gun belt and holster, slipping the Colt into the holster. The Sharps was in the scabbard. In short order Billy was in a gallop, headed back toward town. Ollie was glad Cassie didn't ask him where exactly he was going, because he had left something undone that his dad had asked him to take care of. It was no time at all before Ollie reined up in front of Smitty and Rebecca's and was greeted with a cheery welcome.

"Hello, Ollie, come on up and sit a spell." Rebecca welcomed him as she seated herself on the front porch. Ollie tied off Billy and headed toward a woven hickory chair as a spring breeze caught his curly black hair and made it into a rooster's tail.

"Don't mind if I do, Rebecca. I needed to git back to you and talk a little," Ollie explained.

"Now, boy, that's an understatement if I ever heard one." Rebecca laughed. "You come gallopin' up here double saddled with one of th' most handsome fillies God ever put a mold to and then head off in th' dust and leave my ol' nosy—oops, I mean curious—nature just wonderin' 'n wonderin'. It's a good thing you come back to enlighten me." Rebecca added this with her face loaded with merriment.

Ollie had a good laugh with Rebecca; on the inside he was thanking God he had come back. With Captain Lyons, Sergeant Damron, Cassie, and his dad to think about his cup was full to running over with things to stretch this youthful mind. All he had purposed to share about (which was why he had made the trip back) was the promise to his dad to tell Rebecca about Cassie using his mother and Sue Ellen's clothes. He had not thought about all this information the kind lady just brought up. Rebecca certainly deserved better treatment and should know all about Cassie.

"I suppose you know about Cindy Lou and the murdering gang who killed her folks, around the first of th' week, huh Rebecca?" Ollie began.

"Well, yes, Ollie, Sheriff Allison came by purposeful to bring us up to date about that. I even made one trip out to John and Milly's to see th' little one. She is a sweetheart and I understand y'all may take her if'n her kinfolks don't show up."

"Well, that was the start and we met up with Cassie over in Blainetown in Shirley Bradley's eatin' place." Ollie went on to tell of meeting Cassie, her losing her job, and their meeting her later in the livery barn as they were leaving. He left out the part about the personal feeling that was obvious between John and Cassie, but went on to tell about his dad offering Cassie his help. He was going back to meet his dad tonight but Cassie would be a permanent fixture at the Burke cabin because she had no place else to stay.

Rebecca interrupted. "My guess—although it may be too early to tell—is that John better not let this one get away."

"What do you mean?" Ollie asked innocently.

"You need never mind, Ollie. You just tell your dad that's my message to him. He'll know what I mean."

"Well, anyway, Dad wants you to know that he has given Cassie leave to take Mother's dresses and things, as well as Sue Ellen's, if'n she can use them. He just wanted you and your girls to know privately so you wouldn't think Cassie was takin' leave without permission. He wanted to make sure no one was shamed, and Cassie had his permission."

"Isn't that something. That is so thoughtful of John Burke, to tell me 'n th' girls as well as to see to th' needs of this young woman. I'll tell you, Ollie, John was always a good judge of character—both men and women. I am going to make it my business to see to that young woman. She is particular to John already, I can tell! You tell him not to worry about her, and I will see she meets John and Milly as well as Cindy Lou."

Rebecca hesitated, then looked at Ollie and said, "How do you feel about all this goin' on, son? I mean with Cassie and all?"

Ollie smiled and started toward his horse. Turning, he said, "Rebecca, I think that outside of my own mother, this lady already has a special place in my heart. I am really excited about the future for my dad and me for th' first time since Mom and Sue Ellen left. I haven't even told Dad this feelin' yet, but that's th' way I feel."

Rebecca came over and hugged Ollie close to her. "Ollie, don't wait too long before you tell your dad just what you told me. You are a distinguished young man, son. Elizabeth Burke would be ever so proud of you."

FOURTEEN

Neither Shall the Cruse of Oil Fail

OLLIE SHOWED CASSIE EVERYTHING ABOUT THE LITTLE PATCH OF GROUND they called home: where they had the garden last year, the smokehouse and all that was stored there, the pantry, and every nook and cranny of the house. He even showed her where he kept his money, in case she needed any. He offered her some extra money. Cassie smiled at him.

"Ollie, you're just like your dad. He gave me ten dollars when we were alone, before we parted, and I already had the $5.50, remember?" Ollie nodded.

"If I have need of the money, I promise you I'll use it, but that would only be in an emergency. We're trusting in God and I know all will be well. Does that satisfy you, Ollie, dear?"

"Sure, it does, Cassie, and I will feel good in tellin' Dad what you said, 'cause he'll ask me. By th' way, feel free to call on Rebecca. And she'll be checkin' on you, too. I think she'll come by and take you to see Cindy Lou and the Birchets out at Deephole Branch next week for sure.

"Cassie, I been meanin' to ask you, do you have anythin' at all of a personal nature; furniture 'n such at the farm where you stayed with your dad? We could arrange to pick it up for you, if you wanted."

"Ollie, it's just like I told you and John in the livery barn; I took everything I wanted from the old place when I left. Dad was a man of simple means, and I have never been a collector of things. The few things I had there I simply left for the landlord to do with as he wished. It is good of you to think about me, but I sort of left there without looking over my shoulder. I only kept the few good memories I had when I left—and I will always have those."

Ollie and Cassie had a simple dinner together then he packed Zeb's saddlebag with a few things to replenish their food supply and made ready for the troops.

Sergeant Damron and six men rode into the front yard ten minutes later, just before one o'clock. Cassie came out to say her good-byes, and Ollie introduced her to the sergeant. He brightened up at the sight of this beautiful young lady, giving her a salute. Sergeant Damron then introduced his men to Ollie and Cassie. He began with his brother, John. Private Damron appeared older than his sergeant brother, and was every bit as handsome. The remaining men were privates, and seemed to be pleased to see such a pretty lady. Sergeant Damron snapped to attention and spoke to Ollie.

"Ollie, we are prepared to ride out as soon as you want to lead off."

Ollie hugged Cassie and she kissed him on the cheek, causing him to blush, but he enjoyed it. He mounted Billy and headed due south through the Two Mile pass, bypassing Louisa and heading toward the main Blainetown road.

Ollie led the men at a good clip, staying with the main road, and they didn't rein up until he reached the West Side of Busseyville.

There they took a break and watered the horses, joking with Ollie about being a rough taskmaster. After about fifteen minutes, Ollie didn't say anything, just mounted, and waited. Everyone took the hint, and they were off again. Ollie didn't see any reason to hide their movements since this was Union-occupied territory. He had decided he would rather be early than late. They passed a couple of local farmers on the road; one leading a team all harnessed for some task, and another hauling some grain. They just spoke as they passed and kept moving.

Ollie's meeting time was 8 P.M. and they were an hour and a half early by Sergeant Damron's watch. The men set out to make a picket line for the horses and gave them a good rubdown after taking them to water. Ollie set about making a campfire, and before long had water on the boil for coffee. By popular appointment Private Bennie Sparks was designated as cook. The other men knew his love for eating so they teased him into the task. It wasn't much really, since most everything was prepared except for coffee. He put on a pot of beans, and after awhile they smelled pretty good. Sergeant Damron had his brother take the first watch and asked the men, rather than ordering them, to keep the noise level down. It would be pretty dark by the meeting time.

Ollie stayed pretty close to Lewis. He was really drawn to this young officer, which was fine with Lewis for he enjoyed being with Ollie, too. Ollie propped himself against a smooth sycamore tree and got to think that John Burke might be watching them right now. John was like that. He would check everything out before entering the campsite. One thing was for sure, John would not be late; he detested tardiness. This was self-imposed, and more for himself than anyone else. He was forgiving to anyone else for being late, but not for himself. If he made an appointment, or agreed to be somewhere, he was there and on time, or an unavoidable emergency had occurred. Ollie was destined to be just like him. After all, he was his father's son. Early was OK; late was not to be tolerated!

John Burke was a God-fearing man, but not a strong church-going one. He took his family to church on occasion, back through Ollie's earlier years. He always tried to keep Sunday as the Lord's day, a day of rest, but did not always appear in church services. This was not a deliberate act on John's part, because he loved to fellowship and worship with God's people. He also loved to hear a preacher teach on God's Word, especially the evangelistic fervor of the United Baptist preaching. But it was usually a far distance to a church and, before the war, he had not kept horses so had no transportation. So on Sundays John would simply call his family together, pull out his Bible, read the Word, and teach it himself. He would sometimes ask Elizabeth to share a lesson, sometimes Sue Ellen; he would even encourage Ollie to do so.

As they ate and waited all these thoughts were flooding in on Ollie because tomorrow was Sunday. He knew also that this Sunday would be different from last Sunday and he didn't know what the near future would hold. The sound of a horse arriving disturbed his thinking and brought everyone to a standing position as John Burke rode into the camp light on Silky.

Ollie ran to his dad, joyfully greeting him. Everyone could see that John was delighted to see his son. Ollie pointed. "Dad, our cousin, Sergeant Lewis Damron, is in charge of the patrol." John Damron walked over as Ollie was speaking. "And this is his brother, John. I'm sure you know him, too! I'll jus' let Lewis introduce you to the other men."

Introductions being completed, John fixed himself a plate of beans and updated the men about the Rebel hideout Zeb had led him to. He told them that Zeb had stayed to keep an eye on the place and watch the activity of the Confederate troops who were pilfering local farmers' food and livestock. There were about twelve men, John guessed, but only two remained in camp at this time. The others were probably transporting their cache to larger bivouac area. John guessed it must not be too far from here, because these men would not operate a great distance from a larger company of soldiers. John's objective was to put this group out of business and also to find out where the looters' headquarters were located.

"John, we are at your disposal," Sergeant Damron said. "I turn myself and these men over to you to command. Ollie has a complete outfit and clothing for Zeb, and he is to act under this Union patrol to return with me when we have finished whatever you need us to do. Those were Captain Lyons' orders."

"Good," John said. "We'll break camp here and head up Brushy Creek. I'll lead you to the Reb hideout. We'll move softly—no talking once we start. We'll decide our next move once we're back with Zeb."

Sergeant Damron stood up. "Break camp, men, you know the routine. Get your mounts ready to move out."

A good two hours later found the men in the cave above the Rebel cabin, meeting a grateful Zeb. He has been nervous ever since John had left to meet the soldiers. His black face actually brightened when Ollie produced a Union uniform as well as a horse. Zeb wasted no time changing, and found that everything was a good fit. He examined his rifle and smiled from ear to ear.

"Mista John, you is a man what can be trusted. Yes, suh, you sure has made me one happy man, um-uhh! You sure has."

The men all joined in this former slave's gratitude by laughing and backslapping. Zeb was immediately made to feel a part of the patrol, and Sergeant Damron liked the man without reservation. As John called the men together in a circle, he included Ollie right by his side.

"OK, Zeb, what has happened since we have been separated?" he asked.

"Well, suh, Mista John, ain't nothin' been takin' place since you done went an' left. Dah two Rebs has been heah mos' da time. Thet skinny one, he done went and wuz gone a sho't period—maybe one hour or so. He done comed back and I jus' dunno why he wuz gone." Zeb explained. John spoke up on the heels of Zeb's remarks.

"Well, boys, if one of the men decides to leave again, we'll follow him. In the meantime, we'll wait until th' main group returns to camp. I'd like to find out where the headquarters is, so we'll just play a game of wait and see for th' time being. Lewis, why don't you post a guard to watch these two in camp." John then turned to Ollie.

"Son, early in the mornin', before light, I want you to take your rifle, lead Ginger out on foot and scout around the other side of th' cabin. I want you to keep your eyes peeled for th' main detail of Rebs. While you're out there, you're jus' a local boy huntin' for food. You sure look th' part dressed in your buckskins. As far as thet goes, some wild game would be good to go with beans. You may be able to stumble on somethin' thet would be a big help." John turned to the men and spoke to them as a group.

"G'night men. Ollie and me have some visitin' 'n catchin' up to do so we'll turn in."

Ollie took the hint and pulled his bedroll off Ginger, who stomped and snorted her greeting. She was noticeably delighted to see her young master. Ollie hugged her and patted her neck, acknowledging her welcome, then followed his dad to where John had his bedroll laid out near the cave entrance. Delighted to be together, father and son reclined against a huge rock and small tree. John smiled at his boy and spoke to him with obvious pride.

"You did good, son. You did real good. Now, tell me about your trip."

Ollie knew where his dad was headed. He knew John wanted to know about Cassie—so he deliberately avoided referring to her except in a general way. He wanted to see if John would be straight-forward and ask about her specifically.

"Well, Dad, we had a safe trip. Cassie let me ride in front of her to lead th' way. We jus' met a couple of wagons on th' road and we got to Rebecca's at about three o'clock or so. We had a good trip and th' weather was good, too. I left Cassie and Rebecca together to fix supper while I went to th' captain and gave him your letter. Dad, he sure is th' nicest man. He called me his young-est scout, 'n introduced me to everyone that way." Ollie beamed, grinning widely.

John smiled his appreciation and felt pleased that Captain Lyons approved of Ollie.

"What about Cassie, son, did Rebecca take to her?"

"Oh, they seemed to get along jus' fine, Dad," Ollie answered indifferently. He then hesitated and came back with, "Boy, Dad, that Rebecca sure fixed one good meal, she had me sit at the head of the table and ask the blessin', since I was th' only man there. I felt sorta funny. I sure would like to have had you there, too."

John was getting a little fidgety by this time, as well as per-plexed. He was at a loss of what to do about the situation without being obvious. He wanted to know about this lady who had so recently come into his life, but expressing this interest to his eleven-year-old son was difficult—to say the least! John had, for the most part, treated both of his children as small adults. This had been good in the wilderness lifestyle he had chosen. Ollie had devel-oped in skills and education far beyond his years. What John had not learned to do was bring the adult part of a man-and-woman relationship into his son's education. He had not counted on the developments of this last week; they had really overtaken him, leaving him unsure which way to turn. He tried again.

"Ollie, the clothes, what about the clothes?"

Ollie knew very well what his dad meant, but he couldn't resist this game he was playing, although he was feeling a bit guilty by now.

"Oh, Dad, that was easy. I jus' told th' captain to get Zeb clothes 'n uniform to fit himself; they looked about th' same size to me."

By now John was totally exasperated, on the verge of anger. He bent over, slapped his leg, raised his voice.

"No, Ollie, no! Not Zeb's clothes. Cassie—I'm talkin' about Cassie. Th' clothes I told you to show to her—I mean give her—your mother's clothes, Sue Ellen's clothes. Do you understand, son?"

Ollie knew he had pushed a little bit over John Burke's patience level, so he changed direction. He looked his dad squarely in the face and asked point-blank, "Dad, do you love her? Cassie, I mean—do you love her?"

John's face became ashen. He looked at his young son and opened his mouth as if to speak, but no words came forth.

"Dad, I'm askin' you this question man to man, do you love this lady, Cassie Martin? 'Cause she loves you with all her heart—and I'm needin' to know! Do you love her back?"

John still was not speaking; he was perspiring. Even though he had regained his color, he found himself breathing heavily. He still did not know what to say to his young son, who had caught him in an adult-life drama in which he was inexperienced. Ollie helped him out by speaking again.

"Dad, I want to be honest with you and let you know somethin', Before—I mean when you was askin' me questions about th' trip 'n all, I knew all you really wanted to know about was Cassie. I was sorta playin' a game with you 'n not answerin' th' way you wanted. I'm sorry for that; I didn't mean to make you mad. I really know more about things than you think. I really know th' answer to th' question I asked about Cassie better than you. I know you love Cassie. Great day in th' mornin', Dad, a person would be blind not to see it.

I think you're probably the only person that doesn't know that you love Cassie. Even Cassie knows you love her. She's jus' waitin' till you—well—till *you* figure out that you love her and admit it."

Ollie stopped talking to watch his dad's reaction. Ollie knew his words came as a shock to John. His dad was still in trauma, squirming and speechless like a mischievous child who got caught doing something wrong and not knowing what to say.

"I'm sorry, Ollie, I'm sorry."

"Aw, Dad, you don't have to be sorry." Ollie spoke tenderly. "I didn't say all that to make you feel bad. I want you to feel good! I know you're worried about me, but you don't have to. You remember when you let me stay up late to write in the journal, th' night before we went to Blainetown?"

John leaned forward, putting his hand to his brow thoughtfully. "Yes, I remember that night. What has that got to do with it?"

"Well," Ollie said, " I did some powerful thinkin' that night. I thought about Mom bein' gone, Sue Ellen bein' gone, and you and me all alone. I thought about you, Dad, and that you was lonely, jus' like me—and maybe even more, although I knew you wouldn't admit it. I pictured in my mind: what if another lady would come into our home and be your wife? Dad, you are not an old man!"

John caught that statement and the expression on Ollie's face and began to be himself again. He smiled and his eyes twinkled through the moisture that has gathered. He answered his young adult son. "Thanks for that, Ollie, I hope I'm not too old."

Ollie took courage with this hint of his dad being himself again, and continued.

"Anyway, I thought about all this stuff before we ever met Cassie! I had to ask myself th' questions about another lady in my mother's place. In her home with my dad. I even thought about the—" Ollie hesitated and continued somewhat embarrassed. "The—aw, you know, Dad, th' baby thing. You could have more

211

children with another lady. Well, I thought about all that and you know what?"

"What, Ollie?" John asked with much interest.

"I didn't have any problem with any of that stuff. I know that no other lady will ever be my mother. My mother will always be my mother even though she's gone. I also know that I can love someone else, jus' like you can. Th' love we have for someone is not used up. What I mean is that love keeps on going. It's like we have a great big water bucket that we keep dipping water out of, and it never runs dry. You remember th' story in th' Bible, Dad, about th' widow that never ran out of oil?"

John nodded, his eyes filling up with tears as Ollie continued.

"What I mean is that God has given us love like He gave that widow woman oil. It never runs out. That love we have for another person, or another lady, never will take away th' love we had for Mother or Sue Ellen. That love will always be there, won't it?"

"Ollie, your wisdom for your age astounds me. It shocks and sometimes completely overwhelms me. I sometimes wonder how you got so smart. It must have been from Elizabeth—most assuredly from God in His infinite wisdom—it wasn't from me. To answer your question, Ollie—No! Loving someone else will not ever take the love away that we had for your mother and sister. That will always be there, and so will the memories we shared with 'em as long as we both shall live. Your word picture of the love in a water bucket—" John shook his head. "Son, that's prob'ly th' best I ever heard."

Ollie had not finished his story so he continued. "Dad, after that night on the hill, well th' very next day Cassie came into our lives. I jus' have to feel it was God workin' things out. It was sure strange how this pretty lady dropped into our life jus' like Cindy Lou—smack-dab after me havin' all this thinkin'. You see I was prepared for it! It was more of a surprise to you than me. And,

Dad, I want to tell you right here and now—God did good. I mean, He did real good! I never have seen a lady so pretty and so nice in all my borned days. Yes, sir, God did good!"

John could not help bursting out with laughter at this last outpouring of his son. Ollie joined in and John pulled his son over to him, hugging him tightly as the two enjoyed the bonding of father and son love.

John had listened intently to the expressions of this child-man and knew he had nothing left to hold back from the relationship that the two of them enjoyed. He had been made to look into the mirror, so to speak, and face the truth that was battering away at his insides ever since the meeting that destiny had arranged between John Burke and Cassandra Martin. He had one last hurdle, but he could deal with that now with his best friend—his eleven-year-old son.

"Ollie," John said, "what about Cassie's age? She is years younger than me. Why she could marry anyone she wanted. She's so beautiful and intelligent. She is also God-fearing, and knows the Lord as her Savior."

"Well, Dad, I'll tell you. Gene Yates put it best to you—she is a woman full-grown. Anyone can see that! Dad, she's twenty years old. Why, that's twice my age. Sure, she could have anyone she wants, and Dad—that's you. You're who she wants! The fact that she knows God, and loves Him, is in our favor. I know she loves you, 'cause she told me so, and further more she'll marry you. She's made up her mind."

"She told you that, Ollie Burke?" John blurted out. "What made her tell you that?"

"I asked her," responded Ollie. "And she was beatin' around th' bush a little, but I could tell about that and told her so."

"You have more nerve than General Garfield, Ollie Burke. What possessed you to do such a thing?"

"I think it was th' Lord that possessed me to. Besides that I jus' wanted to know. Th' Bible says 'Ye have not if ye ask not'—so I was askin'. Dad, I approve of this lady; she is special, and I think you know it too. You're special too. You deserve Cassie Martin, and Rebecca told me to tell you, 'Don't let her get away,' or somethin' like that."

"Well, Ollie, you are certainly right about one thing. Everyone but me knows what's goin' on." John let that sink in a bit and then added a postscript.

"Yes, Ollie, I do love her. God in heaven knows I love her—and I can't help myself. Now you know! I wasn't lookin' for love, I wasn't even thinkin' of a woman. But when I laid eyes on her in that restaurant in Blainetown, I was smitten. I never had an experience like that in my whole life, not even when I was courtin' your mother. That was why I was fighting it off. But I jus' couldn't get her outa my mind. I was also having to deal with telling you, and I didn't know how to approach th' subject with you. I can see now my concern in talking to you was unfounded. I've sure learned my lesson about that."

"Dad," Ollie interrupted, "I already knew that and so did Cassie. I knew I was going to have to help you face this love-thing with Mom only being gone a short time. Rebecca saw it right away, and I talked with her about it. She knew you never would let jus' anyone into our little home and Mom's clothes without somethin' exceptional being there. Heck fire, Dad, even Captain Lyons figured it out."

"Don't swear, Ollie!"

"Sorry, Dad. You know what I mean."

"Yeah, Ollie—I do know what you mean. I'm beginning to understand a lot that's been going on inside me. At least I can be honest with my emotions and myself now. I have had these battles of conscience; mostly brought about by social pressures, I'm sure.

I do love that girl, and I admit it—to you and to myself. Now, young man! Since this is out of the way, can you please tell me about th' trip and especially about the party of the second part, Cassie Martin." He grinned and gave Ollie a playful punch on the shoulder.

Ollie joined in the grin and went into detail about Cassie, from the time he put her on the spot while riding back to Louisa, up until the time he rode off with Lewis and the boys. He especially exposed her feelings about John that she had shared with Ollie. He told about the visit with Captain Lyons and the captain's observations, the feelings Ollie had shared with Rebecca and her message for John. He said, too, that Rebecca would watch out for Cassie, and probably take her to meet Cindy Lou.

He told about the last breakfast they shared and how Cassie was exploring every nook and cranny of the property. He shared about waking up and finding her out milking Daisy, and how thrilled Cassie was as she examined each piece of clothing Ollie had turned over to her.

Ollie also told about some of his own speculations. He told his dad that Cassie was comfortable with people and would soon befriend the whole town. He spoke of his feeling that by now, Captain Lyons would already have ridden out to the cabin to meet her for himself. This got a laugh out of John, as he shook his head. Ollie figured that by the time they returned, Cassie would have the cabin looking like a dollhouse, and would probably have Cindy Lou there with her.

"Do you really think so, Ollie? I mean do you think she will bring Cindy back to the cabin?"

"Sure I do, Dad. She's that kind of a woman. She'll see something that needs to be done, and she'll do it. You see, Dad, in her mind she's already promised to you! She knows you belong to her and she's not hiding that she knows it. Not taking it for granted mind you. She jus' has a lot of confidence that God has brought you together and, sooner or later, you'll get the message too! Yes, sir, she'll have Cindy there as sure as I'm Ollie Burke—'cause she'll think that would please you, 'n that is what she will want to do. She will do things to please you. She loves you, Dad."

"My dear God," John said. "What a treasure. Not that I did the findin', mind you. God did all that Himself. I'm jus' so blessed to be the one who gits her. I am also doubly blessed to have you as my friend, as well as my son. Ollie, God has his hand on your life and you are under divine protection. Sure as I am your earthly father, you have certain destiny to fulfil and God will lead you by His Spirit—all the way.

C'mere son." John placed a warm hand on Ollie's bare head and ran his fingers through the dark curls. "The things I jus' said— I pronounce as a blessing on you, son. It is partly declaration of my love, partly blessing of a father to a son, and the rest is pure prophecy. I proclaim it and according to God's Word, He will perform it." Ollie was moved to tears with this pronouncement. After he took control of himself, he said, "Thank you, Dad. That means a whole lot to me."

"Good boy, son. We both better git some shut-eye. We may be busy tomorrow. By th' way, I love you son—an' g'night."

FIFTEEN

He Shall Deliver Thee

B EFORE LIGHT OF DAY THAT SUNDAY MORNING IN 1862, THE LITTLE UNION camp was busy with activity. Sergeant Damron squatted by a small fire, out of sight of the Rebel camp, holding a tin of hot coffee between his hands, blowing the steam off to sip a little. By his orders, the guard was in the process of being changed. Ollie was busy saddling Ginger and checking his supplies. He had plenty of cartridges for both rifle and revolver. He added some jerky and dried fruit for food and checked his canteen. He made sure he had a couple of lengths of rope, then added his bedroll and felt satisfied.

When he was done he joined the men for hardtack biscuit and had some well-sweetened coffee. John came over to join the men at the campfire for coffee, giving Ollie some last minute instructions.

"Ollie, when you leave it's best you lead Ginger out until you're away on th' other side of th' cabin. Don't fire at any game unless you're a mile or so from their camp; they may send someone to investigate. If they do, just play dumb. You don't need instructions in that—you were playin' dumb with me when I first asked you questions last night. You're sure well-equipped to handle thet," he said with a grin and good-natured sarcasm. Ollie caught the quip and smiled back. The men glanced at one another and shrugged, but John left it unexplained.

"If by chance you hear rifle fire over in this direction, don't git anxious, 'n by all means, don't come rushing back here. Do things with thought, and remember—sometimes slow is better than fast, even when everythin' inside your gut says rush. You understand what I'm sayin', son?"

"Yes, sir, I understand."

Then more seriously, John continued. "Ollie, three quick shots in the air with your Colt tells us you're in trouble. OK?" John waited for an assenting nod. "Three quick shots, a pause, and one more shot will mean fer us to watch out. In other words—you are telling us to watch out for some danger, OK?"

"I got it, Dad. You can tell the difference in the blast from the rifle 'n the Colt." John smiled. "You're a quick student, Ollie. Go git 'em." He patted his son with affection on the shoulder.

John was sending his son out of danger. He knew that when the rest of the Confederate troop arrived back at camp that there could well be a confrontation and perhaps bloodshed. He knew Ollie was capable, but John wanted to keep him from the horrors of war as long as possible. He smiled to himself as he saw the boy trudge off, leading his mare. He knew that Ollie was smart enough to figure out what his dad was doing.

Ollie finished his meager breakfast and said good-bye, nodding and waving at the men and his dad. He picked up Ginger's reins and left by way of the north side of the cave. Slowly and methodically he headed west until he crossed Brushy Creek, where he paused to allow Ginger to drink her fill while he topped up his canteen with water. He was well out of sight of the cabin when he began to climb to the west through a bed of birch trees as the morning light showed a promise of overcast skies. Ollie looked up through treetops that were bending with a pretty stiff wind and thought, *We may be in for another spring rain.* He mounted Ginger, who seemed to think it was about time. She gave a little welcome shudder as Ollie climbed into the saddle. He patted her neck bending over talking to her in her right ear.

"You're a sweet lady, Ginger. Yes you are, you're my baby, aren't you? Nice lady, nice lady." Ginger responded by virtually prancing. Ollie almost laughed with glee, but he remembered his mission and held himself back.

The wind had not let up and was making a howling sound through the branches as Ollie climbed gradually to the southwest in a rocky terrain of oak trees with lots of underbrush. He pulled up, dismounted, and tied Ginger to a scrub oak. Pulling the rifle out of the scabbard, he began to zigzag south up the gradual incline.

Before long he crossed a trail of cattle and horses heading south. It led away from the cabin and had to be the trail of the Confederate raiders as they herded the cattle toward their main camp. The trail was several days old, but easy to follow since it had not rained. After following on foot for a hundred yards or so, he decided to overlap the trail to the right and left. Ollie quickly turned and climbed back on Ginger, following the trail south. As he overlapped the trail, he would zigzag first to the left a dozen yards or so diagonally, and then back to the right across the trail a dozen yards.

Ollie followed this pattern for fifteen minutes or so and found himself widening his swath. Suddenly he stopped, frozen in his tracks! There, in the damp dirt and leaves were recent tracks going in the opposite direction, headed toward the cabin, not away from it. He dismounted and examined them more closely. Sure enough, several shod horses, moving at a quick pace had passed through here not more than a couple of hours ago. Ollie led Ginger and followed the tracks. He began to have a sinking feeling in the pit of his stomach when he discovered they were bent on only one direction! Suddenly it dawned on Ollie—the men at the camp were in trouble. He knew it in his gut. He was sure of it. He concluded that the lone rider who had left the Reb camp yesterday figured into this. They had somehow discovered Zeb's stakeout and that lone rider had ridden ahead to warn the returning detachment. Without any more hesitation, he pulled out his Colt and shot into the air. Bang—bang—bang. A one-second pause and one more—bang.

Ollie had no way of knowing what was taking place in camp, but he knew that the raiders as well as the Union soldiers would hear those shots. Putting Ginger into a fast trot, he headed back toward camp. Not five minutes had passed before he heard rifle fire from that direction. At first he couldn't tell from which camp. Then he heard more shots that sounded closer. Those shots, no doubt, were the Rebel soldiers. There was fairly steady rifle fire now, back and forth. Ollie slowed down but stayed mounted as he drew closer.

The wind had become boisterous, and there were occasional drops of rain Ollie noticed as he dismounted and tied Ginger by just dropping her reins. She stayed where Ollie left her. He headed downhill toward the Rebel cabin on the south side. Moving silently from rock to rock, he suddenly came to a clearing that gave him a high vantage point and he was able to see the rifle fire from both camps. The Rebel group was superior in number to the Union force, and it looked like the only advantage that Lewis and his men had was the elevation. They were looking downhill at the Rebel band. Otherwise, they were pinned down by Rebel crossfire. The cliff and the cave backed up the Union soldiers so they could not retreat. Rebel forces were well placed in front of them and on each flank. As Ollie viewed this scene in front of him, he knew he had done the right thing by firing those shots. His dad and the others were in big trouble. These Rebels were moving in close for the kill, no doubt, when he fired off those warning shots.

Ollie quickly pulled out his Colt and reloaded the chambers; he checked his Sharps and began to make his plan. He knew his dad, Sergeant Damron, and the other men were in danger. No way could he sit on the sideline and watch them get wiped out. He had to take action! He studied the situation by watching the puffs of powder as shots sounded off. He figured the right flank was the weakest for the Rebels, so that was where he would take a piece of the action. He knew his dad would not approve. He also knew that his dad had probably sent him on this errand to get him out of their way. But after all, at this moment he was on his own and it was his decision to make—so he made it.

Ollie carefully moved around to the right, staying to the uphill side of the clearing, memorizing where the puffs of smoke were coming from. It looked like three men on the Reb side were in the right flank position so he decided to take out the man on the extreme end first, and move in from there. Ollie was struggling with himself at this point. Here he was thinking of taking a man's life, maybe more than one. *How—Oh God—how can I?* He thought! He paused and prayed silently.

Lord, we are in a war; this is part of it. The war takes in the young and the old alike. I'm young, and I know these men are older. They think they are right, and we are forced to defend ourselves, and we think we are right. I know in my heart you are against men and women being made slaves. I know you are not against us defending our family. I am fighting and could lose my life. I am fighting to protect my dad like he is fighting to protect me. If I die, I'll be with you—if he dies, he will be with you. Maybe the men whose lives we take today in war will be with you when they die. I pray this is true and they will be with you. I pray for all men mixed up in this fighting today both sides. I pray my aim will be true when—I shoot, and that our side will win this battle—Amen.

Rain was dropping steadily now, building up to a downpour. He slowly maneuvered himself through the wet leaves and grass closer to the enemy. Finally, he was at the extreme right of the skirmish line, where small puffs of smoke erupted at intervals. They were aiming up the hill. The Rebel soldier he spotted was exchanging shots with a Union man. It seemed that the soldier on this man's left was firing at the same Union soldier. He checked the breech of his Sharps, making sure a round of ammunition was in place. He lifted his rear sight, estimating the enemy soldier was about 100 yards away. As he carefully sighted down the long barrel, tears filled his eyes and blurred his vision. Not once did Ollie consider that this man might turn and shoot him.

He waited until his eyes were clear again. The Rebel soldier had a red crop of hair projecting from under his forage cap and he was bearing down on someone in the Union band of men—maybe even Ollie's father. The man was camouflaged well from the front, but Ollie could see the man's entire back and head. His presence had not been discovered so he quickly aimed again, cocked the rifle, placed his finger on the trigger, and began to squeeze. At the last second, Ollie yelled. The man turned, and Ollie fired at his chest. As the man rolled over, Ollie heard the bark of the Sharps simultaneously.

Ollie buried his head a second, feeling a bit shaky and nauseated. Knowing he could not give in to these feelings he regained his composure and quickly reloaded. He surveyed the situation, keeping very low, and saw that nothing had changed, except the puffs of smoke. They were no longer coming from the spot where the redheaded soldier had been hiding, but the exchange of gunfire between the Rebel and Union lines continued.

The deathly drama just played out between a redheaded Rebel soldier and an eleven-year-old Union scout had not been witnessed by anyone, as far as it appeared to Ollie. The boy caught his breath and knew he must continue. The other Reb was firing deadly rifle fire at his companions and must be stopped.

Ollie slipped through the downpour on his belly, slithering like a reptile. He was quiet on the outside, but his mind was inflamed. *Is the man dead? Is he just pretending? Did I, Ollie Burke, actually take another person's life? What will I do when I get to the location?* On and on the thoughts went, while his body kept moving ahead to do the duty that must be done.

With the rain steadily beating on his bare head, Ollie looked down at the body of a man that, only five minutes ago, had been full of life and anger. Now it was silent. He carefully turned the body over and two unseeing eyes seemed to stare up at him. Ollie began to shake again; his knees felt weak, and he was slightly dizzy. The rain was beating down on the dead soldier's face. His eyes were not blinking. Ollie almost lost it right then and there, but he choked back his crying as he moved to the side and quietly lost everything in his stomach. *Control your thoughts, Ollie, control yourself!* Regaining his composure and controlling his thoughts were not easy, but Ollie had a strong will and took courage from his reflection of God.

He reached over and closed the man's eyes, noticing the small hole through the chest; no doubt the heart. The man never knew what happened. No suffering, no pain. Just quietness—and a divine meeting with his God. Ollie took courage from that, then began to focus on the next man who was still directing steady fire at his friends in the Union camp. The Union soldier who had been returning the fire toward the dead Rebel, now directed his shots toward the enemy elsewhere on the skirmish line.

Putting his attention toward the next soldier to his left and carefully watching for the telltale signs of rifle fire, Ollie waited for the right moment. The dim light of the overcast day, plus the poor visibility brought about by the gusting rain, blocked any action or movement. The rain was coming in harder now with a steady beating on Ollie's brow and showed no sign of decreasing. And then, there it was again—a puff of rifle smoke rising from a pile of brush some seventy-five yards away. Immediately there was a return of rifle fire from two locations up the hill. Other rifle fire back and forth beat a steady staccato in time to the beating of the rain.

Ollie's mind wandered, remembering the Scripture his dad often quoted from St. Matthew: "The rain falls on the just and unjust." He brought his mind back to focus on the brush where he had seen the smoke, and he saw movement. A Confederate gray cap moved up until Ollie could see the bearded soldier's head for an instant. It went out of sight again as the soldier ducked into his hideaway. Ollie needed to be closer for a certain shot. A shot that missed the mark might mean the end of him. *This is war, and I must have the upper hand if I'm going to come out alive. I'm younger, I lack the experience of these men, and I purpose to see more of this war, if it should last more than this one battle. I must be alive at the end of this battle—so I cannot miss a single shot!*

This thought kept Ollie low on his belly as he began to slide through the grass, being careful not to lose his Colt. He was within 100 feet of the clump of bushes when he crept up to a fallen tree that covered a low spot in the ground. He heard several exchanges of fire as he maneuvered himself to this position, so he knew the man was still active. Ollie slid under the tree, finding there was just enough room for someone his size. His wet-to-the-skin buckskins were a perfect blend to the grass, leaves, and dead tree branches to make good cover. He sighted down the Sharps with the rear sight in the down position.

After a minute he saw another puff of smoke followed by more movement. He was very close, and there, through the brush, he saw the figure of the man. He was sitting on something, perhaps a stump, slumped in a forward position. Ollie could make him out well except for his legs. No wonder he could not be hit—there was a huge boulder in front of him with a natural crevice for supporting his weapon.

As he was about to aim his rifle and pull back the hammer, he had a second thought. He reached for his Colt, cocked it, and put it at his right side. Concealed well under the fallen tree and clump of brush, he had the Rebel soldier right in his sight. Ollie had to aim at a forty-five degree angle and for some reason he needed the comfort of that Colt as a backup. There was no moisture in his eyes this time, except for the rain. Ollie aimed, held his breath, and squeezed the trigger.

What happened next took place in a matter of seconds though to Ollie it seemed like a lifetime. The Rebel soldier let out a scream of pain jumped out of the brush with his rifle cocked and ready, heading straight for Ollie. He actually was reacting from the rifle sound, for he had not seen the lad. Nevertheless he gave a frightful yell as he came out of the brush. Then suddenly, there he was—standing over Ollie, looking down at him.

Ollie felt the Colt buck in his right hand. The bullet struck the Reb exactly between the eyes, and he fell over the tree, dead. Ollie was instantly in motion. Slipping the Colt in the holster as he scrambled out of his ditch, he grabbed the rifle and headed toward the cabin, dodging from tree to tree. His heart was pumping as if it was in his mouth, but he let out no sound except his breathing. Noticing the Rebel's blood mixing with the rainwater on his jumper chilled him to the bone. About fifty yards up the hill he crouched behind a tree, listening for sounds of pursuit. Hearing none, he breathed a sigh of relief. Quickly he checked his rifle, reloaded, and listened. It was quieter than it should be. Then a yell from the Union camp echoed down to him.

"What's goin' on down there, boys?" Ollie thrilled; it sounded like his dad.

"I don't exactly know, John—I think we got some help down there somewhere."

Ollie listened; nothing came back except the sound of the rain. He knew he had stirred up both sides now, so he had to be extremely cautious. He headed back in an indirect way to where he had left Ginger above the cabin on the west side. The faithful horse had wandered just a few feet from where Ollie left her, grazing in the new spring grass. Ollie thought about the last storm and spoke reassuringly to his horse.

"Well, little lady, at least the only thunder we got this time is gunfire, and the only lightening is being spit outa rifle barrels. Boy, am I glad to see you here where I left you." Ginger stomped and shook her head up and down as if she knew exactly what Ollie said.

Mounted on Ginger again Ollie rode straight up the hill out of the clearing to the timberline, then headed due north to the left side of the skirmish-line. In the meanwhile rifle fire began again in fury as Ollie slowly made his way down the hill eastward, watching for those telltale puffs of smoke. He was also wrapped up in thoughts about the Rebel soldier who had charged him.

I'm sure I killed that man the first shot, and he was all but dead. That sure taught me a lesson about the endurance of the human spirit an' body.

The man furthermost to the left of the flank was now in Ollie's view. He dismounted and again dropped Ginger's reins. Just as he pulled out his rifle he heard a cry from the center of the skirmish line.

"I'm hit." The cry came from the Rebel side.

"How bad is it?" came back a voice closer to Ollie.

"I dunno, it's my shoulder—it hurts."

"All men hold your positions. I'm on the way to Billings. Come on now, let's wipe out these damn Yanks," the closer voice ordered.

That last order put a fresh resolve into Ollie. *No bunch of stealing Rebs is going to wipe out my dad and his friends, even if they are Yanks!*

Ollie Burke, an eleven-year-old scout, was now in this Civil War. He was no longer on the sidelines listening to the talk. He had faced fighting, he had been under attack, and he had killed two men. This was not playing games—it was life and death. Again he purposed to be alive when the battle was over!

With this determination firmly planted in his mind and in his heart, he moved in on the puffs of smoke and suddenly came into sight of the Rebel firing those shots. About 150 yards down the hill, behind an oak tree stood a tall skinny Reb soldier. He seemed to be bearing down on the north side of the cave where the horses of the Union camp were kept. The oak stood near Brushy Creek, which was now running full and muddy from the rain runoff. Ollie had picked off deer and game many times at this distance, and remembering how that last Rebel charged at 25 yards, he decided he could handle this situation from right where he was. The rain had let up a little now and the sky was brighter, so Ollie figured this for an easy shot.

Unknown to Ollie, John had put two and two together and come up with Ollie after Lewis had called back to John that it seemed as if they had help down there. He figured out the strategy his son was working and moved himself into a good position near the horses. He passed the word to his troops, through Sergeant Damron, to be ready to charge down the hill when he made a high-pitched yell and fired his weapon. They continued to return the Rebel fire, waiting for John to give the signal.

John had the benefit of the telescope and had caught sight of his son as he moved from tree to tree at the edge of the timberline. He followed Ollie's deliberate stalking of the Rebel soldier on his extreme left, John's right. The distance was far, even for the tele-scope, but the size of the rider and the way he was dressed were unmistakable. He watched Ollie dismount and begin to plot the end of a Rebel soldier who was hidden from John's view behind a big oak tree. John had exchanged shots with this Rebel soldier, but never had a clear shot at him. He put away the telescope and mo-tioned for the men to be ready. He waited for Ollie's shot, smiling to himself and bursting with pride. He was proud because his son had made his own grown-up decision about entering this fight, and it looked like the small Union force was going to come out on top just because of Ollie's decision. He knew Ollie would not miss.

Ollie was getting ready to instigate an all-out attack on the Rebel raiders and he did not know it. Once again he pulled back his hammer, lifted the sight, and held his breath while he squeezed the trigger. He aimed at the back of the Rebel soldier's head. The man never knew what hit him. He tumbled into Brushy Creek and was instantly out of sight in the swollen creek's muddy water.

Suddenly there was a high-pitched yell and Union soldiers plunged down the opposite hill shooting and yelling. Two Rebels were killed in the attack, three surrendered, including the wounded man, and it was all over in five minutes. The leader and several of his men panicked, mounted their horses, and fled up the hill to the west. Sergeant Damron counted four fleeing up the hill. Only two Union soldiers were wounded. Zeb had been hit in the calf of his left leg; fortunately, no bones were hit. Another private had suffered a wound in the upper right arm. They felt they had been blessed by God—and spared!

The men bound their prisoners and took them up to the cave. Not one enemy soldier would say anything except his name. The Union soldiers investigated the Rebel camp, took the remaining horses, and found two of the men Ollie had eliminated from the battle. Sergeant Damron and John Burke examined the bodies and removed their weapons. Lewis looked at John and shook his head.

"Well, John, I'm glad that boy is on our side and not the Rebs'. He's a terror. I never have seen such shootin' anywhere. You know he saved our hide, don't you?"

"Yep, I reckon I do, Lewis. He gave us that warning and kept us from being totally surprised. In addition to that he weakened the enemy flanks by th' removal of three men and completely demoralized the raiders."

"Let's rejoin th' boys. I'll have burial detail attend to these brave men," the sergeant said.

Ollie had joined the men at the hideout, and was a sight to behold. Grass stained and wet to the skin was just the description of his clothing. The blood had been washed away. Briars had scratched him and his hair was a disheveled mess—but he was smiling. John went over to the mule and rummaged through the pack, coming up with a flannel shirt, underclothes, dry trousers and some moccasins. He tossed them to his son.

"Change into these, son, and come on back to th' fire and get some heat on those wet bones."

Sergeant Damron announced, "Men, Private Damron will head up a burial detail with three of you that can dig. There are four Rebel soldiers down there that died for the cause they believed in. We have the time so we'll pay them our last respects. One man we have not recovered. The swollen creek water took him. When you have the graves dug, I'll bring these captives down and let them pay their last respects to their buddies. It may seem odd to do this, but we have the time and these men were brave soldiers."

The Rebel men looked at one another with surprised approval, and the Union soldiers came back in unison, "Hear, hear!"

The rain had stopped at the end of the skirmish, and after the burial service took place the Union men checked out the cabin and took the contraband that was left. They confiscated everything of value and packed it on the horses left by the soldiers fallen in battle. Ollie and Zeb prepared a hot lunch for everyone, including the prisoners-of-war; these men were then taken to the far end of the cave. One man was left on guard, and John asked Sergeant Damron to gather the other men together out of earshot of the prisoners.

"Men," John began, "the first thing that I want to do is open the conversation up to all of you and let you say your piece. I mean, anything goes: opinions about the battle, frustrations, questions, comments. Let's say it all right now and be open about it. Anyone want to go first?"

"Question, sir," said Private John Damron.

"Go ahead, Private."

"Well, sir, what happened? I mean—we were watching the camp close; only two men were present to our knowledge, then suddenly there were the warning shots, by Ollie no doubt, and all hell broke loose. We were surrounded and pinned against the rocks."

"Anyone care to explain to the private, as well as the rest of us, what they think happened?" asked John.

"I'll offer my opinion boys," Lewis said, waiting before continuing. "The main body of Rebs slipped in without any of us spotting them, and were sneaking up on us to close a trap when Ollie fired off those shots, which halted their advancement. What I don't know is, what made Ollie fire off the warning?"

John looked at Ollie, sitting close by. "What about it, Ollie? Can you shed some light on this for us?"

"Yes, sir, I think so," Ollie said. "I was doin' what you said—checkin' out the tracks going away from th' cabin, and I started a zigzag pattern, overlappin' to each side, when I come upon tracks headin' toward the cabin that was fresh. I mean they was—real fresh. I sorta figured the man that Zeb had seen earlier, before we all got here, had left to warn the main group that there was someone watchin' 'em. I figured that somehow th' two that stayed behind saw Zeb, or Dad, or the horses, or somethin' and went off to give warnin'. We didn't know about that, and so it gave th' Reb's time to plan a raid on us. When I thought on this, I didn't know how close they had come to th' camp so I figured I had to warn you, even if I was wrong. I had not seen th' men, but to me seein' th' tracks headin' in that direction was jus' like I saw 'em."

John thanked Ollie. "Anyone else?"

"Yes, sir," said Private Young. "Ollie, this is to you—I want to thank you, son. You probably saved my life. Not only the warning shots, but when you took that Reb out of the running on the south side, you probably saved me. I was exposed and he had my number. If you hadn't yelled and shot him, he probably would have got me. I am grateful and beholden to ye son, I want to thank you and I'm sure others feel the same."

Ollie was embarrassed and nodded back to Private Young, but didn't say anything. Sergeant Damron spoke up again.

"Let me say something for all of us, Ollie. We're all in your debt for being the hero of this battle! You were the element of surprise to the Rebel force, which was superior in number to us. You weakened their flanks and you spread panic through their camp because they did not see you and could not know what—or whom—they were dealing with. It gave us the edge and we prevailed. You are the reason why—and we all know it." The men all applauded in agreement.

"Is there anything else anyone has to say?" John asked. "If not, I want to address you all. First off, I want to thank you all for your individual participation in this battle. The surprise attack was not anyone's fault; it simply took place. They saw us, they were warned and set a trap, which failed because we had a secret weapon: Ollie! Everyone did a good job, and Ollie went far beyond even his own expectations of himself. He did this because of the position that destiny placed him in. I have no doubt that anyone of you would have acted the same way, if you had been in Ollie's geographical location. It was jus' Ollie that God picked for this job today. Now to the heart of the matter." Putting his hand on Ollie's shoulder, he continued.

"Ollie and I are scouts—and spies. Our normal job is not fightin', it's finding out things and reportin' 'em so that you men can do a better job with th' enemy, and win battles. I am fixin' to send you back to Louisa with your sergeant, th' prisoners and th' wounded, who need attention. Ollie and me will stay and try to track th' men who ran off; we really need to find th' main camp. I asked all you men to speak today and get what was on your mind said. Th' reason is, it can't be said anywhere else except th' report to Captain Lyons. Ollie and me depend on your keepin' it quiet. Our very lives may depend on it! We all like to be a hero, but let us give all the glory of this victory—and Ollie's being a hero—to God. We know it, Ollie knows it, and God knows it! We'd just as soon let it stop there. Can we depend on you to do this?"

One by one the men came, pledging their support to John and Ollie with a handshake. Each one added his personal thanks and Lewis said he would brief the man on guard duty when he could. John personally thanked Zeb and Sergeant Damron and asked that a message be taken back to Cassie. He got some paper and quickly wrote out a note . . .

Sunday May 11, 1862

My Dear Cassie,

Ollie and me are fine. He came back with the men and supplies on schedule. We had a little battle today and we came out all right. Zeb was hurt in the leg, but should be OK. It rained all morning here. Ollie and me miss you all the time. I think about you every hour. You sure did change my thinking and it is nice to have you to think about. We will look forward to coming home and seeing you. I pray for you every day.

God bless you,
Love John

He sealed the envelope and handed it to Lewis. "It isn't long, but I'm not used to letter writin'. I know you'll tell Captain Lyons everythin' and so I won't write him. He'll be hearin' from us before long. I want to get on thet trail before it rains again, so I will say good bye until we get back."

Sergeant Damron had his men mounted up; able-bodied men aiding the wounded first, followed by the prisoners and guards. The captured horses were loaded with contraband and weapons, with Private Young in charge of leading the pack animals. Lewis saluted both John and Ollie and signed off with a hearty "God bless you."

John and Ollie were already packed ready to move out, so John started across Brushy Creek, pointing Silky in the direction that the Rebels had escaped. It wasn't long before they picked up the trail in the soft wet ground. They steadily followed the easy tracks the galloping horses had left behind. After about fifteen minutes John noticed that the escaping men had slowed their mounts to a fast trot.

It was late afternoon before John let up the pace they had fallen into, with only two breather stops to rest the horses. Not a dozen words had exchanged between John and Ollie since they left; both were busy living over the thoughts of the bloody morning. John felt bad that he had not taken time for devotions or prayer, honoring the Lord's day of rest. He always tried to be very faithful to that, but in this case he was concerned about more rain taking out the tracks left by the raiders. As the five o'clock shadows began to deepen, the overcast skies gave way to sunshine and beautiful blue sky. The signs of rain had passed so John slowed down the pace and finally broke the silence.

"Ollie, over to th' north of us we passed Blainetown hours ago. We have been making a straight course to the connection of Lawrence and Morgan Counties. We only have about an hour or so to go and we'll leave Lawrence County behind us. You notice we haven't met a soul—and we've crossed several well-traveled trails. This is partly 'cause of it's Sunday; th' other part is thet these men knew their business and picked an off-th'-road way to travel, unnoticed, through the enemy lines. Now, I want you to put your thinkin' cap on! Why do you suppose they knew to pick this route?"

Ollie leaned on his saddle horn and thought for a minute. "Well, it could be by accident or careful map makin', but I allow it's because they've a local man, or men, in their outfit, don't you?"

John smiled. "I think you hit th' nail right on th' head, son. Thet's why they knew where to raid, find cattle and, for th' most part, dodge th' local folks who live in these hills. There is local help all right. We are goin to keep travelin' to the county line 'cause I figure they're a headin' fer Sandy Hook area. I think that's where we'll find th' main body of Confederate soldiers."

Having come to this conclusion, they headed out again and th' next time they stopped, they were on the edge of Lawrence County, actually in Morgan County. The trail had continued on toward Sandy Hook just as John had figured. They made camp and Ollie took extra time rubbing down the horses before he fed them. John attended to supper, which was a switch of duties. John had not said anything to Ollie, but his leg was giving him fits. Both man and boy felt the effects of a long, hard day. A good hot supper with hot coffee had its desired effect in settling down the two Union scouts. John rose and went over to the mule's packet. After a little search he came back to the campfire with the Bible. He motioned to Ollie and said, "We'll honor God and His Word, son. I know you understand why we couldn't until jus' now. But more important—God knows and understands. I'm goin' to read some from Psalm 91, verse 1 to verse 7. I think you'll see why.

"*'He that dwelleth in the secret place of the most High shall abide under the shadow of the Almighty. I will say to the Lord, He is my refuge and my fortress: my God; in him will I trust. Surely he shall deliver thee from the snare of the fowler, and from the noisome pestilence. He shall cover thee with his feathers, and under his wings shalt thou trust: his truth shall be thy shield and buckler. Thou shalt not be afraid for the terror by night; nor for the arrow that flieth by day; nor from the pestilence that walketh in darkness; nor for the destruction that wasteth at noonday.'*

"That last verse really kinda comforted me today, Ollie. In all the fightin' this mornin' I wasn't afraid for myself, or even for th' men. But when I discovered you had taken a hand in th' fight, a shudder of fear went through me, until I thought on this chapter. I jus' put my hand in th' Lord's hand at thet time and prayed this Scripture over you. I knew then thet you'd be all right. First I was angry at you for gettin' yourself into th' fight." He paused and laughed.

"Then I was mad at myself for bringin' you along into a dangerous war game. Finally, I jus' put it into God's hand and figured he would see you through it all. What a comfort His Word is, son. Never be without it. These word's from the Lord to us just proves His great provision for us. I had to realize that God loves you even more than I do. He will provide for you as well as for me." John looked at Ollie with a quizzical expression.

"Son, you've had quite a day! I'm anxious to hear all you want to tell me."

"Well, sir," Ollie began, "I don't know exactly where to start in tellin'. I sorta knew that you wouldn't let me get into the fight if you had been there for me to ask; I also knew that I was in a place

I couldn't ask. I could see the whole battle goin' on from where I was—like a show, and I had th' only ticket to get in. From where I was, judgin' from th' rifle fire, it looked bad for our side. I figured I would be in a real bad mess if I just sat there and let the battle go on and you lost. I didn't think I could live with that. I jus' had to make up my own mind. So I did!

"Th' next hardest thing was shootin' a man, or men, and takin' their life. I remembered what you said at Uncle John's, and I prayed for those men—and our men—and me. After I did that I was OK, until I shot th' first man. When I crawled up to him and turned him over, his eyes that couldn't see any more looked up at me and I lost my breakfast. I guess th' rifle fire to my left made me realize that it was still goin' on—th' fightin' I mean, and I still had a job to do.

I crept pretty close to th' next man 'cause he was so well hidden. That was really th' first time I was scared for myself. I pulled th' Colt out before I shot him with my rifle, and when th' man yelled somethin' awful and charged at me, I thought I was done for. I think the Colt saved me, and I shot him again between th' eyes while he looked down on me.

"You know, Dad, as I think back on that, I don't even know why I put th' revolver beside me. It was really after I had already aimed and cocked my rifle that I—well—I sorta stopped, pulled that gun out and cocked it so it was ready."

John interrupted. "I think I have an insight into thet Ollie. Remember th' Scripture we just read?"

"Yes, sir."

"Well," John continued, "in the 11th verse of that same chapter it says, 'For he shall give his angels charge over thee, to keep thee in all thy ways.' I think thet an angel was probably at your right hand and sorta nudged you tellin' you to pull thet Colt out and cock it. You see God knows th' things thet are goin' to happen before they happen. He has placed His angels for our protection. I believe God was protecting you all th' while, son."

"Dad, you must be right, 'cause I don't know why I did it, unless it was God doin' it. Boy, that sure is somethin', He was right there with me all the time."

"All of us, son, all of us—even those Rebel men, I'm sure. It must of been His will for us to win this battle, but it sure wasn't His will for us to burn that railroad track in Georgia. I've thought a heap on thet, too." John pulled out his pipe, packed it, and lit it with a coal, the first time he had done so since he was with Uncle John, several days ago. He spoke again to his young student.

"Son, you're no longer an outsider in this Civil War. You're a soldier, as sure as I am. You have fought and found out th' tragedy of taking a life. It ain't easy, even when you're in th' right. It will never be th' same again, 'cause you are no longer innocent. I know you'll think long and hard on this and you'll wake up nights thinkin' on it. Jus' don't let this affect your judgment. Give your conscience over to prayer, like you already have done, and remember those men would have shot you or me jus' as easy as anything. Remember th' Rebel leader yelling to his men to 'Wipe out those damn Yanks,' or somethin' like thet? Don't let th' dyin' of those men keep you from good wisdom th' next time you're in battle."

Ollie agreed with his Dad's advice and noticed that John was winding down. He was almost ready to retire. Ollie decided to update the journal and did so while he watched his dad sleep. It took awhile, because Ollie was behind in his entries. He finished and was also asleep very soon.

Power to Become
 the Sons of God

I T WAS NOON ON MONDAY BEFORE JOHN CALLED A REST FOR DINNER. THEY had nibbled on a cold breakfast and were coming close enough to Sandy Hook to start recognizing their surroundings. The tracks were still clear and it was obvious that the men were not afraid of pursuit at this point.

The animals were allowed to graze nearby while John and Ollie fried sliced potatoes and ham for dinner. As John sipped a hot cup of coffee, he spoke to Ollie about the plan of action for the next few days. He pulled out a military field compass and gave Ollie some basic instruction. Ollie was fascinated with the needle that always stayed to the magnetic north as he turned it in different directions. John pulled his hunting knife out of its sheath and placed it near the compass to show Ollie how metal would pull the needle away from the true north. Ollie tried the Colt, the rifle, and other metal objects, which all affected the compass. As John poured himself another cup of coffee, Ollie served up the food and his dad taught as they ate.

"You see, Ollie, this compass will help you in makin' maps and drawings to take back to the captain about our findin's in the coming days around th' Sandy Hook area; thet is, if we find what I think we'll find there. I'll show you how to use it and it'll help you in bein' more accurate in your maps."

"I can see that there sure is a lot to know in this scoutin' business, as well as the spy business, Dad. I sure thank you for bein' willin' to teach all this to me. I'll put my memory to work and sure try to remember what you tell me."

John laughed as he finished off the last big bite of ham. "Well, son, you're a good student and you make teachin' easy for a teacher. Not jus' me, but I've noticed thet with anyone who is tellin' you somethin'. I want to give you a piece of homespun philosophy, Ollie. In life, we have an opportunity to learn a lot of things—good, as well as bad. Some things we learn are neither good or bad, they are just things to help us get along better in life in what we are doin' at the time. Do you understand what I jus' said, son?"

"I think so, Dad—like learnin' to fight in a war, 'cause there is a war. Like learnin' to use a compass, 'cause you need to know how to make a map. Is that what you mean, Dad?"

"Exactly right, son. Now the bit of philosophy is this: Everything you learn to do, learn it as well as you can. In life, you never know when you have to call upon what you know in order to make a livin'. In other words, if you are skinning squirrels or cleaning chickens, learn to do it well; it may earn you money to live on sometime." John instructed.

"Like me hunting to sell rabbits and squirrels to th' Ellers and Louisa folks, huh, Dad?"

"Perfect example, son. You hunt well and you are selling your services and talent to do what other folks don't have th' time or ability to do themselves."

"Dad, I think I know, but that word you used—'philosophy'—what does it mean?"

"I don't know thet I can give you a dictionary definition, Ollie, but basically it means a belief, or sometimes a religion. When I said 'a bit of homespun philosophy,' it was like sayin' I want to tell you a belief thet I made up myself. Even thet isn't th' whole truth, 'cause I learned thet philosophy through th' years in livin', and partly from other fellers who also believe thet way. I jus' kinda put it into words."

Ollie thought on this a minute and followed up with another question.

"Dad, that means that religion is a philosophy, doesn't it?"

This young son of mine can come up with some good questions. Better questions than I have answers. Nevertheless, John believed every question deserved an answer, so he attempted to teach his son through his answers.

"Yes, Ollie, to some folks religion is a philosophy. I really should say religions! There are many religions in th' world, son. Some have to do with th' God we know and serve and some have to do with other gods men have made up. All of these are philosophies, of a sort. There are other types of philosophy thet you read about that man has made up, which have nothing to do with religion. You'll learn a little about these ideas as you continue in schoolin'. I mean schoolin' in th' sense of a formal education, or in readin'. Now my personal belief in God, and in Jesus Christ, His Son—well, I don't account it to be a religion, or a philosophy. Let me explain what I'm sayin'. My description of Jesus as my personal savior is a *relationship*, not a religion. It is based on my knowledge about my God, through His Son. For example: You are my son; we have a relationship. We are relatives—father and son, right?"

"Right."

"That's not a religion, is it?"

"No, sir. I know you're my dad, 'cause you told me so, and so did my mother."

"I know God is my Father, and His Son is my Savior and older brother th' same way. He told me so, in His Word," John continued.

"Th' Bible," Ollie advanced.

"Absolutely. Th' Bible says to me, and to you: 'But as many as received him, to them gave he power to become The sons of God, even to them that believe on his name.' John 1:12.

"That's why religion and philosophy to me are different than a relationship. I know we sing about th' old-time religion, an' thet's all right. What we mean is somethin' different than th' most of th' world understands as religion. Did I help you, Ollie, or make you more confused?" John laughed a little.

"I think I'll always remember this, Dad, and it helps me to have a picture in my mind about who Jesus, my older brother and Savior is, and who God is as my heavenly Father. God really loved us Dad, to give His only Son for just country folks like us."

"Not only country folks like us, Ollie, but the whole wide world, every color and every race of mankind—wherever they are and whenever they lived. Now let's me and you clean up our camp and I'll start you in some lessons on how to use thet compass."

That afternoon John taught Ollie the simplicity of reading a compass and how to draw maps according to the compass. They moved in and out of their camp and crossed several streams within a five-mile radius.

On the road to Sandy Hook they came across a farm where a middle-aged couple were pulling weeds in a good-sized garden. Both wore large straw hats, and the woman could be distinguished from the man by her large flowing cotton dress. They seemed the same size in height and weight and actually resembled one another in facial features. The garden was at least half an acre, and the piles of wilted weeds told John they had been at it all day. John leaned against a chestnut fence post as he spoke to the folks.

"Now thet's a well-cared-for garden if I ever did see one."

They both looked up and the man removed his hat, speaking to John and Ollie as he wiped his damp brow with a blue bandanna that showed signs of much use.

"Wal, sir, thanks, we try ta keep after it. After thet good rain we had yestiday, we couldn't hoe fer nothin,' but th' groun' was so soft it made pullin' weeds purty easy. We kinda gotta keep up on it if'n we wanta good yield fer th' winter. You fellers new ta these parts ain't ya?"

John answered by introducing Ollie and himself,

"This here is my son, Ollie Burke, and my name is John Burke. We come from over Louisa way and we're jus' over here to git a look at some caves 'n such. I'm actually a spelunker, and I been sorta teachin' it to my boy. I heard about some pretty good-size caves over 'n aroun' these parts. I jus' got a natural-born curiosity when it comes to snoopin' into rock formations."

"Wal, I'll be consarned," said the farmer, "I never heard of anybody jus' a goin' out to find caves. A spee—a spee-lunker ya say? Is thet what they call it? I can't stand caves myself, they kinda spook me—but there's a heap of 'em around here ta look at, that's fer sure. Best uns are over inta Carter County, thet's where ya otta go," the man added. "By th' way, my name's Bob McPherson and this is my wife, Mary. Why don't y'all come up on th' porch 'n sit a spell. We've kinda been lookin' fer a excuse ta quit fer th' day, anyhow. We don't git ta sit and visit much, 'n we don't git any outside news ta speak of. You boys could use a cup o' cold water now, couldn't ya?"

"Well, Bob," John said, "you done hit my want button. I'd sure be pleased to have a cup of cold water and we'd be happy to visit a spell. Them caves are never in no hurry to get anywhere, so we got th' time."

Ollie followed his dad and the McPhersons up to the humble farmer's cottage with a vine-laden front porch. Mary disappeared into the house to fetch the cold drinks. Ollie couldn't get over his dad's comeback as a "spelunker." It was the first time Ollie had heard that word. He knew it must be real or his dad wouldn't have used it. He laughed to himself as he thought about the recent caves and rock formations they had been through, mostly to camp, or to hide, or for shelter. Yes, John and Ollie had an interest in caves.

As they sat and visited, Mary brought a big pitcher of cold tea and joined the men for a short time. Soon she stood, asking John and Ollie to stay for supper.

"We sure would be pleased to take you up on thet offer, Mrs. McPherson. Ollie 'n me has been cookin' fer ourselves fer a week now and a good home-cooked meal would be hard to refuse," John said with enthusiasm.

Ollie spoke up to Mr. McPherson.

"Sir, I'd be glad to see to your chores, if you like. If you got livestock to feed, or milkin' chores?"

Bob gladly took Ollie up on his offer and he and John walked along toward the barn and outbuildings as the men continued talking. It seems that Bob and Mary had lost their team of horses last year to thieves, and they were never recovered. There had been a widespread rash of stealing from local farmers last winter, and it ended as quickly as it started. Some had lost livestock such as sheep and cattle and goats as well as some poultry. Bob only had the one milk cow, but had had a good team of horses that he depended on for his gardening and farming. It had been hard this spring putting in the garden by hand and also planting and preparing for several acres of corn and hay. A neighbor had kindly done the initial plowing and preparing the soil, but he didn't know about the rest of the year because everyone was busy with their own problems.

As the men talked, Ollie took care of the chores. He fed the chickens and turkeys, slopped the two hogs and milked the cow. He put down feed for her while he milked, then the men followed him back to the house as he carried in a pail of fresh milk. He filled the water buckets for Mrs. McPherson and brought wood in for her kitchen stove.

John remarked to Bob, "The same thing has been happening recently over around Blainetown. The Confederate soldiers have been seen doing th' stealing over in thet area."

"I don't have any proof who did the stealin' over here, but it might be the same group. I can't help but wonder how and why it stopped so quick though."

"I may have th' answer to thet, Bob. I think those boys are holed up around here, or somewhere between here and Sandy Hook. They were stealin' too close to their home camp, and figured thet might put too much pressure on 'em to move their camp," John speculated.

"Supper time," Mary called out from the kitchen. She had done herself proud. Chicken and dumplings, green beans, mashed potatoes and gravy, and a fresh green salad out of the new garden. After a good visit around the table, John and Ollie gave their thanks and headed back to their camp and the horses before dark. After they had walked about a half-mile in silence, Ollie began to laugh and slap his knee. John laughed with him at first and then began to question what was so funny.

"All right, Ollie," he said. "What's so all-fired funny? Let your dad in on the joke."

Ollie finally caught his breath and sputtered between breaths, "I—was—was—jus'—a—thinkin' about being a—spe—spe—lunker; that's a new one on me, Dad. I jus' started thinkin' about it and it hit me funny. How did you come up with that? You did it so easy, and I never even heard of th' word before."

John smiled. "Well it jus' came to me when I started talkin'. It seemed to fit with all th' caves we been in th' last week. I don't like to lie, and sometimes you git caught up in doin' jus' thet in this spy business. Bein' a spelunker sounded pretty impressive to me and it jus' rolled out. By th' way, Mr. Ollie, it really happens to be a word thet describes people who explore caves for real!"

"Oh, I knew that. I knew you wouldn't make up a word that sounds so funny, unless it was true. It jus' came as a surprise to me, and I won't forget it any time soon."

John and Ollie arrived at their camp and checked the horses, deciding to turn in early. After an hour of tossing and turning over and over in his bedroll, John sat up.

"Are you asleep, son?"

"No, sir, I can't seem to get to sleep."

"Me neither. What's on *your* mind, son?" John was particularly sensitive to Ollie's behavior right now. He wanted to allow him ample opportunity to talk about the recent events if he needed to. He also wanted to make himself available to counsel him, if it was needed.

"Well, several things, I suppose. I was thinkin' about those three fellers—th' Rebels . . ."

"Th' ones thet died in the skirmish," John finished for him.

"Yeah, them. I was wonderin' if they had family, or folks at home, or children—like me?"

"Those thoughts are normal to have, son, but it would be good if you got it out of your mind as soon as you can. You see, all of us who go off to war leave someone behind. Remember last Christmas? I had thet same thing to face when I left you, your mother and Sue Ellen. The odd thing is, I came back to you, and the girls were dead. They wasn't in the war, but they still died. You see, son, it could be the same with those men. We jus' don't know about those things. The thing is: when a man—or a boy—goes off to war to shoot at other men—and be shot at—the odds are greater thet he won't come back. I mean we take a chance jus' bein' a farmer like Bob and Mary McPherson; all kinds of things *can* happen. Whether they do or not, well, no one ever knows what's goin' to happen? Th' business of war is th' business of killin' and dyin'. It's like a game where you play for keeps. Those men knew thet when they left home, and when they started shootin' at us on thet hill, they knew we would shoot back. Those men played th' game of war and for them—well—they lost. You played the game and won. If you would have lost, I would have been burying you. So don't let it get you down, son."

"Well, I won't Dad. It was jus' th' thought and I know what you said will help me when it happens again. By th' way, what was keepin' you awake?" Ollie returned the question to his dad.

"Well," John said, "her hair has sorta red highlights, when th' sun hits it jus' right; she is pretty as a speckled pup, and—"

"And her name is Cassie Martin!" Ollie ended the sentence.

"You sure got thet one right, son. My mind has been actin' like th' mind of a youngster thet jus' met his first sweetheart. Can you believe thet, Ollie?" John confided.

"I don't know if I understand exactly what you're feelin', Dad; I never have had that to happen to me yet. But I can sure see what you have to think about in Cassie; she is th' most beautiful and kindly lady I ever did meet. Now that we are friends, as well as you being my dad, I can tell you something that I prob'ly never would've before."

John immediately gave his attention to the serious tone of this young *friend*.

"What's thet, Ollie?"

"Remember when we stopped to see Uncle John? Well, I was sort of taken by Eliza Birchet." Ollie blushed as he heard himself say these words.

John smiled and sat back against a tree.

"You don't say! Well, I can sure see why a man would look at Eliza thet way," John continued. "She is one beautiful little lady, and she has th' ways of an uncommon woman. Yes, sir, I can see how you could be taken by such beauty as thet. Th' problem is, as I see it—"

"Yeah, I know," Ollie interrupted, "She is way too old for me and jus' sees me as a little ol' kid. But what I mean Dad, is I found myself watchin' her at th' table. I watched her hands, her eyes, her smile, and her tiny little waist—Gosh! I can't believe I said that, 'n to my dad!" He put his head between his hands and hid his face in the dim light of the night.

John reached over and pulled him to his side, pulled his hands down, and looking into his eyes said softly, "It's all right, Ollie. It's all right, friend! We are friends, remember? We can talk about intimate things between men. Intimate means—well, you know—private things. Friends do thet and so do fathers and sons. Thet's why I spoke to you about my private thoughts of Cassie. I trust you, Ollie, and sometimes we need to have someone to confide in, someone to tell our innermost feelings and thoughts to. Now, I know we all have the Lord for thet, but we all need to have the human kind of friendship, too. We need to hear each other, confide in each other, and sometimes even give advice to each other.

"Now, the thoughts you had about Eliza were a little bit grownup for your age, but you, Ollie, are not a normal eleven-year-old boy. You are far advanced in your thoughts, actions, your skills, and in your education for a boy your age. That is all good, not bad. Th' thoughts you had about Eliza were honorable thoughts, and she would be complimented if you ever shared them with her. Thet's not what I'm sayin' to do, but I will guarantee you she would be honored if you ever told her. For you to notice a woman's softness, her beauty, and her feminine charms, means only thet you're growing into manhood. It also means thet I can share manhood-type things with you as your father—and friend—and you will understand them."

Ollie listened carefully and realized the sensitive nature that John Burke possessed. He did feel secure in sharing his private thoughts with his dad. He felt he could bring anything to his dad and it would be treated with respect. He was quite awhile, just thinking and taking in John's words.

"Well, Dad, I don't know that I'll ever tell Eliza, but I know it helps me understand your thoughts about Cassie, because, until I saw Cassie, I thought Eliza was th' most beautiful girl I ever met, but when I met Cassie—I changed my mind."

"Hear, Hear, Ollie Burke. I'll have no competition from you tryin' to take my girl away from me, will I?" John said as he roughed up his son's hair.

Ollie started laughing. "Aw, Dad, no man or boy could take Cassie Martin away from you; she don't have any eyes or thoughts for anybody else. And that's th' gospel truth!"

"Ollie, I know somethin' else thet's th' truth. If we don't get to sleep, we'll still be talkin' about this favorite subject come mornin'." Father and son rediscovered their bedrolls and soon were wrapped in individual thoughts about Cassie, Eliza, and each other. Sleep came to both before too many minutes passed.

John was restless during the night. Two or three times he awakened with sharp, shooting pains in his leg. He rubbed the back of his knee through his buckskins and the pain eased up somewhat but recurred. Each time he would rub and soon he would drift off into sleep again. Consequently, when morning came, he was glad the night was over. When Ollie rolled out he noticed that his dad was still sitting on his bedroll, so he began to move around getting ready for breakfast. John smiled sheepishly and nodded at Ollie.

"Son, I'll just sit here a spell, if you don't mind. My bad leg gave me fits last night; I'm kinda favorin' it this mornin'."

'Sure, Dad, you jus' sit there. I'll tend to the horses first, then I'll fix us somethin' to eat; it won't take me long at all."

John tried to stand, but shooting pains hit his leg as if someone had a knife cutting on him. He smiled painfully. "Think I'll take you up on thet offer, son. Jus' go on. I'll be all right soon's I get to lettin' th' blood circulate."

Ollie took the animals to water. He then measured out some grain for them and returned with food for a hearty breakfast. His dad had managed to get a fire started and had some water on for coffee. Ollie gave him a quick once-over and didn't like the color of his face. He was pale and he looked ill, even to his son's inexperienced eyes.

"Dad, are you goin' to be all right?"

"I reckon so." Looking Ollie straight in the eyes, he continued, "I guess with all th' excitement of trackin' th' Rebels, th' skirmish and all th' walkin' yesterday, I plumb forgot this bad leg. It's been a hurtin' all along for sure, but I ain't been payin' it no attention." He smiled out of the corner of his mouth. "It's now yellin' for some attention, I s'pose. Don't fix me anythin' much for breakfast, son; I'll jus' have my coffee and some dried fruit."

Ollie obeyed, getting the fruit and coffee, but he knew this was not normal for John Burke. John loved his breakfast, so this caused Ollie real concern. He did not have the heart for cooking anyway, so he joined his dad in a cold breakfast and some coffee. After an interval of silence, John slowly rose and turned toward the horses, limping more than Ollie had ever seen before. Then he noticed a dark spot behind John's knee. Trying not to let his voice show his deep concern, he said, "Dad, I—I believe you're bleeding. It's—coming through your—your buckskins. You'd better come back over here and sit down."

John turned with a surprised look, and followed his son's advice, sitting very carefully on a rock. Ollie slowly began to roll up the left leg of John's buckskins. By the time it got past the calf of John's muscular leg, both could see that wasn't going to work. Still very much in control for an eleven-year-old, Ollie was giving his dad orders like any sergeant John had ever heard.

"Take off your trousers and let me have a look at your leg. It looks like your wound has opened up because of all it's been put through th' last week. Why don't you pull them britches off and lay down on your bedroll?"

John painfully followed Ollie's orders, lying on his stomach with his left leg stretched out. Ollie examined the bloody leg, then went to get water and a clean cloth from the pack to wipe away the blood around a hole in the back of John's knee. A sharp piece of metal was visible to the naked eye. Ollie felt the leg, moving his fingers gingerly toward the puncture. The bleeding seemed to subside after washing with the damp cloth, but as he probed closer to the wound, ever so gently, John flinched and moaned, and Ollie quickly stopped.

"Sorry, Ollie. It hurts like th' blazes all of a sudden. Feels jus' like a knife cuttin' right through my leg. Go ahead, son. What do you see?"

"Well, Dad—it's a knife!" He moved up so he could see John full in the face. "There's a piece of metal comin' from the inside, tryin' to get out! It has poked a hole through your leg and that's where th' bleedin' is comin' from." Ollie couldn't keep a hint of alarm in his voice.

John was quiet for several minutes while Ollie patiently waited for his dad to take over this dilemma and make it disappear. But it wasn't going to be that easy. John finally spoke.

"First things first, Ollie. Go over to th' pack and you'll find an oilskin packet in th' right side. Bring it over here."

John untied a cord wrapped around the square-shaped bundle, unfolding it on the bedroll. A razor sharp knife, a pair of scissors, and a whisky flask lay on top of several clean, white bandages. Also among the equipment were a packet of assorted needles and a spool of white cotton thread. John went to work with the bandage packet. He folded a square of white cloth many times until it was bulky and thick then, handing it to Ollie, proceeded to fold a long piece of cloth three times, making a bandage about three feet long and four inches wide. John handed the steel flask and gave it to Ollie.

"Son, take the flask and dab some alcohol on the wound. Be sure to clean all around it. Then put this square bandage on top of the wound and wrap the long bandage over the square one several times. Leave enough room to tie it at the end."

Ollie moved into position as John turned with the back of the knee facing upward. He opened the flask and the smell of strong sipping whiskey reached his nose. Instinctively his head recoiled. "Dad, this alcohol has turned into straight corn whiskey, sure as shootin'."

Managing a slight laugh, John said, "Thet is plumb down-right deliberate on purpose, Ollie; there is a two-fold purpose to that flask—one's for th' inside and th' other is for th' outside. Believe me, it'll do th' job!"

Ollie simply shook his head and smiled, continuing this task for his dad. Following John's instructions to the letter, he soon had his dad all bandaged up. John carefully arose and put his trousers back on, taking care not to put any weight on the bandaged leg. He sat back against a tree, allowing his left leg to stay straight.

"We're a long way from bein' done, Ollie. But, as I said before, first things first. I want you to search this area and find one of them 'spelunker' objects." He said this with a smile. "We need a place with shelter, out of th' way of th' trail; we need a good place for th' horses; a place to make a campfire; and as private as you can find. We are liable to be there for several days. OK, Ollie? Take Ginger and be careful, son."

Ollie left with a few dozen unanswered questions in his young mind, but he knew this was serious business. He obeyed his father without asking a single question—for now anyway.

John's leg began to throb as he waited for his young partner. He tried to get his mind off the hurting wound and what had to be done. His mind went to a story his dad told him many years ago.

T.C. Burke had a younger and two older brothers that John and his sister Marcy never had seen. In fact, T.C.'s wife Amanda never met any of the Burke family from Yorktown, Virginia, near the Atlantic coast, where T.C. was born. On rare occasions T.C. had talked of his brother George. He never discussed the older brothers, Stephen and William, other than mentioning their names. George was three years younger than T.C., who was born in 1800. When the boys were small, they played and roamed the fields together. Once, when T.C. was thirteen, they explored part of an old battlefield from the Revolutionary war days in the Battle of Yorktown. They were running and young T.C. fell on a piece of metal that turned out to be a half-buried British bayonet. It cut into his thigh and made an ugly wound.

John remembered his dad telling him that when they got home their father, Calvin Burke, had scolded the boys and then, setting T.C. on the kitchen table, he had cleaned the wound with corn whiskey and sewed it up himself. He even made brother George, John's uncle, watch the proceeding as punishment for exploring in a forbidden area. T.C. had showed John the scar when he told the story. John recalled asking about his uncle. His dad told him they had drifted apart as years went on.

George married young, and became a farmer. He never thought much of T.C.'s inclination to see what was on the other side of the mountain. The last T.C. saw of George, he had several sons and was quite prosperous. When T.C. asked him to cross over the Big Sandy Country and visit, he just remarked, "Probably never will, Thomas. Probably never will." John thought of this part of his family he never met, but never had the time or money to go looking for them.

SEVENTEEN

The Steps of a Good Man

O LLIE RODE OFF TO THE SOUTH, WEAVING IN AND OUT BETWEEN GIANT oaks, marking the trail well in his mind for his return trip. He noticed a rise in the lay of the land to his left, which meant an uphill climb. On impulse, he turned Ginger abruptly to the east and climbed, noticing the increase in rock formations. Less than five minutes later Ollie discovered the ideal place.

A spelunker's delight, thought Ollie, grinning as if he were sharing it with his dad. A huge rock formation loomed up into a projecting cliff, under which he could walk Ginger while still mounted. The depth of the overhang was at least fifty feet and perhaps three times that across the front. The overhead stone shelter declined as he went to the rear of the cave, so he dismounted and Ginger could go no further. To the right of the center, at the rear of the cliff, the overhead was higher, with an opening into what seemed to be complete darkness. Ollie peered inside; he could remain standing in the opening, but a grown man his dad's height would have to stoop over. He could see that inside the opening was a large room with many possible directions to explore.

The location satisfied Ollie. Now arose the question of water. How far was it to water? He had not crossed a stream in his trek to this location, so he would have to check that out on his way back. His mind was full of thoughts about his dad and the pending medical need. He could not fathom the depth of this problem, but he knew it had to be serious if his dad stopped his quest for the Rebel raiders mid-stream, so to speak.

On Ollie's short journey back to the campsite, he found a good branch of water. So there was plenty of water only a ten-minute walk from the cave. He felt satisfied with everything and was back to his father by mid-morning. Ollie found John right where he had left him.

"Well, son, you look like the fox thet stole the egg. I guess thet means we're movin' to a new location?"

"You've got that right, Dad. I guess th' McPherson's were right about this country bein' full of caves. Didn't take me long to find a dandy."

"I'll take your judgment on thet, son! You best get the horse and mule all loaded up. I'll help you lift th' pack when you have everythin' ready. We'll do thet last, so you can help me walk over to th' mule. I want to try my best to keep th' bandage in place, and keep th' bleedin' down to a minimum."

Ollie made short work of breaking down the camp, erasing any evidence that they had ever been there. Finally, he went over to help. John stood up, putting all his weight on his right leg. Ollie supported John by standing at his left side, allowing his dad to place his arm around his neck, resting on his shoulders. They slowly made it over to the mule and John helped Ollie place the pack on Fred. The biggest difficulty was in helping his dad to mount Silky, especially from the right side. This accomplished, John was still in a great deal of pain.

An hour later they were settled in their new rocky location. John readily approved of his son's choice. Ollie placed his dad's bedroll well inside the shelter of the cliff then went to tend the stock and build a good campfire to make ready for the noon meal. John had suggested the fire, but did not totally have the meal in mind. Food would have to come later.

He then sent Ollie to the branch to bring back plenty of water. Ollie took both canteens as well as the bean pot, filling them all. John told Ollie to fill the smaller metal cooking pot half-full and put it on the fire to heat. Then John spoke very seriously.

"Ollie, I need to tell you what th' plan of th' day is. I know you're concerned about me—and this infernal leg wound of mine. Well, I am too, son! I must say, however, thet if we're careful, it's not life threatening. But it must be taken care of right away. Th' choices we have are several: first, we try to make it back to the infirmary in Louisa. Thet's a bad choice, because of th' distance and the shrapnel poking through my skin. Second, make it the shorter distance to Sandy Hook with the possibility of finding a doctor. I don't like thet choice either; it's five miles at least, and any travel at all could be dangerous with thet metal cutting through my leg. Besides, I'm not especially trustin' to doctors right now, even if one was in town. Th' third choice is to take care of it ourselves and thet leaves it mostly up to you! What I need to know from you, Ollie, is—are you able to stand up to it?"

Ollie looked a little nervous. "What would I have to do?"

"Son, I need you to actually operate on my leg an' get thet hunk o' metal out o' there. *It has to come out* Thet's th' only choice I got!"

"B—but, Dad—I've never done anything like that before. I'm scared of—I mean what—what if I hurt you?" Ollie's fear was evident. "Oh, Dad, what would I do?"

John smiled at his young son and knowingly patted him on the shoulder, building assurance. "You can do it, Ollie! Let me tell you—I would ten times rather have you here to do this than thet sawbones thet was ready to chop my leg off! Besides, son, I'll walk you through it step by step, and I know thet you follow instructions better then most full-grown men, or women, too for thet matter. Do you think you can do what I tell you?" asked John.

"Well—yes, sir—I always did what you told me to do—as best as I knowed how—but—somehow, this seems a mite different," Ollie stated. Then, straightening his shoulders, raising his head, and standing tall, he made up his mind. "OK, Dad. Let's get at it. What do you want me to do?"

John laughed, but in the middle of his laughter, he winced as he accidentally moved his leg. He hesitated a second and smiled back his response.

"Thet's th' spirit, son. I knew you had it in you to do—an' jus' in time, too; th' water is startin' to boil." Pointing to the small pot on the coals, John began his instruction to his new surgeon.

"As I said before, son, first things first. Preparation is the first thing to do, and we already started thet with the boiling water. Get the small knife in th' bandage pack and th' large needle and thread. Might as well bring th' whole pack over to have it close by."

Ollie brought out the oilskin package again, picking out the items requested.

"Thread the needle with about two or three yards of thet white thread. I know you can do thet; I remember seein' you sew up your britches before. Thet's it! Leave one end shorter than th' other 'n knot it on th' end. Now, put th' knife and th' needle 'n thread in the boilin' pot of water to sterilize 'em thoroughly. You see, son, the danger is not goin' to be in th' cuttin, or in the removal of the metal, or even in sewin' me up; it's the danger of infection. Thet's why you need to use th' flask for antiseptic, and boilin' water for killin' germs. Before you start, you need to wash your hands with good hot water 'n soap and have everythin' laid out. After you wash, make up two new bandages jus' like we did earlier. Now, thet's th' preparation part. You get thet all done and I'll get myself ready."

John wriggled out of his trousers and removed the existing bandage, which showed very little blood. *This is good,* he thought. John removed his moccasin from the left foot and maneuvered himself into a reclining position on his bedroll. Ollie, in the meantime, brought everything close to him and easy to reach. The bandages were made up, the flask was sitting straight up, and the scissors handy. He had removed his shirt and was wearing only his short-sleeved undershirt and trousers. Very carefully, he had washed thoroughly all the way up to his elbows even cleaning under his fingernails. He felt proud that he had thought of that himself. The knife and threaded needle were still in the boiling water.

"I'm ready for th' next lesson, Dad, whenever you are," Ollie bravely announced, taking a deep breath.

"OK, son. Lesson number two will be th' final lesson. Then it will all be up to you." Ollie let out an involuntary sigh, and John continued.

"Put a towel under my leg, about th' knee and double it, 'cause there will be blood! Lay out a clean bandage rag and place your knife and needle on it; you'll need th' knife first, of course. Wash the leg all around to the front and up and down four or five inches in each direction with hot water—not with soap. Then go over thet same area with alcohol, using a piece of bandage material. Now, you're ready for th' cutting part. Ollie, take your finger and go lightly over the metal under th' skin. It will help you to outline th' way to cut and remove th' metal.

"After you've done this, make your first cut in a straight line over th' shrapnel. It will tell you where, and when to stop. It will bleed, but don't let thet scare you. Jus' pretend you're takin' a big piece of buck-shot out of a rabbit—and—I'm th' rabbit!" Ollie deliberately shook himself as he shuddered.

"But, Dad, won't thet hurt? You won't be asleep or anything?"

"Son, your part is to do th' cuttin, th' removal, 'n th' sewin'—in thet order! My job is to do th' standin' it and th' prayin'. Don't worry none about me; it's gotta be done, and I can do what I have to do when it's necessary. If I flinch or moan, or even cry, you jus' keep doin' your job—OK?"

Ollie said timidly, "OK, Dad, I'm with you. Go ahead with your teachin'."

"Well, son, I'm almost to th' end. After you have the metal out, put the skin and flesh back together and sew it up. Mind you, there will be wiping up, and dabbing blood, but you have your water handy with a white cloth to do thet with. You sew one stitch at a time, cut it with the scissors, and tie it in a knot, putting th' skin back together. Take another stitch and do th' same thing until you have it all sewed back together. Then you wash off all th' blood, sterilize again with th' alcohol and apply th' bandages jus' like we did before. Put th' bandages on firm with th' compress over th' wound then wrap it and tie it off. Have you got all thet, son?" John asked one last time.

Ollie shook one final time and let out a breath. Then sucked in a fresh lungful. "I—I guess there is no time like this time. Let's get—get—that shrapnel out of you, Dad."

Ollie set out to work. He fished the knife and threaded needle out of the hot water, laying them side-by-side on some bandage material. Next, he brought over the hot water, dropping in a good-size white prepared bandage. He set out the bandages he intended for the wound after the metal removal, and looked around.

"I'm ready as I think I can be." Looking at his dad he forced a smile and said, "Roll over, rabbit! I've got some buck-shot to take out." John laughed out loud, rolled over on his stomach, then made a request.

"One last favor, Doc. Let me have a swig of thet antiseptic!" Ollie smiled back and gave him the flask, understanding the need for the healthy swallow that John took.

Ollie began the most memorable event of his young life by washing his dad's leg thoroughly with hot water, taking care not to snag the protruding metal. Following John's instructions, he swabbed the whole area down, including the open cut, which caused John to tense up as the alcohol bit into the wound. As he probed the piece of metal that was just under the surface, he could feel it extend for about an inch as it went deeper. He thought he felt it extend in a different direction at that point, but he wasn't sure. He picked up the sharp surgeon's knife and spoke, partly to himself, partly to his dad.

"I'm picking up th' knife to make th' first cut; it looks like it will be about a one-inch straight cut. It will probably hurt; I have to start at th' point of th' metal and follow it."

Blood was oozing out of the wound. As Ollie put the point of the scalpel at the metal's edge, he felt his patient tense up. Ollie was perspiring, but his hand was steady as he uttered a prayer when he made the first incision. He did it quickly, following the metal under the surface and he stopped just a little past the metal end. The blood came forth freely, but not as bad as Ollie had imagined. No major blood vessels were involved. He sponged off the blood quickly, wringing out his cloth. He could now see the ugly uninvited metal, and he had made a good estimate. The end was deeper, but in view, and, as he probed with the scalpel, his patient moaned and tensed again, holding tight to his bedroll. Ollie was right; the metal was shaped like the letter "L." He said as much out loud.

"I have to make another cut, Dad—looks like about the same length." He sponged again, picked up the scalpel and announced, "Making another cut. It's a little longer than the other incision—

about an inch and a half." Ollie sponged, probed with the knife, and could see the piece of shrapnel move. It was all John could do to keep from screaming with pain, but he just groaned and shuddered, straining again. More than anything Ollie wanted to get this procedure over with; he was feeling the pain for his dad, so he worked feverishly.

With his right thumb and forefinger he grasped the shrapnel and felt it move. He lifted slightly and felt it give way until it was out halfway. He sponged the blood again, continuing to work the metal, taking care not to tear any tissue as he put leverage on the object. He had to take the scalpel and make a short cut in the muscle to release the other end and suddenly it was free. He had it in his hand!

Quickly he dropped it in the wash pan and proceeded to put the cut and torn flesh back together. Washing away the blood, he could see he had made an almost perfect L-shaped cut. He put the flesh and skin back together as his dad had instructed, then picked up the needle and thread and put one stitch in and cut the thread, leaving enough to tie a knot. He proceeded with this method until he had made sixteen stitches. *Perhaps a little wide, but pretty neat for my first time* he thought. *Dear God, I hope this is th' last time.* He was wiping down the wound with alcohol when his dad finally spoke.

"How is it goin', son?" whispered John weakly.

"Down to the end, Dad."

Ollie finished off with the compress, tying it into place with enough pressure on the wound to hold back the bleeding. Ollie cleaned up washing the tools and bandages completely and replacing all except the wet bandages in the oilskin. After hanging the bandages to dry, Ollie noticed he was soaked with perspiration and so was his dad.

John carefully rolled over to look at the neat bandage, sitting up on his bedroll, keeping his left leg extended.

"Well, Ollie, how do you feel now thet it is over?"

Ollie laughed. "How do I feel? How do *you* feel? You were the rabbit!"

John was pale, but this was understandable, for when Ollie removed the towel he saw there was more blood lost than he thought. The towel was soaked with blood! John finally answered. "I feel a little weak, but my leg feels better—no knife cutting into me anymore. You did good, son, I can jus' feel it."

"Dad, can I pray?" Ollie asked. "I'd feel a lot better about this. You remember when Jesus said, 'If ye shall ask any thing in my name, I will do it.' I want to do that right now."

John answered by reaching out and pulling his son close. "Go right ahead, Ollie—you pray!"

Ollie placed one hand on his dad's leg as he prayed.

"Oh Lord, I am so glad you will listen to me when I talk to you. I know you are always kind to us and provide food and clothing for us. I know you love us and I believe that your Word is real and true today, jus' like when you walked with your disciples. I remember your Word when you said we could ask anything in your name. I do that jus' now, oh Lord Jesus. I ask in your name that you heal my dad's sore leg and keep infection and sickness away from him. Jus' like you healed th' lepers and th' blind man, heal my dad's knee. Thank you, God, in Jesus' name. Amen."

John Burke felt good about his surgery, about the metal being out of his leg, and most of all about his son.

"Let me see thet monster, Ollie" John said, nodding toward the wash pan.

Ollie lifted the piece of sharp metal out of the water. It was shaped like an L, only rough and jagged with sharp edges. It was a couple ounces of ugly and deadly shrapnel. If it had struck his dad in or around the heart, lungs, or other vital organs, he wouldn't have been here to have his young surgeon remove it. *Another thing to praise the Lord for,* he thought.

"Ollie, I'm hungry," John said as he reached over to put his trousers on. He checked his watch. It was fifteen past one P.M., high time to be hungry, especially with no breakfast. Ollie was delighted to see his dad back to normal—almost! He felt like a year had gone by since this morning—at least off his life.

"Don't worry, Dad, I'll have you some dinner before you can say Jack Robinson."

After a good hot meal, John began more instruction.

"I need you to do some things while I rest up here for a day or two and heal. I want you to get your journal and also a tablet. You need to make your maps and directions in th' tablet so it can get to Captain Lyons at the proper time. You may even have to copy some of th' journal entries, because we don't want to let thet book get away." John paused to allow Ollie to get his writing materials. Once he was seated alongside his dad, John began with a basic instruction aimed at helping the youngster make accurate maps to pass on to headquarters through Lyons.

"I want to talk to you, Ollie, about distances so you can take your compass and draw directions, like north, south, east an' west, as well as estimate how far it is to a point on thet map. Do you understand so far?" John asked.

"I think so, Dad, if I don't understand, I'll jus' pretend I'm in school and raise my hand, OK?" he said with a grin.

"Sounds good to me." John returned his smile. "Now, you already know how to estimate pretty good in shooting a deer, or some animal. Fer instance, how far was the last shot you made at th' Rebel thet fell into th' creek?"

"About a hundred 'n fifty yards, I imagine," Ollie answered without hesitation.

"Good. Thet's prob'ly right on the money. Now you know thet a yard is—how many feet, Ollie?"

"That one's easy, Dad. It's three feet, and a yard in a box. I mean a yard going this way, and this way, and this way and closing in th' box is a square yard or nine square feet," Ollie offered proudly.

Ollie drew a picture with his finger on the dirt in front of him, making a square to illustrate.

"Thet's very good, son. Now it will git a little harder as we go on. I want you to write these things I'm goin' to tell you in your journal, so you can refer back to them. Remember this, you're not a surveyor. You an' me are jus' amateur mapmakers. Now thet's all right, jus' so we do them th' same way every time. This way someone else can follow what we do, even if we ain't told 'em. Use a symbol for where you take your bearings from. Lots o' times thet's you! Where you stand can be th' point you are measurin' from. I like to make a circle with an X in the center as a symbol to mean me. If thet's OK for you, jus' put thet down in your book. If you are measurin' from a tree, say so, or use a symbol. A cross would be for a church (they use thet on big maps), and so on." John carefully stood up without putting weight on his bad leg, stretched, changed his position, and continued his instruction.

"Do you follow me so far, son?"

"Yes, sir, I believe it's pretty clear. A circled X to mean me, and a cross for a church, and other symbols for trees and houses and things, right?"

"Exactly," John said. "Now, we'll go ahead; put this down— 5,280 feet in a straight line is th' same as one mile. What I mean is, thet if you walked back toward th' camp we left this morning, in a straight line 5,280 feet, it would be exactly one mile. Thet, of course, means thet 2,640 feet is a half-mile an' 1,320 feet is a quarter mile. If you transfer thet into yards, 1,760 yards equal th' same as a mile. Th' reason I'm havin' you write this down, is for you to refer back to until you get it down to memory. Do you have any questions so far, Ollie?" John waited for Ollie to answer, as Ollie thought over the "so far."

"No, sir. I think all this you're tellin' me is jus' information for me to know to help make maps. I jus' am wonderin' how I'm goin' to use all this to make maps?"

John laughed and slapped Ollie gently on the back. "You see? You do have a question, and a good one, too. Well, thet part all comes from practice. Thet's what you're goin' to start for th' rest of th' day. Th' first part will be th' hardest; it involves thinkin', measurin' and walkin'. Go over to my saddlebag, in th' left side and you'll find an oilskin tape measure." John waited while Ollie dropped his tablet and the journal to search out the tape. He came back shortly, allowing the tape measure to unroll as he came.

"This is one yard?" he asked as he examined the tape.

"Thet's right, son. Now see thet big ol' white oak tree I'm pointin' at?" John asked.

"Yes, sir."

"How far do you say it is from here?" John inquired.

"I'd say, oh, about 25 yards, or close to that," Ollie speculated.

John neither confirmed nor denied Ollie's guess, he simply said, "All right, Ollie, prove it. Take thet measuring tape and measure all th' way to thet oak, one yard at a time. Now, keep in a straight line all th' way to th' tree."

Ollie began by laying the tape down on the ground straight toward the tree, making a line on the ground then put the tape down again and made another line. He continued this method for about six yards and stopped. Leaving the tape at the last measured yard to mark his place, he put his hands on his hips, and looked around until he spied a small patch of hickory saplings off to the right. Pulling out his hunting knife, he walked over to the saplings and carefully selected a nice straight one, about one inch in diameter at the base. He cut the sapling, trimming the trunk of all sprouts, leaving the top until he returned to his measuring tape. Marking the place he left off at six yards, he used the tape to find out how long his hickory stick was. It was a little over seven feet, or two yards with a foot left over. He hesitated a minute and turned to his dad to ask a question.

"Dad, you don't mind if I make this a little easier do you? You did say one yard at a time!"

John kept a serious look on his face. "You're in charge, Ollie. What you decide is up to you. Jus' git th' job done."

"Yes, sir."

Ollie cut off the top of the sapling at exactly six feet, which was two yards, and ended up with a measuring stick that was straight, one inch thick at the bottom tapering to about one-half inch. He marked the stick by grooving around in the bark at one yard, and measured one foot at the small end, cutting a circle there also.

John could hardly believe he was seeing this from an eleven-year-old boy. He was overflowing with pride What a marvel to see a boy who knew how to think, and was bold enough to do so. In these modern times a lot of farm boys and girls were strong and serious-minded and did much more work than play. It was the normal way rural folks lived and raised their children. But from among all these children once in awhile there was an exceptional child. John Burke figured he was the most blessed, to have one of these designated children for his son.

Ollie was finished and on the way back. He had rolled up the tape and put it in his pocket. Taking the hickory measuring stick, he used it end-over-end, all the way to the tree.

Ollie had a smile on his face as large as all out-doors when he said, "Missed it by one yard, Dad. It's actually 26 yards to that tree."

"Great, Ollie, I knew you were close. Now thet you've got a measurin' stick, I want you to measure a straight mile. Why don't you take a straight line back to our old camping place we left this morning? Now, let's check you out! How long is your stick?" asked John.

"It's two yards, Dad—six feet," Ollie answered.

"Do you remember how many straight yards to a mile? It's all right if you have to look at your notes."

"I remember that one, Dad, it's 1,760 yards," Ollie related.

"Good, son. Now how many of the 'Ollie sticks' would it take to make a mile?"

Ollie laughed and looked at his dad; John's eyes twinkled though he did not have even the shadow of a smile on his face.

"Ollie sticks?" Repeated Ollie quizzically. "I never heard of no 'Ollie sticks' before, Dad."

John broke into a big smile and joined in the merriment of his fruitful youngster.

"Why, yes. Didn't you know?" John took on a pompous air and continued importantly. "An 'Ollie stick' is a unit of measure, measurin' exactly six feet or two yards, th' same as one fathom in nautical terms. The term was invented by thet popular and well-known surgeon, and spelunker, Dr. Oliver Thomas Burke of eastern Kentucky fame." John ended his pompous verbal display with circling gestures with his right hand and a little bow with his head.

Ollie was in fits of laughter, enjoying his dad's looseness and good humor after such a painful morning. It was such a contrast and they both needed a good laugh from all the seriousness of the last forty-eight hours. After a few minutes of enjoyment together and in one another, John became serious.

"Getting back to th' question, Ollie, I was serious about wantin' to know th' answer. What is th' answer?"

Ollie had to think a minute to remember the question, and as he did so he picked up his tablet and put down the number, 1,760 divided by two and came up with the answer 880.

"Well, sir, it would take 880 'Ollie sticks' to make a single mile."

"Good, Ollie. I want you to take thet 'Ollie stick' of yours and measure your way back to th' old campground we stayed at last night. Before you go, I want to tell you, son, I don't even have a twinge of pain in my leg; not even an ache. I don't know if it's due to havin' an expert surgeon, or a tremendous prayer of faith, but I do know I am grateful to th' Lord and to you. By th' way, please bring my Bible over to me, and also my book of poems. They're in th' pack."

After Ollie got the Bible and poetry book for his dad he began the slow job of measuring out a mile on foot. John began by reading several chapters in the Bible and reflecting on his favorite verses in the book of Psalms . . .

The steps of a good man are ordered by the Lord: and he delighteth in his way. Though he fall, he shall not be utterly cast down: for the Lord upholdeth him with his hand. Psalm 37:23 & 24.

This familiar scripture had captured John's thoughts many times in the past. It had upheld him when, at times, he felt he had fallen from grace with the Lord, or even with his family. Not necessarily in outright sin, such as breaking the Ten Commandments, but more in trying to measure up in goodness and endeavoring to be a good man. John meditated on this, knowing that God's Word says to "hide the Word in your heart so that you might not sin against Him." It was this Word that kept him going when all else seemed to fail, even his own reasoning.

John knew it was impossible to be good enough to measure up to the goodness that the Psalmist spoke about. God's word itself spoke of man's righteousness being no better than "filthy rags," in Isaiah 64:6. Further, it is written in Romans 3:10: "*There is none righteous, no not one.*" In that self-same chapter further down it says, "*For all have sinned and come short of the glory of God.*"

John knew all these Scriptures by memory. So how then can one be a "good man" and allow the Lord to uphold him when he falls? John reasoned in his mind it was by that perfect gift, Jesus Christ, that he, John Burke, was a good man. Not by anything that he, or any earthly man could do, but only because of John 3:16: *"For God so loved the world, that he gave his only begotten Son, that whosoever believeth in him should not perish, but have everlasting life."*

So it was by God's goodness that John could declare himself good. John mused, *I am a good man, saved from sin and made good by the righteousness of God's gift to all man-kind, Jesus Christ, His only begotten Son.* John leaned back against the tree and had great joy. This was reflected on his face as he counted his many blessings: The metal and pain in his leg was gone; he had a loving son who was godly; he had been given a precious new daughter; he had been given a beautiful woman to love; and most of all He was declared to be good by the righteousness of Jesus Christ.

His reverie was disturbed by Ollie's return, a big grin on his face, which was damp with perspiration.

"Got it done, Dad. Measured straight back to th' camp and you were right, it was jus' about a mile; closer than anythin' to argue about. I marked it and high-tailed it back. What do you want me to do next?"

"C'mere son." As Ollie moved closer, he pulled out his treasured Waltham watch. "Until I get you a watch of your own, I want you to use this for th' next few days. Ollie, your mother gave me this, so I don't have to say how important it is to me. The next project I want you to do is goin' to be hard work, pure 'n simple."

Ollie was admiring the watch and looked on as his dad took the key and wound it up tight, dropping the key back inside the cover. The key was attached with a little gold chain to prevent it from being lost. There was no photograph or likeness of his mother, but an inscription on the back cover read, "From Elizabeth to John with Love." Ollie was elated to be able to even handle this treasure of his dad's; let alone carry it. He looked at his dad seriously and promised, "I'll guard it with my life, Dad."

"No you won't, Ollie Burke!" John commanded. "Your life is more important to me than any watch or trinket. I know you will take care of it, and thet's all I expect. It has sentimental value and I don't want to lose it, but if it comes to a choice, well—there's no choice at all; you come first! Understand this, young man?"

"Yes, sir." Ollie responded with a hand-salute and a grin.

"All right, smart aleck!" John came back, smiling at his sprightly son. "Let's get back to work. I want you to take your journal with you so you can record your findin's. Check th' time, then walk back th' measured mile in a normal walk, like you were goin' somewhere. Don't rush, jus' walk normal. When you get there, see how long it took and put thet down in th' book, and turn right around and come back at th' same speed, OK?"

"Then you want me to put down th' time again, right?"

"Right! Next I want you to saddle Ginger and get in th' saddle, and let her walk her normal walk to and from th' measured mile, puttin' down th' times in th' book. Thet's the assignment, Ollie. Get to it!"

Ollie picked up the journal, checked the time, and was off toward his assignment. John continued reading, switching now to the book of poetry that Sue Ellen had purchased for him a couple of years ago. He appreciated and enjoyed reading this particular book from time to time for that reason. It was a book of poems by English poets; all of them dead, and some of them very profane men in their time, judging by their writings. John was broad-minded enough to examine their thoughts and ideas through their sonnets and prose, which spoke a lot about death, battles, and romance. He had read Shelley, Lord Byron and even William Shakespeare, but his two favorites were William Wordsworth, who had just died in 1850, and William Cowper, who died fifty years or so before. He loved Wordsworth's, "The Daffodils," because he loved nature and flowers. He had read "The Daffodils" over so many times he had it down for memory.

Today he decided on some of Cowper's work. He read the "Loss of the Royal George" through several times. It was about a ship that had been lost at sea with all her crew on board, as well as the "Brave Kampenfelt," a well-known sea captain. Eight hundred men were lost in this vessel, "The Royal George." John had tried before, and could not find any reference material about this great ship and her captain and crew. Anyway, it was a good story.

He also read "The Poplar Field," one that always saddened him because there were many poplar trees in eastern Kentucky. This was a story about a man who either owned, or knew of a great "Poplar Field," which he enjoyed seeing and visiting. After being absent for a period of time, he came back to find all the poplars gone. They were evidently cut down or destroyed and no more could he see the breeze flow through the leaves and watch the poplars display their beauty. *How sad,* John thought, *to cut so many beautiful trees until there were none left; yet that was happening in parts of Kentucky, even at this very time.*

The William Cowper poem that stopped him in his tracks was the short poem called "To a Young Lady." Immediately John's thoughts settled on Cassie as he began to read this comparison between a mountain stream (at least it was like a mountain stream in his imagination) and a pretty lady. John began to think upon his love for Cassie. Certainly it must have been a lady like Cassie in Mr. Cowper's mind when he wrote about the young lady in his poem. *Cassie really fits this writing,* thought John. *I'll have to share this with her when I get back to Louisa.* He knew there was a specific reason he was drawn to this poet's writings today. *Dear God,* he thought, *I'm like a lovesick puppy over this beautiful lady that so recently came into my life.*

To a Young Lady
BY WILLIAM COWPER

Sweet stream, that winds through yonder glade,
    Apt emblem of a virtuous maid—
    Silent and chaste she steals along,
    Far from the world's gay busy throng:
    With gentle yet prevailing force,
    Intent upon her destined course;
    Graceful and useful all she does,
    Blessing and blest where're she goes;
    Pure-bosom'd as that watery glass,
    And heaven reflected in her face.

John reflected on the poem and on his beloved lady. He wondered what she was doing right now, knowing full well that she was in God's hands and that his friends would look after her if a need arose. John thought back into the lives of his lost wife and daughter. They were neither lost in his memory, nor in eternity, because of the provision that was made by God in sending his Son, Jesus Christ, to die that they may live. They both were strong believers in that certain hope of the resurrection, as were he and Ollie.

And now, wasn't it just like God to give him Cassie, to protect and care for, as she would care for him? It was just the goodness of God to bless and bless and bless again. John felt in his heart—in the very depths of his heart, so very full to overflowing—gratefulness toward his God. He felt worship and praise rising up within him as his eyes filled with tears that overflowed and trickled down his cheeks.

In this pensive mood, John reached over and picked up the tablet Ollie had left behind, and he began to write his feelings in a prayer. He knew he could never use mere words to express the love he felt for God, or Ollie and now even Cassie. He remembered the thankfulness again of lovable Sue Ellen when she prayed, last Christmas Eve. Still John felt he must indeed write something about his thoughts, he knew God could read between the lines and see into his heart that was over-flowing.

My Prayer Oh God this Day

As I survey my thoughts in line,
My God and Savior who art sublime.
An undeniable uppermost place to rest,
Releases sin-burden from my chest.
My Family gone, beneath the sod,
From their grave; yet with their God.
My son named Ollie, thou gavest me,
For comfort, solace, and enjoyment be.
Thou givest more than my share,
Cassie—a Lady beyond compare.
With fire-lined hair, that softly unfolds,
Surrounds a face that an admirer beholds.
Perfection, from a near-by angel reflected?
A gift to me that my God has selected.
I thank you Lord for giving me so much,
My lovely Cassie, to love, to see, and to touch.
Amen

John smiled as he wrote. *I am not much of a poet; but I am sincere about what I pray to the Lord, and He understands.* Through the trees John noticed the sun beginning to set in the west, and he heard the clip clop of Ginger as she made her return trip from Ollie's mile.

After Ollie cared for his horse and the other animals, he prepared for supper, excitedly telling his dad of his afternoon's learning experience. John enjoyed listening to him rattle on and on as he prepared a meal that would make some women envious.

After clean-up, Ollie said he would be right back. He went to the pack and rummaged around a bit, coming up with a hand-ax. Without offering any explanation, he disappeared from view and John heard him thrashing about in some tree branches off to the right. It was still dusk, so visibility was not a problem; it was just that Ollie was beyond John's vision. Finally, there he was holding a cleaned, forked branch cut from oak. He smiled triumphantly.

"See if this fits you, Dad." He held out the crude crutch to John.

John shook his head, again amazed at his son. He took the sturdy homemade walking stick to lift himself, fitting the fork under his left arm. He took a step, then another.

"Ollie, this is great," he said. "You jus' think of everythin' for your ol' man, don't you?"

Ollie frowned and was visibly upset.

"Dad, please don't say that. I mean—you're not an old man.— I don't think of you as an old man. I don't call you an old man and even when th' kids at school says somethin' about you bein' an old man, I change their mind's real quick."

John knew he had struck a nerve and he was not prepared for this response. He quickly apologized.

"Ollie, please forgive me, I didn't know this was offensive to you. I certainly agree with you. I'm not an old man; it's jus' an expression people use. I appreciate your attitude and I won't use th' term agin, even in jest."

"Aw, it's OK, Dad—it's jus' a sore spot with me and I shouldn't have sounded off that way."

EIGHTEEN

The Camp of the Enemy

I T WAS TIME FOR JOHN TO LAY OUT INSTRUCTIONS FOR HIS SON FOR THE next few days because he knew it would be at least that long before he should try to walk on his healing leg.

"Ollie, it's important thet you pay attention to th' next instruction I'm goin' to give you. I don't think you need to write it down because you have a good memory. I'm goin' to be laid up here for two, maybe three days while I let this leg get well. I don't want to tear those stitches you did such a good job fixin', 'cause th' bleedin' might start up again."

"You bet, Dad. I sure will do whatever you want an' you don't have to worry about me."

"I know thet is true, Ollie. I am jus' goin' to outline what needs to be done 'n let you do th' plannin' as to th' way it's done. First off, I suggest you dress jus' in your farm clothes—overalls or somethin'. Don't wear your holster. Put your Colt in th' saddlebag out o' sight. Leave your Sharps here with me and take th' musket outa th' pack.

277

You don't want anyone to see them new firearms with you out alone. Take your bedroll and some food jus' in case you get caught out overnight." At this point John hesitated while he thought over what he had said. "Ollie, do you have some money in your pouch?"

Ollie took his leather pouch that was folded over his belt and counted his coins.

"I have four dollars and fifty cents."

John took his pouch and counted out ten silver dollars, handing them to Ollie.

"Wrap these so they don't jingle, son; we don't want to attract some poor wandering bum to a young lad, out here with more money than most children see. How is our supplies gettin' on?" John asked.

"We could use some stuff, Dad. We're low on grain for the animals and we could use some potatoes 'n—I'll check what else before I leave."

"OK," John said, "leave th' grain for me and you can graze Ginger until you get to town, Sandy Hook I mean. Thet's th' closest place! Get what you need with thet money, son. Jus' get a receipt or mark it in your journal. By th' way, always do your journal entries away from folks; it might raise some thinkin' and cause someone to want to see thet book. Oh, and take some fishin' line and hooks, an' anythin' else you might need. I think thet's everythin' about preparin' to go.

"Now, what I need for you to do is go back to th' tracks and find thet Rebel camp. Make maps about where it is and any movements or information thet you think is important. Get to town and get some supplies. Anythin' you hear there thet seems important, write it down and we'll get it back to Captain Lyons. Bob and Mary McPherson are friends, and you can depend on them if you need to." John hesitated and it was plain to Ollie that he was getting very tired.

"Do you have any questions, son?"

"No, sir. If I think of any, I'll ask you in th' morning at breakfast time. We prob'ly should get some rest," he suggested, thinking more of John than himself.

"Good thought, Ollie. I'm really tired 'n sleepy."

John pulled over his bedroll with the aid of his new crutch, and within five minutes was in a deep sleep. Ollie cleaned up, stoked the fire, and decided to catch up on journal entries. He lit a lantern and picked up his journal and the tablet. He decided not to take the whole tablet with him, so he began to tear off some loose pages on which to draw maps. He flipped a page and noticed his dad's writing. John had copied a poem by William Cowper, and on the next page had written his poem-prayer. As Ollie read his dad's thoughts, he had to hold back the tears. He glanced over to his sleeping father and thought how much he loved and respected his dad.

After copying the prayer, he picked up his dad's Bible and began to read out of Proverbs. Then he prayed—for his dad, Cassie, Sergeant Damron, John Damron, Zeb and the soldiers he had met. Ollie also prayed for little Cindy Lou, Captain Lyons, and th' Birchets and ended with prayer for himself. He then began his journal work, starting with the day, time, and date: Tuesday, 8:00 P.M., May 13th, 1862.

Ollie enjoyed the responsibility his dad had given him in this scouting business. It made him feel as if he were contributing to the war effort for the Union cause and President Lincoln. Most of all he had been a big help to his dad. That piece of shrapnel would have worked its way out whether he had been on the trip with his dad or not. It would have been terrible if John had been alone when that happened. The wound was in a place that John could not have dealt with it himself. It was a big undertaking for such a young person, but Ollie felt good that his dad trusted and challenged him to do it.

It was still early enough to get some other things done after Ollie finished his journal entry of that day's events, so he went over to the pack and took out the musket. He took a supply of wadding, musket balls, and a full powder horn. The musket was a flintlock smoothbore weapon and accurate up to 150 yards in the hands of a marksman. Ollie was very proficient using this firearm; he had hunted with it even after his dad brought home his Sharps.

Ollie then checked the grain supply for the animals, the food, kerosene, and supplies in general. Ginger neighed at him, turning her head as if to ask for some attention. Ollie obliged by pouring sugar into his hand and allowing Ginger to help herself. He patted her a little and rubbed her nose and she was content. Ollie decided he had better turn in himself so he could attend to breakfast early for his sleeping patient.

Ollie was up before daylight because he had a distinct plan for breakfast. He took his musket and equipment and headed toward the old camp, where he had seen a hickory tree and a whole family of squirrels busy cutting on last year's hickory crop. He had watched the squirrels jumping from tree to tree, as well as running along the ground. Digging out the old musket fired up the hunting blood in Ollie, and also caused him to start thinking about a mouth-watering breakfast. He slipped quietly through the damp morning, being careful not to step on twigs. Before dawn he was in full view of the silhouette of the large hickory, and already he could hear the squirrels chattering and playing. It was too early to see them well. Ollie patiently sat back and waited until the daylight began to filter through the forest. He wasn't in a big rush, but he was hungry. In thirty minute's time, Ollie had fired four shots and had four squirrels ready to dress. He accomplished this on the way back to their camp, stopping by the branch, which was their water supply.

John was awakened by the first musket shot. When he saw that Ollie was out of his bedroll he knew what was going on. He stirred up the fire from the hot embers and put on some more dried tree branches. Soon he had a good breakfast fire going. Coffee fixings were nearby, so John had coffee brewing and water heating in the bean pot when Ollie returned with four plump dressed squirrels. He smiled at his dad as John spoke.

"I wondered how long you would go before you had to have a bit of wild game for food. You're a man after my own heart, Ollie."

Ollie just smiled and cut up the squirrels, dropping them into the bubbling water. He added salt and pepper and began to mix up a batter of water, flour, and butter, with seasoning. Soon the aroma of the fresh meat filled the air and Ollie backed the pot to a cooler spot, placing a couple of stones to lift it a bit. He dropped in chunks of batter with a spoon, and soon had a pot of fresh meat and dumplings. Ollie allowed the squirrels to cook until they were so tender the meat was falling off the bones. These two friends and scouts sipped on coffee and filled up on a scrumptious breakfast without much chatter, just enjoying the food and being together.

Breakfast over Ollie busied himself cleaning up and leaving things presentable for John, knowing his dad would not be able to get around easily. Before long Ginger was saddled, with the musket in the rifle boot and the revolver in his saddlebag. Ollie also included a couple of empty burlap sacks and two fifty-foot lengths of rope. He had fishing line, hooks and enough food for a couple of days. He left all the grain as his dad had requested, but did give Ginger a half-ration before they left. The last thing on Ollie's agenda was to change out of his buckskins into normal farm-boy clothes. He wore a cotton shirt, partially hidden by rough, well-worn overalls and brogan shoes that had more than a few miles on them. Ollie was still bareheaded; he had never cared too much for hats. He did have a coon-skin cap that his dad had cured-out and made for him, complete with pull-down flaps to keep his ears warm, and the ringed 'coon tail coming down the back, but he only wore it in winter when it was cold.

"Well, you look ready to take to the trail," John remarked, with a twinkle in his eye. He had been admiring his son as he put his things together. He was a pleasure to watch because he seldom missed an item.

"Now remember, Ollie, you ain't a Yankee or a Rebel; you're a country boy bent on hunting an' fishin'. You don't talk near as much as you listen and remember. Always remember—'cause everythin's important. You are a friend to everyone, unless thet person makes himself your enemy. Don't be defensive unless you are directly attacked, 'n if you are attacked, you strike th' first blow and make it do some damage. Lots of battles are won with only one blow bein' used. Who wins, sometimes jus' depends on who hits first."

Ollie shook hands with his dad, and then gave him a hug for good measure. As he hugged his dad, he couldn't help noticing that his dad was bareheaded, which was not usual. This reminded him that it had been too warm for his coonskin cap. Ollie made a mental note about this, before answering his dad.

"Thanks, Dad, I 'most always remember th' things you teach me, and it sure does help a lot sometimes. It keeps me out o' trouble," he said with a laugh. Then he mounted Ginger and headed southwest, toward where they had left off following the raiders' trail on Monday.

In a short time Ollie began to climb and he picked up the trail, which was still fresh enough, because it had not rained since Sunday. He realized he was crossing on the south side of the McPherson farmhouse; it was probably up the hill about half a mile. He made a mental note to draw some preliminary maps, showing Bob and Mary's farm as well as where John was holed up and their original Monday night camp location. He had the foresight to check the time before leaving, and he was deliberately riding Ginger at a normal stride; his dad was sure smart. That was why John had wanted his son to time Ginger walking the mile back and forth.

That way he could measure distance by just looking at his watch and keeping Ginger at a normal pace. Of course, it was just common sense if you knew how to think ahead. Ollie sure was bent on learning, and his dad was a good teacher.

The tracks led straight southwest and, although there were low-lying areas and grassy meadows here and there, most of the area was thick with forest. There were many trees native to the area, mostly various types of oak interspersed with black walnut, hickory, elm, and poplar. It was beautiful to see all the trees and the many animals he came across in their native habitat. Several times he came across deer and once the track of a bear near a stream, where the animal had probably been looking for fish.

Ollie lost track of the time, but felt it must be close to ten miles since he had left camp. When he looked at his watch it was 11:50 A.M. He shook his head at the ground he had covered and how time had slipped away. He made a notation, did some calculations and sure enough he had traveled about nine and a half miles, based on Ginger's gait and the time he left. He thought a minute and realized he would have to allow a little for times he slowed down for crossing a stream, dodging a rock formation and trees, but still it would not be less than nine miles, nor more than nine and a half.

He glanced at his compass; according to it he had not veered much off the steady southwest direction. That would mean that Sandy Hook would be due north from where he stood, but he didn't know how far, since he did not know how to figure how far south he had traveled. He was not hungry so he decided to keep on the trail for awhile; he was still living on the squirrel and dumplings from this morning.

He made his calculations, put down the new time, and continued for a good fifteen minutes before he started to see other tracks crossing the raiders' trail. These tracks had been made since the rain and, like the Rebels, they had trailed from over on Brushy

Creek. In a matter of minutes Ollie came to a halt. Suddenly there were too many tracks to keep up with, and most of them converged with the trail he had followed, so he knew he must be near the camp. Ollie figured it was time he left the trail so he turned south and allowed Ginger to pick her way through the trees, following a stream. There were no tracks here and Ollie could see he was climbing. Soon the stream rounded a bend into a level open area lush with grass surrounded by rocks and forest. It was a beautiful meadow and the sun was brilliant this warm day in May.

Dismounting, he began walking around the perimeter, leading Ginger, who was already sampling this fine grass. Ollie found a perfect campsite on the south end of the meadow, hidden from the open area and backed by a huge boulder. There was no shelter in the meadow, or even a cave, but there was a low place that dropped off at the base of the boulder; it would hide a mounted horse and rider from view of the large meadow, unless they were right on top of the rim. It looked as if a giant had dropped this massive boulder on the soft ground many years ago, making the indentation, then rolled it away leaving the hollow. Well, whatever had happened, it was made to order for Ollie so he unsaddled Ginger and took the bit out of her mouth. Leaving the bridle on and tying the reins up around her neck, he put hobbles on her front legs and turned her loose to graze.

Ollie ate a cold lunch of jerky and dried fruit then hid his saddlebag, bedroll, rifle, and supplies under the edge of the boulder so he could travel light. He kept only two silver dollars and fifty cents in his pouch and started off in a slow run, backtracking to the trail he had been following.

An hour later Ollie, hidden from view, was watching a bivouac area of a hundred Confederate soldiers, more or less. There were several campfires, with men huddled around talking and drinking coffee. There were rows of tents with muskets and rifles propped outside, military fashion. Some men were marching in close-order drill with a squad leader barking out commands; others were sitting around the tent enclosures talking and laughing. He could hear them, but was too far away to distinguish the words.

As he studied the camp, memorizing the layout, he noticed one tent with an awning of sorts angling out in front. Perhaps twenty-five feet in front of that tent was a homemade flagpole flying the Confederate flag. This tent was larger than the others and was, without a doubt, the commanding officer's headquarters. The soldiers' tents, made of dingy canvas that buttoned together at the top, were noticeably smaller; each would sleep two men. John had spoken about them before; they were called "dog tents," and they were assembled in two rows, four in a grouping. Ollie counted forty-four of the dog tents and two tents that were larger but similar in shape, as if to house several men for sleeping.

There was a corral at the far end with cows, steers, horses, and some sheep. From Ollie's location, it seemed as if they were partitioned off; no doubt some of them were the contraband taken from near Blaine Creek. *Maybe even those workhorses of the McPherson's were enclosed there,* thought Ollie.

The camp was in a good location, abundantly supplied with water from a stream almost as large as Blaine Creek. The campground was mostly bare ground, the underbrush and grass having been beaten down by the many feet of marching soldiers. The surrounding area was a meadow of lush grass encircled by forest. As the soldiers raised a cloud of dust in close-order drill, Ollie paced off the entire area and studied the camp. He looked it over from every angle, but stayed out of sight of the guards and remained unobserved by anyone in camp.

With all these figures stored in his head he wanted to get to his campsite as quickly as possible to record his information. Taking a more direct route this time, he cut off at least two miles compared to about five miles following the stream. As he got closer to his camp, he remembered a deep water hole, full of fish, that he noticed earlier. As he neared the stream, he cut a slender sapling about six feet long and sharpened the point until it was a dangerous weapon—dangerous for the fish, especially with Ollie holding the other end.

The sun was not out of sight yet when this eleven-year-old boy, with pant legs rolled up, waded silently into knee-deep water, stalking a big one. Quick as a cat, Ollie nabbed a large bass when it swam within three feet of him. It was speared and thrown on the upper bank high and dry before it knew what had happened. Ollie captured it while still flopping in the grass and, putting his fingers through the gills, carried it back to the camp. Ginger spied him from a hundred yards off and came to him as fast as her hobbles would allow her, letting out a little whinny of pleasure, making Ollie feel like he had a real homecoming welcome.

Ollie cleaned the bass, which dressed out at about three pounds, he guessed, and soon had fire going and a potato in the coals. They were getting low on potatoes so Ollie brought only two with him and left the remaining ones for his dad. Before long Ollie was dining on fish, cooked on the same spear that had captured it, and baked potato with salt and pepper, washing it all down with cool water from his canteen. He set up his lantern before the last light disappeared and curried Ginger, tethered close by. He spread out his bedroll and began to work in his journal, recording his findings of the day; copying everything twice, except for the maps. One copy was in the journal; the other was for Captain Lyons.

Ollie included maps of the camp site, McPherson's farm, the trail they followed, the place he was now camping and the Rebel camp, including tents, officer's quarters and the other larger tents. He included the corral and a brush area in the center of the camp, which looked about 20 feet by 20 feet. It was a type of shelter consisting of about 16 cut trees tied together at the top with smaller trees, and covered with brush and branches on the top. It looked like an area for shade, or eating, maybe both. It took several hours of painstaking work for Ollie to complete his maps, and he was proud of his work.

Tired after a hard day of riding, walking, planning and writing, Ollie was ready to turn in. He placed the Colt by his head and was soon asleep, thinking about his dad but really not worried. His dreams, however, were on a totally different subject. He saw himself stalking fish with a spear and he saw a Confederate officer grinning at him as he pointed at a burlap sack that was jumping and wiggling. He saw himself bend over, pull up the bottom of the sack, and bunches of flopping fish tumbled out of the sack. Suddenly, Ollie awakened with a start. Ginger was close by and looked at him in surprise, twitching her ears in the lantern light that Ollie had left burning low; allowing just enough light to see the campsite.

"Well, Ginger, I guess th' Lord jus' showed me my plan for tomorrow. I'm going to go to the Rebel camp, bringing a gift. You'll have th' whole day to fatten up." Ollie turned over and slept undisturbed until dawn.

Finishing off a portion of bass left from supper, along with some dried fruit and nuts, he started his day with a nourishing breakfast. He placed all his belongings back as before, making sure they would stay dry if it rained. He sharpened his spear, took a burlap sack, and headed back to the fishing hole. In less than one hour Ollie had twenty fish, each of them a pound or more. Since he would have to carry them himself, he stayed away from the really big ones. He left Ginger to gorge on the fine grass, then headed for the Rebel camp.

Ollie Burke came into the Confederate camp on the main trail as bold as a lion, carrying a sack that had become heavier and heavier as he finished the last mile of his journey. The guard yelled at him, but let him pass, seeing it was only a kid. He laughed and shouted something obscene toward the camp.

A Rebel soldier approached him. "What's goin' on there, kid? Whatcha doin' here an' where ya headin'?"

Ollie put his sack down in the dust, wiped the perspiration from his brow with a sleeve, and answered the gathering throng. "Wal—I wuz agoin' right here! I wuz hankerin' for some grub—an' I hain't actually headin' for nowhere." Ollie stumbled with his answer.

"Well, Judd, I guess he told you," one of the soldiers shouted, and everybody laughed. There was back-slapping and knee-slapping and Judd joined in the humor, returning with, "Whatcha got in th' sack, kid? Somethin' alive looks like!

Ollie carried the sack over to a grassy spot and dumped the fish on the grass—just as in his dream. Some were still alive and flopping around. The Confederate soldiers gathered around, their eyes widening at the sight of fresh fish. "I'll take two, lightly buttered, please!" one joked. Ollie took in all this excitement and finally spoke. "Ya see fellers, there's more 'n I can eat, an' I jus' tho't I'd share 'em with you'uns—if'n ya want to, now." All of a sudden an aisle began to open up when a tall, clean-shaven captain interfered. The men became very quiet and Ollie found himself looking into the brown eyes of a very serious man. He looked at the men, looked back at Ollie, looked at the fish, then spoke politely to Ollie.

My name is Captain Graham Rutledge, and I am commanding officer at this camp. What is your name sonny-boy?"

Ollie had no way of knowing that Captain Rutledge was a very austere officer, a southern aristocrat from South Carolina. He was the son of a prominent plantation owner who raised tons of cotton and owned 125 slaves. He was the epitome of southern aristocracy and a former aide-de-camp to General Marshal Humphrey who had led the southern raid on Middle Creek. Captain Rutledge was one of two officers in General Marshal's command who was born into wealth. He was accustomed to having his every whim and order obeyed. Along with Lieutenant Martin Jones, of this command, he was a graduate of West Point and had a spotless military record.

"My name is Ollie Thomas, sir." Ollie licked his lips nervously.

"And where are you from, Master Thomas?"

"I'm from over close ta th' Big Sandy, near Fallsburg." Ollie answered truthfully.

Ollie had not planned ahead for such questioning and he wanted to stay as near the truth as he could, but he realized he might have to make up a story. He liked the looks of this young officer, very impressive in his uniform. Ollie waited for the next question, preparing to sort of make up his answer as he went along. *Boy, the spy business is enough to make a person a nervous wreck*, he thought.

"Now, Tom—you did say your name was Tom, didn't you?" queried the captain, trying to trick Ollie.

"No, sir—didn't say nary sech thing. I said Ollie, that's my name. My other name is Thomas, but nobody calls me anythin' but Ollie. You can call me thet too, if'n ya want to."

"Excuse me, Ollie. I guess I misunderstood. Now tell me, what are you doing clear over here so far away from home."

"Fishin'," Ollie answered wryly, as if that explained everything. Ollie was determined not to make this easy.

"Now, Ollie, don't tell me you came all the way, some forty or fifty miles just to fish, and by yourself?" continued the officer.

"Didn't say I come over here alone, I jus said I was fishin'. Anyone can plainly see thet that's what I'm doin'—there's the fish!"

The southern officer, used to being respected and catered to, was beginning to lose patience with this exasperating youngster. "Now listen here, young man. Tell me who you came with and what you are doing in this camp with all these fish—and right now!"

"Well, ya don't hafta git so all-fired put-out 'bout it. I'll tell ya, an' I'll jus' pick up my fish and go. I comed over ta this area with my uncle, who is doin' some cattle tradin', and he jus' turned me loose ta fish 'n sech until he got ready ta go back. I comed ta this camp 'cause you was here, and th' fishin place is over there." Ollie pointed to the creek. "And I brought 'em here 'cause I thought you'd want some too, and maybe I could have 'em cooked."

"If you caught them, where is your line and pole?" A crimson flush crept up the captain's face, indicating his anger.

Ollie sighed and put his hands on his hips, which infuriated the captain.

"Anyone can see I speared 'em. Jus' look at the fish 'n you can tell," Ollie said, disgusted.

"Do you mean to tell me you speared all these fish yourself?"

Impudently, Ollie didn't answer! He just bent over and started putting the fish back in the sack. He was mumbling to himself, radiating contempt, when a not-too-kind hand took his shoulder and abruptly turned him around. Ollie wrested himself free from the captain. The men stood back aghast as Ollie showed defiance to their officer in charge, who had become tired of looking bad before his men—and at the hands of a dumb hick country boy.

"Ya keep your han's offen me. I'm takin' my fish 'n leavin'. It 'peers ta me you'uns jus' ain't friendly. Ya don't know my name after I tell ya. Ya don't believe me when I say I caught th' fish. An' ya ain't got no biz'ness askin' me a whole bunch o' dumb questions," Ollie blurted at the captain. This boy humiliated Captain Graham Rutledge and he had to hold back his rage to save face with his men.

"Boy—I have in mind placing you into custody just for your insolence. You show no respect for my rank or my position." The captain wasn't going to let this upstart have the last word.

Ollie knew he was taking a chance in going so far, but he was in too deep now to back down, so he continued!

"Your rank don't mean anythin' ta me, 'n you ain't th' sheriff o' these parts ta put me under no custody. If'n you lay a hand on me my uncle will be over here ta take you ta hand. He knows where I am and will come a lookin'," Ollie bluffed. "In fact, I gotta mind o' gittin' my musket 'n shootin' ya myself."

At this the men laughed, but instantly hushed when the captain glared at them. He had taken all he was going to take from this disrespectful, good-for-nothing hick. The captain figured Ollie had built himself a trap—and now it was payback time!

"Oh, I see—you shoot a musket too, do you?" He addressed Ollie with a phony smile. "Sergeant Judd, bring this boy a long gun and ammunition."

He turned back to Ollie. "Well, young man, I'm going to call your bluff. We'll just see how well you shoot a musket!"

Ollie was now beginning to have fun with this game. It was totally out of character for him to argue and infuriate adults, whether they were of Union or Confederate persuasion. He would not act this way to a private, let alone an officer, if he did not want to accomplish a purpose. He knew that once he had the attention of this officer he could make him like him as well as be angry at him. Right now this was a fun game to Ollie. He could always apologize later, so he continued his charade.

"Thet's jus' fine with me," Ollie said, not backing down one inch.

Sergeant Judd was the man Ollie had first encountered when the guard let him pass. He was a burley man with a salt-and-pepper beard and hair to match. His sideburns were long and his hair edged from under his Rebel forage cap. He had the cadet gray trousers and wore suspenders over his undershirt. Like many of the on-lookers he was without his uniform shirt. He was enjoying the show this farm boy was putting on at their captain's expense. The sergeant returned with a musket and stood waiting for further orders. Captain Rutledge spit out his orders with a smug expression on his face, assured he was going to best this smart aleck kid.

"All right, Sergeant, give Mr. Ollie Thomas three balls of ammunition and the other equipment to allow him to fire a musket."

Ollie received the gun, the ammunition, powder horn. The sergeant backed off with a grin. Ollie looked up to the captain. "Well, who do you want me ta shoot?"

This time the captain laughed with the men, and shook his head. Turning again to the sergeant, he said, "Judd, take three of those food cans with light-colored labels and place them on that old log over there," gesturing to the creek bank about fifty yards or so away. "Sit them side by side."

"All right, Mr. Ollie. We will shoot not 'who', but 'what'. I want to see if you can hit those cans—or for that matter any single one of them. My guess is you can't even load that musket, much less shoot it and hit something with it," he laughed unkindly.

"All right, sir," Ollie replied, showing a little more respect. "Looks purty easy ta me, if'n ya want holes in them cans, holes it will be!"

More quickly than anyone expected or could imagine, Ollie methodically loaded the musket, aimed, and fired three times, hitting each can dead-center, and sending it flying over the bank. Ollie accomplished this in less than two minutes, which was better than any man in his command. It was quiet, except for some under-the-breath whisperings.

Captain Graham Rutledge took off his big hat, strolled over to a stool, sat down, and, for a minute, didn't say a thing. Captain Rutledge was a good man, even though a defiant one, but he had just undergone the most exasperating morning of his life at the hands of a hick country kid. He had been bested and the only thing he knew to do now was confess it as diplomatically as he could manage. He sent the sergeant over to examine the cans, raised his head and looked at Ollie.

"Son, do you want to enlist in the army?" It was half in jest and half serious; but it was all the men needed to start laughing and coming up to congratulate Ollie and shake his hand. Shortly Judd came back with the targets. Every one of them was hit in the exact middle. The captain suddenly shouted, "Sergeant Judd. Get some men to clean these fish and cook 'em; divide them as far as they'll go. Let's have a fish-fry."

"Yes, suh." Judd started barking orders before coming over to make Ollie officially welcome. Ollie remembered his dad's words, "First things first."

"Jus' a minute, Sarge. I got me somethin' to do." He walked over to the captain and stuck out his hand.

"Captain, sir. I didn't mean ta be disrespectin' to ya, but I guess I jus' got riled when ya wouldn't take my fish 'n fix 'em. I jus' want to 'polagize," Ollie said sheepishly.

"That's all right, Ollie. I shouldn't have been so suspicious of you, but you know, we don't have farm lads bringing us fish every day. Apology accepted, young man." He accepted Ollie's extended hand. Formalities over, the captain strolled back to his tent with his hands folded behind his back, still shaking his head.

Ollie spent most of the day in the Rebel camp joking with the men, but mostly just listening. The cooks fried up the fish and, although there was not enough for everyone to have a meal, all that wanted had a taste. Sergeant Judd took it upon himself to be Ollie's guide and treated him like royalty; introducing him first to this one and then that. There were four other officers on hand; two lieutenants and two 2nd lieutenants. They were bunked in the larger tent, as Ollie had supposed. There was a sergeant who was an aide and orderly to the captain, while Sergeant Judd was the sergeant major of the command.

Another sergeant was in charge of supplies, and Ollie learned that this was the man, Sergeant David Runyan, that he and his dad had been tracking. He was the leader at the skirmish. Ollie learned that two of the men with Sergeant Runyan in the raiding detail were local boys out of Sandy Hook. Ollie studied them, so he could recognize them if he ever saw them again. One was a man in his thirties; bald in front with sandy hair. In fact, they called him Sandy, Private Sandy Tibbett. The other, Sam Blainey, also a private, was a surly man about five-feet ten-inches tall with dark brown hair and a sweeping mustache, who never said much but always seemed to have a scowl on his face. Ollie learned that these men went to and from Sandy Hook at their leisure with Captain Rutledge's blessing. Most of the time they dressed in civilian clothes, gathering information and acting as informants for the camp.

Captain Rutledge was under the command of General Marshal Humphrey, who was several days away by courier. The captain was put in place with these soldiers to give the Confederates a toehold into Louisa as a prime target. The reason, of course, was easy enough to guess. Louisa had access to the Big Sandy River, which flowed down to the Ohio River and, finally, to the Mississippi. It was a gateway into the north.

The men visited easily in front of Ollie and he picked up recent war news. Just three or four days ago a large ship called the *Monitor*, made of iron from the north, had fought it out with an iron ship from the south called the *Merrimack*. They evidently fought each other to a standstill and the south had to back off and destroy its own vessel because of the advancing Union Army ashore. This happened off the coast of Virginia.

Strasburg, Kentucky was the scene of another big battle, according to the camp talk. This battle was still continuing, even now. Confederate General Nathaniel Banks was confronting some federal general. Naturally the camp was enthusiastic about the outcome for the South.

Ollie listened to these men in earnest, hearing about their battles and prospective victories. He found he could like them all, and prayed he would never have to confront them in battle. The camp consisted of good men who cared about the outcome of the war, and men who were indifferent and just putting in their time. These soldiers were men just like you would find in any given crowd in this war.

The talk about the defeat of Sergeant Runyan and his men at Brushy Creek was still being relived throughout the camp. Sergeant Runyan still could not fully understand what had happened.

"We had the enemy cornered, dead to rights, and were slipping in for the kill, when all of a sudden there were warning shots—shots, at least, that warned the enemy—who then went into action. The rain started coming at that time—just bad timing," Runyan said. "We still had the upper hand and crossfire, and—then—out of nowhere something started killing off my men who had pinned down the Yanks."

"You mean some*one* started killing off your men—not some*thing*. Great day, man, you talk like it was a spook or something like that," Judd remarked.

"Well, what would you think?" asked Runyan. "No one saw anything, no one heard anything—except for th' shots—and at least three of my men were killed outright. I tell you it wasn't human!"

"Well, some person was out there and was good enough to slip in on you and was dead shot enough—like Ollie here—to pick off your men, right, Ollie?" Judd said with a grin and winking at Ollie.

"I guess so, Sarge, if'n ya say so, although I don't rightly know what you'uns are talkin' about." Ollie shrugged his shoulders.

The subject was dropped, and that pleased Ollie. That was just too close a guess for comfort.

Ollie wandered around the camp, scrutinizing the animals in the corral, where he noticed a large team of horses that looked like domestic draft animals. They had the unmistakable harness marks of workhorses, were gray in color, and stood out from the smaller animals. This team was probably the McPhersons' stolen animals. He noticed the guard's location; the way the rail fence was constructed, and tried to figure out the easiest way to enter the corral unseen. Ollie was trying to work out a plan, without appearing obvious, to liberate the McPhersons' team and return them to their rightful owners. He didn't want to be noticed, so he turned and headed back toward Judd's tent.

Having left his dad's watch back at camp, Ollie had to estimate the time of day. Some of the men were having their noon meal so he figured the time between twelve and one P.M. He noticed that the men all attended to their own needs, including cooking.

Sergeant Judd offered to show him the items an average soldier carried in his pack. From what Ollie had seen so far, this was sort of a ragged army in terms of dress and private gear. Obviously, he did not make this unkind observation to his host. A man in this outfit was fortunate if he had one blanket, two or three tin cups of varying sizes, a metal skillet, a ladle, a fold-up spoon and fork, a mess tin, and a small metal nut bowl. All men had a wooden box or someplace where they stored personal gear such as soap, a shaving kit, and such.

They were issued hardtack, which looked like a cracker, and beans or whatever edibles they happened to come across in the way of contraband. The men had candles for the evening and a small tent lantern, if they were lucky. The candleholders resembled a bell-shaped brass base with a tack projecting from the top to hold the candle. Most men had a tobacco pouch of cloth or leather.

A lot of pipes were made of oak or hickory branches, with a hollow stem made from some type of reed. All the men carried matches in their personal effects. Aside from weapons, this was their gear.

Ollie felt it was an education, but it left an empty feeling in the pit of his stomach to know how little these men existed on. Despite this, he did not hear much complaining. In fact there were men sitting around singing hymns that Ollie recognized and joined in singing. Other songs were ballads about sweethearts, tents, camping, and war, most of which he had never heard before. Men maintained various postures during their leisure time, reclining, squatting, or standing while drinking weak coffee, herb tea, or some other variation of heated brew. Some were writing letters home as they tried to pass the time waiting for orders.

Ollie was enjoying this close-up look at a soldier's camp-life. There seemed to be little difference between the foot soldiers and the officers, except that the officers had more luxuries and more-or-less stayed to themselves in a social setting. It was about three o'clock when Sergeant Judd sought Ollie out at the officers' tent and asked if he would like to help in a daily camp project. Ollie smiled from ear to ear. "I'd be happy ta help out. What-cha want me ta do?"

"About this time each day we water th' stock in th' crick. Would ya like ta help us?" the sergeant asked, knowing that all boys liked to be around animals.

Ollie wasted no time in giving an excited whoopee.

"Boy-ee, I sure would, Sarge. What can I do ta help?"

The sergeant sent him off with two men, who recruited eight others. Ollie followed them toward the corral. He soon saw why they needed so many men. There were about twenty horses, as many cattle, and a dozen or so sheep. They did not tie them individually, but let them go to water as a group.

The corral was built of split rails with slender slide-poles as the gates. There was a gate on the meadow side and between each partition in the corral; but what Ollie had missed when he looked before was on the downhill side facing the creek, was that each section had a gate that opened toward the creek. This made watering the animals easier. They simply opened the partitions one at a time by sliding the poles back. One man would go into the pen and drive the livestock toward the gate while the other men formed two lines to the creek, allowing the animals to pass through to the water. One man would be the point man at the water's edge to avert any animal from trying to cross over. The creek was perhaps fifty feet or more across at this point, and it was shallow enough to wade. Ollie stood in one of the lines on the end toward the water. After the animals drank, the men called out.

"Hi-yah—git—ho there—git—along now!" and whatever else came to mind to yell at them to keep them moving back to the pen. It was a good system and Ollie was elated because it gave him an idea. Yes, it was the beginning of a good plan for an eleven-year-old Yankee spy—for, in fact, that was his role now. Ollie observed the bank across the creek, making a mental picture of the heavy forest that came right down to the edge of the water. It was time for Ollie to say his good-byes; he had a plan to execute. On the way back through camp he talked to one of the soldiers on the watering detail.

"By th' way, Randy, how far would ya say it was ta Sandy Hook?" Ollie innocently asked.

"Oh, I'd say about five or six miles—thet away." He pointed in a northerly direction.

Ollie tried to seem casual, but he was racing inside. He knew he had a mission to accomplish while he still had light so he went from campfire to campfire saying good-bye to those he had met, and heard a welcome extended from one and all, "Y'all come back now, d'ya hear?"

NINETEEN

The Moon and Stars
Rule the Night

O LLIE HAD A LOT TO ACCOMPLISH BY NIGHTFALL AND HE RAN ALL THE way from the Rebel camp. He met Ginger in the high grass of the meadow where she had been left to do her grazing. By 4:30 Ollie was mounted with all his gear. He leaned down to Ginger's ear. "Now, listen up, girl. We have to burn up some of that fat you been storing up th' last day or so; so let's make some travel time."

Ollie chuckled because Ginger seemed to understand his urgency. As she felt the loose reins, she took off so quickly Ollie almost lost his balance. The summer breeze hit him in the face and he felt an exhilarating rush of excitement as he steered Ginger toward the trail along the bed of the stream. Soon Ollie reached the crossroads where all the tracks converged and where he had left the trail yesterday. He headed due north toward Sandy Hook. Judging from the tracks, this was a well-traveled path.

Ginger covered the miles quickly. Within an hour they were coming into a community that was not unlike Blainetown, with a livery stable, a feed store, a cafe that seemed to be a local meeting place, a post office in the general store as well as a tavern or two, and a few other stores. Ollie picked the livery stable to ask his question. He approached a tall bearded man in a felt hat with dirty denim jeans. The man looked up, smiling. "Hi-dy do, young feller. What can I do fer you?"

"I'm kinda new in these parts. I'm a wonderin' if you could point me to the McPherson farm."

"If'n you mean ol' Bob McPherson, I sure can. Just folly th' main street here through town thet-away and make a left jus' past th' eatin' place and head up thet trail—oh, about five or six miles, I'd say. It's not a road, mind ya, jus' a sort of wagon trail. You kinfolks of his'n?" the man asked.

"No, sir. Jus' a friend who wants to say hello."

"Well, he 'n Mary will be right glad to see ya. It gits kinda lonely out there since th' war; all th' young folks gone 'n all. Tell him Jim Henderson says to say howdy. He'll know who ya mean."

"Much obliged, Mr. Henderson. I'll sure be givin' him your howdy. Thanks for th' directions." Ollie turned Ginger and was on his way. Ginger's canter was a mile-eating gait and she could go for hours with this stride. About an hour later Bob and Mary were surprised to see the "spelunker" man's son rein up at the gate. It was getting on near seven o'clock, so Bob had the chores finished and was sitting on the porch with Mary.

"Well, I'll be," the farmer remarked. "Ollie, what in th' world are you doin' here? An' comin' from thet direction, too. I sure am pleased to see ya, but this is a surprise."

Ollie ground tied Ginger, came up to the porch, and sat on the steps while Mary went right in to get him a glass of cool tea. Ollie welcomed the drink and said first off, "Jim Henderson in town said to tell you howdy for him. He was askin' 'bout you folks."

Because Ollie was still working to a schedule, he had to cut his visiting time. He came right to his point. "I need your help, Mr. McPherson, and I need this help so I can—help you! First off, are the horses that were taken from you a heavy duty matchin' pair of dapple gray?"

"Well, thet sure describes 'em. How'd you know, boy?"

"Well, I think I know where they are, and there might be a chance on you gittin' 'em back. But right now I need you to jus' listen because I'm runnin' out of daylight." Bob looked at Mary and back to Ollie and nodded.

"OK, Mr. McPherson. My dad is about a mile and a half from here and I don't have time to check in with him. I left him gettin' well from an injured leg and he still can't get around jus' yet. I need you to go to him and tell him about this meeting and what I'm sayin' and tell him not to worry about me. He's in a big cave near th' top of th' hill; jus' ten minutes up from the stream. He has his horse and a mule there and is jus' mostly gettin' well. I need you to go do that as soon as I leave."

"Consider it tended to, son; I know thet place very well and I'll take him some milk 'n eggs. Mary go git 'em ready, honey, will ya?" Mary nodded and scurried off to the kitchen.

"Please tell my dad that I'll see him by tomorrow evening with a lot to tell him. He'll understand what I mean. Now, what I need from you is two bridles—th' ones you used for th' team you had, if'n you still have them. I also need some of their favorite mix thet you fed 'em; somethin' they'll be able to smell and recognize. If you have enough of that mix, put twenty pounds or so in a sack for me. I'll need that for my plan."

Bob went off to get it right away.

Ollie topped up his canteen from the McPherson well and watered Ginger at the trough. Bob was back soon with a sack of grain

301

mix, smelling of molasses, and two well-worn but serviceable bridles. There were two nose feeders with a measure of grain in each one and a third measure in a bucket.

"For your horse before ya head out," Bob said with a smile.

"Ginger'll sure thank you for that, Mr. McPherson," Ollie said as he put the bucket under her nose.

Mary came back with a bundle for Bob and one for Ollie.

"Somethin' fer you to nibble on when you git th' time, son. I know you'll be hungry when you stop fer a spell."

"You've been more than helpful, folks, and I must be off. Oh—one more thing, if you happen to wake up some time before morning with strange noises in your barn, don't come out with a shotgun, It'll jus' be me bringin' in your team. By th' way, what's your horse's names?"

After glancing again at his wife, Bob said, "Th' darker one I call Mike and th' other one is Dick—'n if you come back here with 'em, I think we'll run you fer sheriff."

With that, Ollie was on Ginger with his goods and she was off at a canter; taking the same trail back toward town. He pulled out his watch. It was 7:15. Still more than an hour before dark.

Ollie ended up skirting Sandy Hook to the south for he didn't want to be seen riding through town just as it turned dark. He headed over to the trail, slowing down a bit as visibility diminished. *The time between dusk and the lighting of the moon and stars is the darkest time*, Ollie recalled. He knew the moon and stars were up in their orbits all the time, but he had a vivid imagination and liked to picture God sending angels out to turn on the lights of the heavens to light the way by night. It always gave him a good feeling knowing that God was watching over him and giving him light for his path in the night.

It was nine o'clock before he stopped Ginger and dismounted. He knew he was nearing the north side of the creek that flowed past the Confederate camp. Ollie left the trail, entering the much darker forest, where he used his instinct to feel his way along. Within thirty minutes he began seeing campfires flickering through the trees. He tied Ginger to a tree, making sure her hooves were clear of twigs and breakable branches as she moved around. He took the bridles, the sack of grain mix as well as the two nose-feeders and, sticking his food bundle under his arm, began maneuvering himself stealthily through the trees until he was in line with the corral on the other side of the creek. He then settled down for the supper that Mary had prepared for him.

She had put in some crisp fried chicken, two boiled eggs, some cleaned raw carrots, and some big biscuits. Ollie thoroughly enjoyed the feast. It made him think of that big meal Aunt Milly had made for them just before they left the Birchets' farm, which then led him to think about Cindy Lou, Wiley, Rhoda and Eliza. Pretty, pretty Eliza. Goodness, he wished he were older. Well now, Susan was more his age and it sure wouldn't hurt any to think on her. Putting these thoughts aside, he decided to focus on the business at hand. It would be late before he could attempt any move on the corral. He'd have to be sure the men were all asleep except for guards. He decided to pray and then take a short nap.

Ollie prayed that God would give him guidance, protect him, the animals, and also the enemy. He wasn't there to hurt; only take back something that did not rightfully belong to these men. He asked God to forgive him if this was wrong, but, in his mind, it was only doing what was right to return something those older folks needed. He asked God to bless his dad and everybody else: Cassie, Cindy Lou, the Birchets and, last of all, himself. He leaned up against the tree and soon was asleep.

When Ollie awoke it seemed like he had been asleep for only a few minutes, but it was midnight according to his watch, which he could see well by moonlight. He noticed the campfires were down to a glow of embers. *Now is the time,* he thought as he scooped up the food leftovers so as not to leave a trace for someone to find. He raked his fingers through the leaves and grass where he had rested, to give the area an undisturbed look. Then he picked up the bridles and the grain and moved silently through the trees toward the water. He had noticed earlier that there was one place that was easier to descend because the bank incline was not as steep. Once he found that spot he took off his shoes and, tying the rawhide strings together, swung them around his neck.

Working his way carefully to the water's edge, he put the bundle of supper leavings into the water and allowed it to be carried swiftly down stream. Not bothering to roll up his trousers, Ollie waded into the cold water and was soon up to his waist; holding the grain, bridles and feeders high to keep them dry. There was no sound except for the water rippling around him as he slowly made his way, feeling each step to insure his footing and keep from falling. He heard the noises of the cattle and sheep, and occasional movements of the horses from the corral. This was his greatest concern—that the animals themselves would give him away. The guard could not see him from his location in front of the corral. When he reached the incline leading up to the corral watering gates, he stood motionless and allowed the animals to get used to his presence.

He could already make out their shapes as he inched closer. The horses were in the middle section and the sheep were in the end section away from the camp. After five minutes or so, Ollie maneuvered himself within five feet of the horses. Some of them came to the fence and looked him over as if expecting something, but they remained silent, which, in Ollie's experience, was a miracle in itself. Either God was working out his prayer request, or these animals were familiar with so many men it didn't bother them to see a mere boy. Whatever the reason, Ollie thanked God for it!

He could not see over the backs of the horses, so Ollie put down his gear, including his shoes, and crept over to the sheep pen for a better view. When he arrived on hands and knees in back of the sheep pen he slowly raised his head and saw the guard on the opposite end, in front of the cattle, leaning back against the rails smoking a pipe. He glanced back at the cattle and straightened up as if to yawn. Ollie could see no rifle or musket—not that it made any difference, but Ollie just did not want to be seen at all. He hunkered back down behind the sheep. *It would be great if I had a diversion to take the attention of the guard elsewhere.* After another five minutes, he arose to see the guard headed off toward the camp's outhouse area. *God is still helping,* Ollie thought, and he almost said out loud, "Praise the Lord!"

Now for the diversion. Ollie quietly slid into the sheep pen and worked his way through the animals to the front, quickly untying some knots in the rawhide ties on the lower rails. He slid two rails aside to leave an opening and pushed two ewes out into the campground. The first one out immediately went leaping toward the grass meadow. The second larger ewe bleated then kicked up her heels and went leaping across the campground. He quickly edged out another ewe and a ram; soon others were exploring the hole to freedom, and Ollie backed behind the pen, returning to the horses just in time. The guard let out an oath when he saw the sheep wandering all over, then ran around trying to catch them. The guard was not the ideal shepherd, but started loudly calling to the animals.

"Here sheepie, sheepie, sheepie—dad gum it, come here you woolly critters." The sheep ignored him. They were bleating, leaping, kicking up their cloven hooves, and grazing the tender grass. The ram just stood there looking at the other sheep, watching the guard, and looked like he was trying to decide whether to have a good time or do something constructive.

Ollie worked fast. He located Mike and Dick and began to bait the horses out with handfuls of grain. He had slid the poles to open the gate, leaving enough room for one animal at a time. Soon, Mike, the larger of the two, came within arm's reach and Ollie baited him with some of the familiar grain, which he immediately recognized. After a handful, Ollie slipped the bridle over his head, buckled it, and eased on the nosebag. As he led him out it was an easy matter to have Dick follow. He led the McPherson team into the water while he threw some handfuls of feed on the bank to bait the other horses.

One by one the horses came out of the gate, eating the feed. Ollie picked up his shoes and forded the creek with the two horses. Climbing the bank on the other side, he could hear the guard trying to round up the sheep, making enough noise to wake the whole camp; and sure enough, he did. All kinds of bad language was coming from the tents, mostly aimed at the guard, as men were coming out of their sleep in their bare feet and underclothes. From his elevation across the creek, Ollie could see what was going on and just had to stop and watch; it was like a stage performance. By this time the sheep were all out in front and the horses were all out on the waterside. Some horses crossed the creek; some were in the creek; and still others were galloping across the meadow.

The captain wandered out and the way he was dressed was an exhibition. Captain Graham Rutledge was wearing his officer's high-crowned hat, his underclothes and, instead of his military boots, he had pulled on some kind of lace-up shoes. The moon was so bright Ollie could even make out the laces. Ollie had to hold in his laughter until it hurt; he thought he was going to burst. The officer shouted some orders, and men were running to answer his command.

The captain bent over to tie a shoelace, and the guardian ram evidently made a decision—he was going to do something constructive. The ram bleated, threw up some dirt with his front hooves, and was off like a shot out of a cannon. He hit his target precisely where he aimed, and Captain Graham Rutledge went sailing about ten feet in the air. Ollie had a fit. He was rolling on the ground and tears were flowing down his face. But he had to maintain silence. He finally stood up, looked, and sure enough, the ram was still standing where the captain began his flying lesson.

Ollie put on his shoes, left Mike and Dick a minute involved in heavy duty eating from their nosebags, and slipped down the bank to remove any traces of his bare feet in the soft mud. He was still holding back the laughter, but he had to get his mind off of what he had witnessed in order to accomplish his mission. He quickly led the team over grass to where Ginger was tied. He slung the remaining feed over Ginger's saddle horn and was off toward Sandy Hook, leading the McPherson team. "Boy, God sure helped us out of that one, Ginger." He laughed out loud with the picture of that whole rebel camp in a midnight uproar, chasing sheep and horses all over the place. *I sure hope our friend Judd don't find out I did it. It will totally destroy his faith in me,* and he began laughing all over again.

It was past three before Ollie led Mike and Dick into their own barn. It was plain to see these work animals knew their home and were elated to be there. They neighed, snorted, and stomped up a cloud of dust and straw. Soon a smiling Bob McPherson came down the path from the house swinging a lantern, with a jubilant Mary right behind him.

"Well, I'll be—well, I'll be—well, I'll be," Bob kept saying over and over.

"You'll be what? Bob McPherson. That's what you'll be." Mary laughed, petting Dick on the nose.

Ollie just stood there grinning, elated at the happiness that God had brought to these two dear people.

Bob was beside himself and tears brimmed as he looked to Mary, then back to the team, and then to Ollie.

"Well, sir," he said finally, "John Burke said to me last evening, 'If Ollie said you may be seein' your horses before mornin', you better fork some hay in their mangers, fer as sure as I'm John Burke—they'll be there come mornin'.' And, sure enough, here they are!"

Ollie was a little embarrassed and lowered his head, saying nothing. He just continued to hold Ginger and stroke her nose.

He spent the rest of the night with the McPhersons and, after a good breakfast of ham and eggs, biscuits and gravy with home fries, he spent an hour on the porch catching up on journal entries and maps. He drew a new map, including Sandy Hook in relationship to the Rebel camp and the McPherson farm. He also jotted down the information he'd picked up at the Confederates camp. Just before he left for Sandy Hook, Bob came out to thank him again and visit a moment while Mary was still in the kitchen cleaning up after breakfast.

"Ollie, your dad said his laig was feelin' so good he could run a foot race with thet pretty horse of his'n." This produced a big smile from Ollie. Bob continued, "He accounted it was more th' prayer you prayed fer him 'n th' Lord's healin' than anythin' else. Fine man, thet paw of your'n. By th' way, you can forget about th' taters you're goin' ta git in town. I'm takin' him a good supply of taters, a ten-day supply of feed fer your livestock and a passel o' eggs. Thet's th' least I can do after what you did fer me. Say, tell me about thet, how'd it happen thet you comed across Mike 'n Dick?"

Ollie told how he was out looking for caves and such while John was laid up and he stumbled across the Confederate camp. The Rebs gave him the run of the camp and showed him around, him just being a kid and all. And when he saw the corral, he noticed the two draft animals among the riding horses.

"They stood out like a black snake at a frog convention. I jus' decided on liberating those two animals and save the Confederates a feeding expense."

Ollie and Bob had a laugh about this. Ollie went on to tell him how he turned the sheep loose to cause a diversion, and how funny it looked when the whole camp aroused to sheep and horses running every which way. They laughed some more, then Ollie turned solemnly to Bob.

"Mr. McPherson, I jus' need to ask you one awful big favor. I would jus' as soon no people should know 'bout th' part I had in bringin' th' team home."

"Ollie, I hear whut yore sayin' and so far as anyone knows— why, Ol' Mike n' Dick jus' wandered in here las' night by themselves," Bob said with a mischievous grin.

TWENTY

∼ℓ Glory, Glory to the Father

J OHN BURKE HAD WATCHED HIS GROWN-UP ELEVEN-YEAR-OLD SON RIDE
off that Wednesday morning with a touch of sadness mingled
with pride, a sort of bittersweet regret that his youngster had to
ferret out the job that John had been sent to accomplish. Here he
was on the threshold of locating the Confederate camp—his prime
goal—and he had to send his son to do it. This was the bitter.

The overwhelming pride was that he had complete confidence
in his son, first because he knew that God was with this lad, and
secondly because Ollie had the resourcefulness to get the job done.
He was extremely grateful to Captain Lyons for allowing Ollie to
accompany him on this trip. It had started as companionship for
John and training for Ollie, but quickly developed into a full-fledged
partnership in which Ollie had become John's equal as an able-
bodied soldier and scout. More than this, a friendship and confidence had matured between the two of them and enforced the
loyalty they already shared as father and son. The gladness John

311

felt in his heart was resting in the knowledge he had about Ollie's ability to reason and make decisions, and the confidence he had in the Holy Spirit to be his guide.

These reflections led John to feel like worshipping the Lord, so he began to sing in a rich baritone voice, which he often used to worship God. Silky and Fred, his only audience, turned and looked at John, giving their consent. Silky snorted and Fred swished his tail, as if trying to keep time to the music.

John unashamedly lifted his voice to God and sang;

> When I saw the cleans-ing fountain
> O-pen wide for all my sin,
> I o-beyed the Spir-it's woo-ing,
> When He said, "Wilt thou be clean?"
> I will praise Him! I will praise Him!
> Praise the Lamb for sin-ners slain:
> Give Him glo-ry, all ye peo-ple,
> For His blood can wash a-way each stain.

> Glo-ry, glo-ry to the Father! Glo-ry, glo-ry to the Son!
> Glo-ry, glory to the Spir-it! Glo-ry to the Three in One!
> I will praise Him! I will praise Him!
> Praise the Lamb for sin-ners slain:
> Give Him glo-ry, all ye peo-ple,
> For His blood can wash a-way each stain.

The beautiful strains of the hymn wafted out of the crevice of the rock dwelling where John sat, and up to the throne of God where it was received as the sweet-smelling incense that it was.

John spent all day Wednesday staying off his leg to allow it a chance to heal. He didn't unwrap the bandage or even check the wound other than to occasionally feel around the cut softly; surprisingly, it wasn't even sore. John shook his head and thought, *If it wasn't for taking a chance in tempting God, I'd git on Silky and take off after Ollie.* His confidence in Ollie and the wisdom of staying off the leg prevailed. He used the day to catch up on his Bible reading and compose a couple more poems. John also took time to work a tallow mixture into his saddle, bridle and belts, as well as his rifle boot and holster. The sun and weather exposure was hard on leather and this procedure helped weatherproof them and give them long life.

John ate very little and, since the coffee supply was running low, he limited his coffee drinking; having several cups of sassafras tea instead. He turned in early the first evening, wondering about Ollie's day and where he was. He didn't expect to see him that first night, but knew he was safe wherever he was.

He went to sleep as he had many times the past week, thinking about Cassie. He had no trouble at all thinking of her as his darling by this time. He ended each night in prayer for her, Ollie, and Cindy Lou as his family. He prayed a prayer for the Union war effort and his comrades, as well as the friends he held so close. No day was complete without his regular talks with God; for in John's thinking, that's what praying was—just talking to God as a father and friend through Jesus Christ.

On Thursday John awakened at dawn to another beautiful day in the hills of eastern Kentucky. The birds were so plentiful and melodious they were downright noisy. John smiled as he yawned and set out to start up a fire for some breakfast. He sliced the last of the bacon, whipped up some biscuit batter, and sliced a potato to fry in the bacon fat. He spooned coffee in the boiling water and let it boil. After sufficient time he took the coffeepot off the flames, sprinkled in some cold water to help the grounds settle and poured a cup to cool. As he enjoyed a good breakfast he decided, while sipping his coffee, that more grounds remained unsettled in the cup than settled in the pot. He shrugged his shoulders and strained the coffee through his teeth, spitting out the grounds.

John felt tremendous. He had no discomfort in his leg. He had always believed in the power of prayer, but he had felt that the miracles that accompanied Jesus and the original twelve disciples had ended at that time. He thought that God had used miracles to usher in the Christian age, but was not using them today. That is the way the preachers in this part of the country preached, and the way he had been taught to believe. John had never heard any Scripture quoted to back up this thinking, but folks seemed to accept it. What if they were wrong?

One thing was sure and steadfast—John believed he had an open mind to the Word of God and he definitely believed in the power of prayer. Right now he was on the verge of believing that a present-day miracle had occurred in the healing of his leg. *It is altogether possible that a child's prayer has been heard and answered by God,* he thought. Ollie had laid his hand on John's leg and quoted the Scripture; praying a "believing" prayer. John made up his mind he was going to examine his leg more closely today. Anyway, he needed a bath and a fresh dressing on his leg. While he was at it, he would water the animals at the stream.

John felt restless. He picked up his crude crutch and put some weight on his left leg to see if it roused any pain or soreness. Nothing at all happened. He took a step without the aid of the crutch and it was as though the wound had never been there. This was the first time since he was wounded that he had put weight on that leg without pain. He laid down the crutch and walked—without a limp—to the horses, about fifty feet away, turned and walked back to his bedroll. There was no pain, no ache, not even a muscle pull or noticeable weakness. John felt tears begin to flow down his cheek as he felt the joy of thanksgiving swell up within his chest. He said out loud, "Praise be to God! Praise be to God! Thank you Lord Jesus for healing my leg!" With this, John could not wait to see the wound—or where it used to be.

At about ten o'clock, judging from the sun, John prepared for the journey down to the stream. He took his shaving kit to trim his beard, soap, clean bandages, the antiseptic flask and a complete change of clothes. He also threw in Ollie's buckskins and a few dirty clothes to sponge out in the stream. John left the walking aid at the camp and led the animals to the edge of the stream, where they showed their appreciation by drinking long and seriously. In all this, John's walk was normal and he experienced no discomfort. After watering Silky and Fred he found a small clearing, where the grass grew tall, for them to enjoy grazing while he bathed. John had worked up a little sweat, for the day was already very warm, showing signs of coming summer.

John had resolved in his mind how he could see the leg wound. He usually carried with him a mirror, about six inches square, for the infrequent times he trimmed his hair or his beard. On occasion he had used it to send Morse Code since the war had started. John found a fairly man-size hole in the stream with a good flat stone, which came all the way to the water's edge. At the deepest part the water came up to his thighs. He pulled off his buckskins and laid them high on the rock and dangled his feet into the cold water. John proceeded with care in removing Ollie's bandage from the left leg and laying it aside, he noticed there was very little dried blood. He held the mirror to the back of his knee to see the wound in the reflection. There was no wound. What John saw amazed him.

There were two straight tiny blue lines making the letter L like a pencil mark. There were also neat little pinhole marks where a bit of thread came through and was tied. The marks were in neat rows, lining up on either side of the blue lines. All John saw was a very small scar. There was no redness, no inflammation, no scab, or any evidence that on the day before yesterday there had been lots of blood and a large piece of metal protruding.

John laid his bare back on the flat rock, exposing his muscular chest to the sunlight. His eyes again filled with tears of gratitude until he had to sit up to let them flow. God had healed him. There was not a doubt in his mind. John removed the rest of his clothing and plunged into the natural bathtub. The water was so cold it shocked him, but he soon became accustomed to it and found it refreshing. He washed his dark curly locks, and suds rolled down his face and beard, cascading bubbles into the cool stream. He soaked and washed and enjoyed the rare luxury of totally submerging his body, and all the while praised the Lord.

As he sat shoulder deep in water, he reached over on the rock for the mirror. Examining his beard, he decided he could do a little cosmetic work on it. He maneuvered until he found the shaving kit, picking up the scissors first. He looked at his beard again and suddenly the impulse struck him to shave it all off. It was a wild thought, for John had worn his beard since he was eighteen. Ollie had never seen him without it. Very few friends had ever seen John without a thick black beard. John even wondered himself what he looked like beneath all that hair. "Why not?" he said out loud. "I can always grow it back."

Thirty minutes later, he looked in the mirror again to see a stranger. A smiling, handsome man looked back at John Burke. His face was angular and ruggedly handsome, with high cheekbones. He had lean cheeks with large dimples that showed when he smiled. A well-formed nose and protruding chin completed the masculine face set off with blue eyes and even white teeth. The bronzed forehead and nose were in noticeable contrast to the paleness of the rest of his face. Sun would change the shades of color pretty quick. *I don't regret having made the change, but there will be some real surprises to family and friends,* thought John with a grin.

John took time to wash his and Ollie's buckskins, underclothes, and the bandages. He didn't bother to put a dressing on his leg, realizing that the stitches would have to be removed as soon as Ollie returned and perhaps a small dressing would be needed to cover the needle marks left by the thread removal.

John was now faced with the decision of whether to go and round up Ollie, or let him be on his own. He decided to allow Ollie his rein for one more day. If Ollie did not return by Friday, he would head out and chase him down. John was still at ease about the youngster; believing that Ollie would be in touch, if not tonight, by tomorrow.

John hung the wet clothes and bandages on tree limbs, being careful to place the buckskins away from the bright sun, so they would dry slowly. He gathered more fallen branches for firewood and decided on an early supper since he had neglected to eat dinner. By about 4:30, according to the sun, he had beans and ham pieces with coffee. He packed his pipe and lit up, leaning back to enjoy an evening smoke. Reaching his hand up unconsciously to stroke his beard, he was shocked when he touched bare skin. *This is going to take some getting used to.* John picked up his Bible and fell asleep after reading a couple of chapters.

Silky stomped and let out a whinny. John awakened immediately and became rigid, with his Colt in his hand; it was always near when he was camping. Then he heard a voice.

"Hey, John—it's me, Bob McPherson. I'm coming to yore camp. I'm alone. Do ya hear me, John?"

"Hey back to you, Bob. Come on in and sit a spell. We'll heat up some coffee."

Soon the pleasant face of his friend came into the dim light and John shook his hand after Bob put down a package. Bob carried a lantern, but he had not bothered to light it since the trip up from the farm still had enough daylight for finding his way. Bob was puffing and blowing from the climb. While he caught his breath, John poured him a cup of coffee. Bob accepted it gratefully and looked up at John for the first time full in the face, and almost lost his coffee.

He stared at John for a minute and said, "John—some Indian— has done slipped up on ya while you slept and scalped your face. At least tha's whut it looks like ta me."

"Do I look thet bad, Bob?" John asked with a smile, showing two enormous dimples.

"Naw—fer sure you look blamed good ta me, John. Ya just shoulda warned a feller. I coulda died on th' spot. I done tho't I wuz som'ere's else," he chided with merriment. "Here's some fixin's fer supper Mary done sent ya," handing his package to John.

John had a quizzical look on his face as he took the gift. "How'd you know I was up here—and how to find me, Bob?"

"Wal, Ollie done went 'n told me you wuz up here, 'n purt-near described th' place to th' letter," Bob explained. "Thet boy of your'n sure is a prize, John. He rode in ta my place on his mare awhile ago and told me he needed my help.

"Whut he needed my help fer, as much as I could gather, wuz ta help me. Durned if he ain't somethin'! Wouldn't let me talk none. Said he had a race agin nighttime—so fer me ta jus' listen. He tole me where you wuz 'n made me promise to come ta you 'n tell ya he was all right. He'd see ya by tomorrow night, he said, 'n he'd have a lot to tell ya. He said not ta worry."

Bob paused to roll a smoke while John waited without so much as a comment. He knew the ways of these country farm folks, and they would get the story all told if you just give them time.

"Wal, he wanted ol' Mike 'n Dick's bridles; he wanted their feeder bags with a measure of their favorite grain 'n he wanted another sack of grain jus' fer his plan. I didn't ask nary a question; I jus' done whut he said. Dad-gum young'un gives orders like a kernel in th' army or somethin'. Thing is, you feel like you better do whut he tells ya! Well, anyhow, I also gave him a measure fer his mount and Mary fixed him some supper ta take down th' road. He said one thin', 'if'n you hear noises in your barn in th' middle of th' night, don't come totin' a gun; it'll jus' be me 'n your horses'— or somethin' like thet." There was a pause, and again John waited to see if Bob was finished. He added one more thing.

"What do ya think thet boy's got up his sleeve, John? Do ya think he's really found thet team of mine? Do ya reckon he'll be all right?"

John looked the perplexed, hard-working farmer in the face. "First off, Bob, you brung me good news thet Ollie has been with you and he's OK. Th' rest of your question, I already know th' answer to.

"Ollie Burke has a plan and he was rushed to get back to someplace before it got too dark. He'll be all right because he's smart, and also because God has an unusual kinda likin' for thet boy— which doesn't have too much to do with me. And, if he said you might hear noises in your barn, well—you better go home and fork some hay into the stalls o' them two horses o' yours 'cause come mornin' they'll be home sure as I'm John Burke."

John shared a little of his recent history with Bob, about the surgery, the stitching of his leg and about the faith healing that had taken place. John gave all the glory to the Lord. If Bob happened to see Ollie sometime before morning, John asked, "Please don't share about the leg being healed or about shaving off the beard." John wanted to keep that surprise for himself to enjoy.

Bob visited a good while and it was late when he started back to the house. John watched him as he walked, swinging the lantern, through the trees. It was still later when John Burke enjoyed Mary's fried chicken and fixings. He guessed he and Ollie probably would be sharing the same meal, fairly near to the same time, only in different locations.

John awakened early on the morning on the third day of Ollie's absence. It was Friday, May 16th, one week since Cassie had departed with Ollie toward Louisa. He had this ache in his heart for her, just desiring to be with her and talk to her about all that happened this past week. It seemed like a month's worth of activities had taken place in a week's time. He wondered what she was doing and how she was adapting. He wondered if she had indeed met Cindy Lou, and if Ollie was right in his prediction that Cindy Lou would be with her when they came home.

What if she's changed her mind? he thought. *After all she's just a young woman. Don't young women often change their minds? She may have come to her senses, realizing my age and her youth.* John had to shake himself into thinking about another subject, or these thoughts would lead to worry, and worry is a sin. At least that's the way John understood the Bible. He thought on the verse that said something about God not giving us the spirit of fear. After all, worry is fostered by fear. Fear and worry feed off of each other.

John dismissed his worrisome line of thinking and made himself some breakfast. Afterward, he fed the animals. He used the last bit of grain for them, so decided to find them some good grazing. On a grassy knoll on the crest of the hill John hobbled their front legs and turned them loose.

He spent the morning cleaning his weapons, including Ollie's Sharps. He reloaded them after the cleaning and went after Silky and Fred around noon. As he brought the animals down the hill, who should appear but Bob, leading one dapple-gray draft horse and riding the other? His smile was wider than the Big Sandy River, and he had a sparkle in his eyes. "You wuz right! You wuz right—I say John, you wuz surely right. The boy brung Mike and Dick home—and he's a shy one, too. Yes-sir-ee, doodlebug! Made me promise not to tell nary a soul thet he had anythin' to do with bringin' 'em back." Bob let out a cackling sort of laugh and John joined in.

"Well, Bob, there was more than just shyness in Ollie's request," John explained. "No doubt he took those horses back th' same way they was took from you. Nobody come dancing up to give him back them two fine workhorses; he jus' took 'em. He'd jus' as soon th' folks thet he took 'em from not know it was him thet took 'em."

"Anyhow, I done brung you some grain fer a ten-day supply, a sack of taters, some milk and eggs. I can't thank you fellers enough fer bein' there 'n bringin' these horses back. They're a goin' ta make me 'n Mary's summer a lot easier. I know it was Ollie thet done it, but he couldn't a done it if'n he didn't have a paw thet was teachin' him right."

"You didn't have to go and do thet, Bob. Ollie didn't bring your team back fer a reward; it was jus' because he knew it was th' thing to do!"

"Oh heck! Don't ya think I knowed thet? It's jus' I wanted ta show thet our heart's in the right place, too. Me 'n Mary are purfek'ly agreed on thet."

Bob went on to tell of Ollie's "workin' on papers 'n sech on the porch," and of him eating a good breakfast after getting some sleep. Bob had assured Ollie that John was getting along better, but didn't go into detail about the leg, as John had requested. He had also told Ollie about the potatoes and grain he was bringin, so that Ollie wouldn't purchase more in Sandy Hook.

"When he left this morning, headin' for town, he said ta tell ya he'd prob'ly see ya afore dark t'night," Bob said.

John insisted on Bob staying to keep him company and he fixed a good dinner for the two of them, after taking the animals to water. John sure admired those big draft horses. "Gentle giants" he called Mike and Dick, and they were as friendly as purring kittens. Bob did remark on how well they worked together. He said Mike was the slow one of the two, but Dick picked up the stride and Mike was jealous so he would work himself silly to not be outdone.

After dinner Bob visited a good while then climbed aboard Dick and headed for the farm. "I sure can't git over thet smooth face o' your'n. It's as smooth as a baby's fanny." Bob launched into that high-pitched laugh of his. John laughed too, reaching up to feel the smooth face for about the umpteenth time. *Well, not quite that smooth,* he thought, *there's already a one-day stubble.* As John thought about this he realized that one of the reasons he let the beard grow, so many years ago, was that he was in the woods so much and it was not always convenient to shave. "Oh well, I guess I can live with shaving regularly for awhile," he said out loud. "I guess it wouldn't hurt for my face to take in some sun."

John got his things together and decided on another bath and shave before the sun went down. The one he had yesterday felt so good he decided he would do it again today. He always preferred shaving in hot water, but didn't want to take the time to start a fire and then for the water to heat up. He took Silky and Fred with him for a good drink of water and let them wait nearby.

TWENTY-ONE

A Fool Makes a Mock of Sin

A FTER OLLIE UPDATED HIS MAPS AT THE McPHERSONS', HE WAS ON THE way to Sandy Hook. Remembering that he still had a little shopping to take care of he had restored his silver to his coin pouch. Ollie was in town by eleven o'clock and got a big welcome from Jim Henderson.

"Hi-dy-do, young feller, did-ja have any trouble with th' directions ta McPherson's? How's Bob 'n Mary gittin' on? Can I hep ya with anythin' else?" The cordial livery man threw rapid questions at Ollie, almost like one sentence. Ollie laughed and gave back answers the same way.

"Howdy back to you, Mr. Henderson, no trouble a'tall with your directions—Bob 'n Mary are jus' fine, and yes, sir—I do need a little help!" Pretending to be all out of breath, Ollie began laughing.

Jim joined in. "Always did appreciate a feller with a sense of humor, one thet I could laugh with. What is it I can hep you with, son."

"My name is Ollie, Mr. Henderson, and I'll be doin' some shoppin' and such today. I'd like to strike up a price and leave Ginger here rather than leave her at some hitchin' rail. What do you charge?

"Oh, if'n you're not stayin' overnight, I'll jus' keep watch and feed her fer jus' th' cost o' grain."

"Sounds like a good bargain to me. Do you want me to take off th' saddle 'n gear, or jus' leave it on?"

"Jus' leave her the way she is and I'll do thet fer ya. I'll take her inside the barn and put it all in a safe place. Now, you go ahead 'n shop 'n have a good time."

Ollie thanked him and strolled across the street to a boardwalk on the south side, where he leisurely walked along, looking in a few store windows. There was a combination gun and leather shop, which also did shoe repairs. Ollie stopped to watch through the window and when the man noticed Ollie he paused in his work to give him a smiling wave. Ollie waved back, then strolled along taking in the sights and sounds of the town. He noticed a group of children playing some game he didn't recognize along the main street. He saw a large boy about twelve years old picking on the smaller children. The big lad took some kind of wooden toy from one little boy, holding it out of his reach to tease him.

The smaller boy was yelling, "Give it back, Tommy—it's mine. Please, give it here!"

Tommy just ignored the child's pleading, until the child began to cry. Then Tommy began to taunt him even more.

"Crybaby, crybaby, Gregory is a crybaby. Go tell yer mama, little baby," he continued mercilessly in a sing-song manner.

A little girl, about the same age as Gregory, began scolding Tommy, "Tommy, it just isn't fair, why don't you go and pick on someone your own size?"

"Polly, you jus' mind yore own bizness. I'll do egg-zactly what I want." With that he reached over and gave a vicious yank on one of Polly's blond curls, almost pulling her down. Polly began crying along with Gregory, who had paused to watch what was taking place with his friend.

Several adults were sitting around on the boardwalk or in chairs in front of the store watching with interest, but not one person was offering to interfere. Two men were chewing tobacco, sharing a spittoon, each carving on a piece of wood, letting their shavings drop to the boardwalk. A proper lady and well-dressed gentleman stood in the doorway of the store, observing the exploits of the young bully, but did not mix in. Ollie was exasperated with the situation, but the fellow was a good several inches taller than him and weighed at least twenty pounds more. He finally decided to at least say something. He boldly stepped off the boardwalk and walked up to Tommy, extending his hand,

"Howdy, I'm Ollie Burke and sorta new in town. If you don't mind, would you please show me around town? I've got some shoppin' to do. I'd be glad to buy you dinner if you help me out." The bully ignored Ollie's hand. "Why don't ya fin' yore own way 'round town. Me? I'm busy. So go off now and mind yore own bizness," he said with disdain.

Ollie was visibly disappointed that he could not move the boy to better things, but at least while he was talking the younger children had a chance to scatter, and Tommy no longer had an audience. Ollie thanked him anyway, and moved back to the boardwalk and walked away. Everyone noticed the way Ollie tried to diplomatically avert the inequity being displayed on the street; there were a few smiles of appreciation.

Ollie wasn't in any big rush. He was taking in the sights when, from behind him, he heard a feminine voice that sounded familiar.

He turned and saw the girlish figure of a young lady backing out of the general store. She had pretty brown curls and arms tanned from the sun. *Is that Susan Birchet? It couldn't be,* he thought. But as she turned and looked right at Ollie, both of the youngsters spoke almost simultaneously.

"Ollie!"

"Susan!"

Automatically, and without thinking, Ollie hugged her and they both blushed as he backed off. "I'm sorry, Susan—I—I—" She interrupted.

"Oh, that's all right, Ollie. We're almost cousins and I'm as glad to see you as you are to see me. What in th' world are you doin' here though?"

"I was about to ask you th' same thing. I was sure surprised to see you."

Unknown to the two friends, Tommy had followed Ollie along th' street. Since he had lost his other audience because of Ollie's intervention, he decided to check Ollie out. After all, this was *his* town and Ollie had interfered. Now Ollie had captivated this new girl who had come into town earlier and whom he had been watching. He was attracted to this pretty little lady, but Tommy didn't know how to be polite or attract attention to himself in any fashion but being obnoxious and over-bearing.

Tommy was a handsome lad, well-developed for his age but, like his dad, he thought the only way to gain attention was through brute strength. This lack of proper training had developed a cruel streak in Tommy and no one had ever stood up to him. He was a reflection of his father, with the same habits that he had learned extremely well.

Tommy slipped up on the boardwalk and, unnoticed by Ollie and Susan, was now lurking in the shadows. When Susan came by, he tripped her by sticking out a foot. Ollie caught her or she would have fallen on her face; instead she only went to her knees. When she arose, she was infuriated at Tommy, who was laughing with glee.

"What did you do that for?" she scolded.

"I was jus' havin' fun. Boy, did you look funny. Ha ha.—Ka-boom!" He gestured with his hands up. "Ha ha."

Ollie had had enough; this was going entirely too far. He moved in front of Susan and spoke directly to Tommy. "Listen, Tommy, your idea of fun is not fun; it's rude and the act of a bully. Now, we're goin' to be on our way and I want to give you some advice—don't bother Miss Susan or me again." Ollie hesitated then continued. "Do you understand what I mean?" Ollie seemed very small in front of Tommy.

Tommy pushed him backward and also pushed Susan. He rasped out in his most fearful voice, "You don' tell me whut ta do, kid; you 'n Miz Susan can go straight to hell. This is my town an' I'll do what I damn well please, so there and there and there." He kept pushing each of them until Ollie tumbled off the boardwalk on to the street, while Susan was pushed up against a post.

Ollie was in the dust—and he did not like it. He remembered what his dad said about striking the first blow. Ollie pulled himself up, methodically dusted his overalls, and came up the two steps with a smile on his face and his right fist doubled into a bony knot. As he approached the laughing bully, he waited until he was right up to him, then he let that fist fly with all that was in him. It connected with the lower part of Tommy's nose, and everyone within earshot heard the crunch of bone. Blood splattered. The blood was all over Ollie's shirt and some on his forehead and cheeks. Tommy went backwards and would have fallen to the boardwalk if a passerby had not caught him. Tommy was blubbering like a baby, shouting, "You broke it—you broke it! You broke my nose!"

Ollie raised his voice slightly. "Yes—I broke it and unless you want a couple of black eyes to dress up your nose, you'd better take th' nose home and leave folks alone." Ollie was surprised at himself, and at what he just said; but he heard it come out of his own lips, so it must have been him that said it.

As Tommy went scurrying down the street and out of sight, Ollie heard something that surprised him—applause. He and Susan looked around and it seemed like the whole town had been watching. All of a sudden, he became his shy self again and blushed. To compound the embarrassment, Susan put her arm through his arm at his elbow, and said to him with a sweet smile, "Come on, Ollie, take me to dinner, I'm sort o' hungry."

Ollie blushed again, but answered very quickly.

"It'll be my pleasure, Miss Susan." They crossed the street, heading toward the cafe. All who heard applauded again.

Susan squeezed his arm and said so only Ollie could hear, "Well, sir, Mr. Ollie, you sure do have a way of attracting attention. I bet I'm th' most noticed girl in town right now."

"Well, certainly th' prettiest," Ollie boldly added. It was now Susan's turn to blush. It seemed that these two youngsters were drawn much closer by what had happened the last few minutes, and Ollie felt every bit a twelve-year-old boy.

The cafe was very busy, with only one table left. Ollie escorted Susan to that table and they occupied two of the four chairs. They were no more than seated when a stout little woman came over with a smile. "I'll tend to you young'uns jus' as quick as I can. As you can see, we're purty busy." She hurried between two swinging doors into the kitchen.

"Before we was so bum-fuzzled with Mr. Tommy what's-his-name," Ollie said, "you had said to me, 'I asked first,' or, somethin' like that. So, I'll tell you my story quick, so we can get into what you're doin' in Sandy Hook. Well, dad and I have been visitin' and huntin' an' you might say I have been alearnin' from him. It's been kinda like goin' to th' school in Louisa, only it's been in th' woods.

You know we stopped in Blainetown by now, 'cause you have met Cassie, haven't you?"

"We sure did and, Ollie—we all jus' love her to death. She was out on Monday and Becky Birchet came with her to introduce her around. Little Cindy Lou took right to her and at the end of th' day, Cindy went back to th' cabin with her. We had a gay time together—went down to Deephole swimmin' hole and played in the water and sand and had a great time. She told us about the way y'all met and we jus' giggled like silly girls. 'Cause that's what we was, I guess." Putting her head down as if thinking a minute, she blurted out, "Ollie, is she and John—I mean your dad—goin' to get married?"

Ollie laughed and said, "If th' Good Lord's a willin' and the creek don't rise, Susan, they'll be hitched afore summer's out."

Susan laughed. As she started to comment the waitress returned. She had a stub of a pencil and a note-pad and asked sweetly, "Now thet I've had a chance ta ketch myself, what will you young'uns have? Our special is pork chops 'n taters with cornbread, or we got catfish 'n taters with cornbread."

Susan and Ollie both ordered the pork chops, which also came with a piece of apple pie. They ordered buttermilk and a glass of water. The waitress disappeared again through the swinging doors.

"I was jus' goin' to say, Ollie, we all felt like they, that is Cassie and John, was a goin' to marry up."

"Well," Ollie said, "Dad jus' come to th' decision makin' place about it on this trip *after* Cassie went on to Louisa. Cassie knew before she left, but she was jus' a waitin' on Dad, knowin' he would make up his mind." Ollie explained.

"Anyway, on with my story. Dad had some trouble that nobody knows about at home; not even Cassie. Remember that piece of shrapnel that caused him to limp? Well, it poked its ugly head out o' th' back of his leg, 'n we had to take it out 'n sew him up.

329

Thet's why I'm here alone. I come to town for some supplies. Dad's restin' up in a cave a little east o' here. We're allowing his leg to heal, so th' stitches can be taken out and the bleedin' won't start back up. Well, that's my story, now you tell me yours," he said with a grin.

The food arrived, piping hot and plentiful. Along with the potatoes and two big crisp pork chops were green beans and slices of pickled beets. Neither Susan nor Ollie could eat that much. While they were eating, in walked Eliza and Rhoda, both of them struck speechless at seeing Ollie sitting there having dinner with their sister. After the initial surprise wore off, they all started talking at once.

Ollie caught the waitress's eye and asked for two clean sets of tableware and ordered milk for the two girls. The waitress caught on to Ollie's plan, and brought back two clean plates as well. Ollie interrupted the girls and asked Eliza and Rhoda to finish their meals, since he and Susan had had more than enough. He placed the two clean plates and extra milk in front of the girls and everyone dined sumptuously. Susan filled the girls in on Ollie's taking up for her—fighting and whipping a boy twice his size. Ollie was embarrassed, but he enjoyed receiving so much attention from three pretty young ladies.

By the time they left, they had discussed John, Cassie, Cindy Lou, and Uncle Robert. The girls had left Deephole Branch yesterday and gone over past Cherokee to Lost Creek, toward Garrison, Kentucky to visit their Uncle Robert Birchet. He was their dad's younger brother by a year or so. Uncle Robert was delighted to see them because he had traded for a good bull to service his beef herd and he needed help driving the bull home. The farmer lived outside of Sandy Hook. The girls brought a change of clothes in the buckboard, and came to assist Uncle Robert in driving the bull home to Lost Creek. This struck Ollie funny but he tried to hold back his laughter. The girls tried to get him to tell his secret.

"I'll tell y'all later. It's not about you, it's jus' somethin' that th' Lord seemed to work out. When I thought on it, it struck me funny. Th' Lord sure has a sense o' humor, I'll say that much," Ollie observed.

He insisted on paying for the meals and they all left together to look for Uncle Robert. After a short walk the girls pointed him out at the feed store, half-block away. He was talking to a couple of men, which caused Ollie to pull up quickly and the girls watched his complexion change from a colorful tan to a winter pallor.

Eliza noticed. "What's th' matter, Ollie? You look like you saw a spook, or somethin'."

They were standing in front of a store so Ollie pulled the girls inside. It happened to be the general store. "That was Uncle Robert talkin' to th' two men, wasn't it?"

"Yes, Ollie, that was him." Susan answered. "Did you know those two men?"

"Well, let me put it this way—they know me—or at least who they think I am. If I had already been introduced to Uncle Robert and knew him it would be all right, but to introduce me in front of those two men ain't a goin' to work out too well."

Eliza took charge. "Let's delay Ollie's meetin' Uncle Robert a few minutes. Me and Rhoda will go to Uncle Robert. Susan, you stay here with Ollie and help him do some shoppin'. You had some things to git, didn't you, Ollie?"

"Thanks, Eliza." Ollie was grateful for her understanding.

Eliza spoke as she and Rhoda went out the door. "When we come back, Ollie Burke, you owe us an explanation, do ya hear?"

Ollie collected his wits, and felt rescued. The two men were Sam Blainey and Sandy Tibbett from the Confederate camp. He felt Susan take hold of his arm, and it made him aware of her presence. He turned to her and smiled, thankful for being with her.

"Welcome back to my side, Ollie. You've been off somewhere else since you saw those men. Do they make you afraid, Ollie?" Susan asked.

Ollie blushed again as he explained. "Naw, Susan. It's nothin' like that. You see, those men are Rebel spies and live here-abouts. Yesterday I was in their camp, and th' story I told them, 'n others in th' camp was sort o'—well—it was made up out o' my head. I jus' wasn't ready to get caught up in a cross-fire with them in front of my friends." Susan looked at him, her eyes growing very wide.

"Ollie Burke! Rebel Spies? Confederate camp? Are you makin' up stories? What in th' world have you got yourself involved in?"

"Later, Susan, later," Ollie said. "Let's do some shoppin'. He dismissed th' subject and pulled her over to the men's hat rack.

Ollie had been eyeing the straw hats ever since their impromptu entrance and, although he was busy, he was still thinking of his dad. He pulled a low-crowned, dark brown straw hat off the rack and asked Susan her opinion—to help change the subject.

"If that is for your dad, Ollie, it is great! I think he'll like it. I sure know John will look mighty handsome in it. If it is for you, it's too big," she added with a giggle.

Just then a short, bald-headed man came over to the two youngsters. "Can I help you young folks with something?"

"Well, yes, sir," Ollie answered, "I'm lookin' at this hat for my dad; I jus' want to make sure it fits."

The man said with a sparkle in his eye, "Is he as big-headed as me?" He put on the wide-brimmed hat as he spoke. The hat was just a little large on the proprietor's head. Ollie studied the man a moment then decided it would probably be OK. As the proprietor pulled off the hat, he said, "Keep in mind, if your dad has hair, instead of bald like me, it will fit much better."

"Yes, sir, he has a lot of hair. I think that hat will work well—and besides Susan likes it too," he said glancing at his companion, as she smiled back. "How much is the hat, sir? I mean th' cost?"

"That hat is $2.50 young man. You've made a good choice; it's a quality hat and very cool in the summer months." The price seemed OK to Ollie and, after all, he was buying this out of his own money. He had purposed to do this ever since he left his dad and had hugged his neck, noticing the absence of his coonskin cap. Ollie dug out his coin purse and pulled out three silver dollars. He smiled as the man took care of the purchase.

"Your father must be a certain kind of man to have such a considerate son. Where is he right now, Ollie? I believe the young lady called you that name?"

"Yes, sir, my name is Ollie Thomas; my dad's name is John and we live over in Lawrence County. He'll be pleased to get this fine hat and I'll see him t'night cause we're camped out o' town a ways," Ollie explained. "This here's my close friend Susan Birchet," he added.

"Well, Susan and Ollie, my name is Anson West. I'm called Ans by my friends. Can I help you with anything else?"

"Yes, Mr. West," Ollie said. "I'm goin' to be needin' a side of bacon, five pounds of flour, five pounds of coffee—'n do you have any canned fruit?"

Mr. West was already putting the supplies on the counter. "Sure do, Ollie, I have some canned peaches and apricots. How many do you need?"

"Four cans; two of each. I sure love canned peaches."

"OK, and what else young man? How about some nice thick steaks to broil over an open fire at your camp?"

"Boy-ee, sure sounds good, but I tell you Mr. West, I think I have spent all my money this time around. Maybe another time."

"I just want to know how many steaks, Ollie, so I can go cut them for you. I am going to give them to you as my gift—to you

333

and your father and friends," Mr. West said. "This is my treat to you—to say thanks."

Ollie was perplexed. When he looked at Susan she shrugged, too, giving him a blank look.

"What's this all about, Mr. West? I don't rightly know what to say. I ain't really did anything!"

"Yes, indeedy you did, Mr. Ollie Thomas. I stood right out there on th' porch and watched you try and accommodate the biggest nuisance in town, Tommy Blainey. What I mean by that is, you tried to diplomatically make a friend while he was annoying the kids in front of th' store. You allowed the smaller children to run away while keeping him occupied and, when he stalked you after they got away, you stepped in and was chivalrous to rescue this young lady. You gave him good sound advice, which he refused, and then you thrashed him soundly for being the bully he was. The whole town has been waiting for that to happen for a long time. I just want to show our appreciation by furnishing you steaks for your supper. OK, Ollie? How many?"

Ollie had turned shy again. So Susan spoke up.

"Mr. West, Ollie is very modest, but he is grateful; there will be six of us dining together tonight."

Anson West smiled at Susan and disappeared into the back. Ten minutes later he returned with a heavy burlap sack and put the rest of Ollie's order in the sack. It was a good-sized bundle. Ollie paid him and waited for change out of five silver dollars.

Ollie asked permission to leave the sack at the store until he brought his horse around to pick it up, and Mr. West was delighted to oblige him. Something was still ringing in Ollie's ears, which had lodged there from something Mr. West had said earlier. Now it came back to him. He turned back to Mr. West just as the girls and Uncle Robert came into the store. "Mr. West, a while ago—did you say, Tommy *Blainey*?"

"Why, yes, son. That's what I said, he's Sam Blainey's son. I regret to say this, but poor Tommy comes by his habits honestly. His dad is every bit the bully that Tommy is. Why?" he asked, "do you know Tommy's pa?"

"Well, sir, in a manner of speaking. I know him to see him, but I don't know much 'bout him. I really hated to hit Tommy, Mr. West, but he jus' was goin' too far, 'n when he was mean to Susan—well, that's all I could take." By this time, Robert Birchet, Eliza and Rhoda were standing in back of Ollie and Susan, facing Mr. West. Ollie noticed them and introduced the girls to Mr. West and waited to be introduced to Uncle Robert. Eliza stepped forward.

"Mr. West, this is my Uncle, Robert Birchet, from over Lost Creek way in Carter County. Uncle Robert, this is our young friend Ollie Thomas Burke. He's th' son of John, who lives over our way."

Uncle Robert engulfed Ollie's hand, shaking it warmly. Uncle Robert was a tall, fairly slender man with salt and pepper hair, and a bronzed complexion from long hours in the sun. He had the Birchet smile and chin, and he was muscular from the many hours of farm work. He was slightly taller than his older brother, John, and a good fifty pounds lighter.

"Glad to meet you, Ollie, I've been hearing stories about you and your dad ever since yestiday. Seems all these nieces of mine can talk about is you, John, Cindy Lou, and Cassie. Now I have th' honest-to-goodness pleasure of meetin' up with ya." He smiled, showing even white teeth.

His appearance and manner warmed Ollie, but he was not surprised. He was really growing to love this Birchet clan, and felt closer to them all the time. He didn't feel backward with Uncle Robert at all and he said so. "Uncle Robert—if you don't mind me callin' you that—I'm as pleased as a hungry cow in a cornfield to meet you." He paused as the girls laughed at his expression. "I feel like I've known Eliza, Rhoda and Susan forever, and I feel like you're my uncle, too."

"Ollie, I'd be honored to have you call me Uncle." Uncle Robert turned and shook hands with Anson West, apologizing for having to leave, but said he had to have a meeting with his family about some business matters.

Ushering the girls out, including Ollie as a family member, he instructed them all to get into a two-seated buckboard. Uncle Robert took the reins and the sprightly team of draft horses pulled the passengers just out of town, where he reined up in the shade of a chestnut tree.

He turned to Ollie, seated with Eliza and Susan on the back seat. "OK, son, do you have some problems with Tibbett and Blainey thet we should know about? Mind you, I'm not tryin' to be nosy, but th' girls jus' happened to mention it to me."

Ollie was caught between a stone and a rock—two hard places. He loved these dear people and they were the closest thing to family that he and his dad knew. On the other hand, he wanted to be true to his dad and the mission they were committed to for Captain Lyons. He would just try to be as honest as he could and do his best. He would first try to copy his dad when he was put on the spot by Uncle John a week or so ago.

"Uncle Robert, can I first ask you a question? I wouldn't want to offend you or th' ladies a'tall," Ollie said.

"Why, of course, boy. Jus' you ask away. I'll answer if I can. If'n I can't, I'll say so," Uncle Robert answered.

"Is your favorite the North or th' South in this here war?" Ollie spoke to the point.

"Don't even hafta think about thet one, Ollie. I'd be fightin' with the Union if I was ten years younger. I guess thet's plain enough of an answer."

"Well, that makes my answer about Blainey 'n Tibbett a little easier to talk about. As you know dad fought with the North at Middle Creek back the first of th' year. Leastways, I figured you knew it." Uncle Robert nodded and Ollie continued. "Well, he was wounded and let out of th' Army, but he kept working for 'em. He's been kind o' using his woodsman knowledge about the area, running errands, and scouting. Th' Union Army in Louisa, our home area, is afraid th' Confederates are mounting up another attack on us folks in Lawrence County, and they have already been stealin' from th' farmers in some areas. We know this for a fact.

"Well, that's what this trip is all about—me 'n dad, I mean. We've been tryin' to help th' farmers who have been victims of th' stealin'.

"While we was doin' this, that piece of metal in dad's leg decided to come out. We sort o' helped it, and Dad bled a lot, and we had to sew him up and that's where he is now. He is healin'." Ollie had them all spellbound, and it was only because they knew Ollie and John Burke that they could believe this story at all.

Ollie continued, "While Dad was waitin' 'til he could ride again, I was out snoopin' around, and I found this Rebel camp over to th' south about five miles or so. There is about a hundred of them, maybe more." Uncle Robert's face showed some doubt. After all, he just had met this young man.

"Uncle Robert, I know it sounds a little hard to believe, but there was forty-four dog-tents, one officer's tent with four officers, an' a captain's tent. You must know how many men sleep in one dog-tent; count 'em up for yourself. Anyway, I figured out a way to get welcomed into th' camp and the captain—Captain Graham Rutledge, by name—was asking me all sorts of questions to trip me up. They finally believed th' story I made up. I told them I was over here from Lawrence County with my uncle to do some cattle tradin' and, while my uncle was tradin', I was fishin' when I came across th' camp."

Ollie looked at the girls individually. "That's why I laughed when you all told me about your trip with Uncle Robert here. I told a fib, but th' Lord come close to makin' it th' truth."

The girls understood what Ollie was referring to, and laughed. Uncle Robert was not amused; this story seemed a little far-fetched to him. Because of the girls he was giving it the benefit of the doubt, but one thing for sure, he still was troubled about Blainey and Tibbett.

"Ollie, what about the two men, Blainey and Tibbett? What do they have to do with this entire story I mean?"

Ollie looked down, then faced Uncle Robert. "I'm sorry, Uncle Robert, I plumb forgot about them. Well, those two are Confederate soldiers and was in th' camp I'm talkin' about. They was there yesterday and saw me, and met me and was th' ones I followed in to find th' camp." Uncle Robert's face turned red and he was truly and obviously angry. He raised his voice so loud he frightened the girls.

"That is an outright lie, Ollie Burke. Now I'll have the truth if I have to thrash it out of you."

Ollie politely excused himself to the girls and jumped nimbly off the back of the buckboard, starting back toward town. Susan called to him and shortly she was beside him, begging him to stay. His eyes were brimming with tears and he could not say anything without becoming very emotional. Uncle Robert pulled the team around and pulled in front of Ollie and Susan, heading them off.

Uncle Robert was still visibly upset, but he could also see that he had pushed Ollie further than he intended with his outburst. In his mind he was still the adult and Ollie was the child. He was convinced he had been the victim of a child's over-active imagination, and wanted to get to the bottom of this situation.

"Just where do you think you are going, boy?" he called out to Ollie.

Susan was still holding Ollie's arm, and he looked at her with affection, holding back the tears that were very close to the surface. After a short interval he collected his composure and looked at Uncle Robert. "Uncle Robert, in due respect, you bein' my elder and kinfolks of a family I love, I will answer you. I'm goin' to town to collect my horse and belongin's and head back to my dad, where I should be goin'," he replied softly and respectfully.

Uncle Robert was plainly exasperated. He was not used to a child talkin' to him like an adult, particularly with as much control as this youngster seemed to possess. He was still not ready to give into this wisp of a boy in front of his nieces. He had demanded of Ollie a satisfactory answer, and by George he was going to get one.

"You're not goin' anywhere until I git to th' bottom of this, Ollie Burke! Now you explain yourself, and right now!"

Ollie had collected his wits and his thinking was back to normal, so he took his time with his answer. Uncle Robert was about out of patience when Ollie began speaking.

"Uncle Robert, because God's Word says I'm supposed to love everyone, and because of who you are, I love you. But you are not my dad, or who I answer to. You have no call to demand anythin' from me. What I already told you I did of my own choosin', not because of you demandin' it. You could believe me, or not believe me, that's your choosin'. It's plain to me you didn't believe me. I don't know if'n you didn't believe about Sam Blainey and Sandy Tibbett, or th' whole story I told you. One thing I do know, is—I told you th' truth, and you not believin' it don't make it into a lie. Th' truth is still the truth."

Robert Birchet was overwhelmed with such reasoning and maturity of speech in a young person. He never had met the equal to the presence of mind and boldness that Ollie Burke, an eleven-year-old boy, possessed. The girls were enthralled at what was going on between their uncle and Ollie; it was apparent that they believed him. There was one thing Uncle Robert had to check out though, to ease his curiosity.

"Ollie, how did you know Sandy Tibbett's first name? I didn't mention it to you, nor did his name come up in the talk I overheard with the storekeeper."

"That's easy, sir," Ollie said, "I was introduced to both men at th' Confederate camp. Their sergeant they work for is Sergeant David Runyan, and Sergeant-Major Judd introduced me to th' both of them. They work in th' detail of supplies and that means they were robbin from th' Union farmers 'n such to feed th' Confederates. I know 'cause we caught 'em at it."

Robert was beginning to believe this exasperating young man, and he was not at liberty to say why he had the doubt in the first place. But the details this boy had in his mind, the capacity to remember names and ranks was too detailed not to be accurate. He still asked one more question. "Ollie, you said, 'We caught 'em at it.' We who? Who do you refer to?"

"Why, me 'n dad—'n some friends," Ollie answered, reluctant to give away the Union soldiers such as Lewis and John Damron, Zeb and the others.

"Well, one thing for sure, I've got to meet your dad before I head back to Lost Creek area; I think thet would be advisable. By th' way, Ollie—I do believe you. I'm sorry I shouted at you and didn't believe you at first. I still have some questions in my mind, but maybe John can clear them up for me."

"I sure would be pleased if you 'n the ladies joined me and Dad for supper. We have some fine steaks that Mr. West gave us. I left Dad on Wednesday and here it is Friday, and so much has happened that I jus' got to get back and catch Dad up on—why don't I make you a map on how to find us?"

"Sounds like a good plan, Ollie. I'll take Rhoda and Eliza with me and after they change into work clothes, we'll get the bull I swapped for and we'll come by way of your camp. In th' meantime, Susan can go with you, Ollie, and keep you company." He smiled knowingly, adding, "That is, if you don't mind?" Ollie was all smiles again. Looking at Susan, he was elated.

"I'd be happy to have her, if'n she don't mind."

"She don't mind at all. As a matter of fact she would be pleased," Susan said.

"Then it's settled," Uncle Robert said, "You two youngsters climb back up here on the buckboard and I'll drop you off at your horse."

Glad Tidings of Good Things

OLLIE PICKED UP HIS SUPPLIES AT ANSON WEST'S STORE. HE DIVIDED them into two sacks to distribute the weight and swung them over Ginger's shoulders in front of the saddle-horn. Then he went to the livery barn to pick up Susan, who had changed into some different clothes. She had put on a pair of old overalls cut off just about the knee, and a work shirt with the sleeves cut off above the elbow. She wore no shoes, and her curly hair, cascading over her shoulders, was tied back with a ribbon. She climbed on a fence rail and swung nimbly aboard Ginger behind Ollie, wrapping her tanned arms around his waist.

They both sat the saddle very well and Ollie felt about ten feet tall as she held him close while he guided Ginger toward the road to the McPhersons' farm. Ollie was enjoying this time with Susan so much that he didn't feel like rushing. Still, as they idly chatted, with Susan snuggled close to him, the miles went by quickly, and they were soon at the McPhersons.

Bob and Mary were on the porch. They waved as they recognized Ollie, walking out to the gate to greet them. Both wore big grins, and Ollie caught a quizzical look as they eyed pretty Susan Birchet. He was getting ready to introduce Susan when Bob spoke up.

"Wal, Ollie Burke, you shore are full of bringin's. Las' time I see'd ya, you brought a team o' horses; now durn me if'n ya don't have a purty little filly," Bob said teasingly.

Mary hit him playfully on the shoulder. "Aw, Bob, stop your kiddin' these young'uns now."

Ollie was blushing as he introduced Susan. "Mr. and Mrs. McPherson, this here is my friend from over Lawrence County way, Susan Birchet. Susan, this here is Mr. and Mrs. Bob McPherson. Her name is Mary, and they're friends of me 'n dad."

Susan nodded from her perch on Ginger and smiled at the older couple. "Mighty pleased to meet you folks. Ollie has told me about you. My Uncle Robert and two sisters, Eliza and Rhoda, will be passin' by later on this evening. They'll be bringin' a big ol' bull my uncle's traded for ta take home ta Carter County."

"My lands," said Mary, "this here road is gettin' so busy it's like downtown Ashland, Kaintuck. You young'ns git off and rest a spell so long as you're here."

"Aw, I guess not this time, Mrs. McPherson. Kinda lookin' forward to seein' my dad. Ain't seen him in three days and seems more like a month," Ollie said.

"Well, we know we'll see you 'n yer paw afore ya leave, Ollie. Me 'n Mary understan' ya wantin' ta see him. Tell him howdy fer us, will ya?"

"Sure will, Mr. McPherson. Pat Mike 'n Dick for me!"

———————

The sun was setting in the west when Ollie and Susan rode into camp, but Ollie did not see John or the horses anywhere. The bedroll, packs, and equipment were all in place so Ollie figured his dad must have taken the animals for water. He dismounted first, catching Susan as she slid off Ginger. It was not that Susan needed the help, but Ollie was enjoying his role of being a gentleman and having a young lady to escort. Susan sure showed off her lady-like charms, whether dressed up in a Sunday-go-to-meeting dress or in work clothes, as she was now. Ollie tried to be careful not to stare, at least not when Susan was watching. After offloading the supplies, Ollie led Ginger away and removed her saddle, slipped his gun belt and Colt out of the saddlebag, strapped it on, then called out to find his dad.

Susan made herself at home, sitting on a stone near the place where they had their campfires. Because it was getting late Ollie decided to start up a fire and put on some coffee. He imagined his dad had not had a good cup of coffee for a day or two. By the time Ollie had some water on to boil, Ginger warned them someone was coming. She whinnied and Ollie saw her ears standing straight up as he followed her gaze into the woods. Well, there was a man in work clothes coming with Fred and Silky and Ollie became alarmed. *Where's Dad?* He shouted out to the stranger, "Hello there—have you seen John Burke?"

A familiar voice came ringing back, as the stranger smiled. "I sure have seen John Burke. What do you want him for?"

Ollie was inquisitively suspicious. Who was this strange man who sounded like his dad?

"Dad—Dad, is that you? What—what—did you do? Well I'll be tarred and feathered. It is you! What in the world happened to your face? It's—it's—it's downright bald!"

Susan was laughing and jumping in glee, clapping her hands. "I never saw anythin' so funny. I jus' never saw anythin' so funny." She continued laughing, and bent over to catch her breath, which caused John to say with mock seriousness, "For goodness sake, Susan. I don't look thet funny, do I?"

"No—nothin' like thet, John. I was laughing at the look on Ollie's face. He looked like he'd lost his best friend or somethin'."

Ollie was still in shock. He ran up to his dad and hugged him and reached up to feel the smooth, pale face.

"I jus' don't believe it. Gosh, Dad, you sure are a handsome feller underneath all that beard." He turned to Susan. "You can laugh if you want to, Susan, but you know, in all my borned days I never did see my dad clean-shaven before. Isn't that right, Dad?"

"Yep, thet's true, son. This is the first time I shaved my beard off in your whole lifetime. In fact, Sue Ellen, God rest her soul, never saw me without my beard, as near as I can remember. I went down to take a good bath in the stream 'n took a lookin' glass. While I was splashin' around in thet water, I took a look at myself and wondered what I looked like. Jus' thet quick, I up 'n shaved her off. I figured I could always grow it back, if'n nobody likes th' way I look without it."

"I think I'd leave it off, John," Susan said seriously. "You look a lot younger—and I think Cassie will think so too."

John immediately perked up when Cassie was mentioned. "What's this about Cassie?"

"I sure have met her, John. Th' whole family has met her—and we all love her. It was jus' Monday that she was with us all day, and all us girls went swimmin' down at th' mouth of Deephole Branch. Cindy Lou went back to the cabin with Cassie. We all figured you 'n Cassie was goin' to get hitched."

John smiled, turned red and looked toward his feet while he got his composure back.

"Sure glad you met up with her, Susan an' I was sure everyone would take to her. I'm glad she took Cindy home to th' cabin. She'll have good company. As for th' other—I—well, I ain't got around to askin' her yet. But I have been thinkin' some on it, ain't I, Ollie?"

"You sure have, Dad, and I'm glad! And they ain't no question about her sayin' yes. Anyone can see that." Ollie changed the subject.

"Dad, I been thinkin' on it for three days and I jus' got to know—how's your leg?"

"Well, Ollie, why don't you check it for yourself. Hold on a minute 'n I'll put on a pair of short trousers." John disappeared over to the pack and stepped behind a tree. Ollie took the opportunity to light a lantern as dusk surrounded them, and he poured his dad a cup of coffee.

He motioned toward Susan, asking if she wanted a cup. She shook her head, wrinkling her suntanned nose. It was plain that Susan didn't care for coffee. John stepped back into view, wearing short pants and moccasins. Ollie gave him the coffee tin and John reclined on his bedroll turning over to expose the back of his leg. Both Ollie and Susan crowded over with the lantern to see something that amazed Ollie.

"Why, Dad, it's—why it's not there anymore. Nothing there but the threads I sewed you up with! He looked at his dad with amazement and John smiled back at him.

"Ollie, did you believe the prayer you prayed?" John asked his son.

"Yes I did, Dad. I did believe it. I guess I jus' wasn't ready for th' answer to happen so quick. What about th' sewing, Dad?"

John told him the stitches should come out—and the sooner the better as far as John was concerned. Ollie got the packet again and produced the scissors, the flask, and a small dressing. Susan watched her young friend go into action and work just as expertly as he had walloped Tommy Blainey on the nose. He clipped the threads on one side of the knot then used the knot to pull the thread out of John's leg with thumb and forefinger. Soon the job was done. A small amount of bleeding occurred, which Ollie quickly swabbed with the bandage soaked with the antiseptic from the flask.

"Dad, I think I'd jus leave on those short pants so nothin' would rub against those small pin holes. I don't think I'd even put a bandage dressing on it tonight," Ollie suggested.

"You're the doctor, son. You've done too well by me for me not to listen to you now." Ollie became embarrassed, then Susan reached over and put her arm around him affectionately, pulled him over and kissed him on the cheek. That did it! Even with the dusk and lantern light you could see the crimson creep up his face. John and Susan both laughed; Ollie quickly raised a new subject.

"Dad, we forgot to tell you—Eliza, Rhoda and Uncle Robert are on the way here to have supper and visit a spell. And I plumb forgot—Mr. West gave us steaks for a good meal tonight."

John could not help but notice that, even though Ollie changed the subject, he was perfectly content to sit with Susan, allowing her arm to stay around him. He enjoyed watching these two unusual children and their innocent infatuation in one another.

"Well," John said, "I kinda knew you'd get around to tellin' me what's been goin' on and how you and Susan wound up together. I'm purty smart, but I ain't learned how to read someone's mind yet. By th' way, Susan, I see you've got some short britches jus' like mine."

It was Susan's turn to blush and become shy as she answered, "Yes, sir, an' if'n pa saw me wearin' 'em here with you 'n Ollie he'd prob'ly skin me for sure. I mostly jus' use 'em for goin' to th' swimmin' hole."

"Well, your secret's safe with us. Ain't thet right, Ollie?"

"That sure is right. Why I like th' way you're dressed," he said innocently.

"I sort o' hoped you would. I kinda dressed thet way for you," she said giggling and blushing again. John just shook his head and began checking out the supplies Ollie had brought.

"Better get some taters out, son. Since we are havin' company, we better make ready for 'em."

It was nearly two hours before the caravan of Birchets reached the camp. Ollie had caught John up on the experiences in town with the Birchet ladies and Uncle Robert. John had never met Uncle Robert, but was looking forward to doing so. Ollie had also briefed his dad on the falling out that he and Uncle Robert had regarding the two men in town. Susan helped by telling the story of Tommy Blainey and how Ollie put him in his place. Ollie was a little shy about bragging on himself, which allowed Susan to make up for it. After Ollie told John the same story he had told Uncle Robert about his first meeting with Blainey and Tibbett, John assured his son that he had nothing to worry about. John told him a lot of adults have had very little experience in dealing with children on an adult level.

"In fact, many folks would have a problem in believing such a story from an adult, let alone a youngster your age. I have an advantage—I know my son and his passion for tellin' th' truth!"

Uncle Robert had a big, stocky white-faced bull that you could tell had good bloodlines. He was a handsome brute but a little disoriented about this trip. He kept giving off a deep, throaty lowing and looking around with curious eyes. He had a massive squared shape head that showed no horns. At least that was the way he looked to Ollie. Rhoda had driven the team of horses and the buckboard with the bull's halter tied to the end. Uncle Robert and Eliza walked behind with switches, encouraging the animal to walk along behind the buckboard. The first hour was a real task, but after that the sturdy fellow picked up on the idea and trudged right along.

Introductions were made and John felt drawn to the older man right away. Like John Birchet, Robert was old enough to be John's father and he always felt a respect for a person who was a generation older than he was. Robert could tell that this young

349

man was everything the girls had made him out to be and more. Of course, he had also heard about John Burke from his older brother. Susan and Ollie familiarized Rhoda and Eliza with the camp layout and they all fixed supper, which gave Robert and John time to get acquainted.

John suddenly recalled that Captain Lyons had told him about a secret partisan leader of Union guerrillas in the Grayson area of Carter County, and he had given John this man's code name as a possible contact. From the information Ollie had shared, John had an idea that Robert might be the man the captain had told him about. Before John went too far, he had to check this out. This man would also be aware of John's code name in the Union spy network. Not even Ollie had been told that name. Ollie simply had not been in the position to have need of this information as yet. As the young folks were busy, John and Robert were enjoying a good visit about family and mutual friends. John felt it an appropriate time to drop his name and see if Robert picked up on it—and he would, if he was the man Captain Lyons had referred to.

"Well, Robert, I guess you know I am kin to th' Damrons over in Wayne County, West Virginy? Them folks all know me in them parts. I got more kin folks in them woods than fleas on a dog's back. They kind o' know me as th' *Northern Woodsman* over in them parts." As John casually unfolded this statement, Robert became alert and his eyes suddenly squinted. He looked quickly into the fire embers. A few moments later he looked back at John.

"Is that a fact, John? Well, I've been over thet way two or three times. I love to fish over in Twelve Pole Creek. They's more catfish in thet creek than you can shake a stick at. I remember one time after a big rain, I was up there to Dunlow an' I threw out a line with a fishworm on th' hook an' thought I hooked a big ol' yeller cat. Well, sir, twarn't no bigger than a *Carter County Tadpole,* but did thet little critter put up a fight!" That was it! John knew he must have a one-to-one conversation with this man.

John stood up and yawned, stretched and said, "I think I'll take a little walk and get th' kinks outa my legs. You care to join me, Robert?"

"Matter of fact, I think I will. It might help ta eat good. You young'uns yell fer us when supper's ready," Robert said.

John led off, directing Robert toward the stream. The night was well lit from the moon and stars, even through the tree branches. After about five minutes of silence, when they were out of sight and hearing of the camp, John stopped.

"You don't know how glad I am to make contact with you, Robert. We've heard great things about th' Carter County Tadpole in Louisa. That is, Captain Lyons and his group, at least, has heard thet information. How's ever' little thin' goin'?"

The big grin on Robert's face became sad. "Not too good, John. We're losin' some of our good men in the underground Union ranks. We have some staunch Confederates thet are not outspoken, but are making themselves felt by cuttin' down some of our people. We've lost three so far the last month; shot down like dogs—all of 'em. Actually, they were ambushed and I got no trace or clue as to who done it."

"Thet's real bad," John said. "Reckon thet's part of th' reason they sent me over here to ferret out th' Confederate build-up and trace down any problems. Th' big concern over at th' garrison in Louisa is thet th' Rebs will mount a large attack and try to swarm Louisa. Thet's our pipeline to supplies and troops from th' North and it would be a big victory for them if the South could capture our town."

"How long have you been out from Louisa this time, John?"

"Well, let's see," John said, thinking back. "It's been nearly two weeks since me 'n Ollie rode off. We left on the mornin' of the fifth. We've been hot on th' trail of a band of Rebs that's been stealin' and raidin' our farm folks. They been takin' our cattle, our sheep and even small stuff like grain 'n taters. Anythin' they can lay their han's on actually. Thanks to th' Good Lord—and Ollie, we got them holed up, for a spell at least."

"Ollie? Thet boy of your'n? Tell me, I'm curious, what did he have ta do with it?"

John smiled because he knew this was coming.

"Oh, jus' about everythin' I reckon. Ollie was trackin' southwest of the hideout where me 'n Sergeant Damron and seven Union soldiers were camped. I sent him out to check on th' trail o' th' raiders. Well, we were jus' finished with breakfast and it rained like—I mean poured, you remember? Last Sunday mornin'?" John paused and Robert nodded.

"Well, all of a sudden we hear these shots ring out—bang, bang, bang, then a pause and one more bang—that was our signal. We made ready and, sure as shootin', we were the targets of 'bout a dozen Reb sharpshooters. They had sneaked up on us and pinned us down. Well, sir, we couldn't move! A cliff in back of us and Rebel soldiers on th' other three sides. We couldn't see much for th' rain comin' down and we was in a pickle, to tell th' truth. Thet boy sneaked up on the south flank and—bang, bang,—picked off two Rebs, stone dead. Well, thet threw them Rebs into a panic, 'cause they couldn't see who or what was shootin' at 'em.

Ollie then hightails it up th' hill, comes over th' top an' behind 'em, and picks off another sharpshooter on their north flank. I saw him through th' telescope and when he hit thet last Reb—clean through th' head. The Reb tumbled into Brushy Creek and was washed clean out o' sight. I yelled, 'Charge'—and it was all over in a few minutes.

"We had two of ours wounded—not bad—and we took three captive. One that we took was bad hurt, so we sent him back to

Louisa with th' other prisoners. Ollie 'n me have been tailin' th' others since Sunday afternoon. He located the Confederate camp while I've been laid up with my leg, but I ain't got th' run-down of thet yet. Susan has been here and we didn't bring up anymore than he already told you this afternoon."

Robert let this story soak in for a minute or two and then came th' call from Rhoda.

"Supper—y'all come 'n git it before it gits cold."

Ollie and the ladies did themselves proud. Fried potatoes, biscuits with lots of beef gravy, green beans and steak. Anson West had cut thick steaks; each one could have fed two people. He was truly a generous man, and everyone took time to say something about it. As Robert and John talked in low tones, the ladies entertained Ollie and talked of Cindy Lou and Cassie. Ollie asked about Shep, Cassie's dog.

"Yes," Rhoda said," he came out to the house with her, and I'm a tellin' you, that dog stayed right at her side everywhere that girl went. He would've made sure that we all stayed away from Cassie, 'cept Cassie scolded him."

"Yes, but did ya see the way that dog took to Cindy Lou? Why, that young'un pulled his hair, opened his mouth 'n even fed him cockle-burrs. Once she even tried to ride him. He jus' stood right there and let her do what-so-ever," Eliza remarked.

As they talked and finished their supper, Ollie suddenly jumped up. In seconds there was a shiny Colt in his hand, cocked and pointed skyward. He held out his free hand saying only loud enough to be heard, "Hush—somebody's a-comin'. They're slippin' up from behind the cliff."

Catlike, John was by his side with his .44 in the same position as Ollie's. He turned facing the other way.

"Are you sure, son?"

"Yes, sir."

Everyone else, including Robert kept perfectly still. John called out into the night. "Anyone thet's out there—you might as well come on into the camp light. We know you're there and we're armed."

From the darkness came an older, yet strong masculine voice. "Now—John Burke, you wouldn't shoot an old Baptist preacher, would ya?" John put the hammer down on his weapon, indicating for Ollie to do the same, speaking to the man in the darkness. "Come on in, Brother Borders. You're welcome at this camp anytime. Who you got with you?"

"Jus' some of my kin, John. Joseph and Joseph are here with me," he said as he came into the light. The men he referred to were Joseph Borders senior and his nineteen-year-old son, Joseph. Rev. John Borders, Brother Borders as John Burke referred to him, was an itinerant Baptist preacher who was famous in eastern Kentucky. He was a fiery evangelist who had held revivals all over this country. At age seventy, he was still strong and agile and rode a mule or walked this entire countryside, lifting up the Gospel message of Jesus Christ. He was an uncle to the senior Joseph Borders.

They came in leading their mounts and Ollie immediately took the horses and one mule over to the other animals and began removing their saddles. Susan jumped up to help him for she knew her way around livestock even better than Ollie. The youngsters put out grain for the animals while John and Robert made the men welcome. There was plenty of food so Eliza and Rhoda attended to the needs of the Borders men, fixing them a large tin of leftovers that were still warm.

Rev. Borders was six feet, two inches tall. He had deep-set dark eyes that could look right through you, it seemed. He wore a black suit and white shirt with a black string tie. He had removed his low-crowned felt hat, and it didn't look as if there was one gray hair in his dark-brown shock of hair. He kept looking at John as he ate.

"John, I always figured you was a Nazarene—with that beard of yours. I just am tryin' to get used to seein' you without it." Both of the other Borders men also knew John and had met the Birchet girls. They all lived in the Walnut Grove area of Lawrence County, to the southeast of Deephole Branch. They were traveling with their well-known uncle, who was on his way to Grayson to preach a revival at the Methodist Church.

John Burke allowed the men to eat before he questioned them about finding their camp. This old fireball of a preacher was a man of God, as far as John was concerned. He loved him dearly and, although no person present was aware of it, John paid his tithes to this man. He supported him whenever possible. Rev. Borders was a man with a message from God and a passion for winning lost folks to Christ. John kept his tenth in a certain place at the cabin, which he added to regularly as God blessed him with wages. John spoke finally to the minister.

"Well, Brother John, how did you find us? Were you lookin' for us? An' who told you where to look?" John laughed. Everyone joined in the humor, including Ollie and Susan who had just returned from their chores.

"Well, John, first off—since I'm friends with you an' know everyone here, I bring nobody bad news! Since a preacher marries folks and buries folks, everyone always expects the worst. I bring you nothin' but glad tidings of Good News." He laughed, pointed in the general direction of Carter County, and said, "but I'll save that for the folks over to Grayson. Answerin' your questions, I found you by followin' th' smell of them steaks from the trail. I was lookin' for you 'cause I brought you a message—which I'll come to in a bit—an' fin'ly, a pretty lady stayin' at your cabin tole me you were over ta Sandy Hook, an was goin' by way of Grayson to come home. Since th' boys an' me were headin' this way anyway, we decided to try and find you. Th' meetin' doesn't start till Sunday night and we wanted to say howdy."

John was delighted to see this dear friend, and he slightly knew the other men from the Borders Chapel, an old Methodist church that was started by old Hezekiah Borders about 1823. It was a sturdy building of poplar logs, reputed to be the oldest church in the county. John had been there several times with Elizabeth, Sue Ellen, and Ollie. John never claimed to be Methodist, Baptist, or Episcopalian. He had worshipped the Lord with brothers and sisters in Christ at all these churches, and he loved them all. He had tithed, at various times, to all of them.

In the past couple of years John had been drawn to this dear man of God who rode the countryside with the message of love, and had supported his ministry. Brother John was inclined to stop regularly at the cabin at Two-Mile and before that, their house near Cassville, West Virginia. If John were away on a hunting or trapping trip, as he was frequently, Elizabeth would go to the secret place and give the Reverend whatever was there. She would also feed him and give him whatever he needed in the way of traveling supplies. People scattered throughout the area were all inclined to help any itinerant man of the cloth passing through their area.

"What about the message for me, Brother Borders?" John asked the preacher.

"Oh that. Well, Cassie—who fixed me a most excellent meal—said to tell you, and I quote, 'I love you, John; I miss you, John; and please hurry home; I'm lonesome without you.' That, my friend, was the exact message, word for word," Rev. Borders said with humor in his eyes. John Burke turned crimson and everyone began laughing.

"Aw, John Borders, did you have to say that in front of everyone?"

"Well, John, you asked me in front of everyone—an' th' lady didn't seem to be embarrassed about tellin' me to give you th' message. By th' way John Burke, speakin' of marryin' and buryin' folks— you wouldn't have somethin' to talk to me about? I mean—no real rush, but maybe after the meetin' over in Grayson? Do you think I should—well, maybe stop by th' little cabin on Two-Mile an' talk to you an' Cassie?"

Ollie put on his most adult-like composure and answered for his red-faced dad. "I think that's a prime idea, Brother Borders. We all feel that you need to sit down and have a good talk to these young'uns."

With that, John Burke peeled off a moccasin and threw it at Ollie. Ollie crouched and avoided the shoe, running toward the horses. Everyone, including the two Josephs and Uncle Robert, laughed at the expression on Ollie's face and his embarrassed dad. John finally joined in the merriment and Ollie came out of hiding. After the laughter, the preacher turned to John in all sincerity. "I will be over, John. When th' meetin' is over, you just look for me." Then Rev. Borders turned to Robert.

"How have you been, Robert? I don't rightly remember when it was I last saw you? Is every little thing all right at home?"

"Well, Brother Borders, we're all tolerable I reckon. You know I ain't livin' over on Lost Creek near Willard anymore. I still run some cattle over there on paw's place though. I actually live over closer to Mount Olive, on the north side closer to them big Carter County caves. I got a two-story log house up there we built. But you know me, I'm over in Grayson more 'n anywhere else."

The younger Joseph Borders seemed really interested in Rhoda and sort of paired off with her in conversation. Susan, Ollie, and Eliza were engrossed in visiting while the senior Joseph and John Burke were listening to Robert and the minister.

"I might say, I was surprised to see you here with the Burkes—and with John Birchets' girls too," the preacher said.

"I say, Brother John—we sure do have a passel o' Johns around here," Robert said. "We got John Burke, John Birchet, and John Borders, not ta mention John Allison, th' sheriff, over Louisa way. We've now added two Joseph's 'n I feel sorta slighted—they's only one Robert." They nodded. John sure seemed to be a popular name in these parts.

"Sorry, Brother Borders," Robert continued, "I guess I was suddenly hit by all these Johns. Anyway, I was over this way to trade fer a bull for my cows pasturing over at Lost Creek. I jus' accidentally run into John here, not aknowin' he was anywhere about. My nieces had come over by way of Cherokee to visit, and I put 'em ta work ta help me bring th' bull back. I'm actually sorry now I got ta go right back, 'cause John and I was jus' gittin' down fer a good visit. But, anyway, I got the bull now and I ain't got no choice but see'n he gits to Lost Creek.

The preacher walked over to see the white-faced bull. "Sure you got a choice, Robert. We're all on th' way to Grayson. Got to go right past Lost Creek and Willard. Me'n th' boys will be glad to take your new bull by Ben's old farm and turn him out to pasture there—if that's what you want?" The elder Joseph spoke up and added his support.

Robert gratefully took the Borders up on their most generous offer.

The preacher said one last thing. "Now, there's a catch to this here arrangement, boys. If you and John—John Burke, that is—get over to Grayson while th' meetin's still goin' on, you got to stop by and hear me preach again," the evangelist said with a glow of humor on his face.

"That would be an honor, Brother John," Robert said. "I'd love to hear you preach again."

John Burke echoed a hearty, "Amen."

TWENTY - THREE

To God Be the Glory

THE LADIES CLEANED UP AFTER SUPPER AND FETCHED THEIR BEDDING from the buckboard. They all said their goodnights and turned in. Earlier John had caught Ollie's attention and told him to stay up after the others had gone to bed. He asked him to bring his notes and maps and follow him to meet uncle Robert.

Ollie and John, each carrying a lantern, went to the extreme end of the cave, on the south side, and found Uncle Robert waiting for them in the dark.

"Now, Robert," John began, "I want you to know that my son is in the middle of all this, and we—that is, Ollie and me—are partners working for the Union Army out o' Louisa under Captain Lyons. We're scouts and spies—and anythin' you say to me, you can say to Ollie." Turning to his son, he said, "Ollie, Robert Birchet is the chief of a band of Union sympathizers who are known as partisans. They fight the Confederate forces as folks without any direct military ties." John paused. "Do you know and understand what I said, son?"

"I think so, Dad. Uncle Robert is like a captain or somethin'; kind of an officer leading a bunch of regular folks who are not in the army, but they fight for the North. How do they fight, Dad?" Ollie asked. John nodded to Robert. "You explain that, Robert!"

"Well, Ollie, let me say first, I owe you a big apology for this afternoon. I really gave you a rough time. Can I say I'm sorry 'n start over?" Ollie grinned from ear to ear and stuck out his hand accepting the apology.

"Well, Ollie, we fight in secret. What I mean by that is, we try to find out who th' local Southern partisans are—and by th' way they have 'em, too, and we try to mess up their plans. If we find ammunition or weapons, we either steal 'em or destroy 'em.

"We try to single out Confederate patrols, or small bands of troops not with their main force. Attacking from ambush, we destroy them when we can. It depends on their size and how many men I can rustle up at th' time. We kind of 'hunt and peck' at their efforts and cause as much damage 'n confusion as possible. I'm the civilian in charge. The folks who support the North picked me to be their commander. We cooperate with the Union Army and keep in touch with them. We do all this because we want to git this war over as quick as possible. Incidentally, the reason I got angry with you was thet Sam Blainey and Sandy Tibbett are lieutenants of mine. It was hard for me to accept what you said about them."

"Well, Uncle Robert, that sure does explain a lot of things to me. I'm sure regrettin' havin' to tell you that bad news; but one thing is sure—they're as Confederate as Atlanta, Georgia! They're workin' on you to get information that can be used agin' you and your local group. They *could* be spyin' for th' North. But if they did that, you'd know about th' Confederate camp. Th' other thing that I'm certain sure about is those are th' very men me 'n dad followed from Brushy Creek—that tried to shoot us. They was stealin' from our farmers, and I saw th' stock they took right there in th' camp. No sir-ee, Uncle Robert," Ollie said with a grimace. "They's Reb's—'n they'll kill you, too, if they get th' chance."

Robert snapped his finger and came alert, turning to John.

"They's th' ones who killed my men! I was tellin' you about 'em, John. We've—I've got to do somethin' about them, and right away—before I lose any more men."

"You were right th' first time Robert—'we.' We're in this too. We'll isolate those men and cut off their double spy work. Of course, we'll have to be careful not to tip our hand. Ollie, it's time for instructions! Lay out your maps of th' camp and th' information you've collected. We need to go over it and get it in our minds before we split up."

Ollie unrolled his papers from the rawhide cylinder he had stored them in. John and Robert studied over Ollie's notes and maps for about forty-five minutes, asking questions from time to time. They agreed that the boy had done an outstanding job. John noted that the commanding officer Captain Rutledge reported to was the general who had led the Southern troops at Middle Creek where John fought under General Garfield back in the winter.

"Don't thet grab you, now?" he asked, not expecting an answer. "Thet shows thet th' intention is still to rout Louisa. We'll see a step up in activities; and soon I'm bettin'. We may be able to slow thet down by eliminatin' their outside pipeline. Robert, were goin' to hafta work together for a few days or so—how do you want to work it?" John asked in deference to the older gentleman.

"Thank you fer considerin' me, *Northern Woodsman*, but I'm jus' a meanderin' lil ol' *Carter County Tadpole*," he said with a twinkle in his eye. "I'll defer leadership of this coalition ta you." Ollie was perplexed. He knew something had passed between the two men, but was hesitant to ask. John saw the question on his son's face and laughed.

"Well, partner," he said. "I suppose it's time to tell you our little secret—but it has to stay jus' thet. In th' spy network here in eastern Kentucky, most all of us have been given a code name for th' purpose of helpin' one another, 'n also to recognize one another. You haven't been in the spy business long enough to be given a name yet, but we'll have to think on thet some." He winked at Robert. "My name is *Northern Woodsman* and Robert's is *Carter County Tadpole*. Thet's how we knew to trust each other tonight. We wouldn't be sharin' this information about maps 'n sech if it warn't for these code names." Ollie felt privileged to be privy to this secret. It made him feel accepted and sort of equal, or at least on the way to being equal.

John took charge. He worked from biblical principles and in military command structure. He always worked that way and remembered those rules. It served to keep him in a humble attitude in following orders, as well as being able to give them. The biblical principles John had down for memory were, *"Be kindly affectioned one to another with brotherly love; in honour preferring one another"* (Rom. 12:10) and, *"Let every soul be subject to the higher powers. For there is no power but of God: the powers that be are ordained of God"* (Rom. 13:1).

"We'll have to split up again. Ollie, you'll be takin' these maps and the information you gathered at th' Rebel camp back to Captain Lyons. Also, you'll tell him what me 'n Robert are about, as far as cuttin' off th' source of information from th' camp. He'll know what's important 'n what's not. I can't give you our exact plan; I don't know thet myself yet. I want you to take th' girls by Uncle John's and see they get home safe. You can put two of them on Silky, 'n one can ride with you. I'll let you take charge of who rides where," he said, teasing Ollie a little. "Stop by th' cabin 'n check on Cassie and Cindy for me—and—"

"I know, Dad," Ollie interrupted. "Give Cassie your love. I'll be glad to do it!" Robert sat in admiration at what he witnessed passing between father and son. Even in their teasing, the warm affection and loyalty was obvious. This was a very rare quality, and Robert felt privileged to see it.

John turned to Robert. "After the men move out toward Grayson with the Bull, and Ollie gets started back with th' girls, you 'n me will take off for Sandy Hook in th' buckboard. I'll keep th' mule with me 'n we'll store some of our supplies at th' McPhersons. Does thet sound all right with you?"

"Whatever pleases you, Mr. Woodsman, jus' plumb tickles me ta pieces," Robert said with jest. But he meant every word.

"Well, it's time for me to say goodnight, afore daylight comes," John said.

Robert stood and said a hearty, "Amen!"

"If you fellers can make out with one light, why, I'll jus' stay here and do a little writin' afore I turn in," Ollie said as he took a lantern.

As Uncle Robert and John retired, he pulled out his journal, making himself comfortable. He had a lot of catching up to do. Pulling out his dad's watch, he remembered that in all the excitement he had forgotten the new hat for his dad! Well, he would lay it out before going to sleep, so he would remember it tomorrow. He glanced at the watch; it was ten thirty-five. Ollie wrote, "Friday Night 10:35 P.M. May 16th, 1862." He started with his trip to Sandy Hook and finished with the meeting between Uncle Robert and his dad. *This journal work takes up a lot of time,* Ollie thought as he carried his lantern back toward the sleeping group of friends and family.

He quietly picked up his gift for his dad and laid it by his bedroll, which was next to Susan's. The young lady had personally attended to his bedroll just before she turned down the blanket on her own. Ollie laid his head on a rolled-up part of the blanket and folded his hands behind his head. He looked out from his sheltered rock ceiling through the trees and at the brilliance of the stars. He was thinking on the good things God does and silently thanked Him for this great day he had had with Susan.

He was innocent in his thoughts of this pretty little friend that God had used to brighten his day. He turned and looked at her sleeping form, not even an arm's-length away. Her soft curls were beautiful, flowing down to her shoulders. Ollie smiled as he turned back and began to pray in a very low voice that he was positive would not awaken anyone.

"God," he started, *"I am so thankful that you love me. I know you love me 'cause you gave your own Son for me, and to me. He is my friend, and He pleases me! I jus' want to please Him th' same way. I also know He loves me 'cause He gives me friends—both grown-up friends like Reverend Borders, and friends like Eliza, Rhoda, and Susan. We had so much fun today. I thank you especially for Susan, God. She was very extra special to me today—and she made me feel so happy jus' to be with her; I know you love her, too. I jus' pray you will watch us, and take care of us, and be with us all tomorrow as we go different ways.*

"Bless and be with my dad and Uncle Robert. Bless and be with Brother Borders and his kinfolks as they go to the revival, and take Uncle Robert's bull home. Bless and be with me, and Susan, and Eliza, and Rhoda as we go back towards Deephole. And—one other thing, God—I almost forgot—please bless Tommy Blainey, and help him to find peace so he won't be a bully anymore. He'd prob'ly be nice enough if he jus' knew people would like him better for being good instead of bad. I love you God, through Jesus Christ. Amen!"

As Ollie said amen, a young lady's soft hand reached out and took his right hand, enfolding her own fingers through his. They tightened in a squeeze then relaxed, just leaving her hand there. It was evident Ollie had another audience besides God. He went to sleep just that way, with Susan holding his hand.

Morning came and Ollie was up before anyone else was stirring. He slipped down to the stream and brought back water. Finding an abundance of wood already gathered, he had the fire going and water heating for coffee in no time. John was awake so he joined Ollie. He spoke softly. "Son, you don't know how good it feels to wake up and not feel a strange metal object in your leg, cutting and gouging. I jus' praise th' Lord; I don't even limp anymore."

"Dad, you ought to tell the preacher and his kin about it—and Uncle Robert. I don't think th' girls, 'ceptin' for Susan, know about it either. It's a miracle, and God should get the glory for th' healin'."

"I'll jus' do thet, Son. Thet's a prime idea."

They both busied themselves making breakfast, working together as an experienced pair of cooks. By this time, the sun was coming up and the girls were busy combing the "rats" out of their curls. Susan had told the girls to expect a change of plans, but she did not tell about how she knew. She would not betray the confidence of the prayer she had heard. The Borders men wasted no time in packing up their gear and joining John and Robert for coffee. Soon all were around the fire eating breakfast, laughing, and talking. Even Susan, who had wrinkled her nose at coffee yesterday, was sipping on a cup this morning.

Ollie went to his bedroll, but found it was already rolled up. Susan had taken it upon herself to care for Ollie. He went over to her and motioned for her to lean over, as if he wanted to whisper in her ear. When she leaned over he kissed her on the cheek and whispered, "Thank you!" Susan blushed, hesitated, and kissed him back. Ollie, holding his composure, picked up his dad's gift and brought it back to the circle of friends. He walked up to John, held it out to him.

"This is for you, Dad."

Looking very surprised, John took the gift, still in store wrapping. He opened it and found a fine dark-brown straw hat.

"My, Ollie. This is great." Turning it over and over, he looked back to Ollie, not knowing what to say.

It was Susan who finally spoke. "Well, John, for goodness sakes, don't jus' wear it out lookin' at it. Try it on so we can see how it looks on you."

He put the hat on and sort of tilted it over his right eye, finding it fit perfectly. Everyone applauded and the girls were oo-ing and making over him.

"John, Cassie will love it, and she is going to just wear out your face touching that bare skin where you shaved off your beard," Eliza commented.

"Well, I'll tell you one thing," Rev. Borders said. "I'm sure Ollie got that hat for John's head, 'cause if it were for his face—it wouldn't fit now!" The senior Joseph spoke up and joined the humor. "I'm mighty sorry I wasn't here when ya shaved off all those whiskers, John. I've been meanin' to pad my saddle, and I guess I plumb missed out." Everyone laughed, and John took it all good-naturedly.

As the laughter subsided, John, still wearing his short pants, said, "I want to tell you all about somethin' that took place right here, this week. It was a miracle—for sure. I mean—there is only One thet's in th' miracle business and that's th' one Brother Borders works for." John took his seat and continued.

"Most all of you are a witness to the fact thet I was in the Army in December of last year and I fought in th' Battle of Middle Creek with General James Garfield. I was wounded by a shell that exploded over me. It also rendered me unconscious with a concussion. I awakened in a hospital tent jus' in time to keep a Union doctor from cutting off my left leg. I had a wound bad enough thet the Army discharged me and some wondered if I'd ever walk agin.

"That was five months ago. This week thet piece of shrapnel started to cut me from th' inside out. I was bleedin' and in terrible pain." He patted his son's shoulder. "Ollie cut thet piece of metal out o' me and sewed me up. I figured I could get back on a horse without reopening th' cut in about three-four days if I was careful. Folks, thet was on Tuesday of this week and I want you all to see thet leg now." John stood up in front of every person. He turned around allowing them to examine his scar. Rev. Borders was amazed and said so. Each one shook their head and glanced at each other.

"How did this happen, John. The miracle, I mean?" The preacher asked.

John took the ugly object and held it up, passing it to Uncle Robert, who examined it, and passed it on.

"Well, after cuttin' out the metal Ollie asked me could he pray for me. He took a Scripture, quoted it, and asked th' Lord to heal up th' wound. Th' upshot of th' thing was—th' Lord heard th' prayer and did it. I jus' wanted to share my joy in this with you, and give all th' glory to God, which I do, right now." With that, John lifted both hands toward heaven, and said, "I thank you, Lord, and I give you th' glory for my healed leg."

As if rehearsed everyone said, "Amen!"

"Now," John announced, "before we all go our separate ways, I want Ollie to tell you a story thet'll make us all laugh. And I would like th' preacher to pray a prayer over all of us. Ollie is takin' th' ladies home; Rev. Borders, Joseph and Joseph are takin' th' bull to Lost Creek on the way to th' meetin'; and Robert 'n me have some business to take care of right here in this Sandy Hook area. Ollie, I want you to tell 'em how you saved the McPhersons' work horses from the Rebel camp."

Eliza glanced at Rhoda and both looked to Susan who had a smile and an "I told you so," look on her face when John spoke of Ollie taking the ladies home.

Ollie loved to tell stories, and he loved to make folks laugh, so he did it up right. He went into the detail of how the camp looked, the name of the captain, how he argued and brought the fish to the camp. Most of all he told about the escape and about the sheep running helter-skelter throughout the camp. When he told about the ram standing there waiting for a cue to do something and how he sent Captain Rutledge sailing, using the bent over rear as a target, there wasn't a dry eye in the circle. Uncle Robert was the only one who managed to say something.

"It had to be a Yankee ram. It jus' had to be," he said, hardly able to talk for laughing so hard!

Standing with hat in hand, the minister stood up to pray, and everyone became silent in respect. John Borders began to pray for the group of travelers and for their journeys as they went their ways. He prayed for safety and protection, for guidance for Robert and John on their mission and for men and women, boys and girls to be brought into the kingdom of God over in Grayson. When he finished, everyone said, "Amen!"

The preacher and his entourage left first; he leading the bull and the two Josephs driving. John and Robert packed up everything except for a few supplies that Ollie had laid out. Robert had brought a saddle in the buckboard and Ollie put it on Silky, leaving his dad's saddle for him. He could use it on the mule or one of Uncle Robert's horses. John and Robert intended to leave their belongings with the McPhersons on the way to town.

After Ollie packed and saddled the horses, he called a meeting with the girls. "We need to go through th' camp and clean up, making it look as unused as we can. We need to stir up the horse droppings with dust, the campfire leavin's, and jus' anythin' thet would make it look like someone has been here. I'll bury the cans and trash and afterwards, if you girls don't mind, I need to stop at th' stream 'n wash up." They nodded and everyone got busy with the assigned task of clean up.

Robert just shook his head and said to John, "Thet boy is a natural-borned leader. He jus' takes over—and them girl's jus' listened ta ever' single thin' he said." John smiled in agreement, and they headed off toward the trail; riding the buckboard and leading Fred the mule.

TWENTY-FOUR

They That Render Evil for Good

OLLIE CAME OUT FROM NATURE'S DRESSING ROOM, THE FOREST, AND stood before the girls a different youngster, wearing his buckskins and boots. The belt of buckskins also held his hunting knife, and he had a sharp-looking gun belt and holster with his Colt .44 on his right hip. *He looks like a miniature Daniel Boone,* Eliza thought. *All he needs is the coonskin cap.*

The girls also freshened up at the stream and were ready for their journey. They still had two full days' travel ahead of them if they traveled at a normal pace, but they all had the feeling that Ollie was not going to travel at a normal pace, yet they were still looking forward to it. Ollie had returned his dad's watch, so he was back to estimating the time again. It was very close to eight o'clock when they set out on Ginger and Silky, with Susan riding once again behind Ollie, and Eliza and Rhoda on Silky, fitting in the saddle perfectly. Ollie chuckled as they rode along, realizing that, in spite of their various ages, they were all pretty close to the same size. Rhoda was a little taller, but all of them were probably within five pounds of each other.

Ollie headed the lead horse down the same trail he and his father had traveled coming toward Sandy Hook nearly a week ago. Wherever the trail was easy enough, he permitted Ginger to lead off with that canter that not only covered miles, but was a gentle ride. The chatter was not easy between horses traveling at this clip, so it was more or less confined to talking with your riding partner which, of course, Ollie didn't mind

_____

John climbed off the buckboard, waving at Bob McPherson, who was working in his garden. He had Dick hitched to a two-spaded plow and had been plowing neat furrows between rows of sweet corn, turning rich loose dirt over on top of weeds. He had the reins knotted, with one strap coming from the harness over his right shoulder, around his back and under the left arm as it led back to the horse on the left side. When he saw John and Robert pull up in front of the house, Bob spoke to Dick as he laid his right arm across the reins, pulling back on the animal and holding the plow up with his left hand.

"Whoa-a there, boy—whoa, Dick." The trained animal stopped in his traces. Bob hooked the reins on the plow handles and walked over to John, wiping his brow with a blue checkered bandanna. He was already wet from waist to his neck, proving he had been following this plow long enough to have a rest coming. Dick was muzzled so he could not nip at the young shoots of corn already about knee high.

"Well, howdy there, John," Bob said as he stuck out his hand. "You always have the best timing, coming along jus' when a feller needs to rest a bit."

John smiled, shaking the farmer's hand. "This here is Robert Birchet, a good friend of mine. We'd like to know if you've got room fer us to store some supplies while we take care of some business together in Sandy Hook?"

"John Burke, whatever I got here is fer you ta use. Ya don't even have ta ask. Now, why don't you fellers sit up on th' porch fer ten minits 'r so while I finish up with this patch o' corn 'n I'll jine up with ya fer some tea sippin'."

John figured this plan was as good as any. He and Robert had to work on some details anyway. As they walked up to the porch, Mary met them with a smile and two glasses of cool sassafras tea.

"Been eavesdroppin'. Howdy, Robert. I'm Mary, Bob's woman fer nigh on ta thirty-two yar's. Howdy, John. Good ta see ya healthy agin. Bob tole me 'bout your healin'. I'll jus' leave th' drinks fer ya 'n git back to my kitchen." Mary scurried back through the house.

"Nice folks, these McPherson's," John said to Robert. "I'm sure they'll help us without too many questions 'bout our comin's 'n goin's. Robert, I've been ponderin' on a partial plan while we've been comin' over here. I think it might play to our advantage if we go into town separate like. I mean it could be we jus' let on like we have never met up with each other before. What do you think?"

"Sounds smart ta me, John. I've been seen in Sandy Hook several times th' last month and folks are beginnin' ta know me. I've been seen in a few spots with Blainey 'n Tibbett, too."

About that time, Bob joined them on the porch and seemed to have something on his mind.

"Boys—I got somethin' ta say. Don't know how ta speak 'ceptin' plain and straight out! I know you fellers are into somethin' with th' guv-a-ment, but don't rightly know what—and it don't matter none. I figure yore Yankees, jus' like Mary 'n me, and yore workin' fer th' North, secret-like. I jus' want ya ta know that you can come 'n go as ya please here. I got a small shed off ta th' side of th' barn thet's dry and big 'nough fer yore horses, buckboard 'n stuff. I ain't askin' ya ta tell me yore story, I'm jus' sayin' you can depend on me 'n Mary ta keep our mouths shut." With that, he waved them on and took off down the well-worn path to the barn. John and Robert glanced at each other, grinning, and followed him.

The shed was just as Bob indicated. There was room for the buckboard, livestock and plenty of room for Robert and John to bed down. A swinging half door led into the barn, and a ladder ascended into the hay loft. Bob told the men to make themselves at home and use the shed as if they owned it. The backside of the shed had a small corral with a water trough and grain buckets nailed to chestnut posts. John dropped the gate, and both men went to the buckboard and led the team and John's mule around through the corral.

In a short time the team was unhitched and the buckboard, harness, saddles and supplies were hidden from view in the shed. Bob returned to his work while John and Robert discussed their plans. John said that the only plan he could come up with now was to try to isolate these men who were killing off good Northern partisans and stealing from the North.

"This is war," John said, "and, even if it takes killin' these men, we must figure th' best way to do whatever it takes to do it without pointin' fingers at th' local folks."

Robert seemed deep in thought for a minute or so. He finally replied. "John, what do ya think o' this? Why don't you go over an' scout 'round thet Reb camp 'n see if you can pick up somethin' thet would give us a clue as to what their about—or if they's jus' there waitin'. I'll go on in ta town and try ta connect up with Blainey and Tibbett. We usually meet at th' feed store close to the livery barn. You 'n me will meet up at th' eatin' place across from th' general store. I disremember what they call it."

"Sounds as good or better than anythin' I could come up with, Robert. I'll saddle Fred and I'll meet you tomorrow afternoon late—'bout 5:30, OK?" "Good. Why don't ya take one o' th' team ta ride on? I'm leavin' th' buckboard here," Robert suggested.

"Thanks, Robert, but someone might recognize thet matchin' team of yours. Fred is broke in fer th' saddle and he'll enjoy doin' somethin' besides carryin' a pack fer a change," John answered.

The curious mule turned when John placed the saddle blanket over his back. It was not like the packs and Fred immediately noticed the difference. As he reached under Fred's belly to bring the girth to the buckle, John noticed that Robert was still sitting—in deep thought. John continued his preparations with the rifle boot and saddlebag, making sure his Sharps was loaded and sighting down the barrel. He placed several boxes of cartridges in the saddlebag along with some jerky and dried fruit. He was giving Robert some time to be alone with his thoughts before he approached him. Something was bothering the older man and John was allowing him to work it out before he disturbed him. Finally, John tied on his bedroll and Fred was ready to travel.

Approaching Robert, John sat down and asked, "Well, do you think we need to cover anythin' else before we split up?"

"Somethin's been botherin' me, John. Why—thet Rebel camp is not more 'n five or six miles from Sandy Hook accordin' ta thet map of your young'un, wouldn't ya say?"

"Thet's about right, Robert."

"Well, how is it thet the town folks and farmers don't git up in arms about it and disturb them Rebs. Why is it they jus' let 'em be?"

"Thet's a good question, Robert. You see, from where we're sitting we can sorta look at th' side lines 'n all—'cause me 'n you are almost military. You're active in the guerrilla warfare, and me, why I'm an active scout and spy on military payroll. So for us thet's a natural question. But let's look at the community here from their standpoint. First off, they's bound to be a lot of 'em like you was yesterday—they jus' don't know thet the Rebs are there.

"Secondly, there are those in this county thet jus' don't care about th' war and don't want to be bothered with it. They know the Rebs are there—but they ain't botherin' nobody, so 'leave sleepin' dogs lie' is their motto.

"Finally, there are those who know, and care, but they're afeared—and they know they don't have the experience or weapons to come against them. Mostly, those are th' folks that make up your partisans—or send word to the Union over to Louisa. Most folks figure if they'll jus' leave 'em alone they'll go away. Let me ask you this, Robert—how many men do you have in your partisan group?"

"Hardly more than twenty-five, I reckon."

"And thet's in two different counties, right?" Robert nodded and John continued. "How many able-bodied men, not in the army right now, are left at home in this county do you figure?"

"I don't reckon they's more than a hundred countin' what's in town. Prob'ly not even fifteen in Sandy Hook." Robert began to see where John was leading him.

"You see, Robert, this Rebel force of one hundred trained and equipped officers and soldiers no doubt have twenty mounted troopers as well as an artillery battery of several cannons. If they wanted to do so, they could take over and control this whole county; Sandy Hook and all."

Robert was looking dejected, pointing his nose between his feet. "Dumb question, huh, John?" He looked up sheepishly.

John slapped him playfully on the back. "Not at all, Robert— no such thing as a dumb question. I would have asked th' same question at one time; th' only difference is th' question had been answered for me once before. This camp bein' so close, and havin' two of your trusted men as traitors to you, jus' came up on your blind side."

Thirty minutes later found Fred winding his way through timber, climbing straight south from the McPherson farm. Fred was a good riding mule, picking his way sure-footedly along a sharp incline. John had decided he was going to come to the camp from the south for two reasons. He wanted to survey the terrain toward the south, and he wanted to mislead anyone who might be watching or tracking him; not that he was suspicious of such an intruder, but he just didn't want to take a chance. As John traveled, he didn't allow much to escape his keen eyes or ears. He was accustomed to living this way as a hunter and woodsman and he was enjoying this time of being alone. His new straw hat, shading his head from the sun, was tilted over his right eye. It made him think of his son's thoughtfulness in buying it for him.

John was several miles south of the raiders' trail that Ollie had traveled, therefore a good distance south of the Confederate camp, when he reached the crest of a tall tree-lined hill. Huge pines were bending in the breeze when suddenly Fred flinched and stopped abruptly. John listened and heard the popping sound of a musket off toward the southwest. It was a long way off, but John could distinguish sound and the direction. He reined Fred toward a tall pine and pulled the telescope out of his saddlebag.

John ground-tied Fred, stood in the saddle to reach a tree limb, and swung himself into the tree. He climbed twenty-five or thirty feet up the tree to get a good view. The sounds of gunfire continued at intervals as he scanned the area until he finally saw puffs of smoke ascending through the dense, forest-covered landscape to the south and west. It was several miles away, in the general direction of West Liberty, a sizable town in Morgan County. John took a bearing on the direction of the firing, and decided to investigate. Fred stood perfectly still until John was once again back in the saddle.

John was an hour or more traveling over rough and rocky landscape, listening to the shots; the noise grew louder as he came closer. He detected the distinctive sound of musket fire as well as one or two more powerful rifles and occasionally a revolver. As he drew near the location, the firing suddenly stopped; he wondered if he had been discovered. He dismounted, tied Fred, and removed his Sharps from the scabbard. As he silently crept toward the area where he last heard the shots, he heard the thunder of several horses traveling at a gallop. They were slightly to the west of him, but he fell to the ground just in time to see three, maybe four, riders through the branches. He could not distinguish their faces, but he was sure they wore Confederate uniforms.

John stayed quietly in place for five minutes, waiting and listening. Hearing nothing, he stood and advanced cautiously toward a clearing and an old farmhouse where the battle had played out. He saw smoke coming out of a front window, so he ran into the house and found a fire burning in the dining area. The fire was not out of control as yet so John tore the drapes off a front window and spread them over the fire. He found water in the kitchen and brought two buckets; dousing the drapes. As soon as the fire was extinguished, John began to take notice of the old home which, from its looks, had been there for some time.

As he walked through the downstairs of the two-story home, he heard a moan. Stepping around an over-turned dining table John found an old man, still clutching a musket, and bleeding from his chest. John carried him to a couch in front of a native-stone fireplace and placed a cushion under his head. John grabbed up the bucket he had just discarded and found the well near the kitchen door. He returned with a glass of water and a wet towel. From the look of the wound, John knew the man did not have much time left. He just tried to make him comfortable. The man looked up at John with glazed eyes.

"Yer—yer not one o' them?"

"No, sir. I jus' heard th' shots an' got here as they rode off. Is there anything I can do for you?"

"R-Reckon not anythin' anyone can do fer me—'ceptin' take a message," he gasped, as a flood of blood and air bubbles spurted from the hole in his chest.

John took the towel and applied pressure to the wound. The man caught his breath and spoke weakly. "Mah—name's—Lloyd Patterson." He coughed up blood and caught his breath. "Mah grandson's—Gus—A'gustus—Patterson—Boston. See sheriff—Sandy Hook." Lloyd gestured with his last remaining strength, pointing toward the floor, saying, "His'n—place." He gurgled his last breath and died in John's arms.

John laid him back and stood, catching his breath, looking around the room. He slowly walked through the old home that must have been a happy place at one time. He found no signs of life inside. At the barn he found a younger man in soiled clothes, shot through the head. The clothing suggested the man was a hired hand, perhaps a relative. A musket lay nearby. John found a fenced family plot in an orchard east of the house. Three graves were obviously cared for. One had a field stone with the name "Amy" etched with a chisel.

Two hours later John had buried the two men side by side in the family plot. On each grave he stuck a cross made out of two pieces of board nailed together, carving Lloyd's name on his marker. John found some tools in a shed and boarded up the house, nailing planks over windows and doors. All this took time, but he could not go off without showing some care for this piece of property as if it were his own. He could see that the men who had brought about this tragedy had taken livestock; the barn was empty of animals except for some scattered chickens and turkeys. John decided to follow the men who had murdered Lloyd and his hired hand, although he felt he knew where the trail would lead.

John studied the hoof prints, which told the story. It looked like these men had been in the middle of a dawn raid at the Patterson place, removing the livestock, when the field hand discovered them. The battle then took place, arousing and bringing the owner into the fracas. It looked to John as though two men held the livestock about five hundred yards away from the farmhouse, while the remaining four overcame the two men. *Such a tragedy*, John thought, as he followed the easy trail. War brought about the destruction of what was left of a man's belongings. Probably Amy was his wife and perhaps the two unmarked graves were children. None left except this grandson, Augustus, perhaps in Boston, if he understood the old gentleman's last request correctly.

John stopped at a stream to water Fred, and he refilled his canteen while chewing on some jerky. He was continuing his tracking when he began to hear the sounds of cattle and horses in front of him. John dismounted, tying Fred to a tree, then listened. The sounds seemed to be those of animals milling around rather than traveling. He quietly crept from tree to tree up a hollow, following a stream, and soon he was hearing the roar of a waterfall. Edging around to the east, he climbed a rocky hill dense with oak and pine, and soon was overlooking a natural corral.

John was amazed at what he saw! Perhaps a hundred cattle and horses were crowded into a dead-end hollow where a cascading waterfall dropped some seventy-five feet into a deep body of water about thirty feet across. Six men guarded the entrance. There was a fence of split rails that had obviously been here for some time. The men were a mixed lot, mostly in Rebel uniforms, but from the looks of things, this was not a Confederate Army operation. One thing is for sure—this is where Lloyd Patterson's stock ended up.

John slipped the telescope out of his side pocket and studied the men and the surroundings. He could hear voices and laughter, but he was not close enough to make out the conversation. He decided to go up and over the waterfall and come down on the opposite side, where the trees were larger. There was one huge beech tree that would be ideal for listening if he could work his way up to it. Thirty minutes later John was creeping up to the beech, which had a hollow large enough for him to hide in. John could hear the voices plainly now. He placed his Colt on his lap and listened.

"Captain Rutledge would sure be surprised if'n he saw all this stock we have holed up here," one man was saying, laughing loudly.

"You sure got thet right, Sarge. He'd git his mind in a total uproar," another laughingly agreed. "Say, Sarge, when are we agoin' ta git rid of this stock? We're gittin' a passel of livestock here and we should be turnin' 'em into some money purty soon, I'm a thinkin'," the man said.

"Soon, Tibbett, soon. We got ta figure out where an' how we're goin' ta market 'em. The closest place is over ta Catlettsburg on th' Big Sandy. Only problem is—thet's pure Yankee country!" Sarge replied.

"Well, what th' hell do we care," a third voice said. "Me 'n Tibbett is jus' as good at bein' Yankees as we is at bein' Rebs. Let's all put on some civilian clothes and herd 'em over there and divide up."

"You know—ya got a point there, Blainey," Sarge's voice came back. "We're in this fer the money anyway, and I sure don't want to stay around 'n git in another fight like thet one a week ago. We almost lost it all right there."

The one called Tibbett called out, "All right you men—come on over here, Sergeant Runyan's got a plan ta tell us about." John took a chance and peered around the edge of the tree. He had to see the faces of these men if at all possible.

Sergeant Runyan was a short stocky man who appeared to be all muscle. He had a barrel chest, thick arms and broad shoulders. His square face had a week's growth of beard and he wore a slough hat, pinned back with a Confederate star. A Remington Army revolver protruded from a holster and he had on well-worn high riding boots with star spurs. John could tell the man had been around and would be as tough as rawhide. John recognized Tibbett by the sandy hair and high forehead Ollie had described. Blainey would be the man with the brown hair and sweeping mustache. Ollie was right, he did seem to have a permanent scowl on his face.

These men gathered with three others and Sergeant Runyan began to talk earnestly. "Men, Tibbett is all for selling out our livestock and splitting up. Blainey feels we should drive these animals to Catlettsburg over on the Big Sandy and sell 'em—th' sooner th' better. I did point out thet's Yankee country—but Blainey feels if we all dressed as civilians we could git by with it. Let's hear from all o' you. What do you think?"

The men didn't take long to decide. "When do we leave?" It was unanimous.

"OK, men, you've decided; so we will leave tomorrow, Sunday morning. I'll take Tibbett, Blainey and Watson on a supply mission tomorrow and we will meet up here at eight A.M. Reynolds and Campbell, you two leave now and hightail it back to th' camp. Take those two sickly cows with you to turn in at the camp. Git yore clothes to change into and be back here at dark. You'll be th' guard here tonight until we git back tomorrow. Th' rest of us will stay here 'till you git back an' then we'll cut out a couple o' head and take 'em into th' camp. It'll take purt-near all week ta git 'em ta market, an' I think market day is Friday.

John watched Reynolds and Campbell head off toward the Rebel camp, driving two poor cows in front of them. He listened while the four remaining raiders discussed the appropriate clothes to wear, and how to allow an unfortunate accident to happen to Reynolds and Campbell—after the livestock had been delivered to market, of course. *Scoundrels, all of them,* John thought.

He smiled to himself as he crept off through the woods, circling back to Fred. He led the mule several hundred yards clear of the outlaw camp and headed toward Sandy Hook. He no longer needed to go by the Confederate camp. His plan had been made for him.

It was dark when John rode into town and he had little trouble finding Jim Henderson and the livery barn. He left Fred there while he carried his rifle and saddlebag down the boardwalk. He passed by the general store and noticed the owner inside sweeping. Anson West stopped his work and gave John the once-over. His eyes settled on the hat and a smile lit his face. "Perfect fit, I'd say." He walked over, extending his hand. "You must be John Burke."

"Well, you sure got thet one right—I jus' got to thank you for them good steaks you sent off with Ollie. I can still taste 'em. And they fed nine hungry folks last night," John said gratefully.

"Nine?" Anson said with surprise. "Why the little lady told me six folks would be dining, I should have sent more," the generous storekeeper said.

"No you shouldn't have, Mr. West. Them other three happened by without us knowing they were coming and we were all finished 'n there was still plenty left. Them girls couldn't eat a whole steak th' size you cut 'em. I'm tellin' you everyone had all they could eat."

"By the way, my name is Anson; just call me Ans—and I'll call you John. Well, anyway I'm glad you enjoyed the steaks. I raise the beef, and butcher them myself, and I take pride in good meat. I have folks from clear over West Liberty way buy beef from me," Mr. West said proudly.

"Speaking of beef, I'm hankerin' for some supper, but I also need to talk to the sheriff if he's in town. I got a message for him," John said.

"You just head over to the cafe across the street and I'll round up the sheriff for you. I'll join you myself in a little bit, if you don't mind."

"Glad for the company, Ans. I'll jus' head over thet way and get us a table." John tipped his hat and strolled out the door.

Walking across to the same cafe, John was aware of his leg—this time for a different reason; he could not help but feel gratitude for being able to walk and not limp. He had been so much in the habit of feeling pain, it was still almost unnatural not to feel it. *How great is our God*, he thought, then said out loud, "Thank you, Lord!" As he went up the steps to the cafe, he wondered where Robert was. As John stepped into the light, he surveyed the room and saw Robert at a table talking with a couple. John didn't acknowledge anyone in particular, but nodded to different folks with a pleasant smile as he passed their tables. He found one unoccupied table with four chairs and seated himself facing the front door. He set his saddlebag and rifle against the window and removed his hat just as a portly waitress came up.

"Let me put up that hat for you, sir." John smiled and handed her the hat. She took it to a hat rack on the front wall and returned to take John's order.

"We have three special features fer supper, sir. Chicken 'n dumplin's, beef stew, and ham 'n lima beans. Bread, butter 'n beverage is served with th' meal; rhubarb cobbler is fer dessert. Th' meal is 35 cents 'n includes th' dessert."

"Let me think on it, ma'am. I got a friend or two joinin' me and I'll wait 'n order when they do. Meanwhile, I'll have some hot coffee please."

Robert seemed to be having a good visit with the couple at his table, and he hardly noticed that John was in the room. *Good man,* thought John. As he glanced around the room he thought back on a meal a little over a week ago when a beautiful lady put his face into his plate. John chuckled as he thought about that. Shortly Anson West came in, leading a large man about fifty years old with a shiny silver badge on his corduroy vest. He wore a felt hat and riding boots, which made him seem taller than his height of six feet. He had a .36 caliber Navy Colt tucked behind a belt, and John was sure he knew how to use it. When they walked over, Anson introduced him as John stood to shake hands with the sheriff, who seemed to tower over him.

"Sheriff Baldwin, this is a friend, John Burke, from over Lawrence County way. John, meet Sheriff Parker Baldwin."

"Sit down, gentlemen, sit down. Let me treat you to some supper and coffee." John waved the waitress back. "Coffee for my guests, ma'am."

As the waitress disappeared, Sheriff Parker spoke to John. "I sure thank you fer th' offer to buy my supper, Mr. Burke, but ya don't hafta do thet. I jus' figured ya had somethin' on yer mind ta speak with me about."

"Well, thet too, Sheriff, but I insist on buying supper for th' both of you. I feel like havin' company and I want to get acquainted. Besides, it helps me feel protected to keep company with th' sheriff," he jokingly added.

"I thought you might want to talk to the sheriff private-like, John," Ans suggested.

"Not at all, Ans; I jus' have a report for him—and a message. I figure we'll order and I'll tell you 'bout it while we wait for our food."

The waitress returned with the coffee and repeated the three menu choices. John ordered the chicken and dumplings; the other two ordered the beef stew.

"Sheriff, do you know a Lloyd Patterson over South of here a ways?" John asked.

Sheriff Parker, sipping his coffee, nodded.

"Sure do know Lloyd—so does Ans here. He's a fine old codger. Has a farm of several hundred acres and an ol' showplace of a house. He built it himself, oh fifty years ago, prob'ly. Why? You got a message from him?"

"I got bad news for th' both of you, then." John put his head down a few seconds. "He died in my arms this mornin'."

"My dear God," Parker said, putting down his coffee cup. "How'd it happen? Why, he was in town last week and looked perfectly fine to me—didn't he to you, Ans?" he asked, turning to the storekeeper.

"Yes, he seemed fine last week. You say he died in your arms? Was his death of natural causes?" Anson asked.

"No, sir, it wasn't a natural death. He had a bullet hole in his chest—lung shot I'm afraid; he was dying when I found him." John related the story about the bandits and the hired man that John had found at the barn. He told of seeing the raiders ride off toward the north. He said that they wore Confederate uniforms. He also told about Lloyd's last words and his death wish about his grandson, Augustus.

"He told me to give the message to the sheriff at Sandy Hook," John said. "So—here I am. I buried him by Amy and the other man."

The meals arrived and the men ate in silence, each thinking about the sobering news of the loss of a friend. John ate his meal, since he had had very little nourishment for all of his travel and activity; but the news affected both Ans' and the Sheriff's appetites. They did eat some, but it was plain they were not as hungry as before. John did not tell the men about the Rebel hideout, and it was evident that the sheriff was up a tree about what to do, because he obviously knew about the camp and was not in position to do anything about it. Anson was also aware and he knew this was a quandary for the lawman. To know where to point the finger, who the culprits were, and not be able to do his duty was frustrating.

"An act of war and my hands are tied," the sheriff said. "I'll write to the boy. He's sixteen an' in school in Boston. His pa's folks are well fixed, 'n his pa is off ta war. Thet's Lloyd's daughter's boy, 'n she's dead too. Buried up there somewhere, I reckon," Parker explained. "Th' man you buried was, in fact, a hired hand but he also was a cousin to Lloyd."

John could not get more involved than he already was. He wished he could tell these men that the killers would be brought to trial—or worse—and pay dearly for the crimes they had committed. He simply could not tip his hand and let them know about the stolen livestock. He noticed Robert was still sipping coffee, and he needed to touch base with him; he raised his voice, loud enough for others to hear.

"Where do travelers spend th' night, Sheriff? Is there a rooming house in town?"

"Absolutely, John. There's a tavern down the street on the right. Next door is a clean rooming house—always accommodating, too." Anson replied first.

Robert stood up and turned to them. "Jus' happened to overhear you, sir. I'm staying at the rooming house myself; I'll take you there and introduce you." "By th' way, my name is Robert Birchet," he said, sticking out his hand. John smiled.

"Pleased to meet you, Robert. I'll be glad to take you up on your offer." Robert and John walked off together, but they left a very curious Anson West.

Anson had met Robert and his nieces yesterday with John's son. He knew that Robert was one of the guests dining on his steaks last night at John Burke's camp. Why would they not know each other today? Well, curious though he was, he was a prudent man and figured he would keep this information to himself.

TWENTY-FIVE

She Maketh
Herself Coverings

OLLIE SLOWED THE HORSES TO A PLEASANT WALK AND THE GIRLS SEEMED more at ease, although they had not complained. It was a beautiful spring day and Ollie felt as if they should be enjoying the time together. Susan squeezed Ollie around the waist as the older girls pulled up along side and they smiled at one another. Ollie pretended not to notice in order to avoid embarrassment. He really was enjoying being with all the Birchet girls, especially Susan. He felt he had become close to her on this trip.

Susan placed her right hand on the handle of the Colt and, as Ollie felt the weight of her hand on his gun, he turned. He smiled at her and allowed her to touch the handle of the weapon.

"Do you know how to use this gun, Ollie? I mean—remember the other night when you heard the Reverend Borders? I mean, before you knew who it was, you jumped up with this gun and it seemed like you were ready to use it. Do you remember?"

"Yes, ma'am, I remember."

"Well—would you use it?" Susan asked.

"I guess that would depend on who it was. I mean, who was out there. If I had to—I would use it."

"Do you *really* know how to use it, Ollie?" asked Susan.

"Yes, ma'am. I know pretty well how to use it." He turned to the other girls who had been listening in. "We'll stop at th' next stream and water 'n rest th' horses."

He had no sooner made this remark when around the next bend in the trail they came to a stream. Ollie helped Susan dismount and then he too dismounted. Eliza and Rhoda were already dismounted and their horses had buried their noses in the cool branch water. Ollie had attempted to change the subject, but Susan was not finished.

"Show us, Ollie—about the gun, I mean. We all have fired muskets and shotguns, but none of us have ever seen a gun like that close up," Susan pleaded. Eliza and Rhoda did not help; they were interested too.

"Oh—I guess it will be all right," Ollie said. "I guess I can tell you what dad told me, and showed me. First, let's all sit down." Making himself comfortable, he pulled out the Colt.

"Now th' first thing you've got to know about is—this is a revolver," he said, holding the weapon skyward. "It's not for hunting varmints, or even jus' plain ol' huntin'—it's a killin' machine! It's used in law enforcement work, and for war. It's used to kill another person and to protect yourself with. Do you all understand that?" His voice was dead serious. He was trying his best to imitate his dad. The girls did not laugh; they knew he was not teasing.

Ollie took the weapon, removed the caps from each nipple and put six of them into Susan's hand. He then removed the six paper-wrapped bullets and placed them in Eliza's hand. He revolved the cylinder, showing the girls how it worked, and pulled back the hammer. Then he pulled the trigger to show how it struck the nipple. He handed the weapon to Rhoda while the other girls watched. She seemed awkward with it as she looked it over. Ollie took the weapon back and showed them how it worked. As the cylinder turned each time he pulled the hammer back, the girls could see the action of the weapon.

"With th' percussion caps here," pointing to Susan's hand, "and the bullets here," pointing to Eliza's hand, "this weapon is only good if you use it as a club. It's also only used to shoot if someone is close to you. It doesn't do good for a long-distance target."

One by one, he put the caps back on and then slid the cartridges back in. "Now," he said, "it's dangerous again." He took the weapon and showed the girls how the hammer had to be pulled back each time in order to fire it.

"Now, stand back to th' side of me and hold your ears when I get ready to fire." Ollie looked around for a target and finally settled on a small birch sapling about two inches in diameter almost forty feet away. He pointed it out to the girls and told them to watch. Ollie aimed, fired and hit the sapling right where he aimed.

"That's wonderful, Ollie," Eliza said, "Could you shoot and hit that each time you fired?"

"Prob'ly not, Eliza," Ollie said, honestly. "I've jus' been practicing for three or four months now." He handed the weapon to Eliza, handle first, and said, "I'll let each one of you shoot one time, jus' to get the feel of the gun." The girls each took their turn; firing one round each. No one scored a hit, but Ollie encouraged them, saying they came close enough. Eliza persuaded Ollie to shoot just once more; he did, hitting the tree the second time. By this time, Ollie Burke had the attention of these young ladies and they knew that he could handle this Colt .44 weapon with no problem.

"Ollie, could you take aim and shoot another person—like you did that tree?"

"Susan, you've been so all-fired interested in that gun o' mine and what I could, or could not do with it. You're—well, you're special to me and I don't want to hurt you—but I'm kinda scared to answer your questions! If I said to you that I could shoot another person—like that tree—what would you think of me?"

Ollie's little speech took Susan off-guard and now she was the one on the spot. Both Eliza and Rhoda were waiting for her answer, along with Ollie. After a full minute, she said, "I—I don't know, Ollie."

"Yesterday, I took a weapon—my fist—and I hit Tommy Blainey in the nose and broke it, th' blood splattered all over th' place. What did you think about that?"

"Why—I was glad! He hurt me and pushed you down, Ollie."

"What if Tommy Blainey's dad, who is a Reb soldier, pulled a gun on you and was goin' to shoot you—and, and—I pulled this Colt and shot him first—what would you think about that?"

"Why, I would be forever grateful, Ollie. Otherwise—I'd be dead."

"Well, Susan, you jus' answered your question to me—for me! Of course, I could pull this gun and shoot a man—especially if I was protecting you—or Eliza—or Rhoda or Dad. Do you see what I mean? I think we all would fight for th' ones we love. And I believe you would do it too—if you had to!"

With the subject closed, Ollie thought, he brought the horses back over and helped the girls all back into the saddle then mounted himself.

Susan was not finished just yet; she had one more question.

"Ollie, have you used that gun on a man?" Ollie stopped Ginger and was silent for a minute while Susan and her sisters waited for him to answer.

Ollie turned toward them, his eyes filled with tears. He looked Susan straight in the eyes. "Yes, Susan—one week ago I shot a man right between the eyes with this Colt and if' I hadn't done it, I wouldn't be here right now to tell th' story," Ollie said with a quivering voice. He turned and they rode on in silence for an hour or more. Susan laid her head on his back and wept while she squeezed her good friend, Ollie Burke, around his waist. She felt like she had pushed him too far and was ashamed. Eliza reined in close and took Ollie's left hand and held it as they rode along together this way until nightfall. Ollie cut past Blainetown and steered them on to Brushy Creek, where he and the Union patrol had camped while they waited for John just one week ago. As they dismounted, Ollie cared for the horses while the girls gathered wood for a campfire. The girls fixed supper and allowed Ollie free time to heal. Susan was feeling so bad that she avoided Ollie.

Finally, he pursued her and took her hand. She had her head down, so Ollie took her chin and tilted it up until he made eye contact.

"It's all right, Susan. I prob'ly needed to say it as much as you needed to hear it. Come on over here; I'll tell you th' rest o' th' story. I know you girls are me 'n Dad's friends, jus' like you're Cindy's and Cassie's, too. You're th' closest thing to a family that me 'n Dad's got." After they had eaten, Ollie told them the story of the Brushy Creek skirmish. When he had finished telling to the point of shooting the soldier who was charging at him, Ollie was quiet awhile, reliving that day, less than a week ago. The girls were in shock that such a young sweet boy, their friend, should be put through such an ordeal at his age. *Almost the same age as Wiley,* Eliza shuddered as she thought of it. She reached out and patted Ollie as she sought to console him. Yet, she felt this was right that he faced this and not let it become a wall inside him.

"That was the end wasn't it, Ollie?" she asked, hoping it was.

"No, ma'am, it wasn't," Ollie said. "I knew that the Lord was my Shepherd and he was with me. I also knew I was doin' right for friends, an' my dad was up there so I had to do somethin'. Then the Rebel Sergeant Runyan yelled, 'Let's wipe out them damn yanks.' I heard him say that with my own ears. Wipe out my cousins—th' Damrons? Wipe out my friends? And—most of all—wipe out my dad? Not if I could help it! I was positive God was with me, so I killed one more Rebel soldier, and he fell right in this creek. It was swollen with all the new rain and run-off and he was carried away while our men charged and we won th' battle. Only four got a way—and that's what brought me to Sandy Hook."

Ollie took Susan's face in his hands and said, "Yes, my sweet Susan—I'd use that Colt to kill again, to save you and Eliza and Rhoda and me." Ollie ended his story emotionally drained and was ready to go to sleep.

At noon, Sunday, May the 18th, Ollie, Eliza, Rhoda, and Susan rode into the barnyard at the Birchet Farm on Deephole Branch. A flock of turkeys scurried off as the travelers unsaddled and removed bedrolls from their mounts. Jim came hurrying out in a trot to take the mounts from the youngsters. He wore a big smile and was full of greetings as he led Silky and Ginger off for a rubdown and some grain.

Uncle John and Aunt Milly were on the porch waving as the young folks rode in. Of course, they were surprised to see Ollie, and more surprised to see their daughters ride in with him.

"Well, what happened to the horses you rode out on?" was John Birchet's first question after the greetings, directing it to Eliza.

"The horses are just fine, Dad," she assured him. "They're still over with Uncle Robert. If'n you come in while we get a bite to eat, we'll tell you th' whole story."

The youngsters had decided to make a straight, fast run to Deephole this morning at Ollie's request. He awakened with a premonition that he shouldn't waste time in getting his dad's message into town. Susan, Eliza and Rhoda agreed to come straight home. They had even decided not to fix breakfast.

Now the girls had talked Ollie into at least staying through dinner, and filling John and Milly in on some of the last forty-eight hours of adventure: Uncle Robert, the bull, Ollie's fight with Tommy Blainey and the big steak supper that was served to everyone including the Reverend Borders and kin. Ollie noticed Wiley's absence and asked about him; he had gone fishing with two of his older brothers who had dropped in.

After Ollie said his good-byes Susan took his hand and led him off toward the barn to give him a proper send off. Eliza and Rhoda glanced at each other and giggled, while Uncle John and Aunt Milly looked curious. Eliza explained.

"Well—you could say—they have sort o' enjoyed each other's company th' last two days, huh, Rhoda? Wouldn't you say?"

"Yes, sister, Eliza. I think you are absolutely right. I think Susan is goin' to feel part of her is missin' in a little while." She looked at her folks and quickly added, "Purely innocent, Ma and Pa. Purely innocent!"

As Uncle John and Aunt Milly sat down on the porch, Aunt Milly slapped her legs and said, "I do declare. Yes, sir, I do declare!" And she laughed.

"Well," John said, "It appears to me thet boy is goin' to have rain on his head afore he gits to Two-Mile. Good boys, them Burkes—I feel like they's both my own. We all need to keep 'em in prayer, now, ya hear?"

Ollie and Susan took longer than necessary for their good-byes. A close bond had developed between the two youngsters on this unusual trip. Susan put Ollie on a pedestal in the past two days, and he enjoyed every minute of it. Susan, who was rarely around any boys except her brothers, found an air of maturity and independence in Ollie that she had never seen displayed in anyone else.

Ollie tightened Ginger's girth and placed his saddlebag and bedroll on her hips while Susan attended to Silky. He placed his Sharps in the scabbard and turned to her,

"Well, I guess I'd better go," he said shyly. "I'm going to miss you, Susan."

"Me, too!" she said, standing first on one foot, then the other. Then, impulsively, she took his face between her two hands and kissed him smack on the mouth.

Ollie looked up and she was gone; out of the barn and off toward the house in a run! He found himself a little dizzy for a minute, then mounted Ginger and led Silky out of the barn and through the barn-lot, waving at his dear friends. As he reached the top of the hill, he turned back in his saddle and there she was—still waving as he dropped out of sight.

Ollie put his heels to Ginger and that was her cue to step up the pace. Silky was a willing participant as they ate up the miles heading across Deephole Branch toward Two-Mile. It was about seven miles to the edge of town in Louisa from Deephole Branch and, as storm clouds swelled up behind him, he felt the wind pick up. Ollie reined up and turning around he took his slicker from his small pack, slipped it on, and buttoned it down to where he straddled Ginger. As they rounded the ridge towards the Carter Graveyard he felt the first drops of rain.

Ollie had not been audience to John Birchet's prediction about the pending rainstorm, but by the time he passed the lonely grave markers, his slicker was shining wet and his legs were soaked. It was a cool rain, mostly because of the wind and, although the thunder and lightening was in evidence, it was not as bad as the storm he and his dad endured the night they rescued little Cindy.

Little Cindy, he thought; it made him warm to think about her. Soon he would be at the cabin and both Cassie and Cindy would greet him. Neither had any idea that he was coming and that thought made him sort of forget the storm as the faithful animals plodded along. He liked to be part of a surprise. *It sure is funny, Ollie thought, three weeks ago me 'n Dad didn't know that there was a Cassie, or a Cindy anywhere. And now we're a family! The Lord sure does work in mysterious and wonderful ways.*

Ollie knew it wasn't nighttime, at least the sun had not gone down, yet the clouds were so dark and the storm was so violent at times that he had to watch close to keep from losing the trail. Finally he pulled up to the little cabin, where lamplight flickered through the window. He dismounted and led the animals into the shed where Cassie's horse, Spot, greeted them with several snorts. Silky whinnied, and the surprise was over. The door opened a crack, letting out light, and a double-barreled shotgun poked through the crack. Ollie could hear Shep, Cassie's dog, rumbling and growling clear down in his throat.

"Who's out there?" called out Cassie. "I have a gun!"

"It's jus' me, Cassie. It's Ollie. Get back inside or you'll get wet; I'll be right in."

"Get wet nothing," she said. "What do I care about a little water?" She rushed out to greet Ollie, with Cindy Lou right behind her.

"Ollie! Oh, Ollie," Cindy cried out as she ran and grabbed him around the waist and began squeezing him. Ginger and Silky took it all in as Cassie squeezed his neck, raining kisses on him. Even Shep knew Ollie and was glad to see him, jumping on him as Ollie pulled off his slicker and hung it in the shed to drip dry.

He was overwhelmed; he could not resist such a welcome as this. As excited and happy as he was, the horses came first. He rubbed them down with dry hay and gave them a goodly portion of grain. It was only a little after five o'clock, but seemed like midnight due to the storm. Ollie brought his things in to dry, being particular about his weapons. Even though summer was just around the corner, Cassie had a fire in the fireplace for cooking supper. There were two lamps lit, and the little cabin smelled as fresh as a spring day with the perfume of flowers and a woman's touch. He had missed this "homey" atmosphere since his mother had been gone, but sure enjoyed the way Cassie had fixed up the place.

Ollie set out to locate his other set of buckskins and soon he was as snug as a June bug on a summer evening. As he dried his hair, Cindy sat on his lap helping, pampering and loving him. This was pleasing to Ollie, since he had wondered at times if she would even remember him—or his father. They had been with Cindy such a short time during the rescue.

Ollie told Cassie he would fill her in on all the news, even if they had to stay up all night. He did want her to know, as before, that he was on a mission to see Captain Lyons for his father. He told her he had awakened this morning with the feeling that he had a short time to get the message to him. "Cassie, I may have to saddle up and go find Captain Lyons before morning. I jus' got this feeling I need to let him know tonight."

"I have good news, Ollie. You won't have to do that. Captain Lyons was over here on Wednesday to check on me, and see if I had heard from John. He said that 'Come—ahem—or high water' he'd come back on Sunday evening to check up on me and Cindy. I told him if he would go to all that trouble just to check on us girls," she playfully hit Cindy, "I'd treat him to some pork stew and blueberry cobbler. I took some of those berries your mom put up last year and whipped up a delicious cobbler. It's baking in the Dutch oven now. S-o-o young man, the captain doesn't know it, but he is coming to see you, too!"

"No wonder this place smells so good." Ollie put Cindy down off of his lap and went about wiping down his guns and putting a light coat of oil over them. He continued to talk about the trip, relating how he met the Birchet girls in Sandy Hook on Friday. He told of his dropping them off at the farm and that everyone sent them their love. He explained that his dad was not alone; he had left Uncle Robert and John together. Eliza and Rhoda rode double on Silky, while Dad was left with Fred the mule, for the time being. Leaving a lot of gaps in his tale Ollie assured her she would know the whole story by evening's end.

Finishing his meticulous care of the Sharps and Colt, he put them away and went over to Cassie and kissed her on the cheek. That's from Dad to you—by the way he didn't tell me to do that exactly, but he did say to give you his love—and you, too, Cindy." He kissed her cheek. Cindy giggled and Cassie blushed a little.

"He—he really did say that, Ollie. You're not kidding me are you?"

"I'm not kidding you at all, Cassie. He really did say that and he meant it too. Let me tell you something funny. You remember, of course, when th' preacher came by here?"

"Yes," she said, her blue eyes became wide.

"Well, he caught up with us in a camp outside of Sandy Hook. Now listen to this: Uncle Robert Birchet, Eliza, Rhoda, Susan and me were all having a big steak cook-out Friday night." Cassie interrupted.

"What is this? The Birchet clan—all th' girls and Uncle Robert—a steak cookout. Why wasn't I invited? I thought you all were roughing it—and me here worrying about you," she said with feigned disgust.

"Now hold on Cassie, you jus' got to hear th' whole story before you make a decision, Oh—I don't know," he said, "maybe I'm gettin' ahead of myself."

"Oh, pshaw! Ollie, I was just teasing; go ahead—tell me about Rev. Borders." Cassie gave him a playful pat.

"Well, he came with some kin o' his and there was plenty left to eat so he was givin' to eatin' and jus' visitin'. Well, he said right off that he didn't have any bad news, but he did have a message for dad, 'n he'd get to it by 'n by." Cassie looked down and blushed a little.

"Well, Dad asked th' preacher how he happened to find us. He said that you had put him on the right trail, and since he was going that way to Grayson for a meetin', he would just swing by and try to locate our camp. Well, th' preacher jus' goes on visitin' and eatin' 'til he finishes. Now Dad was gettin' a little short on patience, so he says to the preacher, 'tell me about thet message for me'. Well th' preacher stands—jus' like he's about to preach—and says, 'Well, I stopped by to see a pretty lady by th' name of Cassie. She fixed me a mighty fine supper' or somethin' like that." Then he goes on to say, 'Tell John I love him; tell John I miss him; and to please hurry home to me; I'm lonesome.' An' th' preacher says, 'And that's the exact words'. Well, Cassie, everyone but Dad jus' went crazy laughing." Cassie blushed.

"And what did John say?"

"Oh, he was red as a beet. At first he didn't say nothin', then he said, 'Oh, Brother Borders what did you have to say thet in front of everybody for?' The preacher says, 'Cause you asked me in front of everybody. By the way, the little lady that sent th' message didn't seem to be embarrassed to send it to you.' That's not all. He said to Dad, 'By th' way John Burke, speaking of marriages, would you and Cassie like for me to come and pay you a little visit after this meetin' in Grayson? Maybe we could have a little heart-to-heart talk?' Well, I had to get my nickel's worth in there, so I stood up and said, 'Yes sir, Rev. Borders, we all think you should stop by and have a heart-to-heart talk with them young'uns.'

"Well, ma'am—my loving dad plumb pulled his shoe off and threw it right at me." Cassie and Cindy were laughing hilariously as Ollie finished.

"Well? Did he hit you?" Cassie asked.

"Naw, I ducked and he missed." With this, Cassie slipped off a house shoe and pasted Ollie good with it.

"I just want to show you—I don't miss." She laughed. "Besides, you had it coming."

Shep, who had curled up by the fire, warned them that someone was approaching. Cassie went to answer the knock at the door.

Captain Lyons stood there, hat in hand and, wearing a wet rain slicker. He bowed graciously to Cassie. "When I made that promise to drop by tonight, dear lady, somethin' about high-water was said? I was not aware I was going to have to prove myself," he said as he stepped in. Then he caught sight of Ollie. At first he was surprised speechless, and then he was beside himself as he came over and began to pump the boy's hand.

"Ollie, Ollie! What a delightful surprise. When did you arrive?" Looking at Cassie," he asked, "Did you know he was coming?" Turning back to Ollie, he said, "Where is John? Great day! Fill me in."

Ollie had not been around too many officers, but he sure was delighted to see the genuine emotion this officer expressed. Captain Lyons was beside himself with excitement.

Cassie took the captain's coat and hat, and Cindy pulled him up a woven seat while Ollie waited until the captain stopped talking in order to answer his many questions.

"Let me say this, sir. Cassie didn't know I was coming. I arrived jus' before you came. Dad is fine and I am here to see you 'cause he sent me. How about your horse, sir? Can I put him in out o' th' rain?"

"Sure, Ollie, you do that, please. I just forgot in all my excitement." Ollie excused himself and was gone for ten minutes attending to the captain's horse. When he came back in Cassie was busy setting the table, with Cindy's help. The two of them worked very efficiently together.

"Ollie, the first thing I want to do is thank you for such a great piece of work in the battle last Sunday. Sergeant Damron and his men have nothing but praises to say about you and, of course, John. But, Son, you saved the day, and—you don't have to worry, nothing is being said about it around the camp with the other men, but Lewis, John, Zeb and the rest that were there credit you, Ollie Burke, in saving their lives."

Cassie was aghast as she heard about the battle for the first time. John had said a little something in a note, but nothing that indicated what she just heard from Captain Lyons. Ollie, on the other hand, was embarrassed and didn't know what to say.

"What are you saying, Captain? What happened last Sunday? Why, Ollie just left here with the men on Saturday," she exclaimed.

As Cassie served the captain and Ollie full plates of food, the captain apologized to Cassie for keeping her in the dark until now. She fixed a plate for Cindy and herself and asked Ollie to ask the blessing. Afterward, the captain told her about the battle; blow by blow, from the warning shots to the capture and burial detail. Cassie's eyes filled with tears as she heard how Ollie had to take the lives of Confederate soldiers in order to save his dad and the troops. There is something that changes within a person, regardless of age or reason, when he has taken another human life.

"Ollie, you no longer are looked on as a boy helper for your Pa." Captain Lyons looked squarely at Ollie. "What I am saying is, you have a place of your own in this Union Army. You're not only on the civilian scout payroll, but you're officially a part of the military record. Senior officers in command are aware of you and the part you have had up until now. If it were not for the risk of exposing your secret, I would personally decorate you for bravery above and beyond the call of duty. It is not that we decorate men for killing other men; rather we decorate them for saving lives, and that's exactly what you did. Don't put your mind on those lives you had to extinguish. Think upon the men you saved, and the innocent farmers you saved from being raided and exploited."

By now Ollie had his composure, and the captain had just reaffirmed what he believed in. He became very business-like.

"Sir, I want to thank you for your confidence in me. I just want you to know that my Dad is my example and my teacher, and I do what he tells me." Then Ollie grinned at the captain.

"That stuff you just talked about—that was all last week's stuff; are you ready to hear about this week's work? And do you mind if I talk in front of Cassie?" The captain pricked up his ears, and motioned for Cassie to put Cindy to bed.

"Ollie, let's get on with it boy. I can't wait. And yes, you can talk in front of Cassie because the information you give me will be acted on out of headquarters." Ollie waited a moment or two for Cassie, then started his narrative about following the Rebel soldiers that escaped after the battle. As he told about cutting the metal out of his dad's leg he held Cassie's hand and she shed tears as she endured the pain that both father and son must have felt. He told about his father's teaching him the use of the compass, and how to figure each mile. Finally, he reported finding the Rebel Camp.

At this point Captain Lyons could contain himself no longer. He jumped out of his seat.

"Hallelujah! I say again, hallelujah. That's an acceptable expression in this cabin, is it not?" he said with a grin, sitting back down. "Go ahead boy, go ahead, I apologize for losing control. By the way, Son—is John all right?"

"He's fit as a fiddle in a Kentucky string band," Ollie said with a wide grin.

Ollie pulled out his rawhide cylinder and unfolded his papers on the table—a map of the hideout where he and his dad stayed, a map of the McPherson farm, the entire Confederate camp with a detailed, hand-drawn picture of the camp layout. There was a map of the Sandy Hook area and all distances between Blainetown and Louisa, complete to Brushy Creek, and the exact skirmish location where the Rebels were holed up.

Cassie looked over each of them with Captain Lyons and her expression was no less surprised than the captain's.

"Did you do all these, Ollie?" she asked with amazement.

"Yes, ma'am, every single one."

"Ollie, all these mileage descriptions and compass markings—how accurate are they?"

"I'd put my life on 'em, sir—both cases. My Dad is a good teacher. And—not braggin', but I'm a good student. 'Sides, I can draw better than him," Ollie said with a grin. The captain began to roll them up and asked, "These are for me—are they not?" as he placed them back into Ollie's rawhide container.

"Yes, sir, but that's not the end of the story!" Ollie got his notes and began to roll out the information he obtained at the Confederate camp—the name of the officers and sergeants and that General Marshal Humphrey was the one that Captain Graham Rutledge reported too.

"What!" shouted Captain Lyons, waking up Cindy, for which he quickly apologized. "You actually went into the camp, and—I just can't believe this. Ollie, I do believe you, I just have never had it this good before." Cassie was having hysterics at the good captain's excitement, as well as the dumbfounded look on Ollie's face. "Go ahead, Ollie," Captain Lyons encouraged, sitting on the edge of his seat.

"Well, sir, I jus' pretended to be a farm boy out doin' some fishin'—so I caught a whole bunch of fish to take into th' camp as a sort of peace offering. It was goin' along fine until this officer—th' commanding officer o' th' camp—started questioning me. Well, I jus' pretended to be a dumb hillbilly and he got outa patience with me, until I showed him how well I could load and shoot a musket. Then he tried to enlist me," Ollie said with a grin.

"What did you say that officer's name was?" asked the captain.

"Captain Graham Rutledge was his name, sir, and he didn't turn out to be half-bad either."

"Graham Rutledge! Well, I'll be dam—oops, excuse me folks— I kinda forgot where I was for a minute. Well, Ollie, Captain Rutledge and I went to West Point together. He is a good man. I'm sorry we are on opposite sides. Well—he is a good southern boy though, raised on a plantation and all. He was in the top grouping in class. Of course, so was I," he said with a twinkle in his eye. "Go on with your story, Son."

"Well, really I spent th' most of th' mornin' and past lunch there in the camp. I visited th' officers, the dog tents, sang a few songs with th' men and got to know some of them. This one, Sergeant-Major Judd, was my host and he showed me everything. I was given a tour and got to see what each man usually carried in his pack—wasn't much I'm tellin' you. They had some discipline about 'em, but at th' same time they was sorta raggedy, 'ceptin' for the officers. Well, I found out who the spies were—who the sergeant was that led the skirmish attack, and met his men, too. That was a Sergeant Runyan, and his two contacts was Sam Blainey and Sandy Tibbett. They was local boys from th' Sandy Hook area and played both sides, I found this out later when I met Robert Birchet."

"Who is Robert, now?" the captain asked.

"Well, you'd know him as the 'Carter County Tadpole,' 'cause that's the way Dad introduced him to me."

"Good—good," said Captain Lyons. "I wanted John to make contact with him. So-oo what did he have to do with Blainey and Tibbett?"

"Nothin' much," Ollie said wryly. "Their jus' his two chief officers—that's all."

"You're sure, Ollie? The captain asked with raised eyebrows.

Ollie told him the whole story and also how he and Uncle Robert had gotten off on the wrong foot when they first met.

Ollie related the relationship with the McPhersons and their help as well as the rescue of the team of horses. He could not pass up telling about the Yankee ram who sent a southern gentleman on a flying mission. Ollie didn't leave a stone unturned in filling the captain in on the happenings, as they related to any military bearing. He didn't go into the personal fracas with Tommy Blainey, the gift of steaks, and especially John Burke's miraculous healing. He had his reasons. It was late when Captain Lyons said his good-byes and Ollie saw him off after saddling up his horse.

"Cassie, that meal was the best meal I have had—since the last home-cooked meal I ate, and I don't remember when that was. Ollie, I will expect you on the post by mid-morning. Remember— as a Yankee scout, you belong to me now!" he laughed and rode off into the wet night.

Ollie and Cassie burned the midnight oil that night. There was much for Ollie to tell, and he had a willing audience. Cassie rejoiced to hear of John's miracle in the wilderness. She laughed when Ollie shared with her his real reason for not telling the captain about the miracle.

"Well, Ollie, I can understand that you may question the captain's ability to understand a simple prayer—and faith to believe that miracles can happen today—but what about the testimony of healing you encouraged your father to give at the camp site that night? Perhaps it would have been an opportunity to share that same testimony to the good captain."

"Well, Cassie—that's not really my biggest problem. OK, supposin' I shared it, and Dad wanted to share it himself?"

"Still, Ollie. You know your dad, and if he didn't tell you not to share it—he wouldn't mind you doing it. You know that!"

"But—but, Cassie," he blurted out, becoming a little exasperated. "OK, OK, th' truth? You're jus' goin to keep on 'til I tell you— what if'n he does believe it—then what?"

"Well—then what?"

"They'll take him back in the Army, Cassie! Don't you see? Dad was discharged because of that shrapnel in his leg, and th' recommendation of th' doctors 'n hospital, don't you see? If'n all of a sudden the problem was gone—and he was healed and didn't limp no more, they could jus' up 'n put him back in the Army."

Cassie began to laugh. Pulling Ollie over to her, she hugged him. As she brushed his hair back and patted his back, she said, "Ollie, I can see that you really had worked yourself up into a pretty good concern over this. Did you discuss it with John?"

"No, ma'am. We never had much chance."

"First off, Ollie, let me make some pretty good observations. I'll do so by asking you some questions, OK? Good!" as she acknowledged his affirmation. "What do you think the military will think was John's greatest service as he served his country—climbing up a hill with several hundred other soldiers and getting himself wounded by enemy fire or routing out a nest of Rebel soldiers that were terrorizing a bunch of innocent farmers of Union persuasion?"

"Prob'ly the routing out thing," considered Ollie.

"Another question, Ollie. Which was more important to the fort and strategic location of Louisa? John marching off with a full regiment toward Middle Creek, or—with the partnership of his young son—finding a hidden Rebel camp with a hundred or so trained troops, living in Lawrence County's back yard?"

"I see what you're sayin' Cassie." Ollie's face brightened. "Dad is more important now than he was before while he was on military duty."

"What do you think, Ollie?"

"Well, yeah. What he is doin' now is more important—I can see that—or they wouldn't have made dad a captain—Uh!" Ollie gasped, realizing he had slipped and let out a secret that only he, John and Captain Lyons knew.

Cassie immediately caught it. "Ollie, I didn't hear what you said. Would you repeat it for me, I must have turned my head at the wrong time."

It didn't fool Ollie; he knew this precious lady was helping him save face.

"Thank you, Cassie; you're special! God hand picked you—special—I jus' knew it!"

"Ollie, one more important thing that you should be aware of—and think about. Your dad, is a special, honorable man who has the ability to make decisions and is not shy about making them. Some six months ago he made the decision, along with a group of friends, that the thing of honor for him at that time was to join the Army and the Union forces. He did so—and at great sacrifice; he left his wife, his children and his home, marching off into battle. He came home wounded and found he had lost two members of his family. He mourned awhile and, without so much as a second thought, he put his life in jeopardy again by becoming a spy and a scout and, even now, he has offered his only son on that same Union altar of sacrifice to serve what he believes is sacred."

Cassie hesitated as she saw the composure changing in Ollie's face; he was very close to tears, but she continued. "Ollie, John Burke is the same man as before and, if he loved his country enough to enlist in this Union Army before, he could do it again. That is, if he thinks it more important than serving as he is now. My guess is that he doesn't and won't. But, don't let that fool you—John Burke belongs to this man's army—and so do you, Ollie Burke. You heard the captain as he rode off; he wasn't kidding. You are in the Army as much as your dad—and—and—God help me—I guess I belong to the Army, too."

Cassie stood up, noticed the time, and said, "Well, sir, do you want to see what I have been busy with since you have been gone? I mean besides the chores and all?"

"Of course, I want to know what you have been busy with, although, I can see a lot of it jus' in th' cabin," Ollie answered.

Cassie told Ollie to wait a bit as she disappeared behind her curtain and rustling sounds indicated she was changing her clothes. *Probably a new dress or outfit*, he thought. In a matter of minutes, Cassie stepped out and what he saw took his breath away. Ollie had never seen a lady dressed in buckskins and moccasins before. The Burkes always had a supply of cured and tanned animal skins. Deer hide was always held in prime consideration, because both man and boy loved the feel and use of buckskin. Cassie had taken great care in making the most beautiful buckskin outfit Ollie had ever seen.

"Cassie, it's beautiful. I mean I have never seen anything so—so—great. Of course, on you—it looks good—you jus' make it look good." He walked around, looking her over from head to toe.

The trousers were cut and double stitched to fit Cassie's form. They were form fitting, but not so tight that she didn't have freedom of movement. The neckline was cut with a V with small colored beads sewn along the edge, looking like a necklace. The waist tapered in and was adorned with five silver flowers decorated with red rawhide bows in each center. They came down in a V, the bottom one centered. The plain sleeves were hemmed halfway to the elbow with rawhide lacing dyed blue. The small waist met the trousers and Ollie could see rawhide lacing on each side under the arms, that drew the blouse into an exact fit. She slipped on a light-colored buckskin jacket decorated with blue fringe from the top of the under arm to the cuff. The jacket was also trimmed with the same ornamental silver flowers and red bows. The moccasins fitted to her tiny feet came halfway up the calf of her leg like boots, with blue rawhide lacing on the outside.

"Cassie, you look like you jus' came out of a picture magazine. I know all the leather, rawhide and dye was here—but where did you get them pretty beads and silver flowers?" he asked.

"Rebecca Birchet took me to the boot and shoe place in Louisa. The owner had them there and I was able to get them for such a little bit of money, I couldn't resist."

Ollie went over to where his things were kept and delved into a drawer. He came up with a pretty rawhide belt with a silver buckle and leather button-type ornaments every two inches.

"Try this on, Cassie. Mother made it for me, but I never used it—'cause I didn't like them button things she put on it."

As she placed the belt around her middle, she found it tied the blouse and trousers together perfectly and fit as if made for her. She spun around with delight. "It even has a sheath for my toothpick, Ollie," she noted. "It's just too grand, thank you so much. I was wondering what to do about a belt, and you have just solved that problem for me."

"A sheath for your toothpick? Cassie, that's not what that sheath is for—" Ollie started to say more, but she interrupted.

"An Arkansas toothpick, Ollie! Let me show you." She went to a large handbag she had carried on her horse, and came back with a slender, double-edged knife with a toothpick-type point. As Ollie took the weapon, he was amazed at how sharp it was.

"It was made for self-protection, Ollie. It is not for whittling, skinning or hunting; it's a little like your Colt. Let me show you something." Taking the knife by the handle, she moved over to the fireplace. She held it by the blade and, more quickly than Ollie could follow, she threw the knife at the heavy-duty front door. The knife buried itself in the center of the hand-hewn timber as straight as an arrow. Ollie stood with his mouth open; he was transfixed.

"Wow, Cassie! You're dangerous!" he exclaimed.

"You might say that, Ollie. I never got a chance to show you my dangerous side." Cassie laughed as she retrieved her toothpick. "I'm just as good with an ax or hatchet. I can shoot that Colt probably almost as good as you and I have killed my share of deer with a musket. As you said earlier, Ollie—about your art work. I'm not bragging, I'm just good at it."

"Looks like God hand-picked you for this family—that's for sure!" Ollie shook his head in amazement. "I want you to teach me how to throw a knife like that; hatchet, too—Cassie! Will you?"

"I sure will, Ollie, as soon as you tell me about—about John. Do you remember our conversations about him—and me—before you left?" she asked shyly, with a blush.

"Sure do, Cassie. I kept my word; I finally pinned Dad down and saw to it that he admitted his love for you. That wasn't too hard to do; he already knew it, he just didn't know how to deal with it so soon, and he had a time knowing how to talk with me about it. That has all been settled, and he talks of you freely now; only in front of me—not anyone else! He still sorta colors up when your name is mentioned. He sits and thinks of you all th' time, jus' like he does th' Lord—almost."

"Oh, Ollie, you're leading me on, now. Tell me the truth—he thinks of me all the time?" she asked with doubt.

"Let me prove it to you." He fetched a tablet from his saddle-bag. "Now, Cassie, what I'm a goin' to share with you—he doesn't know I have, or even that I know he wrote it. I sorta fell on it and copied it down while he was asleep. This is while he was gettin' well from th' leg. You've got to promise me you'll let him share this with you on his own—like it's jus' th' first time, OK?"

"OK, Ollie, OK—show me!" she said excitedly.

"Well he starts writin' with this sentence, 'Dear God, I am like a love-sick puppy about this beautiful young lady that so recently came into my life.' Now, Cassie he wrote that himself."

"Is that all he wrote?"

"No—he had a copied poem by William Cowper called "To A Young Lady." Writin' it made him think of you. Dad has a poem book that Sue Ellen got for him. But here is one I did copy—'cause he wrote it. And you can't see no one but John Burke writin' this—prayer—'cause that's what it is.

My Prayer, Oh God, This Day

As I survey my thoughts in line,
My God and Savior who art sublime.
An undeniable uppermost place to rest,
Releases sin-burden from my chest.

My family gone, beneath the sod,
From their grave; yet with their God,
My son named Ollie, thou givest me,
For comfort, solace, and enjoyment be.

Thou givest me more than my share,
Cassie—a lady beyond compare,
With fire-lined hair, that softly unfolds,
Surrounds a face that an admirer beholds,

Perfection, from a near-by angel reflected.
A gift to me that my God has selected,
I thank you Lord for giving me so much,
My lovely Cassie, to love, to see, to touch.
Amen.

Cassie was moved first to tears and then to silence as Ollie read John's prayer. She finally spoke. "Can—can I keep the copy, Ollie?" Ollie slipped the page into her hand. It was trembling as she took the paper and clutched it to her bosom.

"Good night, Ollie. I'm awfully glad you are here with me tonight!" Ollie picked up the lamp and his journal and went to his bunk.

Fear of the Lord

O LLIE WAS AMIDST THE HUSTLE AND BUSTLE OF THE FORT IN LOUISA BY nine in the morning. He was early, but that was on purpose. As he walked around the military compound, watching all the activity, he was very interested that so much was happening at the same time.

There was a flurry of men in and out of the headquarters area; the infirmary was busy with men in white and military-tan uniforms mixed with a colorful array of the blue and gold of officers' uniforms. Close-order drill was going on in one area; men learning how to use the bayonet in another; and in one section a burly sergeant was teaching a group of men how to defend themselves in hand-to-hand combat.

Ollie was, by most standards, a fearless young man, and his dad had taught him a little about fighting with his fists or hands, but not much. He had wrestled with his dad and even a little with Ernest Newsome, an older friend in school, from time to time.

That was all in fun and games and he felt he did all right, but never really thought about fighting to win—until he hit Tommy Blainey. "I guess I just drew back and let her fly straight at his nose—and got lucky," Ollie said under his breath. But, he did not believe much in luck, just in action and trusting that the Lord's will would be done—or at least to use wisdom in doing the right thing.

Ollie knew that the men stationed here in the Union Army outnumbered the people who lived in Louisa. He had heard his dad say a couple of times that the population of Louisa wasn't even 300 folks, and that was before so many young men had enlisted in the war.

"Ho, Ollie—Ollie Burke—over here!" Lewis Damron called out.

"Sergeant Damron. How are you doin', anyway?" Ollie answered with a big grin.

They made themselves comfortable on the porch at the "Administration Building," now posted in big black letters. They had a nice visit, promising each other a good fishing trip in the near future. Ollie barely had time to share a bit of his and John's recent activities with Sergeant Damron before being called in to see the captain. Captain Lyons' orderly, Private King, came out and greeted him warmly as he informed him that the captain was waiting for him.

In his office, Captain Lyons and a tall distinguished-looking officer with lots of brass and gold greeted Ollie.

"Ollie, this is our commanding officer, Major-General Blair Worthington. He is my superior in command, and the only one at this base I report to concerning our undercover activities in the eastern Kentucky area."

Turning to the general, he said, "Sit down, sir. I would be pleased for you to meet this outstanding young man and personally interview him."

The captain turned back to Ollie and made him comfortable, seated across from the general, who took the captain's chair behind the desk. Captain Lyons seated himself off to the left, and spoke to Ollie.

"Son, I just want you to relax and be at ease with the general—just as you are with me! Simply answer his questions and visit with him, OK?"

Ollie was a bit nervous. He had never met a person of higher rank than captain. He always took for granted that generals talked to no one below a captain's rank. This general was an imposing figure of a man, with white hair and beard, and piercing steel-gray eyes that seemed warm and friendly. Ollie noticed that a hint of a smile danced about his lips as if it wanted to expose itself. He was a tall man, over six feet, wearing cavalry officer's riding breeches with carefully polished high-topped black boots. The general was bareheaded, but wore a non-regulation Union blue jacket adorned with two rows of brass buttons and a single gold star on either shoulder. There was fancy gold scrollwork on both sleeves just above the cuff, and the jacket was form fitting, coming in at the waist, where the jacket and breeches were joined with a wide gold sash. Ollie was pleased to see a holstered Colt, just like the ones he and his dad used.

"Ollie, the captain has told me about your encounter with the enemy, over near Sandy Hook. Why don't you start from there and tell me how you penetrated the enemy camp and—in your own words just tell me what happened."

Ollie immediately felt as easy with General Worthington as he did with Uncle John Birchet. The general reminded him of Uncle John in looks, age, and manner. He started his story with the skirmish where the raiders retreated and he was left to track them. He continued with very little interruption from either the general or Captain Lyons. The time passed quickly as Ollie told about the layout of the Confederate camp. The captain produced Ollie's maps and Ollie stood beside the general, going over every detail. From time to time the general would glance at Captain Lyons and smile, nodding his head as he allowed Ollie to continue his story.

He finished with Uncle Robert and John's schemes to overturn the enemy's plans by removing Blainey and Tibbett. These men were the source of the Confederate Camp's communication with Carter, Morgan and Lawrence Counties, by their knowledge of the local geography and their alliance with the Union partisan group.

"Just how do they plan on accomplishing that, Ollie?" asked General Worthington.

"I don't rightly know, sir," he answered honestly. "When I left with orders to bring you 'n Captain Lyons these maps and to bring you up-to-date, they were not quite sure themselves. They were on their way to town, jus' aknowin' they'd be able to come up with somethin'."

As he spoke, a loud knock sounded and Private King called out. "I need to interrupt you, sir! Emergency, sir!"

The captain quickly rolled up the maps and papers, returning them to their pouch. "Enter, Private. What is it?"

"Man to see you, sir. Very important, sir. Sent by John Burke, sir." The private saluted, and the captain and general returned the salute.

"Show him in, by all means." Lyons glanced from Ollie to the general, shrugging his shoulders.

The private ushered in a very tired Robert Birchet, showing a two-day stubble of beard and signs of exhaustion. Ollie quickly slid his chair to him.

"Sit down, Uncle Robert, you look plumb tuckered out." Ollie realized that neither of the officers knew Uncle Robert, so he took the initiative.

"Gentlemen, this is the *Carter County Tadpole*—Robert Birchet. Uncle Robert, this is Captain Lyons and General Blair Worthington, the commander of this fort." Captain Lyons immediately stuck out his hand and showed his appreciation for meeting Robert; the general followed suit then took his seat.

"Robert, you must have news of grave importance to make this long trip. Please fill us in," the captain requested.

Robert smiled as Private King ushered in an orderly with a pot of steaming coffee and cups for everyone around the table.

"Well, let me say, Ollie, it's good to see you, son. By th' way, I picked up my saddle at Two-Mile jus' in case you miss it. Captain, to meet you and the general was worth th' trip jus' by itself. If'n you folks don't mind, I'm a going to go straight to th' point. John and I split up—me goin' ta Sandy Hook and him goin' ta scout out the Rebel camp again. I know Ollie has told you all about thet, by now. John is purt-near like a hound-dog on a trail, and he sniffed up them varmints Blainey and Tibbett with their leader, Sergeant Runyan, and three other scalawags. Well, it seems thet these men ain't so all-fired Confederate after all. They sure is all-fired thieves though.

"They holed themselves up in a holler with over one hundred cattle and horses. Now, the Confederate camp don't know nothin' about this. They had been doin' the raidin' and stealin' from our farmers all right—even killin'—but fer ever two or three cows they took to the Rebel camp, they took eight or ten fer themselves."

Robert paused, taking a couple of sips of his coffee. "Well, John found them out all right and then he skedaddled inta town, meeting me at the cafe. We slept Saturday night at the boarding house, after we made our plans. Ya see, John came up on them fellers jus' in time. He heard them talking and planning and they was goin' to dress as Yankee farmers 'n sech, and take the livestock to Catlettsburg come Sunday morning at daylight. Well, thet was yestiday, and they'll be nearly a week in takin' 'em thet far—stayin' clear of towns. John is stayin' with 'em, following 'em and waitin' fer me to bring you this message. I knew where Ollie was 'cause I came by Two-Mile and saw Miss Cassie."

"Well, Robert, this is exciting news—and good news I must say, don't you think so, sir?"

"Paramount, Captain Lyons, just paramount," General Worthington said.

"Robert, what does John want from us? How can we help?" Captain Lyons asked.

"Well, sir, John has it all figured out, pretty well. He said to try this plan out on you. He'd like to see a mounted patrol meet him in Catlettsburg, Wednesday evening or Thursday. He said not to worry about contacting him, he would contact the patrol since they'd be hard ta hide. He requested Sergeant Damron's patrol—if they's available. He figures on lettin' these thieves deliver the cattle to the market fer us, then arrest th' men—or worse if'n we hafta—and either sell the stock fer th' North or bring 'em back to Louisa at your pleasure.

He asked me to join the troop a headin' fer Catlettsburg, and he wants his chief lieutenant, Ollie, ta find him and stand by fer messages between the two groups—him being one group by hisself," he said with a smile. "Ta be perfectly honest, gentlemen, either Ollie or John is a group all by themselves. I had me a hard time believin' it—but not any more. I'm convinced!"

The men all laughed and Ollie turned red. All he could say was, "Aw, stop your teasin'. Anyway my dad's not here to defend himself—and—and I don't know how." With that, the general got up and walked around to Ollie taking him by the shoulders and looking down into his eyes.

"Son, it's boys like you who have taken on a man's job—and men like your dad—who fear God and are not afraid to call on Him—you will make the difference in us winning this war. I am extremely proud of you, and I am glad to have had the honor to meet you personally. I will look forward to meeting your dad as well when he returns."

The general then excused himself, shook hands with Robert, and said over his shoulder as he left, "It's in your capable hands, Lyons. I know you will do me right!" Ollie now knew why he felt the pressure of the Holy Spirit on him to hurry in getting the information and maps to Captain Lyons.

By one o'clock that afternoon Robert and Ollie were back at Two-Mile with Cassie. As they rode Robert had passed on John's message to be sure to bring Silky and to check in with the McPhersons for instructions from John. As they briefed Cassie on their plans, Cassie informed them that she was going to be included on this trip. Ollie argued. "But—but, Cassie, what about Cindy Lou? What about Daisy 'n the chickens?"

"Ollie, they'll be fine!" she said firmly. "Cindy can stay with Eliza and the Birchets, and Rebecca's girls can take care of the cabin and Daisy—just like they did before! I want to see John, and besides, I can help. What if two couriers are needed? Robert is going with the Union troop, and I am going with you. It's settled—my mind is made up, and that's that!"

Ollie looked at Robert. Robert just grinned and shrugged his shoulders as if to say, *Don't ask me—I'm not going to say no.* Ollie could see the decision was made. And she did have a point; there might be a need for another courier before this was over. Without further words, he began packing bedrolls and food for the two of them. Robert volunteered to see that Cindy Lou would get to the Birchets safely, since he was going to spend the night there. He was to report back to Captain Lyons in the morning.

As Cassie began to hustle around, changing into her new buckskins and laying out some traveling necessities, Ollie saw Robert and Cindy off toward Deephole. He then rode back into town to check with the Birchets about seeing after the place. Rebecca was disappointed that Cassie hadn't sent Cindy in to her, but of course they'd be glad to care for the place.

Ollie went by the administration building and briefed Captain Lyons that Cassie would be going along, in case she was needed. He felt it was important that the captain knew this since he was in charge of this mission.

"Ollie, are you sure this is all right?" the captain asked with raised eyebrows.

"Well, sir, she can throw a knife better than anyone I've ever seen. And she says she can shoot as good as me and dad—that's pretty good shootin! She rides a horse as good as any man—I know for a fact. I jus' don't have any weapons for her, 'ceptin' that ol' shotgun."

"We'll take care of that right now, as long as you're sure it's OK, Ollie. I trust your judgment," the captain said as he led Ollie to the armory.

"Oh, I think she'll do fine, sir. Anyway—I ain't one to try and stop her 'cause her mind's made up!" They both had a good laugh as the captain indicated he wouldn't want to try talking her out of it either.

Ollie rode toward Two-Mile with a .44 caliber Colt in a holster and an 1859 Sharps, just like his own. He had brought ample ammunition for both weapons, replenished his supply, plus extra for John. As he rode up to the cabin, he saw Silky tied alongside Spot, with a saddle, a blanket and a pack on his back. Cassie had everything ready to go. She put the military holster on her new belt and, strapping the Rifle boot to Spot's saddle, she was ready. She looked absolutely stunning in her new buckskin outfit complete with revolver and her Arkansas toothpick. Her beautiful auburn hair hung down to her shoulders in cascades of curls, set off with a small tendril at each temple.

Ollie set Ginger at a fast trot for he was bent on going as far as possible while there was still light. Shep kept pace right alongside Spot and once in awhile ran out ahead, always returning to stay near Cassie.

Cassie was deep in thought as she traveled, mostly about John. *Will he be upset because I came? Will he be glad to see me? What if I make him angry by this impulsive decision? On the other hand I'm very pleased that Ollie brought me back weapons from the fort. At least he and Captain Lyons trust me.*

Cassie could use these weapons as well as most men, but she had learned not to flaunt it. It wasn't good to let men know about this; it hurt their pride to be bested by a woman. She did feel that this family God had suddenly put her into would not be so intimidated by her abilities. In these times of war she was comforted that, being the only child, her dad had taught her these skills which she had learned so well. Jacob Martin excelled in handling 'most any weapon he ever used, and he had taught his daughter to be as much like a man as he could. She knew he was trying to make her into the son he never had. Although Cassie excelled in the things he taught her, she maintained her femininity and was as comfortable as anyone with lady-like graces and charm. Whether in poverty or in fashion, Cassie felt she was riding high in the saddle as she went forward with Ollie to meet her man.

TWENTY-SEVEN

Buy Wisdom and
Sell It Not . . .

D AWN ON SUNDAY, MAY 18TH FOUND JOHN BURKE DAMP AND ALERT AS he watched while Reynolds and Campbell stirred around the campfire. Sergeant Runyan had given orders for these two to watch the camp; he and the other three raiders would be there by eight o'clock. John had been watching for some time as the eastern sky turned rosy red. *The promise of rain,* John thought, as he remembered the old farmers' saying, *"Morning gray and evening red, sends the traveler on his way. Evening gray and morning red, brings the rain down on his head."*

The murdering thieves gave no hint that they expected anything but good luck as they cheerfully enjoyed a hot breakfast and waited for their Confederate companions. These two were dressed as civilian farmers. The only things setting them apart were their gun belts and ominous revolvers. Not many farmers dressed with handguns. John had been there two hours before dawn, making sure the plans he had overheard yesterday evening had not changed.

The rising sun showed he still had a while to wait. He made himself comfortable and dug out some dried apricots to nibble on.

John had had coffee with Robert before they split up the day before, and Robert headed toward Lost Creek. He knew that his partner in this new adventure was a good man, very capable, and he had complete trust that Robert would get to Louisa to notify Captain Lyons in ample time. His game was going to have to be one of patience and self-control: following these men and keeping out of sight. He still had to get to Bob and Mary's to leave word for Ollie and pick up some of his supplies. He would make the McPhersons' his headquarters. These men would be making slow progress with the animals, and once he knew their direction, he would have plenty of time to go back and forth and leave a plan for meeting with Ollie.

John pulled out his watch. It was 7:35. He focused his attention back on the camp and saw the two men standing, glancing around as they waited. John was perched above the waterfall and had a bird's-eye view of the camp. As long as he remained alert he was in no danger.

Ten minutes later the four men, with Runyan out in front, came riding out of a thicket on the west side, all dressed in civilian clothes. Tibbett and Watson wore denim trousers. Watson, who was a little rotund, had his faded denims tied up with a piece of rope. He also wore a straw hat and had a revolver of some type slipped in behind the rope. Runyan wore a rawhide vest that looked like it had some wear attached to it. He had a plaid shirt and beat up western felt hat, but still wore the same boots he had on before. It was obvious these men knew what they were doing; their disguise looked entirely believable.

An hour and a half later, John was following the herd several hundred yards off the right flank as the men slowly drove the mixed livestock up the streambed in a northeasterly direction. It was obvious that Blainey and Tibbett knew their way around this country. By heading off in this direction, they would miss Sandy Hook and the McPherson farm far to the east, and stay to the west of Blainetown. They would probably pass near Webbville, Willard and east of Grayson if they kept this trail. Plenty of places for supplies; yet far enough out not to attract too much attention. Blainey was riding point, leading the pack, while Runyan and Watson worked the east flank. Campbell and Reynolds worked the west and Tibbett was in the drag position.

John rode way out to the right flank, which was to the south of the herd. Once he crossed over to the other side, dropping way behind Tibbett to the rear. As noon approached, the sky began to darken, the wind picked up, and he could see that the old farmers' saying was going to certainly "bring rain down on their head."

John dropped behind, allowing the herd to gain some time away from him, and cut across in a straight path toward McPherson's farm. *Ain't no sense in all of us gettin' wet,* he thought with a smile. He made it into Bob's shed just as the first drops fell. Bob happened to be at the barn unharnessing Mike and Dick just as John rode in. Bob let out his cackling sort of laugh.

"Wal, now, thet's a feller who knows to come in outa th' rain."

"I'll tell you, Bob McPherson—Mrs. Thomas Burke didn't raise any dumb children!" he joked as he pulled the saddle off of Fred and doled him some grain.

"Wal, reckon you could bring thet smart chile up to th' house to git some hot vittles?" Bob continued with his banter.

"Jus' as soon as I rub ol' Fred down a bit, I'll be right behind you." John picked up two handfuls of straw.

It wasn't long before John and Bob were busy putting away hunks of ham and fried potatoes with black-eyed peas and cornbread. Mary was pouring John the second glass of buttermilk when he looked up at her with his blue eyes.

"It's a good thing this old farmer got to you first, Mary. Anyone thet can cook like you has got to be a national treasure. It kinda makes me wanta take up stealin' for a profession." He looked at Bob with a grin. "I still ain't ruled it out, Bob. You'd better keep your eye on her." Bob just laughed at John's teasing compliment and Mary playfully hit John with a dishtowel.

"John Burke—as purty as you are—I bet you got at least ten or twelve gurls lolly-gaggin' around you. Prob'ly all can cook as good as me, too!"

John became thoughtful and it caused Bob to glance at his wife. She nodded knowingly back at her husband.

"Reckon you lost yore wife—I mean, Ollie's mother, didn't ya, John?" Bob asked tenderly.

"Yes, sir! I sure did, Bob; last winter in thet big smallpox epidemic thet came through our parts. Lost Ollie's sister, too. I was away, mind you. I was fightin' for the Union at Middle Creek when it all took place. While I was wounded, I caught a touch of it, too. Well, I pulled through and they didn't."

John was quiet again for a while and Mary brought her cheerful disposition back to bear on the up side of things.

"Well, thet was then—and it's now I'm talkin about, John Burke! I bet they's a sweet thing in the corner," she said with a twinkle in her eye.

John thought a moment, then smiled back at Mary.

"I knowed it. I knowed it! Ain't no good man as purty as you, John Burke, thet's gonna git away fer long—undiscovered—I jus' knowed it."

John just sat there with a smile, looking first at Bob, then Mary. Bob was getting fidgety. "Wal—is she some kinda secret weepon, John? Are ya gonna tell us about her or not?"

"Bob, you 'n Mary sure have a way o' gettin' right to the bottom o' somethin'! I sorta got to say thet I have a girl. At least, I'd say thet—I *believe* I got a girl. I think, well—I *hope* I got a girl."

"Soun's like ta me, a lotta hopin, believin' an' thinkin'. What I wanta hear 'bout is th' gettin' part," Bob said.

"Now, behave yoreself, Bob McPherson. You jus' let John tell it his own way. Now you go ahead, John," Mary persuaded.

John was in a mood to daydream about Cassie Martin, and he did so in front of these two friends. He went into detail, telling how they met, Ollie's observations and how he saw through everything and, finally, his long talk with Ollie. He even described her looks and hair, the way it seemed as if it were rimmed with fire when the sun or the lantern light hit it. He talked about her cuddling up to him in the evening and putting her head on his shoulder; the only night they were together.

All of a sudden John glanced at his watch and saw it was 4:30. He stopped talking mid-sentence. He pounded his head on the right side above the temple, looked at Bob and Mary crazily, and said, "Bibble-bibble, bam-bam—and another one for the crazy farm."

Bob and Mary went into hysterics and laughed until they cried. After they gained their composure, John said, "Well, folks, I jus' been sitting here babbling away all afternoon. I ain't talked thet much since Ollie was born. Why, I've wasted your entire afternoon." Just then the thunder crashed and they realized the rain was still coming down hard.

"Well, ain't a lot we could o' got done if you had o' stopped talkin', John. We sure warn't agonna plow no taters in all thet rain, thet's fer sure," Bob reminded him.

Mary was shaking her head. She had continued working around the kitchen all through the visit, and now sat at the table in thoughtful reverie.

"Wal, now, if'n I can jus' keep you sittin' here a little longer, I won't even hafta call you fer supper," she said. "John, th' good Lord sure has His hand on you, thet's fer sure. Thet story about thet young'un and her love fer you on sight—my, my, she is probably moonin' over you th' same way you are moonin' over her. I think I'd know her if she walked right through thet door jus' by your description of her. Now, all us gurls, no matter how old we get, like to hear a good love story. I think thet's th' purtiest one I ever heard—and jus' think, I still got the endin' ta look forward to! My, my." She went over to the shelf and lit a lamp. The darkness from the storm had filled the kitchen with shadows.

John and Bob moved into the front room and sat back and lit their pipes. John became serious about the business at hand and told Bob that Robert Birchet would get word to Ollie about where to meet him, and that Ollie would stop here for instructions.

"I don't rightly know where thet will be right now, Bob. I'm following a herd of livestock thet those thieves stole from different folks here 'n about, and I don't know the exact trail to follow jus' yet. I knew they'd be makin' an early camp t'night 'cause of the storm so I decided to wait here in th' dry. I'll leave word with you on where Ollie should meet me." John smiled and continued, "I'll be back tomorrow, before five o'clock, 'n have some more of Mary's good cookin' fer supper.

"Jus' tell Ollie to bring Silky and th' rest of my stuff thet's in th' shed and come to th' meetin' place. I'll let you know what place when I know where. I don't allow Ollie could get here before midnight tomorrow, even if he rides hard. I'll tell you, Bob, thet boy sure is a prize. God gave me th' best he had when he gave me Ollie," he said with a glow in his eyes.

John, Bob and Mary had a late supper and John read some out of the Bible to the McPhersons. He decided to sleep in the shed, where he could be back on the trail toward the raiders before daylight.

Daylight peeping in from the eastern Kentucky sky found John fifty yards from the rustlers. They were not too far from where he left them. He had guessed right; the downpour and the high wind had kept them from traveling. After John saw them get started and heard Runyan's gruff voice giving orders, he decided to back-track.

"All right, Blainey—git out front and git 'em started! We'll fall in an' folly behind. We'll keep a headin' towards Webbville, 'less you say otherwise," he ordered.

John thought he would accomplish a dual purpose; he had not seen the Confederate camp yet, so he decided to sneak in from the south and have a look for himself. He really wanted to make sure they hadn't moved the camp.

Moving slowly on Fred, John reached a spot that he felt was close enough for him to walk to the camp, yet far enough away to risk having a cup of hot coffee before he proceeded. He had a dif-ficult time finding enough dry twigs to build a fire after the rain. By the time he did, he was also ready for a piece or two of bacon. He was sipping coffee and had bacon frying when he knew he had company. He noticed Fred's telltale ears and decided there was too much of an audience to make a stand. He just played dumb, as if he was the only one in the world; even started whistling as he fished a hunk of bacon out of the hot grease and put it in a cold biscuit from Mary's table.

He was glad his audience allowed him to eat but as he poured another cup of coffee a voice came from behind him.

"Keep perfectly still, Mister. Don't make any move towards thet hawg-leg at yore side."

"If'n you don't mind, I'll jus' keep sippin' on my coffee"

Suddenly six men with muzzle-loaded rifles were standing around John. They were obviously a Confederate infantry on pa-trol. The one who spoke to him came from behind and removed John's Colt from his holster, then walked around to face him.

"What do you think you are doing here, Mister?" he snapped.

"What I think I am doin'—must be obvious to the rest of you. I think I am eating some breakfast—or that's what I was doing, when I was interrupted," John answered softly.

The leader was a clean-shaven young man of nineteen or twenty. He had brown hair and hazel eyes and wore corporal's stripes. He didn't like John's answer and he prodded him in the stomach with the rifle muzzle.

"Ya think you're pretty smart, don't ya, Mister? I'm asking you once again—what are you doing here? And I expect an answer—NOW!"

John tilted his coffee tin and dumped the brown liquid on the ground. Without blinking he looked the corporal in the eye. "Corporal, you have disturbed my meal; you have taken my weapon; and you have prodded my belly with your rifle. Now, either shoot me, arrest me, or take me to your commanding officer before you get yourself into more trouble than you can handle. For all you know, I may be a Confederate officer in disguise on my way to your camp—in which case, you are already in serious trouble!"

"Corporal, you better do just what th' man says—let's take him back to camp. Captain Rutledge will git him straightened out real fast," said an older soldier of perhaps forty summers. He was a private, but he looked as though he had been around awhile. There were several assenting nods from the other men.

The corporal backed off for the time being and gave orders for two of the men to pick up the utensils, put them back into the pack, and lead Fred back to camp. John himself casually reached over and put out the fire, throwing some mud on the hot ashes.

"Private Ellis, you lead off. The rest of us will follow." To John he added, "Mister, you follow and we'll all be right behind you—so don't try anything."

Thirty minutes later the Confederate camp that Ollie had described so well came into view as John followed the older private the patrol leader had called Ellis. As they marched into camp, avoiding the puddles of water and mud, a collection of soldiers started gathering toward the flag stand. John was the center of attention while the corporal was out of earshot making a report to an officer. Soon the officer came forward.

"Suh, what is yoah name?"

"My name, sir, is John Burke, and I am a civilian," John answered him sharply.

"Well, Mistah John Burke, civilian, mah name is Lieutenant Mahty Jones and I am going to ask y'all to be patient with us foah awhile. Captain Rutledge is indisposed and we will have to await his arrival; in the meanwhile y'all will be detained."

Lieutenant Marty Jones was a sharp-looking young officer about six feet tall with blond hair, a well-trimmed mustache, and a slender build. A snappy Confederate officer's uniform looked somewhat out of place in this small obscure encampment; however, John felt the lieutenant would look the same way on the battlefield. He walked with apparent ease and had a military bearing that suggested he had been trained at West Point or some military school. A handsome man with a heavy southern accent, he seemed to be a man of considerable charm. He would diplomatically "detain" John—not arrest him; he would be watchful—yet polite. Nevertheless, John could not proceed with anything until the commanding officer showed up.

"Sah-junt Judd," the lieutenant called.

"Yes, suh." A burly experienced sergeant stepped forward, saluting the officer.

"Sah-junt, take personal change of Mistah Burke. I suggest the brush arboh—away from the hot sun. Make sure that Mr. Burke's evah need is looked aftah—while he is detained."

Sergeant Judd came forward and saluted John with a smile.

"Jus' you follow me, suh!" He said, leading John over to the brush arbor, a shade area for the men. The rifle detail stayed around the perimeter, their weapons at the ready, but in a relaxed fashion. Sergeant Judd ordered a man to take John's mule to the corral, remove the saddle, and feed him.

"Make sure the mule is rubbed down, Carlson." As he started toward the arbor, he suddenly noticed John's Sharps in the rifle boot.

"Hold on a minute, Carlson." Judd walked over, removed the weapon, walked back under the shade, and called out, "Who has this man's other weapon?"

"I do, Sarge," the young corporal came over, producing the Colt.

Sergeant Judd came within arm's distance of John and, placing his two weapons on the table in front of him, said, "I sure do admire a man who has good taste in shooting irons, Mr. Burke. You have two fine weapons here; better than any in our camp, I think. Would you mind tellin' me where you got 'em?" he asked, ever so politely.

When Ollie was at this camp last week he was more impressed with Sergeant Judd than any of the others, and John could see why. He seemed likable, polite, and had an air of command about him as if he knew what was going on—in every detail. *Yet*, John cautioned himself, *this is the most dangerous man in the camp.* He probably was the one man he would have to watch like a hawk, and no doubt the captain depended on this man to run the camp.

"Not at all, Sarge. I'd be glad to tell you where I got 'em. Have one of your men bring my saddlebag over, and I'll show you the receipts," John answered agreeably. "By the way, just call me John; I don't cotton much to this 'Mr.' business." John watched as Sergeant Judd sent a man over to bring back his saddlebag.

"Here you are, John—yore saddlebag, as you requested." Judd handed him the leather pouch. John opened the bag and recovered a smaller suede pouch with papers and receipts. He handed two receipts to Sergeant Judd.

"You were curious about my weapons? This will show where I purchased 'em and also what I paid."

Sergeant Judd was quiet as he scrutinized the documents, finally glancing up at John with a frown.

"I'm a little confused, Burke! Says here you purchased the Sharps and Colt at Kingston, Georgia back in April—'n this receipt says you purchased a Sharps in Louisa, Kentucky, this month, in May. Thet's two Sharps the way I count 'em! Thet th' way you count, too?"

John laughed. "Looks like to me you can count, Sarge. I purchased the Colt for me, and th' rifle for my boy in Kingston town. Didn't have enough money to buy me a Sharps too. My son liked it so well that I got another one for me when I came home, in Louisa. Thet's the simple truth o' th' matter." John realized the sergeant was just doing his job. This was probably regular routine for him, checking out a stranger before the captain interviewed him. He figured that if he passed the sergeant's inspection, the captain would be easy.

"Makes sense, but you don't look like you're old enough to have a kid able to handle a Sharps rifle. What is it—a .50 caliber?"

"That's close, Sarge—.52 caliber, 1859 model," John said. "Thanks for the compliment about my age. I actually had a girl older than my son; she died last winter at thirteen—with smallpox. My boy is eleven and been shootin' since he was old enough to prop up a musket—dead shot, too! He can shoot thet Sharps better than most men." Sergeant Judd watched John carefully as he answered each question.

"One more question, Burke! What were you doin' in Kingston, Georgia?"

"I was really all the way to Atlanta—got a friend, a corporal in th' First Georgia Confederate Volunteers. By th' way Sarge, when is this game goin' to end? I'm who I say I am and I've been where I

said I've been. I bought 'n paid for the two guns you're holding."
John looked around and continued. "I've lived here all my life.
This is my home, and you fellers are campin' in my home area. I
should really be th' one askin' th' questions and you should be
givin' the answers. Now, I've had enough! You're goin' to have to
lock me up, shoot me, or let me go. I'm gettin' a little bored with
this question-and-answer game."

With this sudden reversal in the game plan, John took the sergeant off guard and he was speechless. John decided to see how far
he could go with the bluff. He walked over, picked up his Colt, put
it in his holster, and saw the men around him straighten up, with
their weapons cocked. He continued as if it hadn't happened, put
his receipts in the saddlebag, slung it over his shoulder, picked up
the Sharps, and started toward the corral.

"Stop right there, John!" Sergeant Judd had finally snapped
out of his stupor and spoke with authority. "I like you—and maybe
you've been wronged—but I don't figure you're plumb stupid! Th'
odds are a little stacked agin' ya right now, wouldn't ya say?"

John turned around, pushed his straw hat back a little rakishly
and laughed. "Well, you can't blame a feller for tryin', can you, Sarge?"

"Not at all, John, not at all—but we really do have a captain,
and he would be disappointed if he didn't get to meet you, so jus'
put down you're things and relax a little. He'll show up; trust me!"
He returned John's laugh.

John could see why Ollie liked the sergeant. He was an out-
front sort of man and, Confederate or not, he was probably a good
and loyal soldier. He certainly was a far cry from the likes of Blainey,
Tibbett, and the good-for-nothing Sergeant Runyan.

For the rest of the day John and Sergeant Jeremiah (Jerry)
Woodson Judd became well acquainted. At least, in the end John
felt that he knew something about this Confederate sergeant who
had served in the army since before the Mexican War. He had

enlisted in the infantry of the Federal Army when he was eighteen, and by the time he was twenty, he was a corporal fighting in the Mexican War. He had served under Captain Robert E. Lee, who became the young corporal's hero and mentor. He had been with Lee at Mexico City when Federal forces stormed Chapultepec in September of 1847, where Captain Lee was wounded and decorated. Judd's claim to fame at that raid was being side by side many times with young Lee, and he proudly showed John the scar where he had been wounded in the same battle. Jerry had received a saber cut from a Mexican cavalry lieutenant. John noticed it was a pretty wicked scar and Jerry said it took fifty stitches to repair.

The sergeant went on to tell John that the only difference in him being a Confederate soldier or a Union soldier was General Robert E. Lee. When Lincoln offered Lee the job of being the Union field general, Jerry and a lot more of Lee's friends waited to see which way Lee would go. Even Robert E. Lee had a difficult time with that decision. When Virginia seceded from the Union, General Lee went to the South, and "a whole bunch of us Federal Army men followed him," Sergeant Judd reported.

John didn't say so, but he was sorry just the same. This Sergeant Judd was one he could really buddy with and be very close to. The two men walked over to Judd's tent, which he shared with another sergeant, Roger Cook, the captain's orderly. Cook and Captain Rutledge had left about an hour before the patrol picked John up. When John glanced into the sergeant's tent, the first thing he saw was a Bible. That made him smile. As he sat on a stump at the entrance to the tent, he commented to Jerry.

"Jerry, I noticed your readin' material—it's a favorite of mine too!"

The sergeant was busy fixing the two of them some supper and John's comment caught him mid-stride.

"John, you're a Christian, aren't you?"

"Yes, sir, Jerry! I try to serve the Lord with all my heart, and I could never deny Him—'cause He would never deny me!" John had become animated as he answered this simple question. He continued, "I kinda felt there was somethin' between us thet was special when we first met earlier today. You know the Lord, too, don't you?"

"Ever since Chapultepec, John. I had learned about the Lord as I was raised over near Ashland, Kentucky, in a Bible class they had fer us kids on Sunday. Our Bible teacher, Henry Bird, taught a bunch of us kids about Jesus, and I prayed a sinner's prayer with him when I was twelve years old. I sort o' got away from th' Bible, but I always remembered. When I was charging thet hill in Mexico, and I saw the sun hit thet saber as it came at me—I knew I had met my Maker! I yelled right out loud to God—'Jesus, save me!' And He did—right then. Well, ever since that day, He has been with me in a very real and personal way; by the way, Roger Cook, the other sergeant, knows the Lord, too. God put us together in this tent.

John was elated to learn this good news about his new Confederate friend and forgot about his schedule, realizing that God was obviously in control of this meeting and that he was not there by man-made circumstances; although it seemed that way. John and Jerry had a good time sharing about the Lord. Supper stretched into night, and Jerry lit his tent lamp. John was just getting ready to share some personal things about Ollie and his healing, when they heard the sound of horses. Two men in civilian clothing rode into camp, and a couple of privates ran to take their mounts. They immediately walked toward Judd's tent. He stood up quickly, saluting the taller man. "Glad to see you back, suh, and you too, Sarge." He nodded at the man who must have been Sergeant Roger Cook. John stood waiting; taking his lead from Sergeant Judd.

"Captain Rutledge, Sergeant Cook, this is a friend of mine, John Burke, from over in Louisa. He was kind enough to wait for your return, to—perhaps meet you, and tell you about his travels in these parts. He sort of stumbled onto us."

"I see," the captain said. "You said he was a friend of yours. How long have you known John Burke, Sergeant Judd?" Judd glanced at John and grinned. He turned back to the officer. "Oh, I'd say about twenty years—starting about 12:30 this afternoon, suh," he said with a twinkle in his eye. Sergeant Cook was about to laugh outright, but held it back.

"Sergeant Judd, give me twenty minutes to change back into suitable attire, then bring—your 'old friend'—John Burke, over to my tent."

"Cook, change back into your uniform and have Lieutenant Jones join me, right away, please, I'll have his report before talking with these gentlemen." Both sergeants snapped to attention and saluted.

While Cook quickly changed, Jerry spoke to him about John and about him being a brother in the Lord. Roger beamed a radiant smile as he again shook John's hand and gave him an encouragement just before leaving. "Captain Rutledge is a good officer and a good man. Just be straight with him and he'll be the same way with you. God bless you." And he hurried off toward the officer's tent.

Thirty minutes later found John, Sergeant Judd, Sergeant Cook, and Lieutenant Jones sitting in folding cloth seats at a table in Captain Rutledge's command tent. Someone had brought in coffee and the men were waiting to take their lead from Captain Rutledge. After greeting each one, acknowledging the formalities, he began speaking to John.

"Mr. Burke—John, if I may call you that? I've been brought up to date somewhat on how you have come into our company." He grinned as if something amused him, and took a sip of coffee. "My understanding is this: you were in the middle of minding your own business, eating your dinner. A group of my men on patrol came across you, disturbed your meal, prodded you in the belly, brought you to our camp, and then Lieutenant Marty Jones detained you to meet his commanding officer—me. Am I right so far, sir?"

John grinned. "The only thing you left out, sir, was Lieutenant Jones' colorful accent—which I did enjoy, I might add." Jones blushed a little as he smiled, but was not offended at the jesting.

"Fine, fine! Y'all will forgive me if I leave out the accent; I'm not good enough to sound like Lieutenant Jones, yet. John, I know you and Sergeant Judd had a good visit and became close friends, this last twenty years," the captain said with animation in his voice. "So, I just want you to fill in some blank spots for me, if you could. I understand you've lived here locally most of your life; yet your home—Louisa—is over forty miles from our location. Could you enlighten me about your trip over this way?"

"I'd be happy to do thet, captain." John moved his straw hat and picked up his coffee. "I had met a man, several miles south of here, who owned a farm and had been here all his life. There was a raid on his place several days back and someone stole all his livestock, killing him and his hired hand in the process. I sort o' work with the sheriff over in Lawrence County, Johnny Allison, and I'm also a friend of Sheriff Parker Baldwin here in Sandy Hook. I took it on myself to track those men—th' ones who done th' killin'—and was in thet process when your men stumbled on me." John decided not to say too much just yet, so he sat back as if he was finished.

The captain looked from man to man around the table. "Did any of you gentlemen think to ask that simple question of Mr. Burke?" John liked these men and did not want to see them get into hot water on his behalf, so he spoke up.

"Sir—if I may say somethin' to thet? I wasn't as nice and friendly as we all are now—havin' my dinner disturbed 'n all. These men probably wouldn't have been so inclined to believe me then—not only thet, I don't think I would have told them—'cause I knew I'd jus' have to say it agin when you got here!"

Captain Graham Rutledge was a handsome man, and had a winsome smile when he leaned forward and turned on the charm.

"Well, men! That was the best attempt I have ever seen by a man, heretofore a perfect stranger, to save your collective backsides. As a matter of fact, he did so well I'm going to let him get by with it." A barely noticeable sigh of relief went around the table.

The captain turned back to John. "Did you find the men you were chasing? Or maybe I should ask, did you think it was us?" Sergeant Judd was especially interested in this answer; John could see it in his eyes.

"Well, sir, I have to be honest and say the thought did cross my mind. But they'd still be here, now, wouldn't they?" John waited for reaction and was greeted with assenting nods. "No, sir, it was not your men. These men were in civilian clothes—dressed as farmers 'n sech. They also came from a place where th' livestock had been corralled for some time. I trailed them from south o' here, and they made a beeline past your place here, heading toward Catlettsburg. They're tryin' to make the market there by next Friday, market day. I allow thet's their plan."

Questioning looks passed around the table, something unspoken between the officer and his men, but John pretended not to notice.

"John, did you by chance get a look at these men—I mean close up?" the captain asked.

"Well, sir, I'm like an Indian when it comes to the woods. Yes, sir, I could describe everyone, especially the leaders. Th' boss was sort o' short and stocky—all muscle with brown hair and looked as tough as nails; even heard his name called once."

"What was it—the name I mean?" Sergeant Judd asked.

"Why, it was Runyan. Thet was th' name I heard, sure as I'm here." John noticed the captain as he collapsed back into his seat, and suddenly looked very tired. The other men all looked exasperated. Judd spoke up, after looking around the table, and finally his eyes resting on John.

"Describe the others, John; at least the ones you called leaders."

"Well, there was this one—sort of tall with a stoop, brown hair and long mustache. He had a mean look on his face; another was kinda skinny with sandy hair and not much of it in front; and then there was one who was sorta chubby, well-fed lookin'—any of thet ring any remembrances to y'all?"

"You described Blainey, Tibbett and Watson. Any of you men need anything else to prove my case?" the captain asked, as he looked around the table.

All the men looked very disappointed, and John was really sorry to disturb them but it seemed the only thing to do. He had one more bayonet to thrust into them, and hated to do so.

"Well, them men figure on cuttin' some pretty big fancy spendin'. I mean, beef and horses are prime now with the war on. They had over a hundred head, mixed." They reacted as though he had fired an artillery shell into the tent. They exchanged looks and several mouths flew open.

"One hundred head, John—are you sure?" the captain asked.

"Oh, yes, sir! At least! Prob'ly closer to a hundred 'n ten, would be my guess."

"Well, John Burke, I guess it's our turn to do some explaining. Sergeant Cook and I were in Sandy Hook this afternoon; that's why the civilian clothes. We have been suspicious of several men under my command. Sergeant David Runyan and a group of men assigned to him were in charge of supplies, and this led to some dealing in contraband livestock. You are well aware that we are in war times and, ahh—my small camp of Southern soldiers is here—uh, under orders. For all practical reasons we are isolated behind enemy lines— in a holding position. The job—" John could see that the good captain was struggling between the truth and compromising his position to a stranger, and in war times that could be dangerous. John felt he could help get the captain out of this mess.

"Captain, you don't have to explain anything to me. I'm sorta a victim in this thing, too. You had to assign men for the procurement of food and, being discreet, you sent those men out on foraging missions—hopefully away from your camp, but—you had no way of knowing where they went. I understand—this is war and what you are doing is part of your job to feed your troops. Captain, you've been betrayed. The men you assigned to do the job for you are—or at least have become—profiteers. They've been bringin' you a cow here 'n there to keep you happy, but—they have been takin' the most for themselves. They now feel they have a killin' and they've abandoned you, and my guess is you'll never see them again." John paused, watching the men's faces, especially those of Judd and Rutledge.

They were smiling at each other when the captain spoke again. "John, I could not have put it as well as you did. That does not take care of our immediate problem, though. We are not here to take over Louisa, Morgan County, or even Sandy Hook—so we can't even pursue and punish these scoundrels." He looked at Judd and shrugged. Then, glancing at Lieutenant Jones and Sergeant Cook, he added, "Do you see what I mean?"

John nodded and stood to stretch, pouring himself another cup of coffee; while doing so, he pulled out his watch and glanced at the time. His mind was racing miles and miles ahead of his words. Putting his watch away, he again made himself comfortable at the table. Judd saw that something was developing in his new friend's mind.

"Men," John addressed them all. "I want you to know I appreciate your honesty with me! I also realize that you have accepted me at face value—and you don't even know me. In other words, you believe what I have said to be true."

Captain Rutledge and Lieutenant Jones noticed at once that the woodsman in buckskins, born and bred in these hills, who dropped his "g's" and used "thet" for "that," suddenly switched to King's English that would be acceptable at any social function. Even Judd noticed that something was different about John; he moved and talked like one who was in command. John had always taught Ollie what he used as a standard procedure for his way of life. He learned this from the Bible and practiced it openly. God's Word came out, especially in Proverbs, about wisdom: *"How to buy it and sell it not,"* other Scriptures about letting your yes be yes and your no be no, about keeping your mouth shut, and listening instead of talking, and not casting your pearls before swine. All of these Scriptures John had somehow rolled into a great thought, which he taught to Ollie: "Don't advertise something, unless you want to sell it!" He had explained to the youngster that this meant a product, a plan, a story, or just plain bragging about one's self. John was moving into the "advertising" business as he spoke to these men at this time.

"All I have told you is true, and what I am about to share with you is also true! Last December and January I marched against some of your men—or at least Confederate soldiers—at Prestonsburg and was wounded by a Confederate shell. I am a civilian, which is true; I was medically discharged. I am working with the sheriff of this area to track the men who shot and killed Lloyd Patterson.

"Now, you may see me as your enemy, because I wore a Union uniform six months ago. The reason I am well and healthy right now is because God saw fit to heal me—a modern day miracle. At some future time I may be in a battle and face you men—and you may face me. At that point we will all do what we have to do and fight for our comrades and families as well as our country. But right now, I see our enemy being one and the same. Your hands are tied. Mine are not! I will proceed from here with your blessing, I pray, and you will not have to worry about any future embarrassment from Runyan and company. If you continue to trust me, you can consider the job done! Agreed?" John stood and reached out his hand toward Captain Rutledge and waited.

All the men stood, facing one another in a circle for a full minute before anyone spoke. The captain finally put forth his hand with a smile and shook John's warmly; each man in turn followed suit, Jerry being last.

"John, you dropped your local manner of speech and went into such articulate speaking so fast, I wonder how you can put it on," Rutledge said.

"Twarn't put on a'tall, Captain, we'uns jus' talk this a way, because it's easier than all thet high-falutin' stuff. Jus' comes natural with us hill folks. But that doesn't mean that we can't communicate on a more socially accepted level—if it's called for," John said with good humor. The men laughed at the way John changed so easily in manner of speech. Something had been nagging at the back of Sergeant Judd's mind in the last few minutes. There was something vaguely familiar about John's ease of switching speech patterns as well his looks and personality, and what he had said to him earlier in the afternoon.

"Put my mind at ease, John. Do you know a young man—oh, I'd say about ten or so, likes to fish and can shoot a musket better 'n most men at this camp? Called himself—"

"Ollie Thomas," Captain Rutledge cut in, catching Judd's drift.

"You must be talking about Ollie Thomas—Burke!" John said with a twinkle in his eye. "Yes, I am fairly well acquainted with the young man. He taught me every thing I know."

"Well, I'll be dam—darned," Captain Rutledge said. "I knew there was something special about that young man. Well, I'll tell you, John Burke—he sure pulled the wool—I guess being a good southern gentleman I should say cotton—over our eyes. He pulled that country hick routine on us, and everyone of us bought it. I bet later on you two really had a laugh on us."

John became very serious when he looked at the captain. "Not at all, sir. He only laughed at one thing. I'll tell you about that in a minute. Let me say right now—Ollie's words about each of you were of the utmost respect. He said, 'Dad, those men are just like our men; they pray, they believe in God, and they sing some of the same songs we sing. I really hope we never have to fight any of them. He was especially high on Sergeant Judd, and you, Captain. Three men that he memorized the names of that he didn't like were Runyan, Tibbett, and Blainey, and he was very outspoken about them.

"Why was he here? I can hear you all asking that question. Well, he saw two horses in your corral that he knew didn't belong here and the owners are friends of Ollie's. His purpose in being here—besides curiosity—was to return those two horses to the rightful owner. He did so later that night—uh—while you were busy chasing sheep and horses, remember?"

"Now I know—now I know," Captain Rutledge said as he rubbed his backside.

They all caught on and began to laugh until tears rolled down their faces.

"Ollie almost gave himself away when he saw that happen, sir, not because he wanted to—he just couldn't stop laughing. By the way, the ram did that on it's own; it wasn't prompted. And, another thing you should know—I didn't know anything about that until it was all over. That was a total 'Ollie decision' and he acted alone on the whole thing."

By this time, the sharing of these so-called private things had brought these five men—one from the North, and four from the South—into a close bond of friendship that made the war seem far away. They slipped back into their seats around the table and just visited as friends.

"John, can Ollie slip into and out of that local language and speak as you did here tonight just as easy?" Sergeant Cook asked.

"Well, Sarge, with Ollie it's easier. He hasn't had as much practice at forgettin' th' good speech and diction that I have. I have to think about it when I purposefully try to speak so purty," he said grinning.

"I can see why you bought that boy a Sharps, John," Judd said. "I watched him shoot. He loaded, fired and hit the targets with thet ol' musket three times in two minutes flat."

"Well, from what he told me, you made the task too easy for him. He could have hit those targets at a hundred and fifty yards."

John stood again, reminding them he had a job to do and had better get at it. Jerry tried to get him to spend the night, but he declined because of the need to catch up to the rustlers.

"I'm to meet Ollie tonight; he will be with me on this job—he helps keep me out of trouble," he said seriously. John was not joking in this, for Ollie was a very dependable partner.

"Tell Ollie a couple of things for me, John," the captain said. "First, I don't feel bad about him taking that team back where they belonged—we didn't want to eat them, and I don't have a garden or cornfield to plow. Secondly, that ram paid the supreme sacrifice for making me the laughing stock of the camp. We had mutton stew for several days! Oh, and one more thing, I'd still like to sign him up—he could train my recruits!"

They all had a good laugh while Sergeant Cook went to have a guard saddle up John's mule. As John walked toward the corral, he said his good-byes to Jerry Judd: a friend for the afternoon, a friend for life. Both men realized they could be on opposite sides in battle at some time in the future, but nevertheless, they would still be friends till death. Roger Cook was waiting with Fred all saddled. He also shook John's hand warmly.

"One thing, John," he said. "I have a brother who was attached to Company B in the 40th Regiment in Louisa. His name is David. Say hello for me if you are able to, and tell him—tell him I love him, and to keep himself safe."

"I'll be glad to do thet, Roger, though he already may be gone from there. The 40th, or at least some of them, pulled out several weeks ago to join up with Union forces at Shiloh. Anyway, I'll check for you. God bless you too, Roger."

TWENTY-EIGHT

I Am My Beloved's

A S JOHN CAME OUT OF THE WOODS ABOVE THE McPHERSONS' BARN HE spotted the night light hanging on the gatepost. *Bless that Bob and Mary,* John thought. *They left a farmer's beacon out for me and Ollie.* John saw no evidence that Ollie had arrived. The farmhouse showed no lights. Actually, he didn't expect Ollie to be there until after midnight and it was just now coming up on twelve o'clock. He dismounted Fred and led him in, pausing at the watering trough to let him drink his fill. The corral was empty of stock so he unbuckled the girth and noiselessly opened the door to the shed. He lit a match, and to his surprise, there sat Ollie cross-legged on some hay wearing a big grin.

"Why, you ornery rascal," John said as the match went out. "How about lighting a lantern for a feller afore I burn my fingers off." John heard Ollie giggling as he lit a lantern. He bounded up to hug his dad. They embraced affectionately, and John bent back, looking down into his partner's eyes. "You sure do take the butter outa buttermilk, Ollie Burke! I didn't expect you so soon. You must've been burnin' th' wind." Ollie took over rubbing down Fred. He led the animal into the barn and found a stall for him, then returned to his dad. John watched as he fetched a plate covered with a red and white checkered towel.

"This is your supper, Dad. Mary wouldn't let us—uh—me leave until I brought you a platter of fried chicken." John blessed the food and dug in while Ollie hoped, in vain, that his dad had not picked up on his slip.

"What did you mean by 'us', Ollie? Didn't you come alone?"

"Oh, Dad, I just get to thinkin' of Ginger and Silky as bein' people; I even talk to 'em—don't that sound silly? I rode straight to the farmhouse when I got here—about nine, I think. Bob and Mary were still up and really worried about you."

"I know. I told them I'd be here in time for supper. I guess you relaxed 'em some. I didn't see any light on at th' house when I rode in. Son—don't worry 'bout talkin' out loud to your animals; we all do thet, I reckon. Kind o' keeps us company when we're alone. Now—if you told me Ginger started talkin' back to you, I'd start to get worried," he said with a chuckle.

Cassie and Ollie had contrived a plan to surprise John about Cassie's presence. They would put all the animals in stalls in the main barn, then she would take Shep into the adjoining stall and wait for the right moment before walking out. Ollie had assured her that John wouldn't let much time go by before he brought her up in conversation. This idea appealed to Cassie, but Ollie had not prepared her for the fact that John Burke no longer wore a beard.

When Ollie lit the lantern and John turned, full-face, she almost gave up her secret presence. She didn't recognize the man standing just fifteen feet or so away from her. She knew the voice, she knew the hairline and eyes, but the face was so different. *This man was handsome before,* she thought, *but heavens help me, I can't believe how handsome John Burke is without his beard.* As the shock wore off, she listened to every word and watched his every move. Cassie never had believed in "love at first sight," until John and Ollie walked into her life such a short time ago, but there again— it was God who answered her prayers. She believed this as she watched the two men in her life. Cassie could not believe how well Ollie played the game. He had not said one word except to make small talk to his dad.

"Well, Ollie," John finally said with a smile, "how is she? Do I have to beg?"

"Oh, Dad—she is the cutest little thing. And when I got there to the shed, she just ran out an' hugged me around my waist. She is just a beautiful little girl," Ollie said innocently.

"Ollie, I'm so glad Cindy is cute, adorable and fine and—and— hugs you—but you know good and well what I mean, so don't start this 'dumb act' with me again, remember? We're partners! So don't tease me!"

"Dad, I jus' couldn't resist—just a little! Well, all I got to say is—she's prettier than th' last time I saw her—if that's possible." Cassie could feel the crimson on her face as she listened to Ollie and John.

"Dear God, how she has crawled into my skin. Ollie, I can't stop thinkin' about her and I want to see her so—so bad." John gave a shudder and had a painful expression on his face.

"Dad, do you remember the cured buckskin we had with our furs 'n hides?" John nodded as he wiped his finger on the towel after devouring the last piece of chicken.

"She had taken the buckskin and made one of the finest riding outfits I have ever seen. In fact th' very first one I ever did see on a lady! Well, she made boot-length moccasins to match, and I gave her my belt that Mother made for me—you remember? The one I never would wear 'cause o' th' flowers. And it fit her just perfect. She put her toothpick in the sheath and—why—Dad—she looked like she stepped out o' one of those picture books."

"A toothpick? Ollie—do you mean an Arkansas toothpick?"

"Absolutely—that's exactly what I mean. And, Dad, she can throw that knife as quick as you can pull your Colt—maybe quicker. She can throw it and hit her mark every time. She also shoots a revolver and a rifle as good as me 'n you."

"Ollie, you don't lie, so I know what you tell me is the truth. Do you know an Arkansas toothpick is a wicked weapon? And it's only good if you know how to use it. Well, I'll be! That only makes me want to see her more. I'd give anything to see her in that outfit. She must be as handy with a needle as everything else she puts her mind to."

"You say you'd give anything? Just anything, Dad? That's a real temptation, let's see—what do I want—hmm!"

John began to look at Ollie suspiciously when all of a sudden a black and white bundle of fur hit John in the chest and knocked him backwards. John felt his face being washed as he looked into the eyes of a seventy-pound shepherd dog, who was licking his face and making his presence known. Recovering his balance from the unusual greeting, John saw his vision of loveliness in buck-skins. Her hair looked like a fiery halo as she stood there with moist eyes and hands folded in front of her. The buckskins cut and made to her shape clung to her every curve, as revealing as modesty would allow. John took in her beauty and the comeliness of her shape, as the buckskins accented her charms.

"Cassie," John softly said to his beautiful lady, "hold your arms straight out to your side. That's it, now turn around very slowly. Put your hands on your hips. That's it! I—I—think—that is the most beautiful sight I have ever seen." Ollie was nodding in agreement as his dad looked over to him. John was dazed and Cassie was in a pretty blush.

It was a full moment before either did anything, and Ollie remained a silent spectator. It was Cassie who came forward and put both her hands up, feeling John's face, running her fingers gently over his new appearance.

"It looks like we both had surprises in appearance, John Burke. I'm just examining this *new man* in my life. Do you mind?"

"Not at all—I just expect equal privileges." John smiled as he began caressing her face and stroking her hair. Then he tenderly reached around her small waist and squeezed, gently at first, then tighter until he lifted her off her moccasin toes and kissed her soft lips as she entwined her arms about his neck, pulling his lips harder to her own. Both forgot that Ollie was in the room, and he was very glad of it, for he didn't want to miss this meeting of these two very special people.

After the tender greetings, it was time to visit, catching up with each other's activities. John explained about his being arrested and detained by Confederate troops. He brought them up to date, explaining his unique experience with Sergeant Judd and Captain Rutledge. He gave Ollie the captain's message about the mutton stew and his standing offer to recruit Ollie to train his troops. They all laughed and felt complimented at the captain's evaluation of Ollie. Cassie was busy thanking God for the wisdom he gave her man, which, under different circumstances, could have cost John his life. Unusual circumstances had put them in the position of doing the Confederate army a service in capturing or stopping these men, who now were without a country.

Ollie shared the update about Captain Lyons and Robert Birchet, and tried to describe General Blair Worthington. He also informed his dad that he "no longer belonged to his dad; he belonged to

Captain Lyons," in a military sense. He smiled with a twinkle in his eyes as he repeated what Captain Lyons had said.

John looked at Cassie and shrugged. "Well, Cassie, I left Louisa less then a month ago with a son and allegiance to our government. Now, Lyons not only owns me, but my son, too. I wouldn't be surprised if he hasn't laid claims on you! Another thing—I've been working for the Union all this time, and who gets to meet the general? My son—that's who." John feigned disgust, when down underneath he was so elated about Ollie he could pop a button. Cassie could see this—and so could Ollie!

"I think I'll get the lantern from th' post and go to th' loft to bring my journal up to date," Ollie said. "I'll let you kids talk, without me botherin' you." Cassie and John both made a motion toward Ollie as if chasing him, and he ran out into the darkness.

"John, I'd like to see your leg—where Ollie operated, if that's OK?" Cassie requested.

"Sure, little lady, whatever you say. But there isn't much to see now." John went to his saddlebag and felt around for the wrapped piece of shrapnel. He tossed it to her before he went to change into his cut-off trousers. "Examine this while you wait; it's the metal that Ollie cut out."

Cassie shuddered involuntarily as she examined the jagged and ugly L shaped piece of metal. *No wonder he limped. It's a wonder, and a miracle that this didn't cut an artery, as it sawed back and forth in his leg.* John came back in bare feet and short pants. He carried his bedroll under his arm and bent down as he laid it out in front of Cassie. He laid down and stretched his long legs as he turned over on his stomach.

"Well, there it is, what's left of it—after the Lord finished with it." John leaned on his right elbow, looking into Cassie's eyes. "Honey, this is Tuesday already, and I want you to know—just one week ago today Ollie cut thet ugly thing out o' me. I was bleedin',

I was hurtin', and thet piece of metal was cuttin th' daylights out o' me. Now, jus' look at it!"

Cassie brought the light down close and tenderly ran her finger over the two purplish lines that looked like pencil marks. It didn't even look like a scar. She ran her finger over the surface and then her whole hand over his leg. It was a strong handsome leg, outlined with muscles and strength.

"Hey," John said. "You're goin' to hafta give me equal time if you keep that up." Cassie blushed, but made no attempt to stop her caress.

"John, the Bible talks about, 'a little child shall lead them.' Do you remember?"

"Sure do, Cassie. Thought of it many times the last week."

"Do you think that's why God honored Ollie's prayer?"

John was enjoying Cassie's fondling his leg; so much so that it bothered his thinking. Considering the subject matter, he carefully sat up and took her two hands in his, sitting very close.

"Well, Cassie, as I said, I thought of that Scripture many times— but also other Scriptures come to mind that I believe the Lord has given me new understanding on. A scripture in Isaiah says:

No weapon that is formed against thee shall prosper; and every tongue that shall rise against thee in judgment thou shalt condemn. This is the heritage of the servants of the Lord, and their righteousness is of me, saith the Lord. —Isaiah 54:17

"When Ollie prayed for me, he prayed a Scripture. He took John 14:14: *'If ye shall ask any thing in my name, I will do it.'* He prayed that Scripture; he believed that Scripture; and that Scripture was God's Word. There's another place in the Bible where it says that He—God—would hasten His Word to perform it. It was certainly Ollie's child-like faith that brought God's Word to bear on this healing. But, the healing took place because God honors

His Word—and will perform His Word when someone simply is bold enough to use it—with the same child-like faith.

"Remember—when the Lord spoke about the little child, he was using that scene as an example to adults, proving that if they have the same kind of faith, the same miracles could be wrought." John stopped, looked down and when he raised his head he had that glimmer in his eyes that Cassie was becoming more familiar with. "And now—a special song by Sister Cassie Martin," he said in a slightly different tone, and began laughing.

"John Burke—if you think you sounded—a—bit—preachy— well you did! But, so what? It was good, and—Brother Burke that was a mighty fine message. Now, will Brother Ollie please receive the tithes and offerings?" As she said that, playfully finishing the service, Ollie poked his head down from the loft, saying, with a pronounced accent,

"Why, I shuly will receive th' offerin', Sister Cassie, thas mah mos' fav-rite paht of th' suvice."

"Ollie, you should be asleep by now," John called, not very serious about it though.

Not too long after that John and Cassie looked at each other as they heard sounds of regular breathing coming from the loft. Ollie finally had given in to sleep. John laid his head on the elevated part of his bedroll and Cassie laid along his side, resting on an elbow and gazing down into his eyes. Gazing into each other's eyes acted hypnotically on these two people in love. They were looking intently at each other, volumes of love passing between them without words. Tears filled the beautiful blue eyes of the lady and, as they dropped onto his face, caused his eyes to fill also.

Finally, Cassie said, "I love you, John Burke. With all my heart I love you. I have been storing up my love for you all my life and, now that I have met you, it's easy to let you see it!

"My beloved Cassie, I'm nearly thirty-two years old; I thought I had lived a long time and knew love but—much as I loved my wife, and still cherish her memory—I have never known love like this—this burning, overwhelming love that I have for you. I appreciate your patience and, yes—Ollie's patience and understanding with me. I—I—was sort of slow, allowing the light to come in." With that, he placed his hands on her cheeks and drew her willing face to his as he again kissed her beautiful, full lips that transferred such promise of a deeper, more fulfilling love yet to be given.

Cassie laid her head across John's chest and felt the security of a tender, loving masculinity as she drifted off into sleep. John soon slept as well, and Shep settled down with his head across Cassie's legs.

By dawn the horses were saddled and Fred had his pack on. Ollie was up first and helped the McPhersons with their chores while John and Cassie took care of preparing their own animals for travel.

Breakfast was a specialty with Mary: everything from ham and eggs to biscuits and brown gravy, topped with fried apples. Not much was said as everyone ate and enjoyed hot coffee or cold milk. Mary was busy taking survey of her guests and enjoying their appetites.

"Well, John," she said. "I knowed this young'un was your bride-to-be soon's Ollie brought her in last night. She has you written all over her. I could see you in her eyes!" Mary laughed and Bob joined in; John and Cassie took turns being shy as they glanced at each other.

"Good Lawd have mercy, Cassie. You should have heard the way John talked about you—behind your back, too!" Mary said with a serious look.

"Oh? Tell me about it, Mary, just what did he say?" Cassie asked with a smile.

"Oh, honey, he's so love-sick over you—why he down-right reminded me of a sick calf we had last spring thet got a peach seed caught in its throat. He jus' didn't know whether to throw-up or beller." Mary started laughing and slapping her thighs, and every one joined in, including John.

Then, catching his breath and getting to his feet, John said, "Come on if you're goin' with me—afore this lady tells another one."

There was a little touch of sadness in Bob and Mary as they said farewell. Then she said seriously, "All foolin' aside, Cassie, John sat here all afternoon th' other day and all he could talk about was you, and how much he loves you."

"Now thet's the truth, gal," Bob joined in. "We didn't git one lick of work done all aftynoon."

"Go ahead, Bob, now tell her it rained all afternoon, too." As he put his arm about Cassie, squeezing her close, John said, "Well, I cannot tell a lie—it's true, I talked myself silly—and—my subject matter *was* Cassie, and there was nothing silly about that." Cassie reached up and kissed him on the cheek. Shep, who just had some breakfast leftovers, barked, as if in approval.

It was past high noon when John reined Silky in and pointed to the unmistakable trail of many animals. The broken underbrush, trampled grass, and muddy creek-beds had left telltale signs of the recent passing of the livestock and the rustlers. John motioned for Cassie and Ollie to catch up.

"As near as I can see from here, it looks like th' men are heading' the herd south of Grayson and north of Willard. I want th' two of you to take Fred and head straight into Willard. Then wait for me there." John pointed to a mountain pass to the northwest. "As you head right through thet pass you'll come down to th' main trail between Cherokee and Grayson. Th' left would take you back to Webbville, th' right to Willard—shouldn't be more 'n a mile or so into town. There ain't much, jus' a general store and a tavern. I'll meet you both there before dark. I'll scout on ahead and locate th' herd to see if everything is on schedule. I want to make sure we don't have any unwanted surprises."

Followed by Shep, Ollie and Cassie took Fred, waved good-bye, and headed toward Willard. Cassie was really enjoying the trip—the fresh air, and mostly the company of her new family. John had set a fast pace this morning, leaving no room for light chatter once they left the McPhersons. Except for a couple of stops to water and rest the animals, they had not paused.

Cassie had watched John as he sat in the saddle, studying his profile as they traveled. He was one with the horse, so it seemed, as he anticipated Silky's every move and step. His athletic physique was accentuated by his tan buckskins and set off by the new summer hat he wore jauntily over his right eye. His abundance of black curly hair covered his ears and extended to just above his shoulders, framing his handsome face. Cassie studied the features of his clean-shaven face, which she was still becoming accustomed to. Without the beard, his angular face looked much younger than his thirty-one years. When he smiled he revealed two dimples, which she had not noticed when he wore his beard. There was a small scar on his right eyebrow that was barely noticeable. She silently thanked God for His many blessings to her, and especially for bringing her this "knight in shining armor" on his black charger. Well, maybe he didn't have "shining armor" but he wore the armor of the Lord, which was much more important. The providence of the Lord was plainly showing towards Cassie.

John waited until his companions disappeared over the hill before he resumed his quest of the murdering thieves. He watched his young partner, Ollie, following the most beautiful lady he had ever seen, recognizing that they both belonged to him. Watching Cassie as they had traveled, observing her in her form-fitting buckskins, he couldn't help but notice that she rode Spot as if she had spent years in the saddle. As he glanced at the big Colt on her belt he shook his head, wondering if she could handle that revolver the way Ollie said she could. John made a mental note to check this out when he was back with his partners.

John loved Cassie with all his heart and looked back over the short interval of time since they met, and how he came to this miracle—Cassie Martin—soon to be Cassie Burke—Mrs. John Burke, if you please—scarcely believing it.

John ground-tied Silky, dropping his reins as he crept close to the men on the south flank of the herd. It was just as he had feared. The tracks had led him to believe that the number of men with the herd had increased. After two hours of stalking and observing, John confirmed that there were now nine men instead of six. It was just such surprises as this that John wanted to be prepared for—and the reason he sent for Ollie to join him. Ollie would be the one to get word to the Union patrol.

John moved around the herd unseen, studying the faces and clothing of the newcomers. He was certain he had never seen the rough-looking men before. One slender man had stringy blond hair, a thin face, and a scar down his right cheek. He wore a revolver in a well-worn holster low on his right hip. The second man was a giant—or so it seemed. He was probably six and a half feet tall, weighing about two hundred and forty pounds, John guessed, with a brown woolly beard. He wore a large-crown felt hat, carried two revolvers and a bowie knife.

John noticed the contrast between him and the third man, who was diminutive in stature, clean shaven, neat in appearance, and wore a low-crowned felt hat that revealed red hair and long side-burns. He wore a leather vest decorated with silver, and highly polished black boots with silver spurs. The manner in which he wore his two guns suggested he was accomplished in using them. John could not help but wonder if these men had cut themselves in or been hired by Sergeant Runyan. John could see that the odds needed to be cut down in the near future.

At four thirty John rode into Willard to find Cassie and Ollie sitting on a homemade bench in front of the general store, under a sign that read "General Store & Merchandise," and below: "Bert Cooksey, Prop." They were alone, and Ollie broke into a big smile when he saw his dad.

"Howdy, stranger. Pull up and sit a spell."

John laughed. "Before I do—I wonder if'n you have a handout for a poor hungry travelin' drifter?" Now Cassie cut herself in on the teasing.

"Sure do, honey. Jus' what did you have in mind?"

A round fuzzy face peeped around the door, looking John over and allowing his gaze to drift back toward Cassie and Ollie, who did not know they had an audience. Then Ollie started laughing, joined first by Cassie and then by John. Finally the fuzzy faced proprietor, Mr. Cooksey, began laughing too as he realized they knew each other and were just teasing.

"You youngsters sure had me going fer awhile. I didn't know what was going on out here on my front porch. We don't have too many happenin's to talk about here, and I almost thought I had one—shucks!" he laughingly said.

"How's the tavern across th' street for food?" John asked.

"Nothin' fancy, but nobody ever died from eatin' it as fer as I know," the storekeeper commented. "Josiah Webb is kin to th' Webbs over ta Webbville an', although he ain't fancy, he's a good cook!"

"Let's all eat now and save fixin' at camp later." Ollie and Cassie willingly followed John to the tavern. Ollie took Silky's reins and disappeared for a time as Cassie and John mounted the steps to the small sandstone building. The interior felt damp, but cool, due to the thick stone walls. An elderly man led them to a rough-hewn table and chairs, one of only three sets.

"What's easy to fix and good eatin'?" John asked.

"Got some venison stew with either beer or lemonade. Or I can cook you up a steak with fried taters and eggs. I have some ice from the ice house left from winter fer the lemonade, and I have blackberry cobbler fer dessert."

Cassie said the stew and lemonade sounded good.

"OK," John said, "Make it three orders of stew and lemonade with lots of ice—and cobbler to top it off."

Ollie joined them shortly, having put feeders on for all the animals, and picketing them behind the general store. Before long three steaming bowls of venison stew were in front of them, served with hunks of hot cornbread and country butter. Finishing first, John told Ollie and Cassie about the three additional helpers. They knew this was serious business, and figured that these men were at least as dangerous as the men from the Confederate camp.

Ollie could not help but think about Tommy Blainey. *No wonder the boy was such a misfit and a bully—with a father like he had who was a robber.* These thoughts made Ollie indeed grateful for a godly father and mother. His heart went out to Tommy Blainey.

In the Name of
the Lord of Hosts

JUST SLIGHTLY NORTH OF WILLARD IN CARTER COUNTY, NEAR OLD BEN
Birchet's farm, they came to Lost Creek. Ben, the late father of
Robert and John Birchet, had settled in this Lost Creek area many
years ago. He and Susannah Herron Birchet had twelve children and
Ben gave each one of them a generous farm before he passed on.
Cassie, John, and Ollie made camp as quickly as they could for John
had said he wanted to cover "some important things" with them.

"Ollie, bring some ammunition over for the Colts." John called
their attention to a birch tree with a large fork in the trunk about
twelve feet up. "That's our target. Cassie, you go first. Hit as close to
thet fork as you can. It's about fifty feet from here, I'd say." Cassie
smiled, knowing she was on trial. She decided to play with John just
a little.

"Fast or slow, John?" she asked diffidently, with a twinkle in
her eyes.

"You jus' be comfortable, darlin'—whatever suits you!"

Cassie pulled out her revolver, checked the loads, placed her right foot in front of the left foot so she would be balanced, cocked the weapon as she extended her arm and fired—without even aiming, it seemed. The bark flew out of the fork of the tree—dead center.

John's face was animated with pleasure as he beamed at his lady. "Rapid fire, Cassie, rapid-fire!" Cassie smiled back, knowing she had pleased him. Then she placed her revolver into her holster and turned away from the tree as Ollie caught his dad's eye. Cassie whirled around toward the tree, pulled her Colt right-handed, cocked it with her thumb, and fired from her hip, each time hitting the fork within a three-inch spot—five times!

John gracefully walked over to the beautiful sharpshooter, placed a hand on each shoulder, and looked down into her bewitching blue eyes. Their gaze lingered for a moment then, pulling her close, he kissed her, a long and tender kiss, feeling her lips yield under his own. Cassie wrapped her arms, still holding her revolver in one hand, around his neck and squeezed until she lifted herself off the ground, while John's arms circled her waist holding her close. Cassie returned his kiss softly with the fervor of stored up passion. As their lips parted, still looking into her eyes, John said, "Reload, pretty lady—reload!"

She batted her long lashes at him, flashing a seductive smile as she answered.

"And—what would you have me reload, sir? My revolver or myself?" Ollie broke out in a belly laugh, reminding them they were not alone. They joined Ollie in laughter as John walked over to sit on his saddle while Cassie reloaded her Colt, fighting back a slight flush on her cheeks.

"John, you make me forget myself. It's all your fault!" By this time John was blushing too. "I know, Cassie. Yes, ma'am, its all my fault!"

John gathered Ollie and Cassie around him to prepare them for the next few days. The rough-looking newcomers had him concerned; not only because of the increased numbers, but because of an inner feeling that told him that these men were at least as bad as Runyan and his ex-Confederates, and perhaps worse. Ollie had already proved himself under fire, so now his greater concern was for Cassie and how she would do if faced with the possibility of killing someone—if necessary.

"Listen, little Miss Sharpshooter," he started affectionately, "I understand you're jus' as good with a knife as with thet Colt—I'll take yours 'n Ollie's word for thet. But let me ask—at what distance are you good throwin' thet toothpick?"

"I can hit what I aim for accurately up to thirty-five feet, perhaps more." Cassie stood up and threw the knife at the same tree, which was at least fifty feet away, and hit six inches lower than the fork. "See what I mean?" She had to take a stick and jump to knock the knife down. "I aimed for the fork, and it lost momentum by the time it went that far."

John simply shook his head. "Lady, I wouldn't want you to throw thet thing at me at fifty feet—not even at sixty! But, thet brings me to th' next question. I know you can throw down thet six-shooter on a birch tree, and stick thet toothpick at fifty feet—but can you aim and shoot or stick a man with th' purpose of killin'? There's a big difference!"

It was quiet for a minute as Cassie looked down and sort of stirred a stick in the dust at her feet. Lifting her blue eyes to look straight into John's, she began to speak slowly and deliberately.

"My dad taught me to use weapons such as that Arkansas toothpick and a handgun for my self-protection. I—I—have often wondered in the past if I could ever use them on another human being. Now, with the recent loss of my dad—with the closeness of war—and with you and Ollie to consider—the answer would have to be a definite—yes! I have much more than myself to think about now—and, being able to use the Colt or the knife seriously at another person may make the difference of your life—or Ollie's life! So, yes, I could! I would use those weapons to kill—if we were threatened."

"Well, thet's good. I am puttin' you both on notice. Those nine men out there are killers! Count on it—and when you pull your gun, or knife—plan on using it! Now thet's my order to both of you. And when you pull the trigger, shoot to kill jus' like you would if'n a rattlesnake was about to strike. You'll prob'ly only get one chance! Do you both understand?" John squinted his eyes and he seemed to look straight through both of them.

"Dad, it isn't easy to shoot someone else—but it's easier to do that than it is to be dead! I know we are on the side of God's law when we live in His truth; still, I always pray—jus' like I did for those men at Brushy Creek. I didn't want to hit Tommy Blainey either, but he was mean—and it's jus' like you said, hittin' first sometimes wins th' battle. Remember, Dad?"

John smiled at his son. "You got thet right, Son. Now, I got some special instructions jus' for you." Cassie made a move to arise to give them privacy, but John stopped her.

"Don't go away, honey. This instruction is for Ollie, but not a secret from you." Reaching over to take her hand, he gently pulled her to his side, where she curled up beside him while he put his arm around her shoulders. "Ollie, you're going to have to head off for Catlettsburg alone, by dawn. Tomorrow's Wednesday and you need to intercept the Union patrol that Uncle Robert is bringing and give them a message. They need to be warned thet three other tough-lookin' men are with the rustlers—although I plan on takin' 'em down a bit before they get there. But they still need to know. Thet's your job—to inform the patrol and to stay with 'em until Cassie 'n me meet you."

"How will I know when you 'n Cassie get there, Dad?" asked a somewhat apprehensive youngster.

"You don't need to worry about thet, Ollie, I'll get word to you. Jus' stay with the patrol. I'll find you!" John patted Ollie's shoulder with assurance and Ollie relaxed.

John described the three new men in detail, having Ollie repeat the description back to him. He also gave him explicit directions and assured him he could easily make it into town by tomorrow night. John told his son to warn the local sheriff of Boyd County when he arrived, and give him opportunity to work with the Union patrol if he desired.

Ollie and Cassie sat for a few more minutes as they had a Scripture reading and a prayer, thanking God for His watchful eye and praying for His continued protection as they worked to apprehend these criminals and bring them to justice. They joined in prayer also for Cindy Lou and her future, and special care for the Birchets as they watched over her. Ollie added a special prayer for Tommy Blainey, as he had done each night since their unhappy meeting. Prayer ended, Ollie excused himself and went to make ready his saddlebag and supplies for the coming trip. He also had to bring his journal up to date, knowing this would also give his dad and Cassie some time alone.

John loved Cassie with all his heart, but was also aware of the restraint he needed to exercise regarding her physical appeal. He would keep her as close to him as he had the night before, but fully clothed, and he would not try to take advantages unbecoming to a man and woman who had faith in God! Cassie knew this also, but this did not stop her from looking into his eyes and holding him close. She felt his strength, his warmth and sensed the security that was hers. As she looked into his eyes, her fingers caressing his face, they stopped at the small scar that cut diagonally above his right eye into the eyebrow itself.

"What caused this scar?"

"A man's fist gave me that scar to remember him by."

"Was the fight over a sweetheart?" she asked coyly.

John looked into her eyes of deepest blue, as he stroked her unblemished face, considering the answer, knowing he would open up a whole-untold chapter in his life. Cassie waited patiently, realizing that his mind was active even though his answer was not yet forthcoming.

"Darling, if you would rather not answer, it's OK; I'll understand," she offered diffidently.

"No, you won't—I—I mean you won't understand. If I don't answer, you will misunderstand the reason." John took her two hands in his. "I was just being hesitant and choosing exactly what to say—because—everything you think of me is important, and the question you asked will open up a chapter in my life that's in the past. By answering, I'll reveal to you a part of my life that may sound—unbecoming!"

Cassie straightened up and moved as close as she could to her man. Although she didn't speak, her actions showed she would handle anything John had to say to her about his past and not be ashamed!

"First off," John said, "it was not a scar given to me about a girl, sweetheart or wife! In fact—that may seem to be a more honorable alternative. Cassie, from the time I was fifteen years old I was gifted in being able to fight with my fists. I am sure you have heard of bare-knuckle fighting—for sport, I mean?"

"Oh—I did hear something about it up in Boston, when I stayed with Aunt Prudence. It is done for money, isn't it?"

"Exactly—and it is not too pretty. Not very many women would ever be seen at one of those spectacles. Well, I fought for three years in western Virginia and southern Ohio, and I was considered the champion of Cabell, Logan, and Wayne counties. I fought Davey

Otter for that championship in Huntington, Virginia when I was seventeen. I held the same title for wrestling simultaneously. It was Davey who left me this souvenir on the forehead," he smiled wryly.

"John Burke, that isn't anything to be ashamed of," she said as she placed her hands on her hips, then impishly asked, "Did you win a lot of money?"

"Not too much," John answered with evident relief. "The promoters took most of the money, but I did win enough to learn a bit about money, and to help my folks in their last years. This all ended before I met Elizabeth and, consequently, I never told about it. I sort of hid it away. Ollie doesn't even know—I guess, because he never asked."

"What about your folks, John? Where are they?" John became pensive again, but just for a minute.

"My Father, T.C. Burke—which stands for Thomas Christopher—died the year before Ollie was born, 1850, and Mother died a year later, pretty close to the date. Both of them knew the Lord but died young. Dad died of consumption and Mother of a broken heart I guess. She wasn't happy without Dad. I had—have—a sister too. Her name is Marcy Frances. She ran away with a logger when I was eighteen, and no one has ever heard of them since. I suppose they left the country. Well," John said, "there you have it—the forgotten chapter of my life."

"Marcy Frances, what a pretty name. Was she younger, or older than you, John?" Cassie asked.

"Three years younger." Cassie cuddled back into John's arms, laying her head against his chest. "Is that all your family on your dad's side?"

"Well, not exactly, I have an uncle and aunt I never met. Uncle George and Aunt Belva—if they are still living. Dad had two younger brothers also, but I don't know their names."

"Do you know anything about him, the older brother—and his family?"

"Not much," John said. "My dad told me a bit about them playing when they were children. He was three years older than George. He told me George married and took to farming in northern Virginia, and had a number of sons and—maybe daughters too. Dad never knew their names. They lived outside of Yorktown Virginia. The last time they were together Dad invited him to come and visit. He told Dad it wasn't likely.

"You see, it's altogether possible that Dad was not approved of by his brother—and sister! He married twice, and left his first wife without a divorce, had two children and was several years in returning to his first wife. Dad was saved in a Wayne County Revival and fell under conviction. He confessed to Mother, and with her encouragement went back to Yorktown to make amends. His first wife—Sarah, I believe was her name—refused to recognize Dad's second wife and children and still refused to come away with him, even though Mother was willing to accept that relationship. Dad believed Sarah was with child when he left the last time he saw her."

"You think your Uncle George knew of all this?"

"Dad never said, but I think so. After all he lived rather close to Sarah and her father, who also owned a farm and a tavern in Yorktown. I never discussed this with Ollie, or the other family members—but I always felt that someday I would find out."

"John, I marvel at your mother," Cassie said, "to know about this relationship and accept it—even to send your father back, knowing he could bring back another wife? She must have been a special kind of woman."

John smiled. "She was, honey, and she was ready to share Dad—rather than have him be out of favor with God.

"Then you have an uncle, an aunt and lots of cousins on the Burke side. What did your dad say of Aunt Belva?"

"Not one thing, Cassie. That was always a mystery to me. She was ten years younger than dad, born in 1810. He never spoke of her!"

"It's time you told Ollie, John—he needs to know about his family. He also needs to know how to defend himself. On the way from Louisa, he was sharing with me about his interest in learning self-defense, hand-to-hand, even Army style. That little experience he had with the boy in Sandy Hook brought it all to his attention."

"You sure do have thet one figured out, honey. I've been thinkin' some on it myself. Jus' as soon as this trip is over I'll get right on doing somethin' about it."

Cassie smiled to herself as she listened to John talk. It had not gone unnoticed when he spoke very clearly to her concerning this matter of pugilism—and family. No dropped "g's," not one "thet." But now that the discussion of the silent chapter in his life was finished, he was back to the colloquial hill-folk talk. Cassie felt she would bring this up at another time, as she was becoming a little drowsy and in a very comfortable position. She vaguely re-membered someone putting a blanket around her, even though her cushion had not moved—how so?

Ollie had silently crept over to his two favorite people and saw Cassie already well into dreamland. His dad motioned to a blanket and he caught on, wrapping Cassie and John in the warmth of a dry blanket to keep them from the penetration of the May dew.

According to his estimate, by noon of May 21st, Ollie found himself approaching a stream on the edge of Boyd County, after leaving at dawn with last-minute instructions from John. He was two miles off the southern flank of the rustlers when he decided it was time to rest Ginger and get a little nourishment for himself. The rushing stream beckoned to Ollie as he dismounted under a large sycamore tree. He scanned the area for any signs of recent human or animal use. Except for fairly recent signs of deer watering at the stream, he found the place suitable to make a cold camp.

He had followed close enough to the herd for a time to get a glimpse of one or two of the bandits, but backed off to the south in order to give them plenty of room. They would be nearing the Catlettsburg area by mid-afternoon tomorrow, as near as he could tell, but he would be way ahead of them and have ample time to get his message to Sergeant Damron, or whoever the captain had sent on this detail. Ollie figured he would be into town well before dark tonight. He would have to exercise care until he left the herd a couple of miles behind, then he could make good time with Ginger's canter.

Ollie dismounted, unsaddled Ginger, and led her to the stream. After attending to her needs, he took his lunch and sat beside the peaceful stream to gaze at the rippling water. He laid back on the bank as he nibbled on a piece of jerky and soon drifted off to sleep. He awakened with a start. He did not know what had wakened him— the snapping of a twig? An alarm from Ginger? Maybe a splash of a bass in the stream? He climbed the bank to where he left his gear.

As Ollie entered the open area under the sycamore everything looked OK and he breathed a sigh of relief. The saddle, rifle, his saddlebag, and Ginger, grazing off to his left, seemed peaceful enough. He decided it was time to make haste toward his destination when, all of a sudden the largest man he had ever seen came out of the brush—straight in front of him. There was a leer on the man's bearded face and an evil glint in his eye. Ollie recognized him immediately from his dad's description of the three newcomers to the rustler band. The man's appearance was frightening. Adding to that menace was a shining revolver in his right hand. Ollie's hands were empty, and the Colt on his right hip seemed a long way off.

"Well, what do we have here?" The words came out as a deep, guttural growl. "A mere stripling—all dressed up like a great big man? And where do ya thinks yer a goin', sonny-boy?"

"Jus' passin' through," Ollie ventured back calmly, knowing he was one step away from eternity and from meeting his God. In this, he had no fear—though his human body was longing to scream and run. But he was frozen in his tracks.

"Well, I might jus' let you pass on through as if nothing happened, but I kinda took a likin' to yer horse 'n fixin's. I gotta hankerin' to see thet hawg-leg fastened there to yer hip, too! Now, if you ree-aal careful like pull it out an' hand it to me—I might jus' let you go on through here."

Ollie knew his only chance was that Colt. He also knew he could still make it on foot—if he had to. But he knew that without his gun he did not have a chance with this giant of a murdering bandit who would kill him as quick as he would a grown man. He also knew that, even if he gave the man his horse and gun, the man would probably kill him anyway. He made a decision. If this was his day to die—it would be his own choice, in this instance, of how he would do it. God was still with him—and Ollie still believed, frightened though he was—in miracles.

"Kid, I saw death dance in your eyes jus' now," the man rasped. "And I jus' want ya ta know, thet I didn't git this big, or this ugly, or this mean, by bein' stupid an' not bein' able to read sign!" With that, the big man went into a rapid display of his firearm, spinning it and tossing it from one hand to the other; stopping with it aimed straight at Ollie. But Ollie's mind was fixed—his decision had been made. He inched his right hand toward the Colt even as the firearm display was in progress.

Ollie couldn't know it, but the look of John Burke was etched on his face with a blue coolness coming out of his eyes. If he could have seen his reflection, he would have recognized the same look he had seen on his dad's face when he stood up to the man in Shirley Bradley's café, the day he met Cassie.

Daniel MacGruder, better known as Brute MacGruder—killer, thief, bare-knuckle and barroom fighter, with the strength of a bull—did not see or recognize this resolution on a mere boy's face. He was too impressed with his own immunity to death. After all, a dozen or so men had fallen at his hand, some by blows from his powerful fists, and some by his accuracy with his revolver. He would simply pulverize this wart of a boy by breathing on him.

"If you hafta take my horse and gear, mister—I reckon I ain't a goin' to stop you. But if I have to pull this revolver out of my holster, I'll jus' be obliged to shoot you—not that I want to do that, but—if I take it out, I'll pull it in th' name o' th' Lord of Hosts—an' you'll be dead." Ollie said this with conviction and with a smile on his face. He was surprised to find himself perfectly relaxed.

A terrifying laugh came out of the big man that sounded like a cross between a rabid dog and a huge waterfall. He squinted his eyes at Ollie as he deliberately placed his revolver back in his holster. Another, larger, handgun was tucked in his belt, and a huge Bowie hung in a sheath at his side. He pulled the shining knife and allowed it to glint in the sunlight as he slowly turned it.

"I'm goin' ta kill you boy—I'm goin' ta kill you and cut yer heart out and fry it for supper. I just want you ta see the knife I'm goin' ta use to cut you up with! So you come ta me in th' name of the Lord, huh. Haw, haw. I laugh at yer God, boy. I come ta you in th' name of Dan MacGruder, and once I put this knife in my sheath I'm goin' ta pull my gun and shoot ya between yer eyes—whether ya got yer gun out or not."

Big Dan spit out the words like bullets between his teeth. He never took his eyes off Ollie, as he slid the Bowie knife over to his left side and slid the point into the top of a sheath. Ollie knew that when he had dropped it the big man would draw his revolver with his right hand and start shooting. He found he was still relaxed and no longer sweating. He felt dry and calm. It was over in less than five seconds!

Dan dropped the knife and seemed to pull his revolver simultaneously, but Ollie sidestepped to the right, pulling and cocking his Colt as it came to hip level. He felt a burning sting in his left arm as he saw a blank expression appear on Dan MacGruder's face when the .44 caliber slug hit him in the chest. Ollie fired two more times in rapid succession, hitting the big man each time. The second bullet went through his chest on the right, and the third caught him in the throat. A gush of blood came from his mouth and the hole in his throat. He was dead before he hit the ground. Dan MacGruder is in eternity somewhere, meeting the God he chose to laugh at.

Ollie had been hit. If he had not sidestepped when he did, the bullet would have caught him in the heart and he too would be dead. His buckskins were torn on the inside of his left forearm where the bullet had torn through the flesh of his inner arm; leaving a crease on the left side of his upper shirt. Ollie slipped it off and viewed a raw-looking wound. He did not panic. Instead, he went to his saddlebag and took a folded bandage, which was all he had with him in the way of first aid. He cleaned off the blood, then securely wrapped the white cloth around the sore arm and tied it off. He slipped the buckskin shirt back over his head and had the presence of mind to know that the other rustlers would not be far away. It was only a matter of time before someone came to investigate the gunfire.

He turned the huge man over, closed his eyes, and said to himself, *I need to pray. But that will have to come later; right now I must make haste!* Ollie quickly removed the gun belt and second weapon from Big Dan's waist and pried the shining revolver from his fingers. Placing the gun that the man used back in the holster, he put the other weapon behind his own belt. Figuring that Dan had not come on foot, Ollie began to look for signs of his horse. He found a large buckskin horse saddled with a bulging saddlebag and bed-roll, which Ollie did not bother to investigate.

Leading the animal to water, he did things methodically as if rehearsed. He could not leave Dan's body behind—but neither could he lift the big man. The body should be taken to the sheriff in Boyd County and reported as soon as possible. Quickly Ollie saddled Ginger and tied a length of rope around the big man's chest, which took some sweat and muscle strain since he was working with an injured arm. Coiling the end of the rope, he hurled it over a hefty limb of the sycamore and wrapped it around Ginger's saddle pom-mel, then mounted. He guided Ginger away from the tree and slowly she lifted the huge man up high enough for Ollie to lead a horse under the body.

"Stand steady, girl—whoa, steady now!" Ollie dismounted and moved the large buckskin under Big Dan's body, then moved Ginger to lower the huge body of Brute MacGruder across the saddle and quickly secured him. Leaving the buckskin's reins tied to Ginger, he did a quick cleanup and restoration of the area. Most noticeable was the blood, which he scattered with the use of a tree branch, stirring up grass and leaves over the stained area, then hurled the branch into the swiftly moving stream.

Ollie mounted Ginger and headed directly into the stream, lead-ing the buckskin horse. For thirty minutes he rode downstream, aiming to give himself an edge on time. He knew he could not hide his tracks from a good stalker, but perhaps he could slow them down; after all, the herd was their main priority and they could not all leave at once. He knew he would reach civilization of some sort before nightfall, and these men would avoid people contact until they got their herd within range of Catlettsburg.

As Ollie allowed Ginger to climb the grassy bank out of the stream, he stopped, looked backward and listened. He heard no sounds of pursuit, but he realized that his legs were shaking! As he held out his left hand, he could not control it from shaking. His wounded arm was burning and throbbing. He could hear his heart pounding. For a few minutes, he quivered from head to toe.

Initially, he couldn't understand what was taking place in his body, then, as the shaking subsided, he understood. Less than one hour ago, Ollie Burke had stood on the brink of eternity! A brute of a man, almost three times his size, a killer and a blasphemer, had threatened to take his life and—would have succeeded—had God not been his protector. Oh, he knew he pulled the trigger and aimed the gun, but the throbbing left arm reminded him of his own vulnerability. God had aided him in thinking clearly—to automatically do the things that needed to be done, to clean up the area, to make good his escape. Now that it was all over, his emotions were catching up with him.

Did he have any regrets? No! The man had boldly renounced God! Ollie's only regret was that the man probably at one time had an opportunity to receive God, and he had refused the gift of His Son, Jesus Christ. Ollie could shed no tears for Dan MacGruder— but he could pray—giving God the glory for sparing him and being his shield and his protector. Ollie dismounted and fell on his knees before his God and worshipped—tears of thanksgiving, mixed with raw emotion, streamed down his cheeks as he prayed and gave God thanks for several minutes with an audience of two horses, the lifeless body of a killer—and—a host of unseen angels! There, in the Boyd county forest, he found a cathedral of praise!

THIRTY

He Shall Cover Thee

J OHN AND CASSIE CLEANED UP THE BREAKFAST CAMP ON LOST CREEK AS they chatted like there was no such thing as war going on around them. No pursuit. No Catlettsburg rendezvous! John took time to show Cassie the prayer/poem he wrote—and she was thrilled all over again as he read it to her.

"John, have you shared this with Ollie?" she asked innocently.

"No, Cassie, I haven't—and believe me when I say it was not deliberate. I would have allowed him to see it without hesitation. But we have been away from each other so much."

"Well, no worry," she said. "He has seen it!" Catching John's widening eyes, she continued, "Don't be alarmed. It was quite innocent—and by accident! As he was getting his gear together to leave you, on the quest for the raiders, he stumbled onto the prayer in his notebook and he copied it! He just loved it, John, and wanted to take it with him, as the two of you parted company. When he was back with me, and he had to prove to me—that—that—you did love me, he produced the prayer and allowed me to keep it. I have it in my Bible!"

"Well, I'll be—you two are a pair of conspirators—plotting against me," John said with a grin. He took her into his powerful arms, he squeezed her until she gasped for breath and then he kissed her—and he kissed her again—and again!

"Don't worry, honey," he said. "I could never have anything but love for either one of you and little Cindy, too. I promise I'll git to know her some day soon! Well, darlin', we better be movin' so we don't git left at Lost Creek."

Nearing noon Cassie, Shep, and John were on the heels of the herd, and he knew that the rustlers would be within close riding range of Catlettsburg by nightfall. This left John with the task of making some serious moves to bring the odds more into their favor. There were nine men, and he figured that the Union patrol would be six men plus Sergeant Damron. John figured on allowing the rustler band to do most of the work to bring the herd close to the market area before either arresting or eliminating some of the bandits. He and Cassie were on the north flank, and he had already spotted two of the men through his telescope.

Due to the recent spring rains, there was not much show of a dust trail following the herd, for which John was grateful. He was also amazed at how well Cassie was able to keep Shep in check without so much as a growl. *She certainly has that animal well trained,* he thought as he crept close to a scrub oak to get a closer look at the man he was trailing. Cassie was behind him a hundred feet or so with the animals as he surveyed the view from his perch. The herd had not lost much weight in their travel. One thing nagged at John—he had not seen any of the three new men from this position; although it was too early to tell, as yet, because he had only seen Watson and Campbell so far on this northern flank.

Putting his telescope away, he cautiously slipped back to Cassie and Shep, motioning them to follow. Heading out to the north a distance, he led the way toward the front of the herd, trying to spot some of the others. He was more concerned about the newcomers than he was the ex-Confederates, because he felt he already had an insight into the former soldiers and their potential behavior. He did not doubt that Blainey and Tibbett were killers. Runyan, too. Watson? Perhaps! But he doubted that Campbell and Reynolds would hold up in a down-and-out-fight for their lives. From what he had seen of the three newcomers, he sized them up as out-and-out killers and very dangerous. He certainly would not want one of them in back of him!

Leaving Cassie and Shep behind again, John went on foot toward the herd. Hearing their sounds, he hunkered down and became part of the terrain, slipping from tree to tree and shadow to shadow. In the shadow of a large hickory John pulled out his telescope. Three men came into focus, but not all at once. In the extreme front flank was Tibbett, with Runyan seventy yards or so behind, also riding flank. Bringing up the rear, closest to John, was Reynolds—within easy range of the Sharps, should John want to use it. John had left the rifle in its boot in Cassie's care; he was not ready to start the elimination process yet. He just wanted to account for all the men traveling in the rustler band. He had accounted for all the regular soldier/bandits except for Blainey, and he, as before, would be riding point.

That left the three new men unaccounted for, and this really bothered John. He pulled out his watch. 12:45—just past lunchtime. This meant the rustlers were pushing, and not stopping for a noon meal. As he made his way back to Cassie, he heard shots off to the south, beyond the herd. There was a series of four shots, all from handguns. Two shots seemed to be on top of each other, followed by two more in rapid succession. John was on the run, swift, and fleet of foot as he glided effortlessly through the brush. Soon he was back with Cassie, not even winded.

"You heard?" he asked as he boosted her to Spot's saddle and quickly mounted Silky.

"The shots—yes. What do they mean?"

As John headed back over their earlier tracks, he turned, answering Cassie as they traveled. "I don't rightly know, honey, but my first thought was Ollie," he said grimly. "I'm not trying to sound an alarm, for one weapon that I heard could well have been a Colt. It was a heavy caliber handgun. The other? Well, it was a lighter handgun and I heard it muffled by the heavier gun, and it only shot once." They rode quietly for a time, each with their own thoughts, then John cut across toward the south. Cassie interrupted his thinking.

"John—what are you going to do?" John picked up the uneasiness in her voice. He reined Silky up in a sheltered spot and allowed Cassie to come alongside. John took her hand and reached up to brush an auburn tendril from her cheek, speaking to her in quiet tender tones.

"Darling, my excitement and concern for Ollie was only for a minute. This boy of mine—correction, ours—is blessed and has the hand of God on him. If someone came up against Ollie—although he would not start anything—I have no doubt that God would raise up a standard against that person and concern should be for that person, not for Ollie. We'll still investigate, though."

"Thank you, John, for caring how I feel and I know you believe what you're saying—they're not just words. Let's go and find out! Just one moment, John." Cassie slid from Spot's back and fell to her knees. John thought she was gong to pray, but he just watched patiently.

"Shep," she commanded authoritatively. The animal stopped in his tracks, with ears raised and tail straight, looking at Cassie.

"Come here, boy," she ordered affectionately. Shep rushed over and greeted her. Cassie took his head between her hands.

"Listen, Shep—listen!" The animal became totally still and waited. "Ollie, Shep, go find Ollie." The dog bounded away sniffing and leading, first left and then right, enthusiastically but silently. John was transfixed. He continued to watch, puzzled, as Cassie backed off from Spot about twenty-five feet. He could not understand how she was going to mount from that distance.

Suddenly she ran toward Spot and in a flash she was in the air in a coiled somersault and landed astride the saddle perfectly. "What are we waiting for? Let's go!"

John just sat there astonished.

"What did you do that, for?"

"Two reasons, John, dear," she answered flippantly. "First, to mount my horse; second, to show off." She ended her answer with laughter. John simply shook his head with amazement and pleasure as he led off following Shep.

"Cassie, where on earth did you learn to do that, pray tell?" he asked as he pushed his hat back on his head.

"Well, sir! When I stayed in Boston with Aunt Prudence, she took me to see some circus performers on one occasion. I watched a small girl—no older than I was at the time—dazzle the audience with such feats on horseback, and it fascinated me. Then and there, I made up my mind to accomplish such feats, if ever I was back on the farm and had access to a horse. The rest is history! When Dad purchased Spot for me, I spent hours practicing and perfecting stunts—but you, my darling, are my first audience," she said with an exaggerated bow. John smiled and softly applauded as he kept his eye on the sniffing dog who acted in earnest as if he were in search of Ollie—or somebody. As John moved his hat back in place over his right eye, he was secretly thrilled with the recent surprises this lady came up with. He found himself wondering whether

Shep understood who Ollie was and what Cassie told him? *Well, we'll soon find out*, he thought.

As John led Cassie further to the south and away from the herd, Shep suddenly picked up a scent and gave a small yelp. It was as if the animal knew not to make too much noise; his movements were excited as he wagged his bushy tail and danced around with nose to the ground. Cassie quickly dismounted and came alongside Shep. She examined the ground and quickly turned back to John.

"Hoof prints, and recent too." She waited for John's acknowledgment.

"Let's find out where they go," he said. Cassie got Shep's attention by taking his head between her two hands again, "Find, Shep—find!" she said and Shep was off, following the prints.

Soon Shep led them to a clearing near a stream. As John and Cassie halted, the dog examined the whole area slowly, stopping at a spot in the center and you could tell he was trying to tell them something. Finally, he sat down and waited as if to say, "I think this deserves a closer look."

"He's telling us something, honey. He wants us to look closer. Something took place here."

John dismounted, handing his reins to Cassie. He walked the area while Shep remained seated on his haunches, watching. John spoke softly, as if to himself. He stepped out of sight into some brush and returned, walking in a crouch as he read the signs like one would read a good book.

"Several animals have been here, Cassie," he said. "One came here first—alone. A horse grazed here," as he pointed, "perhaps thirty minutes or so. Another larger horse was tethered over in the bushes."

"How do you know he was larger, John?"

"The impression of his prints are much deeper and a third larger—and secondly, he was tethered in an area where he munched on some brush, which showed he was a tall animal." Cassie seemed pleased with his answer. Then her countenance changed and with an impish look she asked, "And—how did you know it was a he, John Burke?"

Realizing immediately she was playing with him, John answered with all seriousness.

"Well, honey—that was the easiest part. When I was over in the brush there, where he was tethered, I found some droppings and picked them up." John bent over and dramatized his story by pretending to pick something up. "I felt of the leavings, ran them through my fingers and sniffed them. Immediately I knew it was a male animal."

"Ooo, John—no—you didn't! How could you?" she said with disgust, making a terrible face and curling her nose. John could no longer keep his face straight; he bent over and began to laugh until he cried. Cassie slid off Spot pounded her fists on his chest, knowing he was teasing. As John caught his breath, he encircled her with his strong arms, trapping her against his muscular chest, smothering her with kisses from her forehead to her chin and—last, but not least—her tempting full lips. They were both slightly breathless and John gazed into her lovely blue eyes.

"Honey, I don't know whether it was a he or a she—and I couldn't care less. I do know—this is a he!" He tapped his cheek. "And I know—this is a she!" He kissed her on the nose. Furthermore, this he—loves this she—with all his heart." Cassie melted in his arms. She was weak with pent-up passion. She had never ever dreamed she could love this much—or—that love would affect her this way.

Shep waited patiently, sitting on his spot as the lovers floated above him. It took them a good five minutes to remember they were still on the ground and in a land of war and brutality.

John picked her up and carried her to the trunk of a fallen tree, where he put her down, after kissing her once again. He brought his attention back to the reason they were in this clearing. He walked over to Shep and squatted, petting the soft black and white fur.

"What do you have here, fellow? You haven't moved since we arrived." Shep still didn't move, except for his nose. He began sniffing and whining.

"OK, fellow—something happened. Right here, you say. Why don't you move over here," John patted a place off to the right, "and I'll examine this grassy spot!" The big dog dutifully went to the place John patted and laid down—as if he understood exactly what he said.

John, on his hands and knees, began to examine the area where Shep had sat, first with his eyes and then with his hands. "Hmm— sticky." Then he parted the grass, feeling the sod; he bent over and sniffed the grass, suddenly straightening up.

"It's blood, Cassie! Due to the amount of blood, I believe someone died on this spot."

"Not Ollie!" Cassie said, getting to her feet.

"Not Ollie!" John said. "Shep would be acting differently if that were the case. One thing for sure—that amazing dog of yours can talk! He brought us where Ollie was and, no doubt, it was Ollie who ended the life of a rustler—right on this spot. He probably has the body of that murdering thief on the way to Catlettsburg right now. These other prints are from at least two others who are probably attempting to track their cohort—and Ollie—right now!"

"Are you sure of this, John?" Cassie asked, her voice worried.

"Honey, I am as sure as if Ollie wrote me a letter telling me just what I told you. I further know that the dead man was probably one of the newcomers—maybe the largest one I described, because of the size and weight of the horse. I also know it is the other two trying to trail Ollie; although I doubt if they know what took place here. They probably think they are trailing their friend."

John walked a couple of steps over to Shep. Taking his head, as Cassie had demonstrated earlier, he said, "You did good, boy—

Good dog, Shep. Good dog." Shep bounded up on John and gave him a bath with his tongue, wagging his whole body with his tail.

"Find Ollie, Shep—find Ollie." The animal was off again with his nose to the ground, as John mounted Silky, reining up beside Cassie, who was already on Spot.

"John Burke, may I make an observation?" she asked, as they followed Shep down the bank to the stream.

"Of course, darling."

"John, you have not dropped one 'g' off your words; like just now—you said darling instead of darlin'; you have not said one 'git' or 'thet' or even a 'jus' instead of just! You speak as well as anyone I've heard—when you want to do so. Can you explain that?"

"Wal now, darlin', you jus' asked to make an observation. Now yer already askin' questions, too. Jus' how fer do you plan to go with this?" He rallied with a playful smile.

"Oh, John," she said with a petulant look. "You—are impossible!" John was quick with a comeback. "Now—thet, my dear, is an observation!" Cassie broke out in a laugh as she playfully hit at him. John caught her hand and kissed it.

Shep was in the stream looking a little perplexed. He was up to his belly looking up at John as if to say, "What now, partner?" John pointed to the south bank.

"Up there, fellow, up on the bank." Sure enough, the sturdy friend leaped up on the bank and began sniffing as John led downstream. Before too long, John found what he was looking for. The trail of two horses, traveling side by side, led off to the left and headed somewhat north. John halted Cassie and followed the trail a hundred yards or so alone before he returned.

"It's as I thought. Those two riders have lost Ollie—and the big man, who is probably dead and tied across his saddle. These two riders are riding side by side, whereas the second horse with Ollie is being led, one horse behind the other. Let's follow on downstream a little longer; I want to confirm my suspicions—to myself, that is."

"And to me," Cassie sweetly added, flashing John an enchanting smile.

My dear God, John thought, *the woman is absolutely beguiling in her innocence and beauty.* But he said, "Dar-ling," with an exaggerated 'ling,' He picked up their earlier conversation and offered an explanation. "I forget my country colloquialism when I am with you, you bring out the best in me and make me want to put my best foot forward. Do you understand now?"

Cassie gave him that beautiful smile again. "I certainly do, John dear. Now you know why I did that somersault and landed in the saddle. I do appreciate you sharing that with me, though; I love you whether you speak correct grammar or not, but I do have to admit—I'm grateful you have been taught well and, when you speak colloquially, it's because you want to—not because you have to."

Shep's whimpering called their attention to a grassy bank sloping up into thick timber. John found tracks leading out of the rocky streambed, up through the thick grass.

"Very clever," John said. "That little rascal found an ideal spot to climb out—leading into that forest. If it weren't for Shep, we might have ridden right on by! The grass is so thick here, you have to look close to see any sign, and in an hour or so it will not be detectable. Cassie, our boy is well on the way to Catlettsburg, and it's high time we had some lunch."

After a quiet, cold lunch of jerky and dried fruit, John put the saddles back on Silky and Spot, and the pack on Fred. The animals had enjoyed a good forty-five minutes of grazing and drinking. John had no way of knowing, but the place they made camp for dinner was not far from where Ollie had worshipped the Lord just after his triumph over Big Dan.

"I think we'll trail those two men who attempted to follow Ollie, Cassie, I'd feel a lot better if we were able to remove those two from the competition before the others. What do you think about that?"

"John, honey, you've seen those men. I haven't, and—I—I don't know if I could make such an evaluation as that, even if I had seen them. I simply trust your judgment and, I would prefer to follow you even if I wasn't sure!" John smiled to himself at Cassie's answer, but he was not surprised.

Cassie was a woman who thought for herself and had been accustomed to doing just that, but now she was in obedience to the wishes of her man—by her own choice—and she loved it. She did not have the normal fears that many women had about men. She had been taught to take care of herself, and was able to do very well in that area; never feeling inferior to men, as others often did. She did, however, respect the place God had given men in His Word, as the stronger sex and the head of the household. She knew that at the proper time, when God would give her the man of her prayers—and her dreams—she would gladly submit to him, under God, and take her place by his side doing his bidding and accepting his leadership cheerfully and willingly.

She knew John Burke was this man, and she had felt that way before she even knew anything about him. God had heard her prayers. She belonged to John Burke and sensed in her heart that he would never "lord it over her," but that he would respect her and admire her, as well as love her and bring her security. Indeed, he had already demonstrated that very thing.

John led back into the stream, back-tracking to the spot where the two horses had veered to the north. They followed the tracks back to the herd, where, with the telescope, John was able to see both newcomers on their horses in a huddle with Runyan. John could see that the discussion was animated but he couldn't hear the remarks. It was obvious that all three men were upset about something. John watched while Cassie patiently waited, keeping Shep quiet. John turned once and motioned to her, allowing her to glance through the glass at what he was watching. She appreciated this, handing the telescope back to John.

As the afternoon wore on, John and Cassie moved three times, watching the herd as it moved closer toward civilization. John guessed they would hold up before too long so as not to arrive in the populated area of Catlettsburg's outskirts too soon. Runyan or someone would ride on ahead to make arrangements to corral the animals, pending market day. Often buyers would arrive early and try to make good deals before market day, in order to cut out the middleman's profit. Runyan just might try that market, rather than chance waiting through market day. John knew he would have to keep a close watch from here on and, if he planned on thinning down the numbers, tonight was the night!

John pulled back out of sight and shared his thoughts with Cassie. She had not been to a cattle and livestock market before, so John explained the workings. He felt more strongly all the time that Runyan would try to hit that "early market" rather than chance a meeting with the unexpected on market day. He would simply make the best deal he could, get the cash and be gone before market day came, if John was right.

In the meantime, John and Cassie kept an eye on the dapper redheaded gunslinger, and his thin scar-faced cohort, as they were back working the herd again. John noticed they were always looking off to the right or left, sometimes behind them, as if expecting someone. John figured they were looking for the large man, who, of course, would not be returning. John was absolutely sure of that. There was an art to reading trail sign and John had been tracking and reading sign in the woods too long not to be able to tell what had taken place that afternoon. If the man had killed Ollie, he would have had no reason to remove the body. Ollie would still have been there. Shep would've found him as easy as he found the trail. The amount of blood, the tracks, the direction, as well as the shots and caliber of weapons used, were all clues as to what took place.

As evening shadows began to creep in, the men began to drive the animals into a closer "man-made corral." John and Cassie crawled in as close as they dared and watched as the two new men approached Runyan again. John saw a look of resignation come over Runyan's face when he seemed to give in to the two men. They rode off around the herd, to the south. John figured they were on their way to try to locate the big man again. Cassie crept close and pulled on John's sleeve. "Are we going after them?"

John nodded and they crept back to their animals. John led them back away from the herd before they mounted.

"I want to get around to the other side, and see if we can find where 'Slim' and 'Red' went to," he explained.

"I sort of figured we'd be heading that way when I saw those two ride off."

John sidestepped Silky over to Spot and reached over to pull Cassie close to him. John looked at her dark hair in the evening light. "You are a girl after my own heart, Cassie Martin." He kissed her soundly on the lips, while Silky and Spot cooperated, standing quietly.

"I am not only *after* your heart, John Burke—I own it. It's mine—all mine." She raised her eyebrows and gave him a tantalizing smile.

"Not only my heart my dear," he said with lowered voice, "but all of me belongs to you."

"I'll take it. I'll take it."

Two hours later, having tied the animals in a safe wooded hollow, John, Cassie and Shep lay side by side peering at a flickering campfire where "Slim" and "Red" were busy eating beans and sipping coffee. They overheard Slim say, "I tell ya, Cort, it ain't like th' Brute to go and not come back. We've been ridin' together too long fer that. I say somethin' has happened to him, probably right when we heard that shootin'."

The smaller man finished his beans, sopping a piece of bread in the juice, then washing it down with a heavy swallow of black coffee. He took his time answering.

"Well, Benton, you may be right, but what I'm remembering is he had a lot of gold in his saddlebag, and part of that belongs to me and you. Now, he stood to gain some by a cut of the loot from these cattle and horses from Runyan. However, if he kept all that he was carrying and just kept going—well, figure it out for yourself. You're not stupid! There was a couple thousand dollars in gold pieces in that bag of his. I was stupid to let him carry it all—without us dividing it up back in Illinois. But, since he busted us out of jail in Centralia, I got all soft-hearted and let him do the carrying."

"Well, he could have been robbed hisself—didja ever think on that?"

A loud guffaw came from Cort. "Can you imagine anyone tangling with that giant? Why, he killed that deputy with one hand—broke his neck without any effort at all. It would be something if he was bested, but it would take some doing. The funny thing is—we didn't even get that cache from a bank; we stole it from crooks who are still rotting in that jail, I reckon—if' they haven't hung 'em yet."

"Well, I find it hard ta believe that anyone bested Dan MacGruder. An' I also find it hard ta believe he run out on us— but, if'n he did—" Benton pulled out his long-barreled revolver and twirled it putting it back in his holster. "Big as he is, he won't be too hard to miss."

"Now you're talking sense. We'll find him for sure—and when we do, he'll go—like the county sheriff back in Illinois. I kind of took a liking to that lawman—before the end, that is," Cort said with another coarse laugh.

John had heard enough. He pulled his Colt and checked the loads. Cassie followed suit.

"Remember," he said, "don't hesitate if you have to shoot. Think of the fork of that birch tree and do likewise. They're killers—you heard it!" Cassie nodded, and John continued. "You control Shep; have him to go wide to the right and come in with us, silently if possible. You stay wide of me on my right and watch the redhead. He'll be the faster of the two. I'll try to make an arrest; but they won't be taken alive."

Cassie caught her breath and turned to Shep, taking his head again. She whispered something low, then pointed. The dog obediently slipped away from her and after he had gone about twenty feet, he stopped and looked back to Cassie. With her right hand she motioned down, like pushing against the ground, and Shep went into a crouch, as if waiting. As Cassie turned back to John, she pulled her .44, cocked it and held it skyward.

"John, I'm ready, whenever you are—and—and—I love you."

"I love you too, darling. Cassie, watch their eyes. Their eyes will tell you when they are going to make their move." John took her left hand an instant and looked toward heaven. "God be with us and be our shield—in Jesus' Name—amen!" He pulled his Colt, cocked it and went six steps wide of Cassie. He turned, motioning to her—now was the time!

John slipped out into the clearing, and could see Cassie out of the corner of his eye; she was staying up with him. As they became visible in the poor fire-light, the two men suddenly came to attention, facing John and Cassie. Cort, the one John had dubbed "Red" was nearest to John; Benton was closer to Cassie.

"What the hell is going on here?" Cort demanded with a raspy voice. "Who are you, and what do you want?" His right hand slid toward his tied-down revolver.

John softly answered, "You two are wanted in connection with a bank robbery, a jail break, and murder in the State of Illinois. We're here to place you under arrest—peacefully, if possible."

"Where's yore authority?" Benton growled. "I don't see no badge—and no damn woman is going ta put me under arrest!"

"This here Colt is my authority," John said smoothly, "and me and this woman will arrest you, or you'll both go in over a saddle— just like the big fella."

At the mention of the "big fella," Cort and Benton exchanged glances, and John saw resolution transfer between them. Then he heard Cassie say loudly, "Shep." A ball of raging fur caught the attention of two outlaws, distracting them just long enough. Fire spit out of the muzzles of four revolvers that night, and two murderers fell to their death. Cort fell into the campfire with a .44 slug between his eyes and Benton fell wide with two shots from Cassie in his chest. Shep made the difference. Even with guns drawn, John and Cassie were not as fast as the two men—professional killers, both of them. When Shep roared and went flying through the air, it surprised the two killers and cost them their lives. John and Cassie did not get a scratch, although John felt the wind from Cort's bullet whiz past his left ear.

John rushed to Cassie and held her close. Her wide eyes were dazed. "I'm OK, honey—I'm OK," she said. "Are you—are you— all right?"

"Just fine, darling. I'm fine—but let's move. The others have heard the shots and may be on their way here. You get their horses. Here Shep, here boy." Shep came running with tail wagging and jumped up on John. John bent over to greet the big dog. He roughed his head up and said affectionately, "You saved us big boy—you did real good." Shep rolled over and allowed John to rub his belly.

The smell of burning flesh caught John's attention, and he turned to roll Cort out of the campfire coals. The body had extinguished the fire so there was not much light. It took John and Cassie less than fifteen minutes to hoist the two bodies across their saddles. John made sure the fire was out, then they led the two horses back to Silky and Spot. John did not take time to clean up the area; he wanted the thieves to wonder what happened. They had set out to reduce the odds and, with God's help and the aid of a shepherd dog, they had succeeded.

As they each led a horse carrying the body of a killer, John turned to Cassie. "Are you all right, sweetheart? I mean, inside! Are you all right?" He tenderly caressed her shoulder.

"I'm perhaps a little in shock right now. I think, it's—it's like a dream—like—it really didn't happen. But I don't have remorse. I'm all right, honey. *We're* all right—that's the main thing!" John reached to touch her cheek, saying, "To God be the glory!"

THIRTY-ONE

What Is His Son's Name?

A BOUT SIX O'CLOCK WEDNESDAY EVENING, SHERIFF VESSIE COMPTON was sitting at his favorite table devouring a huge steak and enjoying the company of his two good friends, Jacob Hardin and Paul Ray Thompson. Paul Ray was auctioneer for the livestock market and Jake Hardin was one of the most prominent cattlemen in Boyd, Lawrence, and Carter Counties. The men were discussing the latest war news as they ate supper and relaxed.

The cafe, full of livestock traders, farmers, and businessmen, was plainly a man's meeting place It served good food, ale, and liquor, and reeked of cigar smoke. Several gentlemen, in custom-made suits, sported fine pipes and blew aromatic circles of smoke. Most of the conversations were about the war or the coming livestock market, which met twice a month. A day or two before market day, the population always surged. Its strategic location on the Big Sandy River, not far from where it merged into the Ohio River, made it an important location for shipping, trading, and commercial enterprise.

This business had increased since the war and, although the town was predominantly Union in loyalty, many Confederate sympathizers were no doubt in and out of Catlettsburg and Boyd County.

"I tell you," said Paul Ray Thompson, "I don't think President Lincoln had any business interfering with General Hunter's order to free the slaves. He was a duly appointed general, acting on behalf of the Union, and, after all—isn't that the reason Lincoln got voted into office? To abolish slavery?" Gesturing with a fork, Paul Ray hit the table to emphasize his point.

"That is precisely the point, Paul!" Jake said, "President Lincoln was *voted into office*—not General David Hunter. I say General Hunter exceeded his authority and jumped the gun on our president. He ought to be attending to military matters and winning battles—not meddling in politics." Jake Hardin finished off his last bite of fried potatoes. It was quiet for a few seconds. "At least, that is my opinion. What do you think, Vessie?"

Vessie Compton reared back in his seat and loosened his belt a notch. Just as he was about to put in his opinion, a small boy ran into the café, shouting at him.

"Sheriff—Sheriff—come quick. A boy—horse—big dead man." He stopped, out of breath. The sheriff bent over and said gently, "Now, calm down, son. Catch your breath and start all over again!" The noise in the room suddenly stopped. Everyone was listening!

"There's a boy—on a horse—got another horse with a big dead man on th' saddle. He is looking fer you, Sheriff," the lad said, pointing toward the street. The sheriff reached over to the hat rack and pulled off a well worn felt hat.

"Just you take me to the boy on the horse, son." He took the boy's hand and allowed him to walk in front of him. Thompson and Hardin pushed back their chairs and followed Compton. Hardin called out to a man in a white apron behind the bar, "Put those meals on my tab, Yance. I'll stop by later and settle up," then caught up with Paul Ray, just a couple of paces behind the sheriff.

Ollie was ramrod straight on Ginger, foam-lathered from her rough trip. He'd had no trouble finding Catlettsburg, although this was his first time here. It was a lot larger than Louisa, and Ollie had not taken into consideration having to look for a law officer. He was glad that the youngster he met in the street knew where the Sheriff ate his supper. There were a lot of strangers in town on the day before market; he had inquired of several folks, but no one knew where to find the sheriff.

Ollie was relieved to see the boy come across the street with the sheriff in tow. He had been a spectacle on the busy street: an eleven-year-old boy leading a horse with a dead man across the saddle was not a common sight. It was a blessing—and practically a miracle—that no one stopped him or asked any questions. Ollie was relieved to see Sheriff Compton's badge; he felt secure again and the uneasiness seemed to leave, even though there seemed to be a group of men following behind him.

"Howdy there, son. I'm Sheriff Vessie Compton. I understand you want to see me?" The sheriff spoke with authority, yet gently, not pushing. This appealed to Ollie. Sheriff Vessie was forty-five years old and stood only five foot nine, but he seemed taller due to his high-crowned hat and high-heeled riding boots. He wore a cotton shirt with rolled up sleeves, a pair of blue denim trousers, and fastened to his belt was a holster with an old revolver. His tight shirt showed off a muscular frame, and his clean-shaven face was oval, set off with steel gray eyes. *There's an honest look in his eyes, and a look of integrity about him,* Ollie thought, feeling even more relaxed with the man.

"Howdy, Sheriff. My name is Ollie Thomas Burke and I'm a friend of Sheriff John Allison over in Louisa—Lawrence County!"

"Ollie? Ollie—let me see," Sheriff Compton said and scratched his head, pushing his hat back to expose a high forehead. "Seems to me I know that name." Suddenly he smiled. "Are you the youngster who helped catch those deserters they hung a few days ago?"

"Oh," Ollie said, "I didn't know they had already hung 'em. It don't come as any surprise to me, though—excuse me, sir! Yes, I'm the same one. I was with my dad, John Burke, and Sheriff John when we rescued little Cindy Lou—she's my sister now."

"Son—I want to shake your hand," the sheriff said as he reached up to Ollie. "That was a tremendous piece of work, Ollie. I'll be happy to shake your Dad's hand, too. Is he with you?"

"No, sir. But he is on the way. He sent me ahead to find you— but . . ." Ollie glanced over at the lifeless form of Dan MacGruder.

"But what, son? Who's this fellow?" The sheriff walked back and surveyed the man and horse, turning up the hatless head to gaze on the still face of Big Dan.

"His name is Dan MacGruder—and—I think he is—a—I mean—was a very bad man."

"Brute Dan MacGruder—Brute—is that who this is?" asked the sheriff with a grave look on his face; his eyes squinting. "He usually travels with Cort Grainger and Slim Benton."

"Yes, sir, that's who he is—and I'd be very grateful if you kinda took him off my hands. I haven't gone through his things yet—saddle-bag, bedroll or nothing—but here's one of his guns." Ollie pulled the second revolver out and handed it butt first to the sheriff.

"Well, son, you're right about him being a very bad man; he and his cohorts are wanted in three states. I have a poster in my office on him, as well as Cort and Slim—if he's who you say he is—and the description sure fits."

At least a couple dozen people had gathered in the street by now, with a few ladies standing off on the boardwalk separate from the crowd around Ollie. Low, whispered conversations made Ollie a little uncomfortable and the sheriff noticed his uneasiness.

"All right, folks—nothing to get excited about. This man is dead and can't hurt anyone so let's all move along about our business, please. I'll attend to this situation; that's what you pay me for." He said it with a smile, and the crowd slowly began to disperse. The sheriff spoke more softly. "Thompson, you and Hardin stay with me, if you can. I may need you."

Ollie noticed two well-dressed men, one a tall, lean man who was bare-headed, showing ample gray in otherwise black hair, and a shorter, handsome man dressed in western-style boots and suit with a new western high-crowned white hat. Both were clean-shaven, business-like men.

"Ollie, these are friends of mine—Jake Hardin and Paul Ray Thompson." The younger man took off his hat and bowed, with a big smile that showed even white teeth. The tall man simply smiled at Ollie.

"Now, Ollie, tell us about Big Dan. Did your dad send him in?"

"Oh no, sir! I don't reckon my dad even knows about it. Dan MacGruder came by me."

"What do you mean—he 'came by you'? I don't understand."

"Well, sir, Dad sent me to deliver a message to you 'bout meeting a patrol of Union troops to arrest a bunch of outlaws who're on their way here now with stolen livestock! I stopped for dinner, to rest my horse and eat, and Dan simply slipped up on me while I was asleep. I feel embarrassed about that—but, there he was—the biggest, meanest-looking man I had ever looked at. He wanted to steal my horse, my saddle and—this Colt" Ollie lifted out his .44 then returned it to his holster.

The Sheriff exchanged glances with his friends. "And what did you do, Ollie?"

"Well, I knew he was up to no good with me. He already told me he was going to kill me and cut my heart out with his big knife—so I warned him, if he tried to take my revolver I would draw it in the name of the Lord and—he would be dead."

The sheriff, with Jake and Paul Ray pressing in, moved close to Ollie, who was still astride Ginger. "Son, do you mean you faced down Dan MacGruder—with a six gun—and shot and killed him all by yourself?" he asked, looking straight into Ollie's eyes.

"Oh, I wasn't alone, sir. The Lord was with me and—the two of us are a considerable team," he said with a hint of a smile; not bragging, just stating the way it was. As the sheriff looked into his eyes, he knew this was not a cocky, smart-aleck answer. He could tell that Ollie believed what he said. The sheriff started laughing— slowly at first, then a good hearty laugh. Although his friends were smiling, they didn't know what to believe—so they just waited.

"A half-grown boy faces down and kills one of the meanest, most-ornery wanted men in the country—and he's as calm as a warm summer night about it. Big Dan didn't even get off a shot— and the boy without a scratch," the sheriff said, still laughing, un- til he caught the look on Ollie's face.

"What's the matter, son, did I say something wrong?"

"I'm sorry if I misled you, sir. Dan did get off a shot—and I did get a scratch. He shot me." Ollie said, very serious. "But, I lived," he added, as he saw the worried look on the sheriff's face.

Vessie started laughing again, but was more controlled. "I—I see you lived, Ollie. Where—where—did you get shot?"

Ollie painfully slipped out of his buckskin shirt and lifted his left arm, showing a blood-soaked bandage. Ollie heard the sheriff give an order to someone, but it sounded so far away.

"Go get Doc Carter. Quick!" He barely heard the sheriff, when he felt himself falling and there was darkness.

There was a faint light as he struggled to raise his head, but he was dizzy and the room, was spinning. Then he heard voices.

"Ollie—Ollie, you're all right, son." He struggled to see who was talking, then his vision became clear and he recognized Sheriff Vessie leaning over him. He was lying on a clean bed in a room with one window. There was a light on a dresser but, as he peered out the window, he could not tell if it was dusk or early morning light.

"Where—where am I, Sheriff? What—what happened?" Ollie noticed that his voice didn't sound natural.

"It's just eight o'clock, son. A little over an hour ago, you passed out—from loss of blood. It seems that in all your hurry to get here and bring me your message, the rough ride caused your wound to keep bleeding. You're all right, now. Doc Carter was here and put a clean dressing and some antiseptic on the wound. He even put in a few stitches, but you'll be fine." Then Ollie heard another voice.

"Ollie, Doc said all you needed was some good food and lots of liquid to build up your strength again. Do you feel like eating now?" Paul Ray asked, as he bent over Ollie. He looked around the room and saw that Jake Hardin was there as well.

"Son, the doctor left on another call and we are in a bedroom in back of the café and tavern," Jake explained. "It's where we were eating when the lad came to get the sheriff." It was plain to Ollie that these men were concerned about him. Being away from his dad and Cassie when he had come so close to death, he felt warmed by their concern. He saw the clean bandage on his arm and noticed that someone had dressed him in a loose cotton shirt, soft to the touch. He felt stronger and moved to sit up, as Sheriff Vessie helped him.

"Yes, sir. You're all very nice to me. I'm beholden to you. I am hungry, come to think on it, but I have a powerful thirst."

Paul Ray held him steady by the shoulders and helped him to his feet.

"Doc Carter said for you not to make any sudden movements or you might fall. At least until you got some food and water down—so just take it slow and easy," Paul Ray advised. The sheriff led the way to a side room set up for private dining. There was a large round table with six chairs evenly spaced around it. Jake Hardin pulled one chair out and motioned for Ollie to be seated while the sheriff got the attention of the bartender.

"Yance, bring this boy a man-sized steak, fried potatoes with green beans and bread. What do you want to drink, son?"

"I'd purely love a big glass of cool water—and—a glass of buttermilk, too, please."

Everyone patiently waited while Ollie ate and examined the room. His steak was done to perfection, and he finished off two glasses of buttermilk—as well as a tall glass of water. He saw Dan's gear and saddle in one corner, and his own saddle and gear in another. His holster and revolver were attached to the saddle pommel. Other than that nothing had been disturbed.

"Ollie, we put your mount—also MacGruder's—in the livery stable and they've been rubbed down and fed. Your stuff is all here, except for your buckskin shirt. Helga, Yance's wife, is cleaning it for you. It was bloody and needed a little care. Dan's things and his gear are waiting for us to inventory; what I mean is, we need to count it and list it together so no one will doubt what was there. That's why we always have someone else to help." Sheriff Compton's explanation answered a couple of questions Ollie had, and accounted for the presence of Hardin and Thompson.

Jake Hardin explained further. "You see, Ollie—" He held up an official-looking book. "As the sheriff reads off each item, I'll list it here; then, after we're finished, we all sign the book as witnesses that the inventory is all there as listed—do you understand, son?"

"Yes, sir, I think I understand. Do I sign it, too?"

"Absolutely, Ollie," the sheriff said. "You're the most important one! Our local law states that after burial expenses are taken out of the man's belongings, if no relative comes forth to claim them—the belongings, I mean, well—they belong to you because you brought in a criminal wanted by the law. Furthermore, I need to wire the sheriff in Centralia, Illinois, because there's a reward of one hundred dollars for this man—dead or alive! Now, what do you think about all that?"

Ollie was embarrassed. He had not killed this man for money or profit—he just wanted to stay alive, and he knew God was with him and aided him. He had not even thought of such a thing and, of course, the men facing him around the table were all aware of that. They were pleased to see his humbleness and innocence in the circumstances. Two or three times Ollie opened his mouth to speak, but nothing would come out. His crimson face and embarrassment said it all.

"Let's get to counting, men," Paul Ray said. "We ain't got all night. Start writing, Jake. One *big* man's buckskin horse," he said, pointing out the window. "One *big* saddle, blanket, and bridle—and a pretty one, too. Hey, look at all this silver." He continued this way through Dan's personal effects until he got to the shining revolver. He brought the holster over to the table and Ollie viewed the bright metal of the weapon that had come within four inches of costing him his life. As Sheriff Compton carefully pulled the five-shot weapon out of the holster, Ollie could see the admiration in the eyes of the lawman. He held it up. It was still loaded, with just one shot fired.

"Do you boys know what this is?" he asked, glancing at each one. As each one shook his head, the sheriff continued. "This is a genuine Beaumont-Adams percussion revolver. It will fire by cocking the hammer or by just pulling the trigger. Son, it was surely God with you that saved your life! This weapon is several seconds faster than that Colt—good weapon though it is—simply because of the trigger mechanism." He slid the revolver back into its holster, shaking his head.

The big surprise was when they unloaded the saddlebag, which was unusually heavy, and unrolled the bedroll. In the bedroll was the factory box for the revolver, complete with accessories, caps, and tools. The saddlebag was laden with twenty-dollar gold pieces—one hundred and five of them—two thousand, one hundred dollars in gold. The men sat back, amazed. Ollie's eyes were as big as saucers.

"Ollie, I'll have to disclose this in the wire to Centralia. I mean— it could be from a bank. These men were bank robbers, and we don't have any idea where it came from. If it is unclaimed—honestly, that is—the money is yours!"

"Sheriff, I killed that man to stay alive and did so because God was with me," Ollie said. "I didn't kill to make money—or even think about it! I'll sign the book for inventory, but I want it in the book that the gun and case goes to Sheriff Vessie Compton, along with the holster that comes with it. That is—if I have anything to say about it, and no one claims it." He watched as Jake Hardin wrote it into the official book. Now it was the sheriff's turn to be speechless.

"Thank you, son, that was a very generous gesture, but don't you think you ought to ask your dad about such a thing?" he asked.

"No, sir, my dad wasn't with me when I shot Dan MacGruder, so it's my decision to make. Besides, he'd say the same thing if he were here. By the way, Sheriff—I wouldn't send that wire to Centralia until my dad comes; he'll prob'ly have the other two men who were his friends." Ollie spoke confidently, knowing his dad well enough to speak without hesitation. Glancing at his friends, the sheriff smiled and raised his eyebrows.

"Ollie, you mentioned the Army patrol when you arrived. I just want you to know that my deputy is watching out for them and as soon as they arrive he'll bring them to you or come and get you—one or the other."

"Whew. Thank you, sheriff. I had plumb forgot about them. What about Big Dan's body? Where is he?"

"With the undertaker, Ollie. We saw to that while you were resting," the sheriff answered with a twinkle in his eyes. "He just walked over, turned himself in and asked Mr. Turner to lay him out." Ollie laughed, surprised that he could appreciate the humor of such a serious thing.

The next forty-eight hours, Thursday and Friday, May 22nd and 23rd in 1862, were crammed full of activity. Events started when Deputy Phil Workman ran into the cafe just as Ollie and the men had signed the inventory list of the late Dan MacGruder.

"Excuse me, fellers," he said, "th' sojers you been waitin' for has jus' rode into town. They're over to the livery barn now. I tole 'em to wait fer a bit; someone was expectin' 'em. Didn't surprise 'em none. They are waitin' fer ya." The sheriff introduced Ollie to Phil, and turned to the others. "If you men don't mind staying here to guard the inventory, I'll just mosey over there with Ollie." While Ollie strapped on his Colt, the sheriff told Phil to stay with Jake and Paul Ray, guarding the gear. Phil acknowledged the order, plainly wondering why he had to help guard a couple of saddles and bedrolls that seemed a little over-guarded anyway.

"Let's go, Ollie." The sheriff and Ollie left the café, with Ollie in the lead. At the edge of the boardwalk, realizing he didn't know the whereabouts of the livery barn, Ollie let the sheriff go in front.

At the livery stable, Ollie was elated to see Sergeant Damron and his troops. Uncle Robert was there, too, and gave him a hearty greeting. The big surprise was that Captain Lyons had accompanied the men. He was about to thump Ollie on the left shoulder when Sheriff Vessie caught his hand, surprising the captain. He rolled back Ollie's shirtsleeve to expose the bandage.

Ollie took care of the introductions.

"Captain Lyons, Sergeant Damron, Uncle Robert Birchet and men: this is th' Sheriff of Boyd County, Vessie Compton. Sheriff, this here is Captain Lyons from Louisa, Sergeant Lewis Damron under his command, Uncle Robert Birchet from over toward Grayson, and th' men of Sergeant Damron's patrol." He paused while everyone shook hands.

"Captain, Dad sent me here ahead of him and asked me to tell you that the odds have changed with the rustlers. He also wanted me to give the same message to the sheriff and ask him if he wanted to be included in the activities. Three real tough-lookin' men—gunfighters—have joined the group that Sergeant Runyan is heading up. Dad was goin' to try an' even up the odds before they arrived here, but felt like it was important enough to send me ahead. We're to wait for his instructions."

"I'll put my two cents worth in—if you don't mind, men," the sheriff said. Captain Lyons nodded. "First off, I consider this a total military operation and action. You men have been well into this problem before it saw fit to move into my county and, as the ranking law officer in Boyd County, I hereby give you authority to move ahead with this operation as you see fit—and I offer my services if and as you need me." He looked at Ollie.

"And one other thing. The odds *have* changed some—in your favor. Ollie was accosted by one of those gunfighters on the way to find me with that message. Brute MacGruder, 'Big Dan', some folks called him, tried to kill Ollie. All I can say is, that was *his* misfortune. Ollie took him out and his body is over at the undertaker's now. Ollie came away with this wounded arm as a souvenir of the fracas. Now, I'll leave you all together, and Ollie can explain the rest."

Sheriff Vessie Compton did a good job of setting Ollie up to do a lot of explaining. And for Captain Lyons and Sergeant Damron those explanations went a lot further than the adventure with Dan MacGruder. After Ollie explained in detail his gunfight with Big Dan, they wanted to know about John and Cassie and their "getting to know each other." More than once Captain Lyons laughed and predicted, "There's going to be a June wedding—just you all wait and see!"

Ollie sat with the men until he realized how tired he was. Then, remembering his journal, he said goodnight and headed for the cafe to pick up his bedroll. He found Yance and Helga waiting for him.

They turned the room behind the bar over to him for his bedroom; his things had already been moved there, including his buckskin shirt, which was clean and dry. He thought for a minute about the very warm feeling he had inside, and how God made it possible to find such good friends everywhere he went. He decided on a Bible reading in the book of John before he filled in his journal. He felt God's love—and that's what First John talked about. Ollie settled on a particular verse that really spoke to him in I John 5:1

> Whosoever believeth that Jesus is the Christ is born of God: and every one that loveth him that begat loveth him also that is begotten of him.

Ollie knew that many good folks said they believed in God, but what they sometimes didn't accept was Jesus, God's Son. Ollie likened that situation to himself and his dad! If someone acknowledged John, they had to recognize Ollie as John Burke's son. You can't have one, without the other. If you say you believe in God, you must believe the Jesus that God sent. If you say you believe in God, but do not accept His Son, then you don't really believe in God. You can't have one without the other. Ollie was very tired and still a bit weak. As soon as he finished his journal entries he laid his head on his pillow and was sound asleep.

Everyone except Sergeant Damron's posted guard was enjoying breakfast in the cafe as daylight broke the next morning. Captain Lyons, Uncle Robert, Sergeant Damron, Ollie, and Sheriff Compton sat at one table and the other troopers were scattered throughout the busy cafe. The guard, a man Ollie had not met, hurried into the café, saluted Captain Lyons then turned, reporting to Sergeant Damron.

"Sergeant, the man you spoke of last night is probably in the stockyard even as we speak. He is stocky, muscular, and the way he is dressed suggests he might be the man. He's definitely trying to put a trade together with some livestock buyers. I overheard him say he had a mixed herd a short distance west of town." Private Ward was not being disrespectful in ignoring Captain Lyons. It was Sergeant Damron who had placed the watch, and Captain Lyons had made it clear that this was the sergeant's operation.

"Private Ward, speak to all the men here in the cafe and tell them to meet me out front as soon as they finish eating." The private moved to obey and soon there was a flurry of activity in the room as men began to pay for their meals and move out the door.

"Who was that? Private Ward—did you say?" asked Captain Lyons.

"Sharp trooper, sir. Private Nathaniel Ward; native born, one of the Kentucky volunteers—comes from down Fallsburg way. He is an adroit trooper and very serious-minded. An excellent horseman, too, sir."

"Good, Lewis, good. We certainly have some good soldiers."

As the men rallied just outside the cafe, the sergeant gave them their orders, with Robert Birchet, Ollie, the sheriff, and Captain Lyons standing by.

"Men, Private Ward believes that the leader of the rustlers—Runyan, is his name—is in the stockyard now. Private Ward will direct you around the perimeter of the stockyard where the six of you will make a circle, leaving the front open. Ollie and I will advance with these men, casually, and when you see us—kind of close in. I doubt if any are with him—the rustlers I mean—but, until we hear from John Burke, we can't take any chances. Lead off, Private Ward."

As Ollie and Sergeant Damron walked into the front opening to the stockyard a bevy of men, dressed in everything from farmers' clothing to business suits, glanced up, noticing the Union uniforms.

Ollie spied David Runyan at once. He was talking with two other men, his back to Ollie. He seemed on the verge of striking a deal. Then he noticed everyone had become silent as Sergeant Damron's entourage approached. Former Confederate Sergeant David Runyan turned slowly and immediately recognized Ollie.

At first, panic went through him, showing all over his face as he looked around for an avenue of escape—only to find that Union soldiers encircled him.

"Well, if it isn't thet dumb hick fisherman kid. Looks like you've taken a likin' to the Yanks, eh boy? Well, what do y'all want—as if'n I didn't know?"

"David Runyan, I hereby arrest you for rustling livestock and for murder, in the name of the United States Government," Sergeant Damron said.

"You damned Yankee! If'n you didn't have all them troopers behind you, I'd teach you—you yellow-bellied Yankee! I'd pull you apart with my bare hands."

Private Ward stepped up to the sergeant. "May I, Sarge? Please allow me the privilege of taking some of the boasting out of his murdering a—er—backside. Excuse me, sir," he said to Captain Lyons, who remained silent, trying hard not to enjoy this spectacle too much.

"I appreciate the offer, Private Ward, but the challenge came to me. If he still has any fight in him when we finish—then you can have what's left." With this, Sergeant Damron pulled off his tunic, handing his holster and clothing to Captain Lyons, who was vainly protesting. Damron squared off in front of the rustler and met his challenge.

"OK, Runyan, you want a chunk of me—here I am; no one will lay a hand on you until we're finished." He began circling around the perimeter made up of men ready to watch a fight. Runyan fell into a rage as he pulled off his shirt, revealing massive muscles and evidence of many brawls. Lewis Damron seemed so young and innocent in comparison. But he was strong and had the advantage of height and arm length, and he seemed like the most relaxed person on earth as he danced around waiting.

With a throaty growl, Runyan charged at him like a bull, his massive hands folded into fists. Just as he almost had him, Lewis sidestepped, quick as a cat, and jabbed Runyan on the temple as he flew past and fell in the dirt. A cheer went up from the troopers. Runyan was shocked. He picked himself up, ready to kill. He flew at Lewis with a rage and it seemed he was going to do the same thing as before; instead he stopped short and threw a mallet of a fist at Lewis's face, catching him on the chin.

The blow landed the sergeant on his back, visibly dazed. He knew he could not survive another blow like that; this man was powerful and was at least twenty pounds heavier. Lewis had been raised around fighting and, most of the time, was able to hold his own. Most of the Damrons were scrappers and Uncle Moses Damron had once said, "If the Damrons didn't have anyone else to fight, they'd fight each other—just to keep in practice."

As Lewis picked himself up slowly he saw Runyan coming in for another killing blow. Lewis met him with a surprise. He pulled back his long right arm with all the weight he had in him and caught Runyan under the chin, partly on the neck. It almost tore his head off. Down he went, choking and gasping for air. He was spitting blood and couldn't breathe for a couple of minutes. The fight was over just that fast.

The men moved in and shackled Runyan, allowing the sheriff to lead him off to the lockup. Sergeant Damron had a blue bruise on his jaw, but seemed hardly out of wind as he dressed in his blues and put his hat back on.

"Well, Ollie, we got their leader and I'd say we clipped their wings," Lewis said as he placed his arm around the boy's shoulders, being careful of his sore arm. Ollie was back in his Buckskins and was feeling pretty good to start the day off this way.

THIRTY-TWO

Thou Art Beautiful, O My Love

J OHN HAD BREAKFAST FIXED BEFORE DAYLIGHT AS HE AND CASSIE MADE their plans Thursday morning. They had stayed with the herd with the two gruesome packages they carried. John had left the two dead outlaws tied to their saddles overnight, even though it was not kind to the horses. Late last evening they had watched Runyan ride off toward town. In spite of his trust in the Lord, John had a gnawing concern about Ollie, knowing that there had been a serious encounter with the third outlaw, who was "big as the side of a barn." He also knew that things were drawing to a conclusive encounter, especially with Runyan in town.

"Cassie, darling, I hate to do this to you—but I need you to take these two dead men to town and bring the patrol up to date. There's also another reason. I'm concerned about our young partner. I'm trying hard not to worry—but I'm human—and, it's the thing *I don't know* that bothers me! He could have been hurt in that fracas with the big man."

"John, honey, I don't mind going. I have the same concerns. And besides, I can send the patrol back to you by giving them explicit directions. Shep can stay with you and I know you'll both be OK—I just know it."

"Cassie, come here," John said softly, holding out open arms. Pulling her close, he tenderly found her inviting lips and kissed her sweetly, acknowledging her understanding about traveling into town alone. As John pulled away from her lips, she surprised him with her reaction.

"Just a minute. You're not getting away with a puny kiss like that." She pulled his lips down and kissed him firmly and passionately, leaving him breathless and tingling from his head to his feet.

"Lady, get on your pony and ride—now, before we both get side-tracked," he said, laughing as he dramatically backed off.

Cassie Martin was an unusual sight as she rode down the main street of town about eight o'clock that morning. Ollie and the sheriff had gone back to the cafe after the fight with Runyan. As he looked out of the cafe window, Ollie saw Cassie riding down the street, leading two horses with a body across each saddle. With a grin he punched Sheriff Compton and pointed to Cassie, who had already spotted Ollie. He ran out to her and reached up, taking her hand as he walked along beside Spot. Cassie let out a sigh of relief when she saw the bright face of this young boy whom she had come to love so deeply. As she squeezed his hand, she only wished she could convey this feeling across the miles to John.

"Where's Shep, Cassie? He's always with you." Ollie was afraid something had happened to her constant companion.

"He's taken up with your dad, Ollie." She shook her head in mock woe. "We'll probably have to shoot him—taking up with the likes of John Burke."

"I don't know what my peaceful little town has come to," said Sheriff Compton. "Yesterday, a boy rides in with a body on a horse; today it ain't even 8:30 and already a fist fight in the street—and—and—a woman rides in with two more bodies on horses; God forbid, what's a sheriff to do?" He put his right hand to his forehead, pretending despair. "Well, this must be Cassie, and these must be the other two you promised me, Ollie—Cort Grainger and Slim Benton—right?"

"Yes sir, Sheriff, you got their names right, and how did you know they were coming?" Cassie inquired.

"Oh," he said, with feigned boredom, "Ollie told me that yesterday when he brought in Dan MacGruder—and in the same position, I might add. Our undertaker, Mr. Turner, will have to go on vacation after this week is over; he should be able to retire while the Burke clan is in town." Cassie began laughing and enjoying this man, who was having a great deal of fun at their expense.

"I think I'm going to like you, Sheriff," she said, flashing him a radiant smile that almost melted him.

"Phil, come on out here. I got a little chore for you," Vessie called inside the cafe.

"Yes sir, Sheriff. What do you need?"

"Take the bodies of these men over to the undertaker, take the gear off at my office, and take the horses over to the livery barn for a rub-down and feed. How about your horse, Miss Cassie?"

"I'll take care of Spot, Sheriff, if you help her in with her gear," Ollie offered.

"Good deal, Ollie. You better chase down that sergeant and captain, too and send 'em up here while I get Cassie something to eat." As he led Cassie inside to a back corner of the cafe, the sheriff apologized. "This is mostly a man's eating and drinking place, Miss Cassie, but we make occasional exceptions—and you are most certainly one of those exceptions! I need to hear the details of how you *did in* these two murderers. But any information about the round-up of the others—you'd better hold until the army gets here; they're in charge of that end."

Cassie filled him in, including the conversation she and John overheard about the gold stolen from other thieves in jail waiting for their hanging. The sheriff decided not to send a wire about the money in Dan's saddlebag; he had made up his mind that the money was going to these folks who risked their lives to bring these culprits in before they rained havoc down on his community. He did send the wire confirming the deaths and asked for all rewards to be sent in care of the Bank of Catlettsburg, Kentucky. He also asked for inquiries to be made concerning kin of the deceased, having any known relatives wire or write to Sheriff Vessie Compton, Catlettsburg, Kentucky.

Ollie came to the table just as Cassie finished her breakfast and third cup of coffee. John had not ventured to start a campfire before daylight so she had made do with some dried fruit and tepid water from her canteen. She beamed as Ollie sat beside her. When she reached over and pulled Ollie close for a hug Sheriff Compton saw him wince, but he didn't stop her.

"Cassie," he said, "you should know something about Ollie. He's been hurt—a little." Seeing Cassie's face change from delight to horror, the sheriff quickly added, "but not too bad, Cassie—not too serious." Seeing the disgust on Ollie's face, the sheriff directed his next statement to Ollie.

"Now, you listen here, young man. I know you don't want to worry this lady, but it's always best to come out with the truth—even if it does surprise someone who cares for you. I saw how it hurt you when Cassie squeezed you and it just isn't fair for her not to know about your arm. There is less worry in knowing than not knowing. Do you understand?" He gave Ollie a stern look, with eyebrows raised.

"Aw, I'm sorry, Sheriff Vessie," he said, looking down. "I'm sorry—to both of you. I just didn't want to make any big deal out of it!" Sheriff Compton reached over and patted his arm.

"Apology accepted." Turning to Cassie,who was patiently waiting, he explained what had happened with Big Dan. "That sidestep, and the Lord—saved his life," he finished, glancing at Ollie. "He took a bullet in his left arm, but it passed through and didn't hit anything vital. When he came into town he had lost considerable amount of blood and passed out. Doc Carter put a few stitches in and bandaged him up. He is doing fine."

Cassie looked at Ollie, her eyes tender and moist. Placing a hand on each side cheek, she pulled his face to her own and placed her forehead against his, gently rolling her forehead back and forth, and finally kissing him on the cheek.

"Show me, Ollie—I mean the bandage," she said. The bandage was still clean, with only a small amount of blood seeping through.

"Thank you, honey, you can put your shirt back on. Remind me when we get home to fix the sleeve and I'll put on buttons or fasteners so the shirt will open down the front for you." As Ollie slipped the buckskin back on Captain Lyons, Sergeant Damron, and Robert Birchet came by to receive their instructions from John. Sheriff Compton excused himself and said he would be at his office if needed.

"Cassie, it's so good to see you, and to know that you and John are OK." Captain Lyons greeted her. "I have been out there with you in spirit and, although I knew everything was in good hands, it still feels good to see you and know that this nasty business with these scalawags is about to come to a conclusion." Cassie greeted all three men

"What happened to you, Sergeant? Don't tell me you ran into a door," she teased, noticing Lewis Damron's bruised chin.

"Not exactly. I sorta ran into Runyan's fist, but it does match my uniform—don't you think?" Then the captain interrupted the joking.

"First things first, folks. I need to hear about John and get this roundup business underway. I understand that we have three men at the undertaker's and Runyan is in the lockup, so that leaves John out there with the rest. What next, Cassie?"

"John—and Shep," Cassie corrected him. She asked for a piece of paper. "John is about here." She made an X and carefully drew a map indicating where he was in relation to the town. She drew in the herd and indicated the best way to circle past the cattle and rustlers to find John, who would be watching for them. "John will tell you the rest once you're with him."

"Sergeant," the captain ordered, "take this map and your men to John. Stay and receive your instructions from him, Then send him—and Shep—back to me here in Catlettsburg. I don't want him in on the roundup; he's done enough! You and your capable troopers can handle the rest. Bring them to town—dead or alive," he said grimly. "Don't let John argue you into staying; that's not his job and I want to buy him and Shep a big steak here at the cafe. I'll expect him by dinner." Sergeant Damron saluted and was on his way toward the stockyard to gather his patrol. Robert Birchet insisted on going along because of Tibbett and Blainey. He knew they were killers and wanted to see them caught.

Cassie gave the captain a pleasing smile and patted his hand. "Thank you, Captain, you're a man after my own heart." Ollie announced his approval with a big smile, showing his white teeth.

"Yes, Cassie, I am a man after your own heart, but I am second in line. In this heart business—that's the same as being last." He laughed, allowing Cassie to wonder if he was serious or teasing. Ollie excused himself to go look in on the animals and hang around the stockyard.

As everyone left, Captain Lyons escorted Cassie to Yance and asked if Helga was free. The jolly-faced young woman, her blond hair pinned across her head in two large braids, put Cassie right at ease and readily visited with her. The captain left her in capable hands and said he was going to find the sheriff.

Helga showed Cassie through the building, including the guestroom downstairs and the apartment on the second floor where she and Yance lived. She took Cassie to an elegant lady's guestroom with an imported cherrywood dresser and vanity with matching water stand. An ornate water pitcher and basin sat on the marble top and two quaint oil lamps adorned the mantle above a fireplace, covered for the summer. There was a four-poster double bed decorated with a bedspread that matched the wallpaper. A huge porcelain-covered iron tub stood in the corner and the room had the luxury of a small closet for hanging one's fine garments. Cassie told Helga she had not seen anything any finer since leaving Boston.

"This is good," said Helga with her charming accent. "You are our guest and will stay here—in this room. Whenever you are ready, I will have a bath prepared for you." Cassie impulsively hugged her.

"You don't know how much I appreciate this, Helga. I will enjoy the luxury of a bath in a real tub—and I may stay in it all afternoon."

"Good, good! Whenever you are ready, just let Helga know."

Cassie took a stroll on the boardwalk and, following Helga's directions, found a lady's shop. The clerk had already heard about the lady dressed in beautiful but soiled buckskins. She still carried her revolver and knife on her belt and did not look like the everyday female shopper. She started to introduce herself, but was interrupted.

"Oh, everyone in town knows who you are, Miss Cassie—is it Burke?" she asked, catching Cassie in a blush.

"Not yet. My name is Cassie Martin—right now. I just wanted to look at a couple of things and perhaps make a purchase which, I could pay for a little later?" she asked.

"Ma'am, in this store you can buy anything you want on credit." The clerk continued. "Everyone knows who you are and—and—

Ollie and about the wanted men you brought into town. Nobody in this town would turn you down. Your credit is certainly good here."

Cassie thanked her and shopped for a simple dress and underclothes to change into later. She also fell in love with a beautiful evening dress. A few days ago John had let it slip that he wanted to get all dressed up and do something special when they got to Catlettsburg, so she needed to prepare. She signed for these things along with stockings, high-heel button shoes, and matching reticule, all at a very modest price.

As Cassie entered the hall entrance to take her things upstairs to her guest room, she was exhilarated to hear a familiar voice coming from the dining area. Running excitedly to the dining area entrance, she saw Captain Lyons, Ollie, and John Burke dining and having pleasant conversation. Spying his radiant Cassie, John jumped up as if it had been weeks since he saw her. They embraced unashamedly. Ollie sat with a big grin on his face.

"Ollie took a steak over to the livery barn to Shep, Cassie—medium-rare," Captain Lyons said happily.

"You're teasing me!" Cassie exclaimed, but John assured her the captain was serious. He had ordered a steak for the grateful Shep and Ollie had delivered it.

Cassie became serious. "Did—did—Ollie tell you about—about his—"

"He most certainly did and he also showed me. God is good to us, honey. He sure kept a watch on our boy through this!" Cassie warmed all over to hear John refer to Ollie as "our boy." She noticed Ollie seemed to enjoy it, too. Indeed, she felt as close to Ollie as if he were her very own. Cassie sat with John and Ollie and, although she did not order dinner, she nibbled a little of the steak and salad left on John's plate. She showed John her packages, but didn't open them. Then John and the captain brought her up to date on the roundup, at least the part John saw.

"I heard shots as I came into town with Shep. Sounded like a good bit of firing, but I wasn't worried about Lewis and his men. They're superior in number and I doubt if Campbell and Reynolds will even fight at all," John speculated. Cassie was a little tired and felt the need of that hot bath she'd been promised. She caught Helga's eye as she brought a steaming plate of stew to a customer.

"I'm ready, Helga."

John kissed her. "Be ready for a downtown date—by dark. Put on some of those new things and we'll go to a great supper." As his tired but beautiful lady gathered her packages, she smiled and tossed her answer over her shoulder as she left.

"How can I refuse such an enchanting offer as that—and from such a handsome man, too!" John blushed as she disappeared into the hall. Captain Lyons and Ollie teased him, but he enjoyed it. He knew he was blessed!

Sergeant Damron and his patrol had success; not one of his men received a scratch. By five o'clock, the rustlers had been routed and those who lived were in custody in the Catlettsburg lockup with Deputy Phil Workman. In custody, were Reynolds, Campbell, and Watson, who was wounded in the shoulder. Doc Carter had attended to his wound and they had all been fed. Tibbett and Blainey didn't make it. They were killed in the shootout and their bodies were at Turner's, who planned on a mass burial Friday morning. To bury five murderers in one day was big doings for Catlettsburg. Sheriff Compton was authorized by Captain Lyons to take the personal effects, horses, and any money that may be found on them for burial expenses. There was more than enough for that, and the excess was turned over to the Union Army. The rest of the patrol, under command of Private Nathaniel Ward, was herding the animals into the stockyard, which would be driven back to Louisa and held for three months to allow farmers in the area to claim their livestock.

John had met with the sheriff and spent time getting acquainted with him. Compton recounted Ollie's close encounter in more detail and told John about Ollie's signing the revolver over to him. John shuddered at hearing about his son's encounter with "Big Dan;" his eyes grew moist as he thought about the close call his partner, friend and son had with death. John unashamedly thanked God in front of his friends. He knew God loved Ollie—even more than John and Cassie loved him, and he said so to Sheriff Compton and Captain Lyons, who was also present. He was aware that again the providence of God was at work for his son.

John was elated about the reward and would not allow himself to think about the gold or personal effects. He told Vessie Compton he did not blame Ollie for signing over the weapon, which belonged to Big Dan. He would have done the same thing and he was proud of Ollie for thinking of it. Both Captain Lyons and Sheriff Compton smiled. Like Ollie, he had not killed for money, but he did have a use for some of it—particularly right now since he was making wedding plans.

The sheriff took John to a clothing store, where he shopped for a complete broadcloth suit and a shiny new pair of dress boots, topped off with a western-style felt hat to match. The suit was dark blue in a western cut with a maroon vest. He chose a white linen shirt and blue string tie. John also purchased a complete outfit for Ollie with the exception of hat and tie; Ollie hated hats and ties.

After shopping he went back to the cafe to bathe and dress in his new clothes. His suit had been neatly hemmed and pressed for the occasion and he looked handsome. John was not finished with his shopping spree yet, so he took a stroll in his new clothes. He felt strange walking down the boardwalk dressed in a fashion—a new experience for him. A new pair of jeans and buckskins was the ultimate for John until now. He had always wondered what he would look like in a store-bought suit of clothes—and now he looked like a prosperous businessman. He was an extremely handsome man, and one would never know this was his first suit as he walked into a store that sold fine gold watches and jewelry.

Cassie soaked and lathered. Stretching out her lovely legs, she watched the soap circles stream down her limbs. Rolling and splashing lightly in the warm sudsy water, she smiled like a little girl. She shampooed her hair and was grateful God had given her hair that was easy to care for. After two good rinses, a good drying, and thirty minutes or so of brushing, it just tumbled back into place, cascading around her shoulders with its red highlights. Cassie sat at the vanity with her towel around her as she dried, then brushed her hair. She had a natural color to her cheeks and with the exception of bath powder under her smooth arms, she used nothing in the way of beauty aids. She walked to the bed and, laying the towel aside, she crawled between the sheets and slept peacefully until dusk, when she awoke and dressed for the much-anticipated evening.

Cassie came down the stairs into the hall in a beautiful evening dress of light blue taffeta, under which she wore soft undergarments that caressed her every curve and clung to her beautiful figure as if she were molded in them. The gown revealed most of her shoulders and had a sweeping neckline, modestly trimmed with lace. The form-fitting bodice that attached to the gathered skirt at the waist accentuated her shapely figure. The dress was full at the bottom and allowed for the proper petticoats, but Cassie only used one—contrary to the fashion. She detested corsets and restraining under garments and would wear them only if John insisted. Anyway, he had never seen her dressed like this, so she did not have to worry about that yet.

Her auburn hair was soft and the outline seemed on fire as the lights from the oil lamps caressed her soft curls, which bounced loosely about her shoulders. She had a small contrasting blue reticule on her right wrist and a white lace scarf covered her bare shoulders and draped over each arm.

Cassie had not seen John since she had left him in the dining room. As she walked down the hall, she had the choice of entering the dining room or going out onto the boardwalk. She didn't want to be on the street at dark and she felt uncomfortable going into the dining area, knowing only men would be there, so she knocked on Ollie's door.

"I'm sorry, ma'am. You must have th' wrong room. This is— why, why Cassie, is it really you?" he asked with mock surprise. Cassie shook him playfully by the shoulders.

"You're a big tease, Ollie Burke. I'm just trying to find your dad and I don't want to go out there—where all the men are! Please find him for me, will you?"

"Cassie, you are beautiful! Every time I see you I think so, and tonight you are something really beautiful to look at. I'm so happy for my dad! He is going to love that dress; you picked his favorite color." He spoke honestly without reservation and Cassie blushed until she was even more beautiful. "Sure, I'll find Dad for you. The only one I know that is as blessed as he is—well—is you!"

He thought to himself, *those two make me twice blessed.* "Thank you, Lord," he said out loud.

Ollie didn't have to go far to find John. He found him pulling up to the hall door in a covered buggy drawn by a team of prancing horses. As John stepped down from the buggy, Ollie took two steps backward to admire him.

"I can't believe this is my dad. Dad, you're—well, you are almost as pretty as the lady who sent me to get you," he blurted out.

"Not pretty, Ollie. A man is not pretty! That's a word to describe ladies. A man can be stunning, handsome, stalwart, or a rascal—but not pretty," John corrected. Ollie laughed.

"Well, John Burke, you are stunning, handsome, stalwart and—." His dad grabbed the next line, grinning, "And you, Ollie Burke, are a rascal. Have you bathed and cleaned up?"

"Yes, sir," he said, wondering why the question.

"Go and put on the new duds that I got you; they're in the room," John directed. "Tonight you are going to be our coachman. Hurry now. Let's not keep our lady waiting."

John caught his breath as he saw the creature of loveliness that was to be his wife. She stood in the doorway as he and Ollie hurried to the room. Ollie stepped behind her, excusing himself as he proceeded to dress around the corner while his dad admired Cassie Martin, God's gift to John—and Ollie and Cindy.

Ollie had humble, appreciative thoughts as he dressed hurriedly. He knew God had a special hand on him. For his dad and Cassie to include him on their particular night together—just like he was part of it, to have a father that considered him important on such a night—meant more to Ollie than he could express as he fought back tears of gratitude. Ollie was perfectly aware that soon his dad would have a new wife—and they needed much time alone, just the two of them.

John asked Cassie to turn around slowly. He had planned the whole evening as a surprise to both Cassie and Ollie, so he expected to see her dressed up, and he knew her beauty well. Yet it seemed that each time he saw this radiant lady, he was totally unprepared all over again for how she looked. Each time she turned, she simply dazzled him. After turning for about the fifth time, she was getting embarrassed and put a stop to it.

"John, I'm getting dizzy. I love to please you and am excited that you want to see me, but, I am just a—a—*people*! I want to look at you, too," she declared. "Now—you turn around and let me see you in your new suit and boots." Ollie joined them as John turned in the hall, and he chuckled loud enough to be heard. John blushed. "All right, Mr. Ollie, no smart remarks! As a matter of fact, it's time for you to be examined—right, Cassie?"

"Absolutely. Stand out here, Ollie. Let's see how you look. My my, new boots for you, too? Where are mine?" she said, teasing the both of them. Ollie quickly changed the subject.

"We better get out there to them horses, Dad. They've been all alone much too long; let's go now." He turned and hurried down the hall.

"Horses?" Cassie asked, raising her eyebrows.

"Let's see, what time is it?" John said, evading the question. "Hmm—it's way past eight o'clock—got to get moving." He took Cassie's arm and maneuvered her out to the boardwalk. Two spirited blacks were prancing as they waited with a nearly new buggy and eleven-year-old coachman-driver standing by.

"My lady," Ollie said, extending his hand as she stepped up. He then reached out for his dad—"My lord, sir," dramatically bowing, John began laughing unable to hold back any longer.

"Ollie, where in the world did you learn this 'my lady' stuff?"

"I read it somewhere, Dad. I thought it was pretty good myself. It worked OK for Cassie, huh Cassie?"

"It sure did, Ollie. I am impressed—with the buggy, the horses, *and the coachman or driver*, or whatever you are tonight. I'll tell you this, I feel safe with the two of you! Oh, by the way—where's Shep? I miss him." John stepped up to take his place beside his lady, motioning to Ollie to take his position in the driver's seat.

"Well, I took that valuable animal a piece of beef and some water and told him to guard Spot and our horses. He's over at the livery barn since we didn't have adequate place for him where we're staying. Junior Akers, the owner of the barn, is keeping an eye on him for us."

"Where do you want me to go, Dad?"

"What? We don't get anymore, 'my lord' and 'my lady'? I'm purely disappointed, Mr. Coachman. Well, just take us to the corner, turn left and go toward the waterfront. I'll tell you when to stop." John placed his left arm around his beautiful date who didn't know where she was going. As he pulled her close to him, he felt an involuntary shudder of contentment. John looked down at her lovely face with admiration.

"Do you know where you are going, 'my lady'?"

"No, 'my lord', I don't know where I am bound—but then—neither does the driver, and we are both quite content in just being with you." John didn't have a comeback to that, so he just held her close and kissed her tenderly on her full, inviting lips—while the coachman giggled.

John took the two particular people in his life with him to a fine waterfront restaurant, with just one small regret—that little Cindy Lou was not here to share this night with them. He kept that thought to himself for the time being. Through the meal the three of them talked and laughed and enjoyed themselves as if there were no war, no rustlers, and no close calls, as though there was nothing important except the three of them, and their unseen guest—their Lord and Savior Jesus Christ who brings peace and providence forevermore.

John and Cassie talked intimately without shame in front of Ollie. He enjoyed the love his two friends and partners had for each other. They did not realize that the full, elegant restaurant was an audience to the three of them as John would bend over and kiss Cassie and she in turn would pull Ollie close and hug him occasionally, just to watch him blush. As the long meal neared dessert, John reached into his left vest pocket and pulled out a round gold object. He held it up to his ear and, seeming satisfied, he reached out, taking Ollie's hand.

"This is for you, Son. Not for a reward, but—because I promised it to you and—because I love you in a very wonderful way, which words cannot express."

Ollie took the engraved gold watch with a beautiful chain and fondled it in a trembling hand. His eyes grew moist as he opened it and read on the inner case:

May 22, 1862
With love
To Ollie Burke from Dad
John Burke

Both John and Cassie were emotional as they watched Ollie open and close the watch, and check the time with his dad's watch. It had a stem to wind it and the manufacturer's name was Elgin. His dad told him it was one of the best and he did not doubt it one bit; it was beautiful.

John turned to Cassie and, taking her two hands in his, he looked into her eyes.

"Darling Cassie, we have shared some precious moments and eventful hours together in the short time since we met. We have faced death and have been fascinated by each other and even shared the words of our love forever. I have, therefore, taken for granted the love and future life we will have together, but here—before God—with Ollie as a witness, I will not do that again. You are too precious a gift from God for me to take for granted—about anything."

John tenderly shared from his heart and he wanted Ollie to hear it. It touched Cassie to the bottom of her heart and tears began to appear in her beautiful blue eyes. She remained silent, because John was not finished.

"Cassie, your father is deceased, so I cannot ask him for your hand, but again, in front of Ollie, I ask you to be my wife and we will make our wedding plans together. Wait just one moment before you answer." He fumbled for something in his right vest pocket and came out with a velvet ring box. Opening it nervously, he took out a diamond solitaire ring and slipped it on her finger. As Cassie pulled a handkerchief out of her reticule to wipe her tear-stained face, she gave her answer to this man she had prayed for, waited for, and saved herself for.

"It—it—fits! Of course I'll marry you, John Burke. I've lived for this day all my life, and the answer has always been, *yes, yes, yes!*" She threw her arms around him. They arose from their seats and their lips met as they stood in the middle of the dining room and embraced—while Ollie and the spectators applauded and cheered.

Author, Lyle T. Burchette

To order additional copies of

Have your credit card ready and call

(877) 421-READ (7323)

or send $15.95 each + $4.95* S&H to

WinePress Publishing
PO Box 428
Enumclaw, WA 98022

*add $2.00 S&H for each additional book ordered